131 Days

Keith C. Blackmore
2013

131 Days
by
Keith C. Blackmore

Edited by Red Adept Publishing
Extra proofreading by Polgarus Studio

Cover by Karri Klawiter www.artbykarri.com
Formatted by Polgarus Studio

131 Days
Copyright © 2013 by Keith C. Blackmore

Thanks to Eric, Sarah, and Miguel
for their help and thoughts.

For George and Shirley Blackmore
(otherwise known as Mom and Dad)

Part I:

131 Days

• 1 •
Baylus and Goll

Thunder.

Except it wasn't really like thunder. It was more like that initial crash of diving headfirst into a deep body of water—that rush of sound and pressure that flattens a man's ears to his skull, setting his skin to tingling with shock, the sensation of being enveloped by the coldness of it all, the *entering*, right up until he breaks the surface of the pool, gasping for breath, and just grateful to be able to do so.

It was more like that.

And it *roared* overhead at that very moment. There were thousands out there. Watching.

Baylus stood in a white tunnel, long and bare, leading upward to a thick portcullis. A gatekeeper stood a few paces in front of him checking his fingernails for dirt. A lever protruded from the wall over his left shoulder. Baylus ignored the gatekeeper and regarded the bench to his right. There for support, he had sat on it once before, toward the end of his first tournament, because he had been tired of it all and couldn't wait to be finished, one way or another. That was five years ago. He had done that five years ago and vowed never to return. Made *promises* to dead men that he'd never return. Yet, here he was. And for what? When he hacked heads off brutes trying to do the same to him, he wished it was finished. He wished it was done, either with him winning it all or just dying in one short, spraying grunt. He had vowed he would never return to the hell of the Sunja's Pit. But here he was, both ashamed and excited.

Baylus had won it all five years ago. The title and the coin as well as the unwanted life celebrity status and routine. In the first year, he basked in the adoration and the attention. Lapped up the praise like a thirsty dog and barked for more. That was the first year. By the second year, he was already tired of the constant scrutiny whenever he walked the streets. He started avoiding crowds here and there, until he gradually shunned them entirely. He despised people wanting stories of the Pit. He got angry with them, got angry at the smiles when they told *their* tales of warriors, of gladiators, when really they didn't know one damned thing. They were spectators, watching men tear the guts out of each other and delighting in it for an afternoon. Or morning. Or whenever the bloodletting was scheduled. All of them believed they knew his strengths and weaknesses. They didn't know anything more than what they saw from the stands high above, far away from harm. One time, a crazy Zhiberian had flung his spear into the masses and pinned two poor unlucky bastards through their gullets. That was the talk of the gladiators that day, and more than one wished *they* had tossed that gut-sticker. Not that the Zhiberian got away with it. Archers had cut him down right and proper, and then the Skarrs dragged him out of Sunja's Pit using meat hooks.

But the Zhiberian had gotten his point across.

The crowds were both grand and… *evil.*

They praised your name in one instant, and called for your head the next. They supported you utterly, then betrayed your guts at the first sign of weakness. They raised you up and were more than happy to let you drop.

And yet, despite it all, here he was. Baylus was back.

All because, Lords save his soul, he *missed* it.

After he had been forgotten, perhaps around the fourth year, he discovered he longed for the attention, almighty Seddon take his black hide. He missed having his name spoken with such honored reverence. He missed the comparisons to the champions of old. He missed the physical challenges, the competition. Lords above, he missed… *hell.*

You're too old, the Gladiatorial Chamber had informed him, when he approached them about returning to the games. *Be chewed up by the younger pups.*

But they relented. It was nothing to them, and insulting to Baylus's intelligence to think they *thought* they could fool him into thinking they cared. They only cared about the coin they could earn on the odds. Think of the promotions! The old champion, back and seeking glory once more on the arena sands, still as dangerous as in his prime.

Baylus didn't feel old at thirty-seven.

Seven years after prime.

Topside roared again, shaking him from his thoughts. Baylus exhaled. He'd wanted back in the Pit. He wanted this more than *anything*, Seddon save him.

And here he was.

He felt the reassuring weight of his armor plates. They covered his front and back completely, hanging in place by thick bands of leather going over his shoulders. A thick leather sleeve protected his sword arm. His other arm had the shield. Strips of crenellated leather draped his legs but, if he took a good hit there, he could be crippled in an instant, or even lose the limb. His helm was wingless and caged. Baylus preferred as little ornamentation as possible. Some of the others loved it, strutted across the sand in their decorations. Not him. He was all business.

He tightened his grip on the sword hilt, the blade still in its scabbard, waiting to taste air and lick flesh. It was good steel. Someone said Mademian-forged, but Baylus didn't believe it. There were no Mademian characters stamped onto the base.

Beyond the portcullis, a voice, loud and harsh, introduced the first fight.

"You ready?" the gatekeeper asked. The older, grizzled man studied him with one cocked eye.

"Aye that," Baylus answered.

"Seddon bless you, then." He raised his arm to the lever.

"Seddon," Baylus breathed from behind his face-cage, "can lick my ass."

That drew a frown from the gatekeeper as he pulled the lever. The portcullis shivered and parted. Sunlight yawned through unobstructed. Baylus jogged up the wide steps swinging his shield to and fro. His brow crinkled in concentration.

This was it.

A rogue wave of sound engulfed him as he entered the arena, crashing down and almost stunning him senseless. *Lords*, how he missed the applause, knowing it was fleeting. From the stands, the crowds greeted the old champion, screaming his name and pumping fists. Women flaunted their bare breasts. The men howled. A few curses perforated the cacophony, and Baylus scowled.

Savages all. Yet he loved it.

"We knew he could not be away for long, and we were right!" At the far end of the sands the Orator appeared as a gray post with his skeletal arms outstretched. To his left was the Gladiatorial Chamber stand, separated and sheltered from the crowds by high walls. The owners and trainers of respected stables would be there, watching their dogs go at it. To Baylus's right, and so much grander, was the raised platform for the king and guests. King Juhn lounged up there, watching perhaps, while servants fed him some rare tropical fruit. The man appeared a distant figure of white. At the base of the platform was a low wall of pole-arm-wielding Axemen, the legendary guardians of the throne.

"He is an eater of flesh," the Orator bawled. "An abomination. And he has chosen to return. To teach the hellpups of this year's tournament the meaning of the word *war.* Years have no effect on this man and he knows no fear, no mercy, as his opponents have discovered time and time again. In his day, he took the heads of a hundred men, and he means to take a hundred more! He is a survivor and *Champion* of the pit from years past. He. Is. *Baylus*! The Butcher of *Balgotha!*"

The crowd roared. They remembered him. Baylus took a deep satisfying breath. But he never took the heads of a hundred men in the past. He'd have to have a talk with the Orator for spewing such gurry.

"His opponent, from the lands of Kree, *Goll!*"

Across the arena, from the shadows of an open portcullis, stepped a man holding a sword and shield. His sword was already out and at guard. Baylus grimaced. Like he was about to charge across some fifty paces to have at him right at the introductions. In that instant, he knew it was the lad's first fight.

Baylus sighed. Lords help him. He hoped his opponent was a criminal.

"Free Trained and bred!" the Orator announced.

Baylus gave the barest shake of his head. *Free Trained.* That meant, for whatever reason, the lad had entered hell of his own free will. The ranks of Free Trained were the most numerous of the games, but they were also the most unskilled, the most barbaric, unlike the hellpups trained by established Houses. The old champion inhaled hot air, and wondered why the warrior entered the games. Then he caught himself and cursed his hypocrisy.

"This is the first fight of many, good people of Sunja. On behalf of the Gladiatorial Chamber and King Juhn's best wishes for you to be entertained, let the games… *begin!*"

Another tsunami of sound hurt Baylus's ears. Next time, he would pretend his ears were two harlots on their monthly time and jam cotton in them.

At the signal, Goll walked toward the Butcher of Balgotha, the champion of games gone by, amidst the screaming spectators.

Baylus watched him for a moment before finally drawing his sword. The crowd approved.

Goll wore leather. Bracers protected his arms, and greaves shielded his legs. His sword was shiny and oiled. A plain helm, caged and scratched, covered his head. The boy had trained by the looks of him; he knew how to hold his blade. Baylus could tell by his foe's stance. *Even better,* Baylus groaned inwardly. The look on the man's face, however, was one of sheer fright.

Nerves.

First fight of his life in front of so many probably, and to be thrown to the Butcher in his opening match. Baylus frowned.

Seddon above could be a bastard.

"Greetings, la—" Baylus began.

Goll attacked with a straight-armed thrust, aimed for the gut. Baylus turned it away with a swipe of his blade. The younger man thrust again and, once more, Baylus knocked it aside. The once champion then sidestepped toward the other's shield arm. Good stabs, but they had come too early in the game.

Goll, however, was of a different mind. He jabbed a third time, bouncing his sword off Baylus's shield. The young gladiator circled to his right and slashed, missing a cheek. He lunged for an exposed knee and stabbed only air. He stepped in and thrust for the same knee a second time. Baylus parried, parried again, then retreated a pace.

The boy was fast.

Goll jerked his arm back. If of a mind, Baylus could have taken the limb off at the elbow, shearing through like a knob of butter. But that would have finished the match too early. And the crowds didn't like quick fights.

"Slow down, lad," Baylus urged, watching the man over the rim of his shield. "Slow down. You'll be spent in seconds at this pace."

Goll didn't listen.

Instead, he jumped to the attack, cutting for the champion's head.

Baylus spiraled his shield, deflecting the blow and allowing his foe's own momentum to carry him past. The once champion made him look clumsy in that one lunge and,

9

for a brief second, Goll's back was exposed.

Baylus did nothing.

Goll recovered and took a breath. Sweat covered his face. He lunged, steel flashing in the sun. A shield turned the blade away. He got in close and whipped his shield's rim at the old champions's head.

Blocked.

Goll stabbed for the gut. It bounced off Baylus's armored plate.

A series of strikes erupted from the young warrior then, a flurry of well-practiced cuts and thrusts meant to gut or decapitate a foe. The strength and speed of the offensive impressed Baylus and backed him up toward a high wall. Each heavy-handed connection brought a grimace to the once champion's face.

The lad was *strong*.

Then the storm broke, and Goll, his strength momentarily depleted, retreated to a chorus of disapproval.

Peeking over his shield, Baylus studied the younger man. The lad was a fighter and he meant to have Baylus's head. He supposed a champion's scalp would be a notable trophy.

"All right then, boy," Baylus mused. "All right."

Amidst a swelling of applause, the champion shook his sword arm, loosening it. Then he did the same for his shield arm. The crowd reacted with screams. Word spread through the stands like an unchecked fire. Those who had seen the old champion fight years ago knew what was coming. With meat on the table, the Butcher was readying his tools.

Goll sensed it as well. Fear glittered in his eyes. He readied his shield and bobbed it up and down, left and right, trying to be everywhere at once.

Baylus's sword arm snapped out. Goll's shield dropped

to deflect the thrust. He realized the feint too late as the Butcher closed and smashed his shield's edge into the face-cage of the young warrior.

Goll staggered to the left. The crowd approved.

"A love-tap to go with those scratches," Baylus said, but he didn't press his attack.

The young Kree collected himself and became more cautious. Baylus could see it in his stance. The boy was tired. Spent. Waiting for his strength to return and wishing it would return quickly.

The Butcher went to work.

Baylus feinted again, and then drove his blade toward the right shin of his foe. The edge licked leather and split it instantly. Goll jerked back, and Baylus whipped his sword up, drawing a fine line inside the man's guard, up the right side of his ribs.

With a yelp Baylus probably heard better than the crowd, Goll jumped back. The younger man checked himself quickly. Another mistake.

The old champion charged.

Where Goll's initial onslaught had been full of strength and adrenalin, the Butcher's was controlled, tight and, as a practitioner of the medicinal arts might comment, surgical. Baylus feinted, stabbed, and slashed in combination, one attack flowing into the other. Goll got behind his shield, but Baylus nicked and skinned him of his leather. The young man retreated, but the champion pressed forward and slashed for his foe's eyes—a ruse—as his foot stomped and crushed three of Goll's toes.

The connection made the hellpup sing.

Struggling to stand upright, Goll hid behind his shield. Baylus circled to the man's left, his shield arm. It was an old tactic of the Butcher's, to draw out the match—immobilize his opponent, then slowly bleed him until the kill. The crowd paid good coin to see a fight, not a quick stabbing. If it was an execution they wanted, they could gather at the public square.

Baylus continued to circle, and a limping Goll struggled to keep up, turning in place to remain facing his adversary.

The Butcher's blade flashed. His steel rebounded off Goll's shield twice, knocking it out of position. A third thrust bit flesh, and Goll's shield arm drooped from the impact. Behind his face-cage, the young man grimaced and made the mistake of checking his shoulder that had just been cut to the bone.

Baylus's sword bit his adversary's right forearm, gnashing through leather and tasting meat. Blood fell from Goll's staggering frame. He backed up a step and almost lost his balance. Baylus stabbed his right shoulder before cracking his shield's rim across the man's jaw.

The connection straightened Goll's neck, and he crashed to the sand.

The spectators cried out for death then, demanded it. Both Baylus and the Orator glanced in the direction of King Juhn and saw the ruler watching with some interest. A servant held grapes mere inches from his lips.

"Kill him!" The audience took up the chant.

Not about to be hurried by the crowd, Baylus looked down on the sprawled form. Goll shook his head, trying to clear his vision of black motes no doubt. His back was to the once champion—bent, beaten, and exposed. His shield was nowhere within reach, yet he managed to cling to his sword.

Baylus could have killed the man right then, stuck his

blade straight through the lower spine of the gladiator and pinned him, twitching, to the sand.

But he didn't.

"Get up," he ordered. "Get up."

Somewhere in his daze, Goll's lifted his head, the face-cage turning in the direction of his opponent. Confusion creased his features.

"Come on," Baylus urged, wondering if he could be heard over the crowd. "No one needs to perish here this day, boy. You started well enough. Now let's finish it."

Goll got to his knees. His face-cage had been smashed in on one side, the lower part of the metal coated in dust and blood. Blood ran freely from his wounds. His left arm hung uselessly, leather and skin shredded alike. His toes were mashed.

Goll was a mess.

But he brought up his sword.

An impressed Baylus considered the man for a moment, ignoring the swelling impatience of the crowd. The youth had made mistakes, guilty only of inexperience, and Baylus sighed in remembrance of his own first match. It was a shame Goll had to draw the Butcher on his first day back.

Baylus stepped forward and feinted, as he had done often throughout the fight, and Goll plunged his blade through the champion's knee. That sudden shock of steel slicing flesh and bone, forgotten for so long, gushed into the champion's mind and paralyzed him as if caught in a crushing vice.

Long enough for Goll to cut his other leg.

Baylus crashed to the ground. Momentarily forgetting how to fall, his head bounced hard off the sand. He clamped down on his tongue, snipping off the very tip. Blood spurted. The impact brought stars to his vision.

He tried to bring up his sword, but Goll was on top of him. Worse, Goll had his knee in the valley of his elbow.

Baylus felt a foot on his opposite forearm. He couldn't summon his strength. The man had him spread like a wounded bird.

The tip of a sword pricked his throat.

Baylus's vision cleared. He gazed into the hard eyes of his younger foe. He realized then he had underestimated the man's will and had played too long with his foe when he should have been killing. His eyes flicked skyward, and he saw a deep, empty blue. Baylus grimaced. To think he had returned to *this*.

"No one needs—" he began.

Goll stabbed with whatever strength remained in his good arm, clamping Baylus's jaw shut, punching through the Butcher's skull, and partially lifting the helm off the man's head.

The young gladiator did not release the blade. Instead, he stared into the eyes of the corpse. Eyes once full of bemused comprehension, now glazed over like white wax. The man from Kree held onto the blade, even as the crescendo of cheers smashed into his senses, even when the Orator announced him as the winner, and slayer of the Butcher of Balgotha. King Juhn himself tipped a goblet to the gladiator's surprising victory.

Goll released his sword. Somehow, he managed to stand. He staggered and cradled his left arm, which was in bloody ribbons. The cheering of thousands racked his senses, rocking him. He'd done it. He'd faced the Butcher of Balgotha and put a length of steel through his brain. With a curse, he raked off his helm, considered it, and flung it into the air. His name was Goll. It was his first match. He wanted to make a name for himself, to become a legend, much like the dead man at his feet. He flung his good arm wide, embracing the crowd, as tears, sweat, and scarlet fell from him.

He smiled.

The Orator looked down on the victorious pit fighter and nodded. The Butcher of Balgotha had played with the young lion and lost his life. Such was fate in Sunja's Pit. He glanced in the direction of the king and saw the man drinking from a goblet, the rush of the surprise victory already waning. But then, only the truly spectacular held the king's attention for long.

The Orator took a breath as he beheld the pulsating arena.

It was the first day, and a good opening for the games.

• 2 •

Vadrian and Bars

They dragged the corpse of Baylus from the arena by the ankles.

When the arena attendants got the body inside the tunnel, they dumped the dead champion into a cart. Three men wheeled the corpse through the general quarters beneath the Pit, passing through dusty cones of light from torches or oil lamps. The procession went through rows of gladiators standing, sitting, performing warm-up rituals, or mentally readying themselves, waiting for their turn upon the arena sands. Baylus's carcass caused a lull to sweep over the works of them. Hundreds of men stopped what they were doing and watched the cart pass. Some were close enough to peer inside with looks of solemn consideration.

"Damnation," spoke Bars from where he sat on a bench. "That's enough to wake a topper up. If he wasn't before."

"What did you expect?" asked a gladiator named Halm, his bright blue eyes leaving the cart's progression and taking in the man sitting next to him.

"I mean…" Bars paused. "That was Baylus the Butcher.

I watched him fight years ago, when I was just a boy. When I saw him earlier this day, I hoped…"

"Hoped what?"

"That I wouldn't be matched with him."

Halm studied the younger man for a moment, then hissed out his breath from between perhaps the worst set of teeth Bars had ever seen. Though Halm still retained a full set, his teeth were chipped and overlapped, corrupted into a brazen collection of yellow and black fangs. Halm was bulky as well as scarred. Where most pit fighters were corded with muscle, both heavy and sinewy, Halm clearly ate heavily of barley and beans to gain fat over his muscular frame.

"Bah," the fat man finally said, scratching at his bare, hairy belly. "He was asking for it. A right and proper punce if you ask me. He had it all. *All.* And wanted back in, and he nearing forty at that. Dogballs. The shagger wanted to die, my thoughts on it."

Bars wasn't so certain. Death was a possibility in the Pit and he had prepared himself for the bloodletting. He believed he could kill a man if he had to, especially when he considered the potential riches he could win at the tournament's end.

"Look," Halm said, breaking Bars from his spiraling thoughts. "That one was a fool. Make no mistake. No one returns to this hell when they've won it all."

"You returned," a muscular man declared, plopping down on a bench across from the pair.

"I didn't win it all," Halm countered.

"But you came back anyway," the newcomer said, and grinned. "With enough scars that if you were on your back with your gut in the air, people would mistake you for one cheek of a very fat ass lashed forty times with a whip."

Halm chuckled. "At least my mother didn't give me a name like yours." He held out a closed fist, which the other man met with his own.

"This is Pig Knot, youngster," he said, introducing the warrior. "You'll encounter no fouler bastard in these games, past or present."

Pig Knot nodded. "You know what, youngster? You're sitting and conversing with perhaps the only two toppers in here that survived all of this fun and dared try it once more, year after year."

"Aye that," Halm agreed with another scratch at his belly.

"Aye that, indeed," Pig Knot said, his dark eyes twinkling. "Can't get enough."

Unlike Halm, Pig Knot was heavy with visible muscle, great forearms and a head covered in black hair. He kept his mane in a tight knot at the back of his skull.

"Don't listen to him," Halm said. "He let slip a cow kiss before going out onto the sands."

Pig Knot's smile faltered. "You didn't have to mention that."

Bars regarded the muscular newcomer with a curious expression.

"Oh, he let loose." Halm elbowed the younger gladiator and nodded at his pit brother from tournaments past. "He was young, like you. Nervous too, unlike you. Got up to the portcullis and, when it opened, his bowels let go. He let slip a cow kiss right there on the threshold. Unfit, it was."

Remembering, Pig Knot's smile returned. "The gatekeeper didn't care too much for me that day."

"Or any other after that. You stank the place to Seddon's high heaven."

"Lad," Pig Knot started, leaning forward. "You are

sitting next to the one man in this whole madness that, when he finally dies, the Skarrs themselves will take his scarred hide, tan it, and make leather enough to outfit a five-thousand-man Klaw."

"That's why I don't mind the scars," Halm added. "Or the holes."

"Aye that," Pig Knot continued. "If they make sails from him, the holes won't catch a wind."

A weak smile spread across Bars's features.

"Ah, well," Halm said. "All's good, then. It's good to see you, Pig Knot of Sunja."

"And you, Halm of Zhiberia."

"May we never meet in the Pit."

"May we never." Pig Knot looked upon the other with fondness. "Or you, youngster."

Bars hoped the same and, when Pig Knot extended his fist, he met it with his own, pressing his knuckles hard.

"The youngster's got push," Pig Knot observed with approval. "I think he'll do well."

"Aye that," Halm agreed. "Let's see your sword."

After a moment's hesitation, Bars adjusted his scabbard at his hip and took out the blade. Observing manners, he laid it across his forearm, pommel first, before offering it. Halm took it with a nod.

"Good weight," the Zhiberian noted. "And Mademian."

"Mademian?" Pig Knot's eyes went wide. "Let's see it, then."

He took the sword and marveled at the characters stamped into its surface. "It *is*. It *is* Mademian. Where did you get this? Steel like this is hard to find these days."

Bars shrugged. "I bought it."

"Nothing but the best, eh?" Pig Knot asked, but Bars

didn't answer. Glancing at Halm, Pig Knot gave the sword back to the younger man and sized him up. "You've got decent leather on you, too, I see. Sunjan made. Excellent. You don't want that Zhiberian shite protecting you."

"Zhiberia makes the best armor in the world," the fat man declared.

"Which is why you aren't wearing any?"

"Too heavy for me. Slows me down."

Pig Knot snorted. "Slows him *down*. You'd think he was lightning pissed out of Seddon himself. Let me see your shield there."

Bars handed him the round, iron-rimmed barrier.

The veteran gladiator fixed it to his left arm and swung it about. He stood and swung it again, gaining glares from a few men nearby. After a moment, he returned it with an approving nod. "That's good weight you have there. Well-made Sunjan craftsmanship. You'll do well. Got a helm?"

Bars showed a wingless helmet, complete with face-cage.

"He's ready for war, I'd say," Halm commented.

"I'd say so, too," Pig Knot agreed. "All the right tools for the bloodletting. Who trained you?"

"School of Nexus," Bars answered with some confidence.

The revelation surprised the other two men.

"Nexus?" exclaimed Halm. "I know I haven't known you for long, but Nexus? And here I was feeling bad for you! Trying to brighten your spirits."

"Aye that," Pig Knot said. "A man with your expensive tools and training… well, I certainly hope we don't cross steel out there."

"Nor I," Halm shook his head.

It was true enough that the School of Nexus had a

reputation, and Bars had done well in his training. Well enough that his instructors had deemed him worthy for the games and given their blessing. *Win it all for the school*, his trainers and taskmasters had told him.

"Nor I," Bars eventually said, and meant it. It wasn't uncommon for friends to meet in the arena; in fact, he heard that most gladiators avoided each other's company during the tournament for that very reason. The chance that, one day, friends just might have to meet and bleed each other was enough to keep one from getting to know a fellow fighter. The rules of the Pit were simple, and a defeated pit fighter lived or died by the inclination of his opponent. A match did not have to end with a death, nor did King Juhn demand it, although it was said he enjoyed *not* knowing what the victor would do to his beaten adversary. The spectators, however, were different. They usually demanded a killing, and the winning gladiator decided whether or not to give them one.

Truth be known, Bars found himself enjoying the company of both fat Halm and hairy Pig Knot. They relaxed him, as odd as it might have seemed. The School of Nexus didn't want their gladiators to interact with any other school, but especially the Free Trained, who held allegiance to no one and were perceived as beneath their level.

"Why in Saimon's hell are you out here conversing with the horseshite?" Pig Knot asked, as if reading his mind. "You lose your way? These are general quarters, you know."

"Of course the lad knows," Halm defended. "But why wouldn't he come out and walk amongst the Free Trained? This pup is wiser than his years are letting on."

Pig Knot considered the youngster in a different light.

"It's true," Bars nodded. "Nexus doesn't like us

wandering in the Pit. But I knew I was fighting next, so I stole away in hopes of getting a glimpse of my opponent. Nexus will have my hide, though, if he finds me astray."

"Generous master, eh?" Pig Knot commented.

"Oh, he's a self-righteous dog blossom, no doubt." Bars smirked, getting a chuckle from both men.

On cue, a man dressed in stately robes—the *Madea*—appeared in an open archway at the end of the general quarters. A half dozen heavily armed Skarr warriors flanked the arena official as he marched up a ramp to a large desk, a bastion of authority positioned between two torch-lit tunnels. A huge matchboard hung on the wall behind the desk, displaying the day's scheduled fights. More torches lit up the surface, illuminating slots for the names of ten pairings for the day. With a flourish, the *Madea* produced a scroll. He consulted it, then checked the matchboard and called out two names, knowing full well several fighters present were unable to read.

Bars's head came up.

"That you?" Halm asked.

Before the younger man could answer, his opponent, Vadrian, jumped to his feet and roared. He was tall, blond, and yelled long and loud enough to turn the heads of several gladiators. Leather armor covered him, with greaves and pads in the necessary places. Bars couldn't get a good look at his face and, as he watched, his opponent-to-be bent and picked up a winged helm fashioned from bronze. It gleamed in the nearby torch light as if taken from a dream.

"For fatherly Seddon above!" Vadrian exclaimed. "Oh, Father! All shall tremble and fear the name of Vadrian, Son of Seddon!"

The pit fighter fitted the helm to his head and, brandishing his sword, stalked off toward the *Madea*. He continued swearing oaths of a faith not often practiced within the ranks.

"A screamer," Pig Knot observed.

"I hate screamers." Halm made a face. "What was your name again, lad?"

"Bars."

"Bars, do us all a favor and shut that one up."

"Right and proper," Pig Knot added.

"Right and proper," Halm agreed. "Never did like the type. All noise, they are."

"And it's noisy enough around here as it is," Pig Knot said.

"Aye that."

With a little smile, Bars got to his feet. He placed his own helm atop his head and hefted his sword and shield. He felt it then, the build-up of nervous energy in his lower legs and arms. His heartbeat quickened, and he took a breath, remembering to control it as his trainers had drilled into him.

He looked to the two gladiators sharing his company. "My thanks. For... talking."

"Plenty of time for more talking." Halm's bright blue eyes narrowed. "When you get back."

"*If* you get back." Pig Knot winked.

"What did I say earlier?" Halm indicated the hairy beast across from him. "A foul bastard."

Bars composed himself and nodded once more to the two men. He made his way to the arena official and his bodyguard of Skarrs. Eyes watched the young gladiator as he moved through general quarters, and Bars was aware of every set.

"Bars?" the *Madea* asked.

He nodded.

"What are you doing in here?" the official asked.

"I got lost."

The *Madea* frowned. "Follow the tunnel on the left, then." He pointed. "Don't lag. When the portcullis opens, there'll be a short introduction. Wait until it's done. Then you are free to beat, maim, or kill. Understood?"

"I understand."

"Then get on," the *Madea* instructed.

Bars left in a jog, heading down the indicated passageway. More armed Skarrs lined the tunnel, spaced apart at regular intervals. None of the visors followed Bars as he passed. That was fine with him. Too much attention made him uneasy.

Around a corner and at the passageway's end, four more Skarrs stood guard. A gatekeeper waited with his back to the wall, a lever just over his shoulder. A bench was opposite him. Bars considered the seat but chose not to use it. He had too much energy.

"The other one in place?" the gatekeeper asked of a nearby Skarr. He didn't hear a reply. The crowd roared from above. He looked up the stairs leading to the surface and saw the mighty portcullis marking the arena entrance.

The Pit.

This was finally it. Two years of hard training all led to this. If he won, *if* he won, the coin would be enough to afford him a villa somewhere away from the city, and the bride of his choice. He tried hard not to think of her. He tried very hard not to think of her worried face. He needed all his wits focused on the task ahead.

"You ready?" the gatekeeper asked. He was older, grizzled, and studied him with a cocked eye.

"I am."

"Maybe Seddon will bless you, then." He raised his hand to the lever in the wall.

The portcullis groaned as it lifted open. The cheering intensified—almost impossibly so. The gatekeeper might have said something more, but his words were drowned out.

Taking a breath, Bars jogged upward into the light. He entered the arena, the noise pounding his senses like beach rocks in a storm swell. Women called out to him. Men shook their fists and cursed. The smell of sweat and heat and something else made the air bad to taste. Bars saw guards ringing the rim of the arena's lower walls. They stood above the special boxes on the lowest level where the dignitaries, the wealthy, and owners of gladiators could view without obstruction. He saw the high box where the king would watch if he wasn't rutting, as the rumors went. Then he centered on the opposite side of the arena.

The Screamer was there, his bronze helm shining as if on fire. The man threw his arms wide and greeted the audience, turning around once. Then, sensing his opponent, the Screamer turned to Bars and raised sword and fist.

The fist caught his attention.

It was a spiked gauntlet of sorts, with a small buckler fixed to his forearm. Bars figured his foe thought himself to be fast. How fast remained to be seen.

From where he stood, in a high, arena-side pulpit, the Orator called for silence.

"From the renowned gladiatorial School of Nexus, I give you Bars, the Sunjan," he introduced with a raised arm. The crowd approved.

"And from the Church of Seddon, Seddon's son himself, Vadrian the Fire!" On cue, Vadrian sunk to one knee and bowed his head. *He's praying*, Bars thought. *He's actually praying.*

The action quieted the crowd, making it easy to hear Vadrian's words. "Sweet Seddon above, give me strength to vanquish my heathen foe this day. Give me strength to deliver him unto you, oh, Heavenly Father, the one true Lord. Give me strength to fight to my fullest power, in your divine name, in your divine light, to do your divine will. Help me now to smite the heathen across from me."

Then it was over. Bars blinked, not sure what to make of such a prayer.

Vadrian rose and spread his arms wide once more, as if receiving holy messages from above. Then, the communal complete, he dropped his arms and regarded Bars across the way.

He pointed his sword at him. "I shall deliver you!"

You can fishhook yourself, Bars thought with distaste, beginning to dislike screamers as well. There was a smugness, a piousness, present in his foe that he didn't care for.

Then, the Orator bellowed, "Good people of Sunja! On behalf of the Gladiatorial Chamber and King Juhn's best wishes for you to be entertained, let… the fight… *begin!*"

Bars assumed a guarded stance and moved toward his foe.

Vadrian raised his arms, holding his blade two-handed and at high guard above his head. Bars could clearly see the spikes on the holy warrior's off-hand. He'd have to be wary of those.

The Screamer came closer. He was large and well-muscled. Bars could see the man's helm had a visor instead of a cage. The Screamer's eyes scrunched as if the rest of his face smiled.

Bars didn't know what was so damn amusing. He

decided to do something about it.

He sidestepped and lunged, stabbing for a leg while raising his shield. Vadrian's leg jerked away, and Bars found himself twisting to deflect the heavy sword coming down from above. Then, his senses exploded as the spiked gauntlet smashed into the back of his head. He dove forward, the force of the blow driving him on, and spun about.

With surprising speed, the bronze-helmed man was on top of him. Bars whirled to face him. He got his shield up and stabbed underneath it, but a sword parried his blade into the sand. A spiked gauntlet cracked across his jaw, the impact ripping the face-cage from his helm. Bars staggered backward.

Seddon's self-proclaimed holy son would not allow him to regain his senses.

Vadrian brought his sword down again and again, raining heavy strikes onto Bars's upraised shield. Each connection numbed Bars's arm. Vadrian stepped in close, grabbed the edge of his rival's shield, and smashed his sword's pommel into Bars's exposed face. The graduate of the School of Nexus felt his teeth shatter from far away, and his world left him.

Something thundered against the side of his head, and Bars distantly realized that he was on his back. But that couldn't be right. The fight had only just *begun*.

Then, the sun darkened. Vadrian towered over him and stabbed him once, twice, and then a third time through his guts. The steel punched through leather and viscera like a long spike through tough cheese.

After the third stab, Vadrian held his bloodstained blade to the heavens. "I send thee the first, oh Lord of Lords! The first of many, I swear unto you!"

The crowd roared. Some booed and cursed the divine one.

From his back, Bars's empty hands found his wounds. The pain in his midsection sparkled and sizzled enough for water to fill his eyes.

It wasn't supposed to end like this, the thought formed in his head. He wanted to be away from here, back in the general quarters. He wanted to listen to Halm and Pig Knot; for certain, they had more tales to tell. He wanted to see *her* face again.

He heard a voice. "Still here, little heathen?"

Bars regarded the form standing over him, black in the sun.

"Fear not," came the words. "I shall send you."

Vadrian put his full strength behind his spiked gauntlet and smashed the face at his feet.

*

The cart rolled past the masses of gladiators, drawing the usual morbid curiosity. Some were close enough to peer inside, but they did not linger on this one, not like Baylus, the Butcher from Balgotha. This one, while a mess, was only a dead hellpup.

Three men moved the cart toward a loading area where the bodies were piled until the day was done. The corpses would receive final rites and be burned as one. It was a foul job, but the men had done it for so long the horror no longer bothered them. And it paid quite well.

A gladiator stepped in front of the cart, stopping them.

It was one of the bigger men, his huge belly bare and quivering. Halm gazed down upon the youngster he had talked to only a short time earlier and sighed. He'd hoped Bars would return to the quarters. He remembered the unease in the pup's face, and how he had politely held out his sword and shield. Not many would do such a thing, thinking it bad luck.

The thought stuck in Halm's mind. Perhaps it was bad luck after all.

"Well, damnation," Pig Knot swore, as he came up to stand alongside the cart. "I had a good feeling about that one."

"As did I," Halm said.

"Shame. He seemed pleasant enough. Even let me have his sword. Not many would do that."

"Not many."

From the other side of the room, Vadrian entered, bellowing praises to his Lord Seddon. He held the youngster's Mademian blade over his head as a trophy, swinging it without heed.

Halm loathed the Screamer even more.

"Not many," he repeated to a pensive Pig Knot. The Zhiberian didn't dwell on the dead man. He had things to do, preparations to complete before his own fight that day.

And the day was far from done.

"The hallowed Father above granted me strength of arm!" Vadrian bellowed from across the way, further grating Halm's nerves. "With his grace and blessing, He granted me the will to vanquish a heathen maggot and, as Seddon is my witness, I shall triumph again in the bloody pit."

Halm gazed down at the dead man in the cart, very much aware of how the voice was growing louder.

"See here!"

The Zhiberian looked up.

The Screamer stood beside the corpse cart and pointed to it in grand fashion. "This one goes to Saimon's hell for daring to stand against a herald of Seddon. As shall all. And perhaps in the afterlife—"

Halm's eyes became slits. "Silence yourself, you unfit kog."

The rebuke quieted Vadrian.

But only for a moment.

"I'll not stop spreading the word of Seddon, heathen," the blond brute yelled and stepped closer. "If my words disturb you, perhaps you should take yourself from the hall. Sed—"

"Seddon can lick my ass," returned Halm, not backing down in the least. "I've been hearing you pig-bastard all morning. Who are you spouting your shite to? Who is listening? Not this heathen shagger. Take your long tongue and lick Seddon's crack."

The insult mortified the larger warrior. "Seddon will strike you down for uttering—"

"I've uttered it and I'm still here." Halm threw his arms wide, inviting disaster. "Dying Seddon take me now if I've offended you. I'm right here, Lord! But by your holy ballsack," he pointed at Vadrian. "I've had enough of his shite in my ears!"

Vadrian's face darkened. "You blasphemous heathen! You ignorant man-child! I'll smite you in Seddon's name!"

"Away with you, you unfit temple slave. Seddon's smarter than to give any attention to the likes of you." The Zhiberian stepped closer to Vadrian as well, and the pair squared off like two violent storm fronts about to meet.

"By the Holy Church, I'll rip out your tongue!"

And with that, Vadrian raised his weapons.

A wall of pit fighters swarmed between the pair, grabbing and holding onto weapon arms. Pig Halm placed himself before Halm while fixing Vadrian with a hostile look. Shouts of restraint cut the air. Some gladiators glanced toward the *Madea* and his cohort of Skarr warriors, but the arena official did nothing but watch from where he sat.

"Saimon's ass, you smell like a pot of shite," Halm barked over Pig Knot's shoulder. "Do all of you Seddon lovers smell as such?"

"Insolent mouth! I'll yank—" The blond struggled against the mass holding him back.

"Get that topper back!" Pig Knot yelled at the knot of men restraining Vadrian. "Clear the space!"

"He-bitch!" Vadrian spat.

"*Enough!*"

All eyes turned to see a red-faced *Madea* standing tall behind his desk and glaring at the two men. The usual handful of Skarrs guarding the arena official had mysteriously increased to a dozen soldiers ready to break heads.

The two feuding gladiators saw the impassive reavers and quickly settled down. The men between them relaxed at the sudden drop in tension, but they did not release the pair.

The *Madea's* eyes flashed from Vadrian to Halm. "Never in my time have I witnessed that which has transpired here this day, on this, the *first* day of the games. Are you both so eager to dishonor these hallowed quarters? Over so minor a quibble? *Enough*, I say! You've shamed yourselves in my eyes and the sword brothers about you, standing upon the very ground where countless others have stood and trained and waited to enter Sunja's Pit, to shed blood in a place that screams for it, but not here."

That quieted the lot of them.

Vadrian scowled and hung his head almost theatrically.

Halm burned with chagrin and he gestured with his chin. "He started—"

"You bastard!" shouted the other, and jerked an arm free to strike.

"*Enough!*"

The harsh command sapped the fight from both captive men, and their postures relaxed.

"If you are *so* determined to have at each other, then I shall arrange it." The *Madea's* dark eyes smoldered. "I'll make it so. Is that what you want Vadrian of Sunja?"

"By Seddon's holiness, yes, the chance to smite—"

"*Is that* what you want, Halm of Zhiberia?" The arena official snapped, cutting off the Sunjan.

But at the mention of Zhiberia, Vadrian's face became unpleasantly sly.

"Oh I want." Halm seethed with a poisoned glare at the other. "I want very much."

"Then it's agreed," the *Madea* declared. "At a time of my choosing, you two shall meet in Sunja's Pit. If you fight each other before your meeting, both of you shall be executed. It is done." The *Madea* slapped his table, causing some to flinch. "I declare blood match."

"Blood match," Vadrian smiled, pleased with the decision.

"Blood match," Halm muttered and scowled back.

· 3 ·

The Masters

They sat at the north end of Sunja's Pit, in viewing boxes afforded only to the top three schools of gladiatorial arts. King Juhn recognized that they were important men and, in some cases, survivors of the Pit themselves. That did not make them of noble blood, however, no matter what they might have thought otherwise. Still, they were of minor importance, and thus allowed some standard of luxury. The king also decided that they would have their viewing box next to the nobles, with servants to wait upon them.

From this lofty perch, the owners watched the opening matches of the games. They had just witnessed another slaughter in the arena, a vicious killing where the victor wasted no time in slaying his fallen opponent in convincing fashion. Of the three owners, only one visibly stiffened at the conclusion of the match, for it was his own highly touted gladiator who perished.

"What in Seddon's blue pisspot has happened?" Nexus cried, not caring in the least what the others thought. Fine silver hair cut to a fashionable length fell over a face aged and sallowed by the years. A sunken chin and black eyes gave him the look of a weasel. Of the three, he was the only one who wasn't a gladiator in his youth, preferring to sharpen other skills in a much different arena. Besides owning his school, he was also a prominent wine producer for the country. He usually left the management of his gladiator school in the hands of his taskmaster and trainers and, though he was intelligent enough to leave them to do their job, this particular year he'd decided to watch the games in the flesh for the first time. Nexus wouldn't hesitate to tell his trainers what he thought of their work if it didn't produce results in the arena. Of all the business ventures Nexus forayed into, the training of warriors for the Pit had become the most exciting, and the most taxing of his limited patience.

"Seddon's rosy ass!" Nexus's normally pallid face became red with outrage. "Who was that asslicker? Sweet Seddon above! Sweet *Seddon*! I'll personally ensure that bastard is buried in a cow kiss! May Saimon *pack* Seddon's rosy ass! He got his bells paddled by a Free Trained! A *Free Trained*! That stupid he-bitch! Dying Seddon! I'll have some maggot's hanging bells for this! It takes money to raise and train those toppers!"

Spittle flew from Nexus's lips, and he paused to sip from a silver goblet. He got a mouthful of his own vintage down before the anger surged again. He resumed cursing, black eyes livid, as wine fell onto the front of his silk shirt.

Gastillo, owner of the School of Gastillo, looked to the sands with a dour expression. Some people called him *Half-Face* behind his back, and to his front if drunk enough, but they would be the last words spoken if done so. The once champion was the victim of an overhand mace that missed crushing his skull, but raked the skin from the right side of his features, almost perfectly down the middle. Half of his nose had been shorn away, leaving only a frightful black hole on one side. Below that, his lips were mangled, and Gastillo forever drooled when he spoke or ate. He wore a mask during the games and in public, one of gold that also covered the top of his head as a cap. A thin slit between his metal lips allowed him to drink, but at times, he lifted the mask when he really wanted to guzzle.

Unlike Nexus, Gastillo had invested substantial coin and effort in his own school, the House of Gastillo, building it up from the very beginning. Though he would mock Nexus in private, to his face he was much more respectful. The wine merchant possessed experience in matters of business that interested Gastillo greatly.

At the moment, however, Gastillo felt only a twinge of regret and annoyance. It was never pleasant to see a new fighter die on the sands, especially to a fanatic like Vadrian of the Church of Seddon. *Church of Seddon indeed*, Gastillo scoffed. As if the actual church participated in such bloody events. What was worse, however, was that Vadrian had killed one of Nexus's lads, and Gastillo would have to endure a livid merchant. There would be no talk of business this day.

Sitting to the right and ignoring them both, a sickle of a smile spread across Dark Curge's swarthy features. He was baldheaded and big, retaining most of his musculature for a man in his sixties. He had also been a champion of the Pit and had given his hand and half his forearm to the arena gods as the price for his success. Dark Curge wasn't a merchant like the pair to his right. Well, he conceded he wasn't a merchant like Nexus. Gastillo was a graying war dog snapping at ventures he didn't have the schooling for. Curge did appreciate the business of the Pit, and the irony of how some matches played out. The arena was far superior to the theater; here, the players were real, and their characters shone true until weal or bloody woe.

"What are you grinning about, lout?" Nexus snapped at him. "Perhaps, one of your investments will be struck down later this day."

"No offense meant," Curge rumbled, though his smile lingered. "I was just appreciating your oaths."

"My oaths!" Nexus's nostrils flared. "What damned gurry is that? My oaths! Be professional, you one-armed git! You don't see the nobles laughing at their companions' losses, do you?"

"No need for insults," Curge replied. "Apologies if I offended you."

"Your *apologies*, now! From smiles to fake condolences! I share this box with a one-handed weasel, it seems. As two-faced as this one."

At the slight, Gastillo's golden mask turned ever so slightly.

A furious Nexus rose and threw his goblet at a servant. "I'm going to see what happened out there. Seddon's balls, I'll get an answer. And I'll make certain this doesn't happen again."

With that he stormed out the exit.

The two remaining owners sat for a moment, waiting to see if Nexus would return. He did not.

Gastillo shifted, regarded the closed door behind him, and faced the arena sands. "The dog blossom tore out of here like his ass was on fire."

Curge snorted in amusement. "You'd think this was the

first time he had lost a fighter to one of those rabble."

"Not firsthand. And that one wasn't rabble," Gastillo said in a low voice. "There's skill there, as distasteful as it might be. The games are attracting more and more skilled Free Trained every season. Individual swordsmen without the backing of a formal house or school or what have you. Eventually, you'll see one of them as champion."

Curge arched an eyebrow. "Are you favoring them, Gastillo?"

"Favoring? No. Wary of them, yes. Mark my words; there's a gemstone in every mountain. It's just a matter of it clawing its way to the surface."

"Rabble, the lot."

"Rabble they might be, but that's not to say they're slouches." Gastillo rubbed at his throat. "To think that would be a grave mistake."

Curge scrunched his face and looked into the arena. "Enough of that shite, then. When's the next fight? A man has other things to do during daylight."

"How many do you have fighting this day?"

"None. Samarhead will fight perhaps tomorrow. And you?"

"Tomorrow, as well. I have one in there."

"I wonder how many Nexus has?" Curge thought aloud. "If any more get killed outright, the man might choke on his wine."

"He just might."

The pair became silent as the Orator straightened in his podium and announced the next match. The warriors to fight were both Free Trained, and the news was met with a raucous mix of cheers and boos. The two warriors emerged from their opposite entrances and walked on the sand.

A frowning Curge lifted one ass cheek from his chair and rubbed his face, preparing himself for the show to come.

And as expected, the two pit fighters went at each other's throats like mad dogs. Sand and blood flew, and it took only a few moments before the dust clouds cleared, and one man remained on his feet. The other warrior squirmed on the sands, clutching his thigh cut to the bone. Blood spurted between his fingers.

The crowd roared, loving the violence. Curge suspected they cheered for the quickness of the match.

Robbed of mobility, the fallen gladiator held up a bare palm. The other accepted the surrender, and the fight was done.

Curge scratched at an ear. "That was absolute shite. You see why they'll never advance much farther than a third round."

"Perhaps not those two," Gastillo grated, "but there are hundreds of them. The season's a long one. A handful will show promise."

"The lot of them are pure shite," Curge grumped. "If you found one shiny rock amongst the works, you'd still have to sweat to teach it anything. Not worth the effort."

"So you say."

Curge chuckled and eyed Gastillo with scorn. "How long did you fight in the Pit? One season? Two? I can't remember. I was *born* into that hell. And I've a good enough eye to measure what is and what isn't shite. Even the crowd knows, Gastillo, and they're drunk most of the time."

Curge got to his feet. "All this talk about what is and isn't shite makes a man want to piss. You watch on there, *boy*, and perhaps you'll learn something. Don't get too close, though. Shite flies. Might hit that pretty mask of yours. Then where will you be, hm?"

The gold mask didn't move. Didn't offer a reply.

Chuckling, Curge left. He walked past the manservant attending to them and, upon opening the door, met Nexus.

With a flourish, the larger man stepped back and bade Nexus enter. The merchant glared and did so.

Curge exited a heartbeat later.

"Ignorant punce." Nexus sat down next to Gastillo. "The air's so much fresher with that dog blossom gone."

"It is that," replied the half-faced man. "You returned quickly."

"Too many people in the passageways," Nexus settled into his seat and took a goblet from a servant without thanks. "Cluttered shoulder to shoulder. Angered me even more. I'll talk to my taskmaster when I see him. And I'll have a necklace of balls if it happens again."

A necklace of balls, Gastillo thought. That was an image that would strike fear into anyone. "What are you going to talk about?"

Nexus's goblet paused a hand's breadth from his mouth, and he fixed Gastillo with a disgusted look. "You think I'm about to tell you? Take your best guess, you gold-plated topper. The day I tell you anything is the day I'm permitted to pack the asses off the king's daughters."

Nexus drank deeply, then demanded more.

Keeping his insult in check, Gastillo sipped his own wine carefully between his metal lips. *A necklace of balls, indeed,* he fumed. He decided he would not inquire about vineyards and winemaking this afternoon, and reflected, once again, these assigned 'seats of honor' would be much better if it were only him. He thought about wandering down to the lower levels, where each house had a private chamber looking out onto the arena, where the sands were level with a man's upper chest. But those rooms were crowded with the training staff and house gladiators waiting for their time in Sunja's Pit.

And he reluctantly admitted that the box offered the best view to the games.

*

Curge took his time at the latrines and, when finished, took a detour to the Gate of the Sun. He pushed through folk, leaving a wake of mutters and angry glares. No one challenged him. The owner walked by assembled Skarrs, their visors impassive. Up ahead, the wide corridor ended in a glow of sunshine. Curge stopped, ignored the crowds milling about him, and placed his broad back to one of the arena walls.

There he waited.

People walked by without a word, but some recognized the old bear. Those kept their distance all the more.

All but one. A man with youthful features slipped out of the stream of people. Dressed plainly in a black tunic, breeches, and soft boots, the individual placed a shoulder to the wall and nodded to his employer.

Dark Curge eyed the crowds as he half-turned to speak. "Don't make me wait again, Bezange, or I'll paddle your balls with a mace."

"Apologies, my Lord," the smaller man said.

"I want to you look into this one called Vadrian, see what he's about. Get Omaz to talk with him, but don't reveal anything just yet. And I want you to mind who this 'Son of Seddon' fights in the future. I'll give you further instructions thereafter."

"Understood," Bezange said sleepily.

Curge knew his agent was in his late thirties, but his damn near unwrinkled skin gave him the glow of a newborn babe. "How can you wear black in this heat?"

Bezange shrugged. "It's only hot if I stay in the sun. And I do not."

No, Curge thought, *you're a creature of the shadows. Where you do your best work.*

"Get going," the bald owner growled and shoved the smaller man away with a curse, just to make it look convincing.

When his agent had gone, Curge decided to return to the owners' box, mulling over Vadrian and the potential there. He liked what he saw in the young warrior. He liked the praying before the match. There were enough atheists around to despise such a show, and Curge could see a very lucrative opportunity in side wagers, if he was attentive enough and manipulated the odds in his favor.

That particular thought made Curge smile tightly as he made his way back to the games.

• 4 •

Halm and Muluk

The altercation with Vadrian had been interesting for only a moment before the masses went back to their own personal business. Perched at his desk above a fence of watchful Skarrs, the *Madea* sat and pondered the next match. He frowned and sized up the great matchboard. He took another glance before getting to his feet.

Gathered not too far away from the arena official, Pig Knot and Halm leaned against a stone wall draped by shadows. They were a pair of big men amongst other physically intimidating gladiators moving throughout the underground chamber.

"You unfit bastard," Pig Knot scolded with a smile. "You had to go pick a fight with the nosiest punce in the pack?"

"Pah." Halm bared bad teeth. "I could only put up with that yelling for so long. He's no church man. This Church of Seddon is a jest. Think about it. What church trains and sends a man to fight in these games? Eh? No, when I can, I'll toss that sack of gurry into the streets."

The *Madea* suddenly yelled, his voice carrying in those subterranean halls. "The next pairing will be Halm of Zhiberia and Muluk of Kree. Prepare yourselves."

Halm gave Pig Knot a questioning look.

"So soon," Pig Knot said, his eyes bright. "Interesting times."

Halm scowled at him.

"It's nice to know he remembers you."

Halm continued scowling.

"Need any help with your gear?"

"The day I need help from *you* is the day I perish, Sunjan," the fat man shot back.

"So you need help?"

"Aye that."

Halm bent over and plucked at a huge sack at his feet, where he'd dumped his only tools of the trade. Unlike a good many individuals participating in the games, he actually owned weapons and armor. Some of the poorer Free Trained did not and they relied heavily on what the Pit's armory had in stock, a selection of weapons and armor taken from dead men.

The Zhiberian undid the sack's knot. The smell of foul leather poorly kept flowered the air and soured the faces of both men.

"Did you empty the bull in that?" Pig Knot asked.

"I don't think so."

"You should leave that open, afterwards. Dry it out."

"Who is this Muluk, anyway?" Halm asked, changing the subject.

Pig Knot shook his head. "I don't know. He obviously doesn't belong to a school or the like."

"So we'll be two dogs fighting over scraps." Halm winked.

"But, oh, what scraps." Pig Knot's dark eyes glittered.

"Here then, you." Halm held out a long sleeve of leather padding tacked together with pointed studs. He slipped his sword arm into the sleeve while Pig Knot held it and later fastened the buckles under the portly warrior's armpits and neck. The Zhiberian stooped, picked up his sword, a regular blade the length of his arm, and gave it a quick inspection. He placed it against the wall while he strapped greaves to his legs. Once done, he stood and regarded Pig Knot.

"How do I look?" Halm asked.

"Like a fat piece of shite," Pig Knot remarked without humour. "This yours?"

He held out a helm. It was bronze, conical, with a thick visor that protected the eyes and nose but not the lower jaw.

"It is," Halm said. "Give it here, then. I'm getting the wave from the *Madea*. It's time."

They both looked in the arena organizer's direction. They also saw a brute of a man already conversing with him. He wore a shabby vest of studded leather and carried only a sword and square shield. A pot helm covered his head. Despite his ragged appearance, the man was as tall as Halm.

"Strong looking," Pig Knot commented. "But looks like he got his gear from his father."

"You're one to talk," Halm countered. "Have you looked at what you dress yourself in?"

"Not listening to a dog who struts around with his gut hanging out."

"That's strategy." Halm patted his huge hairy belly, wholly unprotected. "They'll all be swinging for this, while I'll be taking off their heads."

He slapped a roll of fat, making it quiver.

Pig Knot wasn't impressed. "Let's hope you win this one

and can at least buy a girdle."

Halm grunted. "If I win, I'll be feasting this night."

"Daresay you'll perish, though," Pig Knot said.

"Daresay."

"Just don't be quick about it. People pay money to see a show."

"People pay nothing to see these games."

"That's right, my mistake."

Halm squared his shoulders. "They can lick my ass, for all I care."

"That would be a show." Half of Pig Knot's face hitched up in distaste. He held out the man's own square shield and fitted it to the Zhiberian's left arm. Halm picked up his blade again, gave himself a quick look, and announced, "Right, I'm ready. Who do I have to kill?"

"Are all Zhiberians like you?" Pig Knot asked.

"No. Just me."

Pig Knot shook his head and held out a fist. Holding his sword, Halm pressed his knuckles into his companion's.

"Care to wager?" Halm asked.

Pig Knot scoffed his answer to that and walked away.

Halm watched him go, thinking that a simple wager wouldn't have hurt much. He realized he had very little to wager with, and Pig Knot was probably in the same situation. The potential for vast sums of coin had initially lured Halm to the games, but truth be known, the money was secondary. The Zhiberian enjoyed fighting, fully expecting to die before the age of forty. If he lived to be old, he had no idea how he would support himself, and he screwed his nose up at the thought of becoming a merchant. Of course, if he actually *won* the games, or even strung together enough victories then he could consider *spending* coin as a fulltime profession.

That and wenching.

And drinking.

Preferably, both at the same time.

Ignoring the Skarrs and the other pit fighters, he made his way through the white tunnel to the arena. He stopped before the gatekeeper, just below the lowered portcullis. The old man sized up the Zhiberian and shook his head.

"You're a ham waiting to be cut up, my son," the gatekeeper chuckled.

Halm focused on the gate above and the sunlight streaming in. "In your hole, you old tit."

The surprised gatekeeper blinked at the insult.

"Shall I pull that lever?" Halm asked pointedly.

Incensed, the old man yanked down hard on the bar, opening the portcullis.

Halm jogged to his fate. He had more important things to do than exchanging barbs with old men. The light embraced him as he stepped onto the sands. The roar of the crowd washed over him, quickening his blood, but failing to move much else. These weren't his first games, and he'd been around long enough to know the crowd's true fickle nature. Some men loved the adoration of the masses, but Halm knew the truth of it. This day, however, he wondered how many had put coin on him winning, and how many pissers had wagered against.

Those he meant to disappoint.

Across the sands, the one called Muluk waited. He was indeed a tall man, perhaps even a finger or two higher than Halm. And meaty. Powerful-looking. Halm nodded at his adversary, and received one in return. That pleased him. A simple greeting was a good sign. He hated pit fighters who got so consumed in the moment that they forgot common courtesy.

Overhead, the Orator bellowed introductions.

Upon hearing his name, Muluk raised his sword arm in salute.

When Halm heard his name, he raised his arm as well. Some jeers reached his ears, and a rancid smile spread across his face—some still remembered the Zhiberian flinging a spear into the audience. It wasn't him, but he could understand his countryman's reasons for doing so. There were days the crowd was with you, and then days they wanted your head.

The Orator shouted to begin.

Muluk crossed the sand, his arms swinging at his sides, the leather he wore even more worn-looking the closer he got. His old pot helm had a few dents and completely hid the man's face. Halm cringed at the uncomfortable heat his opponent must be feeling.

He took a deep breath and went to meet his foe halfway.

"Hail, Halm of Zhiberia," Muluk said loud enough to be heard over the crowd.

"Hail," Halm yelled back. "Muluk of Kree. It is Kree, isn't it?"

"Aye that."

At least he'd heard that part right. "Is this to the death, then?"

"I've no stomach for it to be so," came Muluk's reply, his words somewhat metallic sounding. "In fact, the sight of blood turns my guts."

That made Halm smile. "You shouldn't have signed up for this butchery then.

"You're right. I shouldn't have."

"So why did you, then?"

"Coin." Muluk circled to his right, raising his weapon and shield. "Need the gold. Times are hard."

"So you entered hell looking for it?" Halm shook his head. He circled right as well, sword and shield at the ready. "That why you wear the rags?"

Muluk swung his sword at Halm's head.

Halm parried with his shield and stabbed with his own blade, driving the other man back. The Zhiberian nodded in approval at the nimble evasion. He took a new grip on his sword and slowly pursued.

"These rags once belonged to my father," Muluk answered, seemingly not bothered by the sword exchange.

"Truly?"

"Aye that."

Halm grunted and threw a combination of strikes.

Muluk blocked each one with his square shield, moving the barrier up and down, left and right as needed. Then he thrust with his own blade, and Halm barely deflected the blade with his own protective barrier.

"You're a strong one, Muluk!" Halm cried and shook his arm. "I felt that last one all the way up my shoulder."

"Aye, you're no slouch yourself—for a fat man," Muluk shot back, but Halm imagined a smile around the words. "I thought this to be an easy mark."

The Zhiberian laughed. "They all think that. I've fooled you, too, I see."

Muluk skipped to his right, and Halm matched him. They narrowed the gap and erupted into a short, violent exchange of swords.

Halm stabbed for his foe's leg and then his head. Both blows were turned aside. They parted, and Halm noted that the Kree's shoulders and chest barely heaved at all. The man had stamina as well as strength. Thoughts of wearing him down exited Halm's head.

"You don't move fast on your feet, but you're quick with the sword and shield," Muluk called over the crowd's growing insistence to liven things up. The man didn't rush things just to please them, however, and that also pleased Halm. He hated the kind who listened to spectators.

"Faster than shite through a sick cow if need be," Halm answered.

Muluk's helm arched back in a chuckle.

Halm shook his own head. "This is quite the place for a conversation."

Perhaps agreeing with him, Muluk charged, bringing his sword down in a ferocious chop. Halm caught it on his shield, then sent his own blade into Muluk's, who turned it away.

They parted, and like two bulls contesting for a cow, they eyed each other.

"It is that," Muluk replied.

"You seem like a friendly sort," Halm said.

"As do you, Zhiberian."

"Then, if you're interested, and don't feel too put out, I'll buy you a roast and drink after the day's fights."

"You'd do that?"

With unexpected speed, Halm stepped in and shield-bashed his foe's face. Muluk blocked with his own shield, but he didn't expect or see Halm's sword pommel.

With his opponent partially blinded, Halm twisted and drove that brutal piece of metal down as if hammering nail, slamming it into the side of Muluk's pot helm with a frightening *gong*!

The impact dazed the Kree long enough for Halm to shield-punch him a second time.

That connection knocked Muluk clean off his feet, and he crashed onto his back, arching his spine as if in great pain. Pressing forward, Halm hooked Muluk's sword and flicked it away before planting a knee on the man's chest. With care, he inserted the tip of his sword under Muluk's helm and tapped its edge twice.

"The least I can do," Halm declared good-naturedly.

Inside the Muluk's pot helm, the face dusty, a pair of dark eyes gleamed. When he didn't answer straight away, Halm feared he might have insulted the fallen Kree gladiator.

But then the prone man carefully raised a hand in surrender.

Cheers blasted overhead, mixed with more than a few boos, but Halm cared little for them.

He'd just won his first match.

"Damnation," Muluk groaned. "Never saw that coming. You took the wind out of me."

"My apologies," Halm said. "It is a rough sport."

Muluk groaned again. "I'll have my revenge, Zhiberian bastard. I can drink like a fish."

He tapped Halm's ankle, and the heavier man stepped back and allowed him to get to his feet.

"We'll see about that, then," Halm said. "I was worried for a moment."

Muluk waved his hand. "I'm just glad to be alive. And with only a few bruises. The Pit's one way to get coin, but not one suited to me. No ill will, Halm of Zhiberia."

He held out his fist.

Halm regarded it. Then, amongst the cheers and the insults of the crowd, he drove the tip of his sword into the arena sand.

He pressed his own fist against Muluk's.

"No ill will, Muluk of… where're you from again?"

Three men took their leave of the Pit for the day, made their way to the public bathhouses and washed away the grime of the arena. Since Pig Knot had not yet fought, and Muluk had lost, Halm declared that the baths, food, and drink would all be gifts this evening. He held his small leather purse containing his winnings by the strings, quite content with the twenty gold coins filling it. Once washed and dressed in regular clothes, Halm led them to an alehouse he had discovered only two days ago which served a wonderful pork roast. They ordered ale, along with enough food for three big men, and proceeded to get drunk well into the night.

Smoke filled the alehouse, some wafting from the kitchen area, some from pipes, and all blending with the ripe smell of body odor. The three men sat in an alcove made of heavy wood, their eighth pitcher in the table's center. Mugs surrounded the container. Gristle and leftover shreds of unappealing fat lay on wooden plates. Halm belched loudly and wiped his mouth. He looked at Pig Knot, who had actually arm-wrestled a local mere moments earlier and won five gold for his efforts. Pig Knot was a strong man. One needed only to look at his swelling arms to see it, but the lad who thought he could take him must have been even drunker. At least he handed over his wager with a smile. Halm disliked fighting in alehouses.

"You are…" Pig Knot slurred and pointed at Muluk, sitting on the inside of the booth. "Perhaps the first man from Kree I've met."

"I am?" Muluk slurred right back. "Daresay I'm the only Kree in these parts. Though I may be mistaken."

"You can hold your drink."

Muluk exhaled dangerously in reply.

Pig Knot was indeed correct—the Kree could hold his alcohol, which was good. Halm also hated watching over quick-tempered drunks.

"I think our paying companion here is the only Zhiberian in Sunja as well," Pig Knot said, turning his finger.

"I think so too," Halm agreed. "Not since the last one…"

The three men smiled. They knew the story.

"So what will you do?" Pig Knot asked Muluk. "Now that you're out of the games, I mean."

The Kree thought about it. "Don't really know. I was a trapper, but I got tired of the life. I could also chop trees, being something of a woodsman as well." He shrugged. "I'll find something."

"Chop trees," Halm said. "That explains our fight. You strike damn hard. It was a good thing I had a shield."

Muluk shrugged. "I might stay awhile, however, sleep in the streets or somewhere, until I can see this fight between you and the church man."

"I'm interested in that one myself," Pig Knot added. "What was it you called him?"

Halm chuckled. "A kog?"

"No."

"Pig-bastard?"

"Not that."

Halm had to think about it. "Heathen shagger?"

"That was it." Pig Knot smiled.

"Wait." Muluk frowned. "I was there, too. He called him a heathen shagger."

"Who? Vadrian?"

"Aye that," Muluk smiled. "You're going to have to kill that one. You could feel the heat from him, he was so angry."

Old wood pressed against Halm's back as he shifted. "My thoughts on it are this… he baits men into fighting him. What's the word? Tempts. He tempts."

"Will you kill him?" Pig Knot asked.

Halm studied Pig Knot. "I don't know."

"He'll kill you. Guaranteed." Pig Knot's dark eyes glittered.

Halm took a drink from his mug. "I'll have forgotten this… by tomorrow. If the lad wishes to back out, I'll let him."

Muluk looked at Pig Knot. "I didn't think one could back out of a blood match."

"Aye that," the Sunjan said. "You can't back out of a blood match, you heathen shagger. I like that. I'm going to call you that whenever I can now. Shagger. *Heathen* shagger."

Halm took another shot from his mug, thinking hard on his companions' words. *You can't back out of a blood match.*

"Can't I?" Halm suppressed a burp.

Red eyes studied him.

"It's to the death," Pig Knot said and almost knocked over his mug as he reached for it. He took a long pull off the lip.

"To the *death*," he repeated and chuckled.

Frowning in drunken puzzlement, Halm drank with him.

Leave it to Pig Knot to make a person feel better.

*

In another part of the city of Sunja, in a dilapidated church that threatened to collapse at any moment, the man called

Vadrian knelt on a mat in front of a hundred lit candles, the only source of light in the building. He had stripped, preferring to pray without clothing. Vadrian clasped his large hands and looked to the heavens, visible through a huge gash torn in the roof high above. He prayed. He prayed as if his life depended on it. He prayed for victory and he prayed that he remained strong during the games. He vowed to restore the church to its former glory with whatever gold he won. Prayers of vengeance came out of him then, against the man known as Halm. To speak out against the Son of Seddon and the Lord who spoke to Vadrian every day, was to speak out against the holy one himself. While Vadrian remained alive, he swore to send all nonbelievers and blasphemers to Seddon's heavenly court, where they would be judged.

He'd made a blood sacrifice of the first man he met in Sunja's Pit.

He would make another of the man called Halm from the barbarous country known as Zhiberia.

Disgust filled Vadrian's face. That fat heathen originated from a feral land where men and women lived in incessant sin. One day, when the church was restored and Vadrian possessed an army of followers as devoted as himself, he would ride into that savage land and put the entire countryside to the sword and torch. All in Seddon's holy name.

But first, there needed to be sacrifice.

An *evening* sacrifice.

Vadrian had sacrificed much to be in Sunja's Pit. He'd sacrificed his mother and his father, and his younger sister and brother. While he had wept as he crushed the lives from his family's earthly forms, he knew a better place awaited them. He saved them from the rampant evil in Seddon's world. There was evil all around. Evil so thick it was only a matter of time before it infected his family. It was best to send those he loved to Seddon before any wickedness could touch them.

Seddon, Vadrian believed, would not be pleased just by saving a few meagre souls, however pure they might be. *Send them all*, Seddon had commanded one night, *and you shall be rewarded*.

So Vadrian sent them.

Every chance he could.

To that end, he unclasped his hands and reached behind him.

Vadrian had spent an hour looking for vagrants, but there were none to be saved. He had hunted in the area before. Perhaps the wretched could somehow sense his divine approach. Such power was an evil ability to have if they could, and bestowed only onto agents of Saimon.

All the better to find them and put take their lives.

One old man, however, hadn't been so quick.

Vadrian pulled the dog into his hands. Blind eyes stared and frail bones trembled as Vadrian slipped one hand around the old man's neck.

Then the other.

Terrified whimpers filled the church.

Vadrian ignored those. Once he secured his grip, Vadrian squeezed. Hands pawed at his forearms, but he increased the pressure, squeezing until his muscles knotted and his fingers ached.

The whimpers ceased.

But Vadrian kept on squeezing.

And somewhere near his strength's end, he twisted.

• 5 •

Milloch and Samarhead

On the morning of the second day, Dark Curge awoke in his bedchamber entangled in blankets. He yawned, stretched, and eventually sat up. The covers fell from his broad, grizzled chest to tumble onto his growing paunch. He brushed them away with his left half-arm and got out of bed. Naked and not caring in the least, he walked to the bedchamber's window and threw open the wooden shutters.

Gray clouds bloated the sky and threatened rain.

Dark Curge scowled. Rain would delay the games, and his man fought this day. He wanted to see what the prized prospect of his house could do. Curge especially wanted to gloat in the company of Nexus and Gastillo. Unknown to the wine merchant, he delighted enjoyed watching Nexus boil to a rave. He enjoyed seeing gold-faced Gastillo squirm.

Then Curge remembered who his lad was fighting. A Free Trained dog.

Not particularly challenging.

He sighed.

Of the ten houses, stables and schools present at the

games, only three were considered major contenders. The House of Curge remained the most consistent in developing not just gladiators, but skilled destroyers of men. The other seven were regarded as inferior, but capable of producing and fielding at least one or two talented pit fighters. Not champion quality, but notable, and Curge felt he was being gracious in admitting that.

The Free Trained, however, were the absolute gurry of the games. Scroff. Trough shite. Unfit and sorely lacking. Yet every season, hundreds of self-proclaimed warriors, under-trained but bursting with visions of coin and glory, were drawn to Sunja's Pit.

Occasionally, however, some actually showed skill.

Like the Vadrian lad.

Curge went through his morning routine with a bored expression. His servants—all young, shapely women dressed in flimsy robes—bathed, dressed, and fed him. Once finished, he stepped outside onto green grass and walked the short distance to his training grounds and accompanying properties, all within a great walled compound that shielded him from the rest of the city. His deceased father had built the House of Curge in the richer part of Sunja, within a stone's toss of the nobility district. It was as close as Curge would ever come to noble and, while he openly scoffed the upper classes and even Sunja's own royalty, he secretly coveted a more regal station in life.

The damp grass covered a wild plot of land, right up to a low wall. Curge went through an open door, ignored a passageway and side corridors, and climbed steps to a second level. He made his way through a series of short halls, drawn to voices giving orders. As he got closer, he heard voices straining from exertion as well.

Dark Curge stepped onto an open balcony and looked down into a courtyard

Twenty-nine pit fighters, hellpups of the highest ability, went through their morning exercises. Sweat gleamed over their well-formed bodies, and their exertions punctuated the air. Trainers walked amongst them, observing the men lift heavy-looking timbers time and time again. None of the gladiators were slaves. They were all free men, paying a modest fee and a portion of their winnings to train within the House of Curge hoping that the taskmasters and trainers could fashion them into the next champion of the games. Curge's family history with the games was so great, that being accepted by the house carried a huge amount of prestige.

The trainers cracked whips when needed.

After a moment Curge caught the attention of his taskmaster, a squat, thick-necked man named Baris. He summoned the man to the balcony.

"Well?" Curge asked, leaning against the balcony's railing.

"All is ready," the taskmaster reported. "Tubrik has gone on to the Pit with Samarhead."

Curge pursed his lips and studied the badly scarred man. "He's still healthy?"

"He is. And in bloody spirits."

"Good."

"He'll be a terror these games. Tubrik and Bechar agree as well."

"I have faith that he will," Curge said.

The House of Curge had several gladiators poised to do very well during the season. It was Curge's belief that Samarhead was his best. The pit fighter was a brute, swift on his feet, and ready to kill. Some pit fighters hesitated to take another's life, but it was Curge's uncontested opinion that a gladiator had to be willing to gut a man, sometimes in the bloodiest fashion possible, to rise above the rest.

Even if it meant inciting the wrath of other houses.

If a pit fighter wasn't willing to slit another's throat, one had no business being in the sport.

Curge folded what he could of his arms and looked to those lifting timbers on the sands below. "I have a good feeling about this season. Might be wise if you're placing wagers this year, Baris. I'd bet my entire fortune if I were able."

A servant appeared and bowed, attracting Curge's attention. He nodded to his taskmaster. "I'm summoned. Whip those dogs in shape."

Baris departed.

Curge motioned for his servant to lead the way. He followed the young woman down a set of steps to the main doors, watching her curves sway underneath her sheer wisps of cloth. Curge cocked an eyebrow. The woman wasn't unattractive. He would have to summon her to his bedchamber later, after the day's events.

She led him to a room just off of the main entrance where, with a wave of her hand, she presented his human weasel, Bezange, who gave a short bow.

Curge whisked the servant away. "Well?"

"There's a problem," Bezange began. "Omaz never returned last night."

"He didn't?" Curge's bald scalp knotted up. "Where is he?"

"I don't know, my Lord," Bezange reported truthfully. "I instructed him to locate this Vadrian fellow, and that was the last I heard of him. I even went out prowling, well after hours, I might add, searching all of Omaz's usual haunts. There was no sign of him."

That puzzled Curge. "Did you pay him?"

"No, my Lord, I did not."

"He's probably still looking, then."

"Possibly."

"It does sound strange, knowing that greedy little bastard. Fear not. Vadrian is giving his bloodhound's nose a challenge is all."

"I'm sure you're correct," agreed Bezange with a subtle bow. "I've also overheard some information regarding the House of Tilo. One of his guards has a loose tongue, especially when plied by a woman and drink. He says Tilo is placing a lot of faith in one called Red Mane."

"Red Mane," Curge repeated, studying the smaller man.

"Yes, my Lord. Apparently the gladiator fights equally well with both hands. Tilo, greatly favors him. Shall I make a wager?"

"He's supposed to be good, eh?" Curge thought about it. "When will he fight?"

"Undecided as of yet, my Lord."

"Keep watch on it, then. See when he fights and who. Especially who. Place gold on him but not so much to frighten off the birds. Where did Tilo find him? What's the man's background. Is he a farmer? Soldier? Mercenary?"

"I shall investigate, my Lord."

"Do that." Curge glowered, thoughts churning. "Also, this afternoon Samarhead fights some Free Trained shite. Make the wager. Make it heavy. He'll be heavily favored after this day."

Bezange bowed once more. All the bowing sometimes

irritated Curge. He wasn't sure the little pisser was mocking him or not.

"Off with you, then," the owner commanded. "And make us some coin."

Yet another bow and Bezange saw himself out. Curge watched him go. The little man was a sly one, wise enough to know where the power rested, and where it was dangerous to tread. He wasn't the first man Curge had employed but, if he was smart, Bezange would live to be the last. Curge remembered his last head of spies and how the man had thought he could steal a little from every wager he placed on behalf of the house. It wasn't long before Curge discovered the thievery and decided to make an example of him. The offender was caught, placed in a very private room, and tied down. Every now and again, when the mood took him, Curge would go to that room.

With a very sharp hand axe.

And Curge had Bezange go with him, so the new agent would witness and remember the very horrifying proceedings. Curge wanted Bezange to see and hear every chop of steel into flesh, every squeal of terror, and every word of pleading.

As warning.

Wrong Dark Curge, and he *would* find out.

After eating his noon meal, Curge left with four of his private guards and made his way to Sunja's Pit. A sizeable crowd gathered about the arena gates despite the overcast sky. It lifted Curge's spirits. Spectators were gold to him.

With his four watchful guards at his back, Curge wandered the outer halls of the great arena. He eavesdropped on commoners, as well as watched some Free Trained gladiators practice in one of the many training and sparring lots. He stayed behind the crowds, studying the men going through their paces, eventually dismissing them as no threat to any of his contenders and of no interest to acquire. Curge liked to scout the Free Trained by himself if possible. He trusted his own eye more than those of his spies. If the gurry contained a gold nugget, he would take the initiative and offer the man a place on his roster, as an investment for the current and later years.

And the dogs usually joined, overjoyed at being recognized with potential.

It didn't always happen, but Curge thought wise to sift through the shite. One never knew.

After having enough of watching and longing to drink something, Curge decided to leave for the manager's box. The fights were already starting inside, and the arena exploded at times with the crowds' enthusiasm.

On his way back, however, Curge spied a familiar figure flanked by his own guards. Standing back from a practice lot, Nexus watched a pair of pit fighters exchange light strikes and parries.

Curge smiled. The silver-haired bastard was a wealthy merchant and vintner in Sunja, and obviously had a shrewd enough mind to search through the shite. The question was, was he a good judge of talent?

He thought about just passing by the old topper when Nexus turned and saw him.

"Curge," the wine man frowned. "What are you doing here?"

"Inspecting the goods. You think you are the only one eyeing the meat?"

"Apparently not," Nexus said, and gazed upon the practicing fighters in the lot. A look of distaste deepened upon the old man's grooved face.

It struck Curge then, that Nexus just might have believed that he was the only one of a mind to inspect potential goods. That amused him. If so, then Nexus was quite naive to the ways of the games.

"Might I stand with you for a moment?" Curge offered a cool half smile.

"Can't get enough of my company in the box?"

"You have me there."

"Or perhaps, you look to see if I have found anything of interest here at the market?" Nexus stated without looking at Curge

The two fighters continued with their exercises.

"Well, have you?" Curge drew closer to the well-dressed wine merchant, imposing his much larger self. The guards of both individuals eyed each other, as well as their respective masters.

"I wouldn't tell you if I did, you one-armed snake," Nexus replied without fear. "You'd usurp my purchases at first chance."

"Well, I might," Curge admitted. "But that's the nature of the games, good Nexus. If I were to learn something from your sharp eye, then I'd be a fool not to take advantage of it."

Which was the truth. All the owners did the very thing, playing at games within games.

"Save the honey for your sluts," Nexus snipped dismissively. "I may be inexperienced to the ways of the Pit, but I can tell you this for free—I'm here now, and I learn fast."

"Apologies, Nexus," Curge said politely. "I meant no offence."

"Get your tongue out of my ass," Nexus muttered. "I get enough of such shite from the merchants I deal with. I thought that you stable owners were of a purer, more direct lot, but I can see that I made a mistake."

"I have a house," Curge corrected in a tone that suggested Nexus remember that.

"House, school, stable," Nexus growled. "All packs of trained dogs. Call yourself what you like if it pleases you."

That silenced Curge, and he regarded the wine man's profile, very tempted to slap it.

Nexus's eyes didn't leave the pit fighters in the practice lots.

"Fair enough, then," Curge said, taking that last insult but unwilling to take another. "I'll speak without honey from here on, when it's just us boys."

That earned a stern look from Nexus, actually breaking his gaze away from the display of arms.

"What have we here, then, hmm?" Dark Curge indicated the two gladiators with his half-arm. "Not much." He sniffed then, hard, clearing his sinuses. "Well-muscled, but with problems. That one there, the tall one. He has tells. He leads with his eyes before he strikes. He'll be gutted by the first intelligent warrior fortunate enough to be paired with him. And his partner there? The one looking as if he eats nothing but meat? What do you see there?"

Nexus bristled at the question and his eyes narrowed. "He's quick to be fooled by a feint."

"Aye that," Curge agreed. "And that tells us what?"

"I'm no novice at this, you brazen ass-packer."

"Indulge me, Nexus," Curge pushed, dropping the

honorific *good*, wanting a sense of how much Nexus actually *did* know about this trade.

"He's nervous."

"And what else?"

Nexus cocked an eyebrow. "He's new to the games?"

"Yes, exactly." *No need to powder the man's ass at all*, Curge decided. Nexus was right on target with his observations. "Anything else?"

The lines in Nexus's face deepened as he concentrated, but he did not add anything more. "No. That's it."

"Not at all," Curge disagreed.

"Seddon's black hanging fruit, that's *it*, I said."

"Of course not. He looks impressive, and all you've said about him is true, but there is one other tell which I'll keep as a secret. Give you something to think upon."

Nexus didn't move, but his face took on a familiar shade of anger. Curge knew his point had sunk home. He inhaled sharply, catching a whiff of unwashed bodies. It was time to get to the box and do some drinking whilst men cut each other open.

"You'll no doubt ask your taskmaster anyway," he said as an afterthought. "Who is your taskmaster, or trainers?"

Nexus pursed his lips. "A man called Clavellus."

"Clavellus?" *The drunkard.* Curge let slip a face of surprise. The name hooked unpleasant memories and once forgotten promises. "You... have him? I recalled him retired from the profession long ago. He has an estate somewhere on the road to Vathia, doesn't he?"

"Aye that, he does."

"Well, you're in good hands, then," Curge said, mulling the name. "I'll leave you to it. The fights start shortly."

Curge departed the wine merchant's company. *Clavellus,*

he mused darkly. That was a name he'd have to investigate further, just to make sure. He suspected the wine man simply said the name to shock him. That alone soured his mood.

With his guards parting the crowds, Curge strode purposely through the outer arena.

He spotted Bezange, who gave him a nod.

Excellent, Curge thought, his mood improving, *wagers are in place. Let the feast begin.*

At the door to the viewing box, Curge left his escort. A manservant opened the door, while a woman just beyond the threshold held out a silver cup. Curge took the wine and moved to the front where Gastillo sat, a similar cup in hand, his golden mask dull under a cloudy sky.

"You're early," Curge muttered as he plopped down across from him.

"You're fashionably late," Gastillo said, and sipped.

"Met my friend Nexus outside," Curge threw out, knowing it would rankle the other man. "We were discussing wine."

"Taken up an interest have you?"

"A slight interest," Curge said. "One shouldn't dwell on the games forever, you know. But I suppose you do know."

Gastillo didn't bother replying. He looked across the arena and took another drink. With his free hand, he lifted his mask and dabbed at his mouth with an expensive-looking hand towel.

Curge noticed the cloth. "Is this what you spend your money on, good Gastillo?"

Gastillo's profile dipped. "It was a gift from a silk merchant."

"Silk? You really are branching out, aren't you? Silk

towels for that mess of a mouth today and silk rags for your ass tomorrow." Dark Curge shook his head. "Maybe these games aren't for you, Gastillo. I haven't seen you outside inspecting the Free Trained. Perhaps your mind isn't in it anymore?"

"Perhaps," Gastillo allowed.

Curge smiled broadly, tickled with the man's short reply. Curge had no real enemies, and Gastillo and Nexus were hardly a match. One was trying to assimilate everything he could in the short time of the games, while the other was doing his utmost to survive. Gastillo had only a fraction of the arena experience Curge possessed, and Nexus had no experience at all. They were both beneath him.

Curge wondered how Nexus had ever gotten into this privileged box. He had probably paid someone to get in, hoping it was private. Curge drank his wine. *Bad luck, indeed.*

The Orator stepped onto the platform, holding his robes about him as it they were about to fall. He held up his hands. "Good citizens of Sunja," he started in a low voice, quieting the onlookers. "This dark afternoon is well-suited for the first match of the day. This afternoon, under heavy clouds and moist air, the House of Curge has delivered unto us a *fiend*. A thing of *hell*. An *abomination* forged of flesh, bone, blood, and steel. A child of *war* and a destructor of man. A creature from the Lands of Great Ice, cut by the same freezing storms that sculpt mountains with their breath. He is a monster of a man, if you dare call him one. He. *Is*. *Samar*head."

The crowd exploded into cheers.

"I wrote that introduction myself," Dark Curge confided to Gastillo, smiling at the rousing introduction. The golden mask remained stoic, but Curge knew he struck a nerve.

The portcullis rose with a cranky voice, and a tall figure dressed in heavy plate armor shambled onto the sands. One hand held a double-bladed battleaxe that most men used with two, while Samarhead's other hand held a massive shield that could have once been a door. A great helm, elaborate in design, had two great bull horns forward mounted, while a red iron visor hid the face completely.

The crowd lost their voices when they saw the warrior, but as Samarhead shambled onto the sand, they began to roar, low at first, then growing into a surge of approval. Samarhead moved as if the weight of his armor burdened him greatly, and it took some time for him to walk to where he wanted to be. He turned and carefully bowed in the direction of the king's platform, though the king was nowhere in sight. Then the beast sighted the box of the top ruling houses and schools and bowed to Dark Curge.

The owner dipped his head in return.

His respect noted, Samarhead turned and waited for his opponent to appear.

The man entering from the opposing side was not small, either. The Orator introduced him as Milloch from Sunja, and there was an uninspired sprinkling of cheers that quickly died away into nothing. The man wore a coat of ring mail that left his muscular arms unprotected. He carried a sword and offhand axe, swishing them as if clearing stubborn brush. His helm was a common pot helm of the variety found in the Pit's armory.

Free Trained.

An eager Curge wondered if the maggot knew he'd been fed to a beast.

With a flourish, the Orator shouted for the match to begin.

A brave Milloch plodded across the arena sand, raising his weapons as he got closer to his larger foe. His fearless march drew jeers from the spectators. The Sunjan stopped midway, having done his part, and planted both feet.

He gestured for the man from the Lands of Great Ice to meet him halfway.

Unmoving, Samarhead stayed where he was.

Taunts and curses prompted the Sunjan beckon his opponent once more.

But the menacing warrior from the Lands of Great Ice showed no indication of having seen or heard.

Frustrated, Milloch trekked the rest of the way, and Curge thought he could hear the man cursing as he marched along.

When Milloch came within three strides of Samarhead, he paused again, appreciating the sheer size of the northern brute for the first time. The crowds swore upon them, screaming for action.

Milloch sprang at the giant. His sword and hand axe stabbed and cut. He lashed out at a head and chopped at an arm, kicked at a knee and thrust for a gut.

Samarhead moved his door-sized shield this way and that, effortlessly it seemed, blocking all of the attacks. The man from the Lands of Great Ice then pushed forward with his shield, blinding his smaller foe for the instant it took to rear back his battleaxe and bring it down on top of the flat pot helm.

Splitting the metal and the head within down the middle.

The crowd exploded with cheers.

Milloch dropped to his knees as if before a king. His weapons fell while blood streamed down his front and back and pooled in the sand. Samarhead stood poised, axe still buried in a dead man's head, as if waiting for something. The spectators eventually became quiet, wondering what manner of hellion Samarhead was. An uncertain silence hushed the arena, and some even wondered if, in death, Milloch had managed to stab his foe through the belly before he died.

Even the Orator looked vexed, and cast a wondering eye in Dark Curge's direction.

Then, at a point of absolute silence, where not even a breath could be heard, Samarhead wrenched his axe free of the ruined skull, the blade squealing against the helm.

Only then did the corpse fall over.

After a short considering moment, Samarhead raised his axe to the gloomy heavens.

Once more the people gushed their praise, and even Curge himself shook a victorious fist. The great Samarhead was indeed his prize in these games and, though the match was short-lived, the effect rippled through the entire arena. Samarhead had just become the gladiator to be feared, and Curge adored it.

"That's my lad," he smiled at a silent Gastillo.

Though under his golden mask, the man's face twitched.

• 6 •

Parched

Halm awoke with a powerful thirst. He slapped a hand to his forehead and dragged it down over his features, as if that might improve things. It did not. A pounding as steady as an axe stroke tormented the width of his skull. He yawned, loudly, sat up and looked around table.

Things did not look better. In fact, they looked terrible.

The alcove they'd occupied since last night was a sty. He had passed out in the back, facedown on the table. There was a pair of feet at the other end, and a buzzing snore caught his attention. *Muluk.* That was Muluk. He was certain of it. The Kree had out-drunk them all. Empty pitchers filled the table, most standing, some upended, but the one that drew his attention was the one Pig Knot had thrown up in. Halm grimaced, baring his yellow and black teeth. Pig Knot had wagered with another Sunjan that he could drink what he had just voided… and he had done so for a handful of gold. He couldn't keep the mouthful down, however, and had spewed everything back in the same pitcher moments later, much to the delight of everyone at the table.

Images came into the Zhiberian's mind and left. Memories of food: sliced apples and pears and peeled oranges, roasts and ale. At some point, someone ordered Sunjan mead. That unfit concoction could make a man lose all ankle support, and that was when the alehouse had begun to spin.

Some women had visited their table but, as usual, they had disappeared with the night. A shame, as there were some right nice ones, and Halm faintly recalled having one well-formed wench on his knee, remembering how she giggled when he tickled her.

He shook his head, cringed at the receding pounding within, and caught the whiff of something foul. He tried hard not to look at the pitcher Pig Knot had filled. A fruit tray on the table drew his attention and the few slices of melon there—though he couldn't rightly remember any melon. Regardless, he took a slice and munched it down, savoring its water. The alehouse was quiet, peaceful, the interior empty and full of gloom. Tossing the finished melon unto the table, Halm eased himself out of the alcove, his bare belly scrubbing the table's edge. Muluk's feet twitched, but he continued snoring, a raspy, nasal sound that Halm had no comparison for. The Zhiberian stood, instantly regretting it as the room began to whirl. He plopped back down on the bench and laid his head on the table.

The cool surface felt wonderful, rooting him to the spot. He didn't want to leave.

"Keeper." Halm grimaced at the parched squawk of his voice. "Keeper, bring me… a pitcher—" he thought of Muluk then, and Pig Knot. "—*three* pitchers. Of water."

The effort took his strength, and he took several deep, settling breaths. Nothing else moved so he leaned out, to see if there was anyone about.

No one, except for a few dead-looking drunks splayed out on the floor.

Halm believed they shared a drink together.

His stomach lurched dangerously, settled, and was replaced by an urgent need to piss. He stood and staggered to a door that led to a latrine. He made it safely, freed his manhood from the folds of his breeches, and relieved himself with a sigh. His forehead knotted up at the soreness down there, but he paid no mind further mind. A hole in the roof let the sky in, and Halm could see only grayness between the planks. As he pissed, he heard noise inside the alehouse. He finished, tucked himself away, and drove his shoulder into the doorframe as he stumbled back inside.

The barkeep walked back from his table. "Good morn to you," he said with a nod. He was a small portly man, wearing pants and a shirt with a clean-looking apron. The barkeep obviously had changed his clothes.

Halm muttered a reply and nodded back. He made it to his table, placed both hands around a clay pitcher, and drank deeply. He stopped once to kick Muluk in the ribs. The man did not wake. Halm considered throwing some water on his face, but decided against it. He drank until only a quarter remained, then he sat down, moving Pig Knot's offensive pitcher to the far end. The smell wafted, causing Halm to shiver and nearly almost retch.

Holding his nose, he picked up the pitcher, intending to dump it in the latrine.

Muluk, on his back and snoring like a babe, caught his hungover attention.

Halm considered the full pitcher in his fist. Muluk's head was right below, his mouth open. Ripe for the jest.

Holding out his arm, Halm began to tip the contents.

"He'll hate ye for it," the barkeep rumbled from across the way.

The words cut through the fog of Halm's brain and he ceased tipping. The barkeep was right. Funny it would have been, but cruel, and the lad would be stinking right up until he could get washed, which was a good question of where and when.

"You're a good man," Halm said, as he unsteadily crossed the floor.

"Not really," the barkeep muttered. "Just didn't want to clean that up."

"Hm," Halm said. "Apologies for thinking it."

The barkeep nodded.

Halm dumped the pitcher's contents into the latrine and held his breath. Once the container emptied, he gave it a deep shake, and retreated back inside. He thumped the pitcher on the bar and returned to his table, where Muluk remained on his back, snoring comfortably.

Halm kicked him again before he sat down.

"Do I owe you anything here?" Halm croaked, his voice a rasp. Memories of singing touched him then. And a mule.

"Nothing," replied the barkeep. "You were more than generous last night."

Halm checked his purse. There was something left inside, and he untied the strings to look. Two gold coins peeked out at him and that made him think. He'd won twenty. The baths, food, drink, and women had taken all of his money. Thoughts lingered on the women. He'd paid a woman for something, he remembered faintly.

Muluk yawned mightily.

Halm gave him yet another kick to the ribs, harder this time.

"I felt... the last one," the Kree moaned, his eyes still closed. "But I thought I was dreaming."

"It's morning," Halm informed him. "Get up. We have things to do."

With an effort, Muluk pulled himself up and sat down across from Halm. He yawned again while scratching at his crotch.

Halm pushed the tray with the food scraps towards him. Muttering thanks, Muluk chewed on a piece of apple. The Zhiberian nudged a pitcher over, which was also gratefully accepted.

"Surprised I'm still alive after last night," Muluk said, but Halm was deep into a morning stare and didn't rouse from it.

"Where's Pig Knot?" the Kree asked.

Halm grunted, still staring off at nothing.

"Pig Knot?"

"Don't know."

"Probably with that wench you paid for."

Halm looked at him. "I paid for a wench?"

"You lost a wager."

"I did?"

"Aye that, you did," Muluk nodded and drank again.

"I don't remember anything..."

The Kree almost choked on his water, startling the other man. When he composed himself, Muluk asked, "You don't remember the mule?"

Halm shook his head.

A broad grin broke across Muluk's face.

"What about the mule?" Halm asked, growing uneasy.

"Morning, lads," Pig Knot called out from the second floor. The men looked up and saw their companion standing amongst the ceiling timbers, his hands on a second floor railing. "Anything to eat or drink?"

"There's water," Muluk said.

Pig Knot joined them. He was missing his shirt and sat bare-chested at the table. He picked at the scraps and gratefully accepted the pitcher. When he finished, he looked at both men and smiled. "That was a time, last night."

"Did I pay for a woman for you?" Halm asked.

"You did. You lost a wager."

"What wager?"

Pig Knot exchanged amused looks with Muluk, and both men chuckled.

"You don't want to know," Pig Knot informed him. "Not even I will bring it up again. Least, not in your presence, anyway."

"And I'm sure the others were too drunk to notice," Muluk added.

Halm fumed and rubbed his coins together. There were more important things to think about this morning and wagers to place. Not that it would be much, and he said that to his companions.

"Fear not," Pig Knot said. "I have a gold piece left. I'll throw it down on the table for the lot of us."

"I cannot offer anything," Muluk said. "Unless I sell my sword. No one will take the rags I have as armor."

"That might be an idea," Pig Knot said. "The sword I mean. You won't be needing it now, since you've been yanked from the games. Wager on us, and you'll get your coin back and more."

"Or you'll be in an even worse state," Halm added.

The idea brightened Muluk. "Why not, then."

"One thing first, this morning," Pig Knot said. "I think

a gold piece will get a better breakfast than this. And a bath."

Both Halm and Muluk declined the food, so the three of them went to the public bath house. They paid a gold coin and were given more fruit and water while soaking in hot water. A deep soak was just the thing needed after a night of drinking.

They finished bathing and, still feeling unable to eat anything beyond soft fruit, they decided to head to the arena and watch the games from the stands. None of them were scheduled to fight, but they would check with the *Madea* to see when they were scheduled. Halm in particular wanted to know when his blood match would happen.

The loud preaching voice of Vadrian greeted them upon entering the general quarters.

"Lords above," breathed Muluk.

"I supposed he didn't see me around," Halm muttered, "And no one's said a word to him."

The Zhiberian glanced around the huge chamber cluttered with men going about their business. A familiar figure caught his eye.

Vadrian was speaking with two men sitting on a bench.

"He has a following," Pig Knot observed.

"So it seems." Halm wondered.

"He's been talking shite," a nearby pit fighter said, catching the three's attention. Shadow covered half of the man's upper torso, and the rest was in hard shape. Bandages sheathed him and he talked through a badly swollen mouth. He balanced himself on a pair of crutches. As the three companions watched, the stricken pit fighter sat down heavily on a bench, baring his teeth as he did so.

"Been listening, have you?" Pig Knot asked. "You certainly can't do much else."

The wounded man shrugged.

"I know you," Muluk said, pointing. "You're Gall."

That summoned a grimace. "*Goll*."

"Goll, then. You killed Baylus the Butcher."

Goll grunted. "Not before he danced on me."

Halm eyed Goll's foot. "Broke your foot?"

"Broke my toes." Goll smiled, his wrecked lips warping his expression. He might've been an ordinary-looking man otherwise, possessing dark eyes, short sandy hair. Dressed as he was, it was easy to see how badly the Butcher had mauled him. "Also, my shoulder and some of my jaw, I think."

"Seeing when you fight next then, are you?" Muluk asked.

"My games are finished," Goll sighed, his dark eyes glittering. "If I can recover quickly enough, I'll make for Kree before winter."

"You're from Kree?" Muluk asked, and release a stream of foreign syllables that brought a smile to the battered man's face. Goll replied in his country's tongue, and both men shared a chuckle.

Shaking his head, Halm turned away and watched Vadrian raise his arms to the ceiling. Armor covered the man, and he abruptly turned and strode toward the arena tunnels, sword and spiked gauntlet swishing at his sides.

Without thinking, Halm walked in Vadrian's wake, until he stopped before the Skarrs standing guard in front of the *Madea's* desk.

"Ho, *Madea*," Halm greeted. "I see that punce is fighting this day. Who is the unfortunate soul?"

The arena official looked up from his documents and sized up the belly and bare chest before him, his expression souring the farther his eyes rose. "He wanted to fight you, Halm of Zhiberia, as his scheduled foe could not fight. We hailed you this morning but, as the start time drew near, we found another to fight him."

Halm closed his eyes. "He was going to fight me this morning?"

"He was but, as I said, you were not here." The *Madea* regarded the man. "Fortunate for you. You look… unfit."

"When will I fight that bastard?"

The *Madea* thought about it. "If he's victorious and not too badly cut up, perhaps the day after tomorrow. Depending on whether you win your match, of course. If you wish it."

"Who will it be?"

"A man called Samarhead," the *Madea* informed him. "From the House of Curge. Formidable, I might add. Killed his last foe."

"I know about the House of Curge," Halm said. "Dark Curge only takes killers under his wing."

"He has one now, I daresay."

"So I fight tomorrow. To the death, I imagine."

The *Madea* said nothing

"'Til tomorrow, then." Halm nodded and turned to go. He walked back to his companions.

Pig Knot saw him and gestured at his brooding face. "Something wrong?"

"No," Halm said and looked to Goll. "Were you to fight Vadrian this day?"

"I was."

"But you couldn't?"

Goll scowled and didn't answer that.

"What I meant was—"

"They were looking for you to fight Vadrian?" Muluk asked.

"Aye that," Halm said.

Muluk winced and looked towards a wall.

"He'll think you're dodging him now." Pig Knot placed his hands on his hips. "Regardless of what you say."

Halm didn't answer right away. "Until I meet him on the sands."

"When will that happen?" Pig Knot asked.

"After my next fight."

"Your *next* fight?"

"Aye that. One of Dark Curge's hellpups. One called Samarhead."

Goll's eyes widened. "You've drawn Samarhead?"

The three men looked at the crippled gladiator.

"You know of him?" Halm asked.

"He split the head open of some poor topper only just now in the Pit. Only moments before you arrived."

The three men strained to hear over the bustling activity around them

"Split the head?" Muluk asked.

Goll nodded. "With a battleaxe. One-handed. I saw the fight. I forget the man's name, but he came out strong. But Samarhead was right evil-looking. He waited for the bastard to get closer, which he did. He also carried a huge shield and stayed behind it until he saw his moment. One cut. Right through the pot helm. Opened his brainpan to the neck and stood there with the dead man until all got quiet. Then he pulled the axe free."

"Dark Curge trains his boys to finish fights," Halm said.

"Curge trains his lads to kill." Pig Knot's lip curled. "No secret there."

"Aye that."

"What are you going to do, then?" Muluk asked.

Halm and Pig Knot exchanged looks.

"What was Samarhead wearing, Goll?" the Zhiberian asked.

"Heavy armor. Plate."

"Well, then, that settles one thing," Halm said. "I'll take the biggest axe I can swing from the armory. Looks like I'll be doing some wood cutting of my own, friend Muluk."

"Trees don't split skulls," Muluk replied.

"They do if they fall on you," Pig Knot remarked. "Many thanks to you, Goll. You've done this Zhiberian a great favor. He's in your debt, I wager."

"Least I can do." Goll's features became dark with some unknown emotion.

From above, a huge cheer went up like a crashing of a monstrous wave. Other pit fighters paused and looked to the ceiling, fearful that it might fall in.

"I think," Pig Knot began, "we just lost the opportunity to make some coin."

"Maybe," Halm said, his eyes still on Goll. "But we'll have coin tomorrow. If you have anything left in your purse, friend Goll, you wager it on whom you wish. But if you are wise, you'll place it on my head."

That lifted Goll's spirits, somewhat. "That so? Can you guarantee it?"

"Of course I can't. But if I die, it'll matter not to me," Halm said. "But if I *win*… if I drive this Samarhead to his knees right and proper…"

Pig Knot couldn't contain himself. He grabbed and shook Muluk by the shoulder. "Best sell that sword of yours for whatever you can get. I can smell the odds now. We fast this day, boys, but we'll eat like kings tomorrow."

"Even you, young Goll," Halm added.

That pleased Goll to a point, but something bothered the man. Halm didn't press him, however, since having only just met. Such prying would be considered rude, even by Free Trained standards.

"To the fights then," Pig Knot said.

"Come with us if you wish, friend Goll."

The battered Kree considered it, and just as Halm believed the man would decline, he surprised them all by accepting.

Goll stood without any help. Halm liked that.

The four of them exited the general quarters only moments before the self-proclaimed Son of Seddon returned, victorious for the second time.

· 7 ·

Seddon's Son

Vadrian did not linger after his victory. He collected his money, cleaned his weapons, sent his two followers away to spread the word of his success, and finally left the general quarters for his church. He walked in public bearing his armor and weapons and the crowds parted for him with expressions of fear. Vadrian didn't pay them any mind as he remembered his second fight, pleased at how quickly he'd dispatched his foe. The man was Free Trained, as was Vadrian, but he wasn't infused with the light and strength of Seddon, and thus he was doomed from the start.

The spectators had sensed it also, and those that had wagered coin on his victory were not disappointed.

It was beginning, and Vadrian knew that in time he'd gather to him a flock of both warriors and commoners. Once that happened, Seddon above would show him the way. Vadrian suspected it would be fraught with war, and on a scale that would dwarf the one on Sunja's borders. And if great Seddon demanded a scouring of the land, then Vadrian would lead the cleansing.

But first Vadrian had to prove his worth even more, prove himself by building a legend in Sunja's Pit. The battles he fought on the arena sands would draw a following to him. They'd find him because of his name and the coin it brought. Then they would find him because of his fighting ability, then his deeds in the Pit, and finally his words. His success in the arena was first step toward a church that would rule the world in Seddon's name, with Vadrian as the warrior prophet.

The Fire knew other gladiators talked about him. He sensed their fear.

That thought stopped him.

The one called Halm, the brazen one who had openly challenged him. Vadrian would make him an example of Seddon's order in the coming world, a world where there would be no mercy for the non-believers and the barbarians of faraway lands. Vadrian wondered if Halm wasn't a test of his resolve. If so, the Zhiberian bastard would be quickly killed and offered.

It would be glorious.

Vadrian would make a name for himself with Halm's death. Make a name first and the rest would follow. Seddon would see to it. Seddon would see to everything.

And behold, there in his path, a man waved for Vadrian's attention, interrupting his thoughts. A little man, looking and smelling like a vagrant. Vadrian scowled until he decided to merciful. At least until he heard what the man had to say.

"Salutations, Vadrian the Fire," the little man said in a formal voice. He bowed before Vadrian's towering visage, and that pleased the holy fighter.

Then Vadrian's eyes narrowed. He wondered if the worm was an agent sent by Seddon.

"My name is Bezange," the man said. He wore only a plain tunic and black pants, but he possessed a youthful face.

Vadrian paused. The man-boy interested him.

"I wish to walk with you for a bit, if I may, and speak as well," Bezange said.

"As you wish." Vadrian resumed walking, but very much aware of Bezange at his side. "Walk with me, but when I tell you to leave me, you shall do so."

The little man nodded. He kept up with the taller warrior, sidestepping others who darted into his path to avoid Vadrian. "My master has watched you twice now upon the arena sands, and he's most impressed."

"I don't care about your master," Vadrian snapped as *his* master was the Seddon above.

"That's why I've been sent to you," Bezange said as he continued to dodge passersby while the masses parted for the hulking fighter like fresh bread cleaved with a knife. Those who did not were shoved out of the way. "My master is the owner of the most honorable and prestigious gladiator school in Sunja. As I've said, he's impressed with your performance as of late, but he believes that, under his teachings, you might very well achieve greatness."

Vadrian pushed aside a young boy barely ten. "I will claim greatness on my own," the gladiator replied gruffly.

An older, portly man cut in front of the gladiator. The Fire grabbed him by the neck and heaved him into a stall of hanging smoked meats.

Then he walked on, ignoring the resulting stares.

Bezange glanced back at the scene. "Well, with my master's support—"

"I have no need of your master."

"You have need of coin, do you not?"

Vadrian didn't reply, his suspicions rising.

"My master is willing to take you into his house and train you—"

"I need no further training."

"But with our instruction, you will truly rise in the rankings."

"I am rising now."

"But only so far," Bezange persisted with a smile. "You won't advance much farther without a proper school. Right now, you are only fighting the Free Trained, and all know what their mettle is. Once you rise above that rabble, as you clearly will, you will need the experience, teaching, and support of a professional school—else the lesser gladiator houses will chew you up."

"I need no one."

"You don't seem to understand," Bezange pressed, leaning in close to Vadrian. "You are *alone* right now. If you've caught the eye of *my* master, you've caught the *others'* attention as well. And if you turn away all suitors, they won't allow you to compete in the later rounds. Not without a school behind you."

"Seddon is behind me."

"Seddon?" a skeptical Bezange spat. "If trained and bled gladiators find you in the streets, even those from the lowest of ranked houses, they will *punish* you for being a mongrel playing at a game meant for lions. You must realize that the established schools don't tolerate Free Trained warriors. That you're looked upon as untrained maggots hacking each other's heads off. Truth be known, if the schools had their say, *none* of you would be in the games at all. The Chamber only permits you to fight as a—a bloody prelude to the *real* games."

Vadrian slowed and he glared at the smaller man. "I no longer like your tone."

"Come, dear Vadrian, you—"

In a street packed with people, Vadrian gripped Bezange by his throat and brought him in close. "I've grown tired of you."

Bezange's face reddened and his tongue protruded. His hands pawed at the gladiator's thick forearms. Vadrian shook him, and then shoved him away, sending him crashing to the ground.

Wasting no further time, Vadrian walked on, fuming at the little hellion's attempt to tempt him. He was the Fire! He had no friends, *needed* no friends, for Seddon provided him with all. All others were nothing more than maggots writhing in their own secretions.

"Unfit heathen," Vadrian murmured and went on his way.

He didn't stop until poorly kept houses, built tightly together, lined both sides. The merchants became fewer, the streets became filthier, and the beggars became louder. The wretched souls sitting in the shadows with their hands out scattered upon spotting his Vadrian's fierce form. The menacing gladiator marched to his Church of Seddon, magnificent in its time, but now old, dilapidated, and on the verge of collapse. He marched past the rusted and failing outer gates, past gardens long since dead, and entered the wreck of a church, closing one of two rotting doors behind him.

The street beggars came out of their holes once the gladiator had gone, but even then, they stayed quiet for fear of attracting attention. There were whispers about the old church, warnings of not to be around the building at night.

Those that did tended to disappear.

· 8 ·

Hurt

Far above the lamp lit streets, above yellow and green banners hanging from building and across well-trodden streets, the stars winked into existence. The games had long since closed for the day.

Underneath the arena and within general quarters, Free Trained gladiators rested. Those who didn't have a home or couldn't afford lodgings were permitted to sleep within the underground hall to avoid sleeping in the streets. Hundreds of men had staked out small individual territories before bedding down for the night. Torches and scattered fire pits illuminated the huge chamber in a red flickering hue, and long shadows moved along the walls. The air was warm, stale, and stunk of lingering blood and the breath of sleeping men. Snores, soft and bone-rattling cut the silence.

In one of the quieter sections, four men hunkered down, near a small iron brazier that Halm had pulled closer to a wall. They were only marginally successful with the day's wagers, but there would be no drinking or wenching that night, however, as the Zhiberian had to fight the next day.

Pig Knot decided to keep him company until there was something to celebrate.

Muluk stayed as he quietly informed his companions his dislike for drinking alone, and that, in a place such as Sunja, it seemed wise to stay with greater numbers to avoid trouble.

The one called Goll remained as well, also finding some security in the presence of the others.

The four of them lay around the small smoldering fire, shifting from their sides or their backs, watching the flames consume the last of the wood.

"So then," Halm said, lying on his back and staring at the high ceiling. "Goll, what else can you tell me of this Samarhead?"

"There isn't much more to tell. The match was over before it began. Big man, from the Lands of Great Ice. Wore plate and swung an axe." He lapsed into silence, remembering the fight. "It was quick. I saw no weakness. He let the other man come to him, let him swing at him for a few moments, and then Samarhead drove his shield into the other's face."

"Them lads from up north can be right and proper brutal," Pig Knot muttered.

"Aye that," Muluk threw in, on his back with his eyes closed.

"Apologies, Halm," Goll said. "For not seeing more."

The Zhiberian *tsked*. "No apologies needed, friend Goll. You've said enough, and for that I'm thankful. I should have been watching the matches myself."

"You'll have plenty of time to watch the games," Pig Knot said. "Especially if you're smashed up like Goll here."

"I hope you don't become like me," Goll said in a dark tone.

Pig Knot peered at the second man from Kree. "Baylus certainly did a dance on you, but it's *you* here talking."

Goll coughed and then took a deep breath. "I killed him, that's true, but I fear…" The man sighed. "I fear I made a mistake in doing so."

"Why do you say that?"

Halm and Muluk both turned their sleepy attention to the battered gladiator.

Goll shifted and grimaced. "That was my first fight in the Pit and, I'm ashamed to say, I was nervous. As nervous as any other, I suppose. But, well… I remember… I remember him talking to me."

"Baylus talked to you?" Halm's questioned, lips drawn pulled back from his bad teeth.

"Aye, he did."

"Well, then?"

Goll thought about it, and Halm exchanged a glance with Pig Knot. There was obviously something on the mind of the badly hurt Kree.

"He was talking to me the whole fight," Goll said. "He was telling me to slow down, at first. I was trying to… to kill the man straight off. I've been told I'm fast, so I believed I could cut up the Butcher before he knew he was dead. All I could think was, 'This is the Butcher of Balgotha,' and if I didn't kill him, he would certainly kill me. So I tried to kill him first, but I couldn't strike the man. I couldn't touch him. He was a wisp of smoke and a stone, all at once. Because he was older, I thought him to be weaker and, for that, he made me look a fool. I remember him saying, 'Alright, boy, alright,' and then shaking his sword arm as if loosening it. That's when I knew he was playing with me. He cut up my armor, broke the toes of my foot, and sliced me up like a roast."

Pig Knot nodded. "Nothing to be ashamed of, lad. Baylus was a champion of champions. To even share the sands with him is considered an honor."

The Kree looked deeply troubled. "I was trained to win by weapon masters in Kree. I traveled to these games to take everything and I was confident I would. Yet, an old man taught me the one lesson I did not learn, and that was the danger of being overconfident. He let me strike at him until I got tired, then he cut me up, left me bleeding on the sand and, *worse*, he let me get angry. I was very angry when I crashed to the sand. I was… stunned when I heard the people calling out for Baylus to finish me… I was supposed to be adored by the masses, and there they were calling for my blood."

Goll shook his head. "But he didn't. He *spared* me. Over the screams for my head he told me to get up, that no one needed to die. He didn't want to kill me. He spared me. *Me*. I know you don't understand, but it was… it was…"

"He was just drawing it out," Pig Knot said. "He was famous for that. He was setting you up for the kill. That was the Butcher from Balgotha."

Goll would have none of it. "He was an old man, past his prime, yet back in the games for… I don't know what. He didn't want to kill me, though. I could see that. He bested me easily. Granted me mercy. And I realized that the Butcher had been leading with his leg and feinting. He had fooled me before. He did so again, and I… recognized it for what it was."

"And you killed the butcher," Halm said quietly, fully understanding why Goll was telling them his story. He wasn't a bad man, although the Kree probably thought of himself as one. He had entered the games thinking he was ready and had been bested by a man who could have been his father. The Butcher could have taken his life, but had spared him. Easily bested, chagrinned, and then spiteful... it struck Halm then that this man from Kree was confessing.

"I killed him," a bitter-sounding Goll finished. "I struck out, brought him to the ground, and pinned him. Even then he was talking to me. Even as I was staring into his eyes and had my blade at his throat, he was speaking. And I killed him. Killed the man who showed me mercy, when so many wanted me dead. When I stuck my sword into his head, the crowds adored me the way I wanted... but as soon as I was below, I limped my way, bleeding from everywhere, to the latrine, not to the healers. When I got there, I emptied my gullet, and I... had no further wish to be in the games."

"None?" Muluk asked.

Goll shook his head. "A final lesson from a dead man. I trained to be a champion, a killer of men. I found out I was not. Men around here slap me on the back for what I did—what they *think* I did... but I wish I could undo it all."

The three listeners said nothing. Pig Knot exhaled and stayed on his back, and Muluk gazed at the fire pit.

"You..." Halm started, but he couldn't finish. A good man had made a mistake, and it was clear that he was stewing in his guilt. Halm knew Goll wanted judgment passed, but he could not give it. The Zhiberian had made enough mistakes himself.

"You sleep on it, young Goll. Sleep on it." Halm thought his words sincere. In truth, he didn't know what else to say.

Nodding, Goll slowly, painfully, made ready to sleep. Once comfortable, he looked at them again. "Since that day, I haven't been able to sleep without nightmares. I hope this night will be different."

He closed his eyes.

"Good idea," Pig Knot said.

Muluk spoke something in Kree, to which Goll did not respond. Muluk then closed his own eyes.

Halm took a little longer, reflecting on the words of Goll.

• 9 •

Halm and Samarhead

In a street-side alehouse, the four gladiators ate a breakfast of cold chicken and bread, drinking mugs of water to help swallow it all down. Halm paid for the meal, leaving only a single gold piece from his earlier winnings. The group then meandered to the arena, moving only as fast as the wounded Goll. The young man didn't say much, but the others were cheerful, and included him in their conversation. Halm intentionally would not let Goll dwell on last night. In his mind, the man had made a mistake and apologized to the ones closest. Seddon only knew how many mistakes Halm had made in the past, and would make in the future.

Upon entering the lower levels of Sunja's Pit, Halm notified the *Madea* that he was present, and the arena official informed him he would be fighting shortly. The four companions moved into general quarters and located the huge cloth sack that belonged to the Zhiberian. It was late morning, but the hall was full of fighting men—some practicing, some resting.

"This place is too damned cramped," Muluk grumbled, looking around.

"Aye it is," Pig Knot agreed. "But there's little choice in the matter."

Muluk said nothing to that. They watched Halm untying the sack's knot. He reached in and pulled out his armor.

The smell of sweaty leather wrinkled Pig Knot's nose. "And they call me Pig. Don't you ever air that out, man?"

"Why?" Halm asked. "No one will steal it if it smells like shite. Here, you," he said to Pig Knot and held out the leather sleeve that would protect his sword arm. "Make yourself useful."

"If I was that, I would've emptied the bull on your armor last night. Freshen it up."

Halm shook the leather, growing impatient. Pig Knot took it and helped his companion slip into the sleeve. Muluk pulled out the metal greaves, noting the rust on the armor and the frayed leather. "You need new greaves."

Worming his arm through the leather protection, Halm bared bad yellow and black teeth. "I could use a woman as well. And a new body. And a new life, come to think of it. Maybe I'll win it all."

"Merely saying," Muluk muttered.

"Cheer up, good Muluk of Kree," Halm said. "I've a special task for you this day."

"What?"

Pig Knot buckled the armor into place and slapped it. Halm nodded thanks and reached for his leather purse. He pulled out his remaining gold coin and handed it to Muluk.

"That's right," Halm said. "Place it all on this poor Zhiberian pig bastard."

Muluk took the coin and made it disappear. "I'll do that. You're not afraid I'll run off with it?"

Halm shook his head. "After all I've done for you?" They

both chuckled. The Zhiberian then looked at Goll's broken toes. "Maybe you can keep an eye on your countryman there?"

"I will," Goll winced. "But I'll be as surprised as you are if he leaves us."

"And miss all your company?" Muluk asked, his spirits suddenly brighter. "It'll be done. May the Lords look after you."

"Daresay they'll be looking after someone." Pig Knot stepped back and inspected the armored Zhiberian.

Muluk reached into the sack, brought forth the conical helm, and held it out.

"Not yet," Halm said. "Let us sit and think for a while."

"What about?" Goll asked.

Halm smiled in answer.

In another part of the Pit, in the designated area for gladiators from established schools and houses, Dark Curge paced the chamber reserved for the warriors of the House of Curge. There were ten gladiators present, but only one was scheduled to fight. The others provided an escort and, as reward, were permitted to watch the day's events and even place wagers. Two pit fighters aided the warrior from the Lands of Great Ice putting on his plate armor. The beast of a man stared forward, his dark eyes unfocused. Curge stopped and inspected Samarhead's great musculature and strength of arms and grunted in satisfaction.

"Your foe is another Free Trained whelp." Curge peered at the Northman's impassive face. "This day, I want you to do something special. This day, I want you to make the death a slow one. No killing in one stroke, do you hear?"

"I hear, Master Curge," the fearsome gladiator replied.

"I want you to bleed him first," Curge continued. "Slowly. Bring the crowds to their feet to see what you are doing. Then take off a limb of your choosing. Savor it. Let the man bleed and beg and moan. Take off another limb if the dog still stands. I want the people to *know* that you are in full control in this match. I want any *gladiator* watching to pause in fear. The House of Curge is to be feared."

"And if the dog falls to the sand?" Samarhead asked.

Curge looked him in the eye. "Cut him up. Standing or on his back, chop him into pieces."

"Pieces, Master Curge."

The impassive owner nodded and glowered at the men suiting up Samarhead. Curge was in foul spirits this day, and it was all because of the one called Vadrian the Fire. The maggot had actually laid hands on Bezange and left the agent in bruises and shaky spirits. There were times when Curge could throttle the little man himself, but no Free Trained topper was permitted to touch his agent. To strike Bezange was to strike Curge himself, especially when he had the good grace to extend an offer. Such insult was unacceptable. He intended to have his revenge with the self-proclaimed Son of Seddon. For now, however, Curge wanted a sacrifice. He met the indifferent expression of Samarhead, his best fighter of the games.

"*Bloody* pieces."

The grim gladiator nodded.

"Halm of Zhibera," shouted the *Madea*. "It is your time."

The four companions regarded each other. Pig Knot quickly fitted the helm to Halm's skull, swatting the metal for luck. Muluk held up his shield and fixed it to the Zhiberian's arm. Halm thought of using an axe but changed his mind. He regarded them all from his eye slits. "Dying Seddon, you bunch look solemn. I feel damn near perfect. Go and put that gold down, Muluk, and I swear by Saimon's black hanging fruit, I'll buy you enough drink to cross your eyes."

Pig Knot held out his fist, and Halm met it with his own.

"Luck to you, Halm of Zhiberia," Goll said in a grave tone.

"The only luck I have is bad."

He slapped his hanging gut, making the fat rolls quiver. Then he stalked off in the direction of the tunnels without looking back. Lamplight illuminated the tunnel painted in white, and his shadow flittered along the walls. Halms thought of Goll as he made his way pass the assembled Skarrs. Above, the crowd roared as one voice shouted out above them all, the Orator announcing the opening of the day's fights.

Halm turned a corner and stopped at a set of steps. Sunlight streamed in from above. He had been there two days ago, and yet it seemed much more recent.

The aged gatekeeper, the same one as before, gazed upon the fat belly of the Zhiberian and shook his head. He smiled, revealing bare pink gums. "You're a fat punce, that's plain to see."

"I'm surprised you see anything, you ancient punce."

The gatekeeper straightened, recognizing the fighter.

Halm indicated the lever in the wall. "Are you going to wait until I'm your age before you pull that thing?"

"Brazen bastard," the old man muttered, yanking down on the device.

Ignoring him, Halm went to his fate, sword and shield swinging as he chugged up the stairs and entered the light. The Zhiberian stepped onto the sand just as the Orator finished introducing him. The crowd heaped both praise and curses on his name. The Zhiberian smiled at the curses. Some toppers had obviously lost coin on him recently.

Served them right, he thought. *They should have a better eye for talent.*

With a raucous roar, the one called Samarhead stepped into the light.

He was dark, tall, and protected by plate armor the likes Halm had never seen before. In one hand, Samarhead held a gruesome double-bladed battleaxe that any other man would have held with two. His helm sported two great horns, his face completely hidden by a red iron visor.

Halm took a steadying breath. He'd heard stories of the warriors from the Lands of Great Ice, and none of them were good. Even as he recalled those tales, the Orator introduced Samarhead, lavishing title upon bloody title on his name.

Halm sighed.

The Orator obviously enjoyed his own words.

"A thing of *hell*. An *abomination* forged of flesh, bone, blood, and steel. A child of *war* and a destructor of man."

A destructor of man? Halm grimaced. His *mother* was a destructor of man. The Orator had a way with—what was the word?—*theatrics*. He had a way with *theatrics*.

"He is a monster of a pit fighter!" The old man continued. "A brute amongst brutes, if you dare call him that. He. *Is*. Samarhead!"

The arena erupted with cheers, letting Halm know who the favourite was.

Unfit, the Zhiberian thought and brought up his sword and shield. He intended to make more than a few of them regret placing wagers this day.

Encased in a tower of armor and taking his time, Samarhead turned and bowed to the king's platform, then to the boxes of the schools and houses. Finally, he turned back to his opponent.

"Begin!" The Orator shouted.

The crowd blared excitement, forcing Halm to concentrate on what Goll had told him.

He just waited for the bastard to get closer, the crippled Kree had said.

Halm glanced at the clear skies and the early afternoon sun high overhead. The temperature was fearsome without wearing armor. He suspected the *destructor of man* cooked in that pot of his.

A plan took form in the Zhiberian's head.

With theatrics of his own, Halm marched out a few steps and threw his arms wide, turning to the right and soaking up the sudden deluge of curses. He thought of asking Samarhead if their fight would be to the death or not, but he guessed what the reply would be… if the imposing brute bothered to answer at all.

Halm completed his turn, faced his opponent, and lowered his weapon and shield.

And there he stayed.

Expecting more action, the crowd grew restless within a few heartbeats, realizing the Zhiberian wasn't going to willingly move. They screamed displeasure.

Halm cocked an eyebrow at the angry voices, refusing to budge. Already the sun warmed his armor and drew sweat from his skin. His leather-draped arm felt slick, as did his head. Moments passed, and the jeering became vicious, matching and even surpassing the heat. Sweat beaded upon Halm's back and slicked earthwards, but he did not move any farther.

The Zhiberian exhaled and sighed at the rising temperatures. The games just had to be in the summertime. Lords above, he would need a bath after this day. Halm didn't move his helm, peering ahead, studying the warrior from the Lands of Great Ice, far from his native clime.

More curses cut the air, the people even more incensed with the lack of action, aiming venomous insults in Halm's direction. They ranted and roared, gesticulated wildly, and even called for the Skarrs to intervene.

That wouldn't do.

Not for Halm.

So he cast an eye in Samarhead's direction, rolled his shoulders, and took another step, followed by another, which evolved into a walk. He trod warily to the center of the Pit.

The people shouted and grinned, applauding themselves for taking the initiative.

Then Zhiberian stopped.

Just shy of the midway point, Halm stopped with fingers flexing on his sword, not taking his attention off the house gladiator.

There, with *theatrics*, he drew a long purposeful line in the sand. Halm dragged his sword across the arena's face and he took his time doing so, making sure that the onlookers saw what he was doing.

Once finished, Halm hefted his weapon and stepped back a pace.

Groans flew from the audience.

Then he gently gestured with his sword, inviting the brute from the Lands of Great Ice to cross it.

The groans became cries of excitement.

But that terrible heat was slowly cooking the Zhiberian.

It was time to get dirty.

"This a fight to the death?" Halm shouted, spreading his arms in a question. "Why don't you meet me halfway, you stupid topper? Haven't the bells? Come on, then, you unfit kog. Cross the line, and I'll ring those bells. Even make it quick. Come on, you shiny pisser. I'll send you back to your snowy mother."

The silent gladiator did not move.

"Dogballs, man," Halm yelled and half-turned as if ready to leave. "You're a stubborn one. Or are you purposely being as thick as that pissy ice you think of as home? Come on, you great steel-plated asslicker! I've come halfway. I'll not come any farther."

Hateful sunlight beamed down on the house warrior, transforming that tower of meat and metal into a dusty ogre. No reaction from the man.

The spectators, however, agreed with the Zhiberian.

They directed their displeasure at the heavily armored gladiator, urging Samarhead to close the distance and use that terrible axe of his. They shouted at him to move, to even say a word or two—something to show he was still alive.

An impassive Samarhead showed no indication of hearing any of it.

Halm wondered if his foe was deaf.

"Get on with you!" shouted someone in the stands.

"You came all the way from the north, what's a few more steps?" came another.

"Move you kogless bull, *move*!"

From where he stood, with the sun's rays pressing down upon him, Halm couldn't help but smile behind his visor. The spectators grew increasingly scathing of Samarhead's lack of interest. More insults scorched the air. Standing as he was in the light of the day, the house gladiator's dark demeanor began to thaw.

Samarhead shifted, from one foot to the other.

Delighted with the weakening of will, Halm bent at the waist and encouraged his adversary with sword and shield. He didn't bother shouting anymore as the crowds drowned him out. He rapped his blade against his shield, thought of something better, then turned and showed the reluctant fighter his ass, giving it a saucy shake.

Laughter amongst the onlookers, the exact effect Halm desired.

"He's offering it to you, lad!" a voice shouted. "Go get it!"

"Ah, these men of the north prefer sheep!"

"Any livestock is fine in that frozen hell!"

"Mount him, lad, mount him, just like your father did that he-bitch of a mother!"

Halm winced at that insult, thinking it particularly poisonous.

That rancid barb struck, however. Samarhead's bull-horned helm turned in the direction of his school's box. The jeering was reaching the *brute amongst men*.

Halm sensed it wouldn't be much longer.

Then, for whatever the reason—the sun's heat, the growing insults of the crowd, the unseen prompting of his manager, or his own chagrin at Halm not playing the way *he* wanted—Samarhead stepped forward.

A single step, then another, and he stopped.

"The bastard moves like an old woman!" someone sang out.

"Perhaps that armor is too heavy for him!" added another.

Samarhead resumed walking, swinging both his massive shield and battle axe, and the crowd's taunts changed to approving roars.

Halm swallowed nervously.

The lad got bigger the closer he got.

"Unfit," Halm muttered to himself, taking a better grip on his own tools. An idea lurked in his head, one he possessed ever since he'd talked to Goll about the grim north man.

Halm had to be wary of the battleaxe. The weapon resembled a ceremonial killing tool purely for the show, but that Samarhead wielded it with one arm was almost bewildering. Frightening, even.

True to their treacherous core, the crowd resumed flinging insults at the Zhiberian. Halm ignored them and adjusted his sword's grip for a backhand thrust.

In just a few heartbeats, he intended on shutting up the works of them.

Samarhead shambled forward, a charging mountain picking up speed. The north man raised his axe until sunlight rippled along its edge. His shield seemed an iron wall, his red visor, inhuman. An immense shadow fell over the Halm and he realized just how damn *big* his opponent truly was.

The spectators' roar reached a peak.

Halm turned slightly and narrowed his stance. *Here it comes...*

Samarhead's mighty axe came crashing down and the Zhiberian lunged *underneath* the cut. The ogre from the

Lands of Great Ice slammed the edge of his shield down into the sand, barring any frontal attack on his legs. But Halm, surprisingly quick for his size, rolled under the axe and past the giant's barrier. He turned and stabbed backward, thrusting his blade's tip deep into the thin armor about the man's ankle.

Steel punched through metal and meat.

Samarhead roared. His foot jerked away, wrenching Halm's sword from his grasp. Blood spurted, a black ribbon that lashed clouds of dust. The armored giant fell, unable to keep his own body weight and that of his heavy armor upright. He crashed to his hands and knees and looked up in time for Halm's greave-covered shin to smash into the side of his helm, jarring the gladiator's remaining senses.

The blow stunned the crowd to silence.

Grunting loud enough to be heard and shattering the illusion of a murderous thing from Saimon's hell, Samarhead recovered enough to swing his axe.

Halm stopped the swipe on his lower greave and chopped his shield's edge into his foe's shoulder. Samarhead dropped his axe and fell flat onto his face. He tried to rise almost immediately, but Halm kicked him square in that iron visor, flipping the gladiator onto his back. The resulting clang of metal on metal briefly echoed.

Grimacing, Halm glanced down. The last kick had dented his greave.

It was time to end it.

The Zhiberian threw away his sword and shield and picked up Samarhead's axe. He held it across his pelvis as he gazed down at the dazed beast at his feet. The axe was heavy, and Halm wondered how in Saimon's hell the big man had managed to swing it with a single arm.

That was a question for another day.

With a groan of effort, Halm brought the axe up over his head and decided to send a message. For an instant, he saw the dark, understanding eyes of Samarhead before the descending axe chopped the bull-horned head off at the shoulders. The axe blade went deep into the arena sand.

Halm left it there. He noticed the spasmodic shiver that coursed through the headless torso. He also didn't miss the little jump of Samarhead's head as it came free of his body. Blood gushed to a steady ooze.

The Zhiberian grimaced, straightened, and adjusted his conical helm. He considered the quiet audience, just for a moment, before he slapped the fat rolls of his belly.

The masses recoiled as if stung by burning pitch.

Feeling good, Halm turned in the direction of the Orator. The old man appeared just as shocked as everyone else.

The Zhiberian raised his fist.

"Your victor!" declared the Orator, finding his voice. "The Free Trained Halm of Zhiberia."

Aye that, a defiant Halm projected and flung his arms wide as cheering mixed dangerously with threats and angry howls.

Not that it bothered Halm. Not in the least.

Arms flung wide, Halm strutted toward the rising portcullis, taking his time, soaking in the moment.

And in short time, the growing cheers drowned out even the most murderous of voices.

*

The sudden stiffness in Dark Curge's posture didn't go unnoticed.

And when the Free Trained fighter raised the axe over

his conical helmet, poised to end Samarhead's miserable life, Gastillo thought Curge was about to cry out in pain. The intimidating owner had even reached forward, clutching at air as if to catch something falling, when the battleaxe flashed down and the blood truly began to flow.

"Ho!" Nexus blurted with an evil grin. "How the big ones fall, eh, Gastillo?"

Curge flinched at the outburst, and Gastillo became aware of the heat rising from the manager's direction.

"Unfortunate round," Gastillo said somberly, his golden mask concealing his delight at seeing a Free Trained dispatch Dark Curge's favorite. "My sympathies. Pains me to see a gladiator fall under the rabble."

Gastillo inserted a cloth underneath his mask and dabbed at the corner of his ruined mouth, soaking up the drool.

"Well, not for me," Nexus bellowed without a care. "Your man was butchered like an ox. And look at all that blood! I've not seen juice spilled like that at even one of my own wineries! That may very well be the kill of the games. What say you there, *Dark* Curge?"

In answer, Curge swung his murderous gaze upon the wine producer. The cords of his muscular neck stood out, his face as red as any grape in the sun. Without a word, the intimidating owner stood, kicked his chair out of the way, and stalked out of the box.

Nexus chuckled merrily at the man's abrupt departure. "Not much to say at all, I see."

Gastillo nodded at the victorious pit fighter disappearing underneath the raised portcullis. "You can be sure that's *one* Free Trained who'll be fortunate to live to see the sun rise. To kill anyone's man is one thing, to kill one of Curge's trained dogs is another. And to make a spectacle of it?"

He shook his head.

Nexus chuckled again. "Really? The great House of Curge can be so vindictive? Unfortunate. It's *only* sport. I must say, this game for the commoners can be an *enjoyable* one after all."

Gastillo considered his own future plans and how they involved Nexus. He took a careful sip from his silver goblet and held the wine in his mouth, savoring it, while dabbing at his face. *Halm of Zhiberia*, he thought pleasantly. He would remember that name. Not that it would matter. The wine merchant had said it all: Dark Curge could indeed be a vindictive one.

Having witnessed several seasons come and go, Gastillo had the good enough sense to avoid Curge when he was in such a mood. He hoped Halm of Zhiberia would be wise and do the same… and to watch his back.

Both in and out of Sunja's Pit.

· 10 ·
Words

"You hellpup!" Pig Knot exclaimed, slapping Halm on his back as he returned from the Pit.

"Did you expect otherwise?" the Zhiberian asked.

"I don't know what I expected," Pig Knot said with a grin. "But I'm happy you're in one whole piece."

"Thanks to this one here," Halm gestured at Goll. "You gave me the idea. Samarhead was an armored giant, so I went low on him and cut out an ankle. Truth be known I wanted his toes, but his shield was too big. I had to change targets."

"I don't think I did much at all," Goll replied. "But I'm glad that you won your match."

"I'm glad you're still alive," Muluk said, as Pig Knot helped the Zhiberian free himself from his leather sleeve. "We ran down here to meet you."

"Did you place the wagers?" Halm asked, suddenly anxious.

"Oh, we did that," The Kree chuckled. "We did that and more. I got five gold coins for my sword, and I dare not think about what I won."

Pig Knot nodded to Goll on his crutches. "That one made a bigger pot."

"How much?" Halm asked.

"All that I had," the injured Kree answered. "Fourteen gold."

"To my one," Halm scoffed. "There's a reason why I'll never be a merchant."

"You don't have to be a merchant," Pig Knot said. "You're a winning gladiator."

Depositing his sword and shield on a bench, Halm began getting out of his greaves. Upon removing the plate he had kicked Samarhead with, he noted the large bruise underneath and the dent in the armor.

"Have to get that pounded out," Muluk said with a critical eye. "I can take care of that for you. For next time."

"I thought you only chopped things?"

"And pound things, when I have to," Muluk replied. "I can fix that easy enough."

"Leave it here for now." Halm wiped the sweat from his body. "Only two things concern me now, collecting my coin and getting to a bathhouse. I'll pay for you all."

"I'll take you up on that," Pig Knot said. "Unlike these two, I haven't a coin to my name."

"You didn't wager?"

Pig Knot shook his head. "Nothing to wager with. But that's talk for another time. And if you lend me a few coins, I'll pay them back when I can."

"I think I can do that."

"Let's be off from here, then," Pig Knot said.

With that, the four made their ways through the fleshy clutter of general quarters, passing the other men who would fight that day. Some of the assembled men congratulated the

Zhiberian. Others got out of his way.

"Halm of Zhiberia!" The *Madea's* voice cut through the good spirits of the companions and caused them all to turn about.

"Tomorrow, Halm of Zhiberia," the *Madea* shouted. "Your blood match will be tomorrow. Are you able to fight?"

Halm sighed. "I am. Tomorrow, then."

"First match, Halm of Zhiberia."

The Zhiberian scowled. "No drinking or wenching this night, lads. Not for me, anyway."

"Harsh words," Pig Knot clapped him on the shoulder. "You almost sound responsible, now."

On the way out, they visited the Pay Master, who handed Halm his prize. The Zhiberian's purse jingled from the weight of twenty gold coins, and he kept a firm grip on it.

Just outside of the Entryway of the Sun, the four companions visited the *Domis* who handled the wagers. They lined up for one of four enclosed booths surrounded by menacing Skarrs. Others who had also won their wagers waited to collect their winnings while, one line over, people made their wagers for the next fight. Goll, Muluk and Halm identified themselves with their scrawl and were given their coin. At four to one odds, each man had won enough to be laughing.

"Well, then, lads," Halm said. "I'm off to the baths. And then an early supper, but no drinking."

"Then neither will I," Goll said.

"Nor I," Muluk threw in.

"I can't, anyway," Pig Knot said. "As I'm living off you until my first match."

"When is that?" Halm asked.

"The day after yours, it seems. I fight some topper called Darcevo."

"Dar—" Halm began, and stopped in his tracks.

Just ahead, standing in the middle of the grounds surrounding Sunja's Pit, stood Vadrian the Fire. He wore armor and carried a scabbard on his hip, but his spiked gauntlet was nowhere to be seen.

"Heathen maggots all," the tall, blond man declared. "Prospering over the deaths. Have you no shame? You're as bad as the Zhiberian shite with you."

Pig Knot spoke first. "Aren't you a part of these games, you brazen kog?"

"I do not partake in the greedy practices of wagering."

"Ah, this one is just like the clergy in my homeland," a smiling Halm said. "One corner of his mouth lies, while the other gives the truth. You're in Sunja's Pit, you pig-bastard. With two victories. You've already collected twice."

"I collect no such coin, hellborn." Vadrian's head arched backward as if he had gotten a whiff of something unpleasant. "I fight for Seddon alone. To collect gold at the death of another, even those as lowly as you, is against his divine word."

"But killing them straight away is fine with Seddon?" Pig Knot asked.

"The faster the better, so that the divine may reclaim those lost souls. But you…" Vadrian pointed at Halm. "You'll be a special case. I'll dispatch you to Saimon's hell. Where you belong. Burning for eternity for mocking the Church of Seddon."

"I only mock ass-lickers," Halm retorted. "Not proper churches."

"The Church of Seddon *is* a proper church. It is *the*

Church to which all will soon be tethered to better embrace the light of Seddon."

"Under your command, I suppose."

"Of course."

Halm had nothing more to say, recognizing Vadrian as one fish hooked through the brainpan. He started walking toward the man calling himself the Fire. The self-proclaimed Son of Seddon tensed and gripped his sword's pommel.

Halm stopped in his tracks. "You're damn quick to go for your blade. Get out of my way, and we won't have a problem."

"You *have* a problem, spawn of Zhiberia," Vadrian hissed.

Standing so close, Halm could see the warrior's eyes were even crazier looking than Pig Knot's.

"I know about Zhiberia," Vadrian continued. "The people there are nothing more than ignorant wastes of flesh. Heathens all. I look forward to traveling there one day, to purify the land in Seddon's name. Only then, with you unfit savages scoured from the face of Seddon's earth, will the smell cease plaguing Sunja by way of the spring winds."

"You're unfit," Halm told him, studying his face.

"I've been touched by the hand of Seddon, dog. Blessed with gifts physical and spiritual, to go forth and do Seddon's bidding. Where better to start a crusade but in the darkest pit? It begins here, maggot, with the souls of all disbelievers sent to Seddon by the strength of my fist and the cut of my steel. When I have purged the arena, I'll scour this entire city. *All* of this place. I tell you this, Zhiberian, because tomorrow I send you to Seddon or Saimon, whoever will take you."

A seething, clearly unstable Vadrian waited for a retort.

Halm gave him one.

KEITH C. BLACKMORE

The Zhiberian looked at his companions and indicated for them to walk around the man in their way. Goll hopped along on crutches while Pig Knot stood eye-to-eye with Vadrian and scowled.

Vadrian kept on speaking, however. "You walk away from me now, Zhiberian pisspot, but there will be no walking away from me tomorrow. You go and enjoy whatever pleasures you have waiting. Enjoy the gluttony and the drink that saps your soul. Tomorrow, it all ends. Tomorrow, I send you."

Still glaring, Pig Knot backed off and circled Vadrian after the others had gone. He eyed the Fire, and retreated a respectable distance before turning his back.

Behind him, Vadrian spoke on, faster, and with greater passion. "Tomorrow, Zhiberian. You shall *feel* the might of *Seddon* on your heathen neck! Seddon has empowered me, *me*, to vanquish *all* that displeases him! I send you to him tomorrow, *Halm*, savage from savage *Zhiberia*! I shall send you!"

A pensive Halm shook his head at the outburst.

"I shall send you!" came the parting shout.

Then nothing, the crowds filled in the space between Vadrian and the departing four.

They walked on for a bit before Muluk leaned into Halm's side. "Are you worried about tomorrow?"

"About him?" Halm frowned and rattled his head again. "But if I wasn't in the games, I'd have chopped him right there. That one is right and proper unfit in the head."

"I'll drink to that," Pig Knot exclaimed.

"Enough of him," the Zhiberian declared. "Seddon will damn me if I don't get to a bathhouse soon. I stink!"

*

Long after the four men had gone, Vadrian the Fire stood in the throngs of milling Sunjans and berated the lot. He preached long and loud enough that Skarrs gathered at a distance. They kept their backs to buildings, waving the masses by at times, and simply watched the angry man shouting at people until no one walked within ten paces of him. He chastised the passing people, warning them of gluttony and wanton pleasures of the flesh. He ranted about the sins of the Sunja and he swore to deliver them all into salvation.

After a while, Vadrian grew tired of speaking. The people remained well out of reach. They were wise to do so. Seddon, however, would bring them to him. He'd gather a flock with each victory in the Pit. The arena was key. If he showed strength of arms, power of will, and might of soul, then the masses would cling to his very person.

Tossing his head back and inhaling deeply, Vadrian decided to make his way back to his church and seek an early night. Tomorrow, he intended to make an example of the fat man. Seddon would enjoy the sacrifice.

With that final thought, Vadrian started walking.

*

After spending the remainder of the afternoon in a public bathhouse, the four friends decided it was time to eat and do a little celebrating. The slaying of Samarhead was an occasion that merited something better than the usual fare, and since they had coin to spend, they meandered through Sunja's streets until locating an alehouse of good reputation. They found a table and ordered roasts of beef with vegetables and covered in rich sauce. Muluk paid for the food, and Goll paid for the drink. When the meal arrived, the serving girl left the victuals on a great platter in the middle of the table, and they tore into it.

"This could be the start of something good," Pig Knot said, as he chewed. "I owe you all for this. And I don't forget my debts."

Muluk shifted a mouthful of food into his right cheek so he could speak. "I'll see that you remember."

"I'll sleep in a real room tonight," Halm said. "Spend a few coins on something good."

"They have rooms here," Goll said. "I already paid for one."

"I'll get one as well." Halm replied.

Muluk grunted. "Might as well, then."

Pig Knot lowered his head and ate.

"Fear not," Halm said and shoved the man's shoulder. "I'll get you a room. You should have at least one night out of general quarters."

"No, that would be unwise," Pig knot said. "As I said, I remember my debts. A night in the general quarters will push me harder to win. Stop me from suckling."

"I've been thinking," Goll said between bites. "About us. Free Trained fighters. And the games."

"What about it?" Pig Knot asked, chewing loudly and wiping his face with a hand.

"We don't have to merely be Free Trained."

"We don't?" Pig Knot smirked, muscular forearms flexing as he reached for more of the roast.

"Not in the least," Goll said. "Think of it. The four of us can fight. Fight well, in fact, but we aren't respected in the least. The established houses and schools in Sunja despise us because we pose a risk to their investments. We have no backing. Our weapons and armor are either our own or taken from the piles left behind by dead gladiators. It doesn't have to be that way."

"What are you saying?" Pig Knot asked. "That we start our own school? Our own house?"

Goll leaned over the table. "Why not?"

"Coin is why not," Muluk said.

The two Krees regarded each other for a moment. Goll then reached under the table and plopped his leather purse onto the surface. That silenced the others and, for a moment, the only sounds heard were those of the alehouse's regular customers eating and socializing.

"Foolishness," Pig Knot muttered. "We can't just announce ourselves as a house of gladiators."

"Why not?" Goll pressed.

"The other houses won't have it, for one."

"And it takes more money than one purse of gold," Muluk added.

"Let the man talk," Halm said with a glimmer of interest. "There's no harm in talk, is there? Unless it's about Pig Knot, that is."

The Sunjan winked at the Zhiberian.

Goll nodded his thanks and went on. "I killed a champion and almost died for it. But that champion did not represent any house when he fought me." He pointed at Halm. "This man here just killed off a gladiator from the House of Curge. Do you think there won't be a challenge there? Another blood fight? They might not even wait to get even. They might gut you outside of the arena. I've heard of such attacks on Free Trained warriors."

Halm nodded. "I have, too."

"As have I," Pig Knot added with a frown.

"I only just got here." Muluk smiled, but became serious

when the others didn't share his humor.

"I've heard stories about fighters disappearing in the night," Pig Knot went on. "Fighters that had killed or wounded a man badly enough that he couldn't continue. Free Trained fighters, who would defeat their foe and walk away, never to be seen again. I figure they were either driven out, or there are more than a few corpses in Sunja's sewers."

"Or bones, after the rats are done with them," Halm added.

Muluk paused in chewing, had an image, dismissed it, and kept on eating.

"That's what I'm talking about," Goll started again. "As we are now, we're nothing. We're the dogs, and we're seen as that. We're set against each other as well as the established schools and, if we win, we're still dismissed. No Free Trained fighter has ever been champion of the games. Never. Think on that. And none of us will until we band together, share our secrets, our knowledge, and watch out for each other. Divided as we are now, no Free Trained gladiator will ever win the games. Because the House of Curge, or Gastillo, or Nexus, or Tilo, or any of them won't *allow* a Free Trained to be champion. One way or the other."

"If…" Halm cocked an eyebrow. "If we *did* do something, what would you suggest?"

"Pig Knot's already said it. We start our own house. A Free Trained house."

"We would not be free then," Muluk said.

"I'm still thinking on that," Goll responded. "But I don't think we have to change anything. Think of it. If a fighter joins us, all he promises is to share his knowledge and train. But no one has to pay any gold. If one of us wins, a portion of the winnings will go into a pot. To finance the house and draw upon as needed."

"We'd need training grounds," Halm said. "Lodgings. Food. That would take a good amount of coin. A huge amount."

"Then we'll have to win. Frequently. Take a portion of each man's winnings, as I just said. Perhaps even place wagers in the house's name. Even the recognized houses do that. It'll add up. In return, we'll offer a place of refuge, a place to train, and a place to sleep without fear of waking up in the sewers."

That quieted the three men.

"Think of this…" Goll challenged. "Right now, there are *hundreds* of Free Trained gladiators here at the games, *all* calling general quarters—which is a rat hole—home. Hundreds. We are already together, yet divided. If we have our own house, *we* become the largest force amongst the schools. We're no longer threatened by the house gladiators who strut about as if they were gods."

"That part will never change," Pig Knot smirked.

"But you understand what it is I'm saying," Goll insisted.

"Understanding is thirsty work." Halm raised his mug.

"Aye that," Pig Knot agreed and drank deeply.

Muluk appeared thoughtful, but in the end, he drank as well.

"Another pitcher here!" Pig Knot called out, lifting the empty one.

"Think on it, lads." Goll hoped his words wouldn't fade into the night. "That's all I ask."

He took a drink from his own mug.

Halm eyed the younger man, saw how his shoulders slumped. What he said made sense. There was a problem in it, however, and that was one of leadership. *And* the question of whether or not the Gladiatorial Chamber would actually allow a new house to form while the games were happening. Saying and *doing* were two different things, and Halm was smart enough to recognize that. He wondered if the wounded Kree sitting at his table recognized it as well.

· 11 ·
Dark Matters

In darkness brimming with dust and the smell of decaying flesh, Vadrian slept on the floor of his church. He slumbered on his back, his head resting on a rough sack filled with a few possessions. He was a light sleeper, the Son of Seddon, but even he didn't sense the figures creeping into his sanctuary, as noiseless as ghosts. The church didn't allow any light from the moon outside, and the gloom was as oppressive as a violated tomb. The invading ghosts, six of them, moved in a line down the center of the church. They edged past broken pews, toward the altar at the front, careful not to disturb the sleeping Vadrian. They carried a single hooded lantern, its narrow beam of light revealing the path as they stepped with caution.

Vadrian slept before the altar, snoring loud enough to cause a few of the intruders to smirk. They spread out around him and, on the signal from one, pounced on the sleeping warrior.

Vadrian woke with his arms and legs held fast. Rough hands gripped his skull. A fury rose up within him, and his efforts to break free tripled.

He roared.

"You black-hearted bastards! Let me up! Let me up! I swear I'll kill you all for violating His church! Let—"

An open hand slapped his face. Hard.

Livid rage flared in Vadrian's eyes.

But then a blade appeared above him, just a flash of metal, and the weapon descended to the bobbing knob of Vadrian's throat.

Feeling that steely sliver against his cheesepipe, Vadrian ceased struggling at once.

"Not pleasant, is it?" asked a voice in the darkness. "To have a knife at your throat."

The lantern's light shone into Vadrian's eyes, blinding him.

"And let me be clear," said the voice. "Move, and the last thing you see will be a fountain of your own blood. A *gurgling* fountain. Understood?"

Vadrian swallowed. The weapon's edge rubbed against the knuckle of his throat.

"Understood." The pit fighter whispered.

"Excellent," the voice said. "I've tried to contact you before, twice in fact. And the one that did find you, you weren't very nice to. My man only wanted to speak business, and you were quite forceful with him. Needlessly so."

"I… will speak now," Vadrian said.

"Far too late for *civilized* talk. But I'm willing to talk like this. Now then, to business, and I'll let you sleep."

Vadrian wasn't certain to which type of sleep the silhouette referred.

"Tomorrow, you fight a man called Halm," the voice declared. "I want him dead. You will kill him. There will be no quarter given. I don't think you would, anyway, but I want to be clear on this. I want that man *dead*. In bloody fashion. Do you understand?"

"I understand." Vadrian understood all too well, but the request was one that he had no trouble in following. It was all part of his grand design.

"Do this for me, and I will be most appreciative. I was actually willing to make you an offer before. I see talent in you. Now, however, I'm wary of offering you anything, including your life."

"I—"

The voice cut him off. "Quiet. Listen. I've heard you rant about Seddon. Well, tonight you are under the knife of *Saimon's* child. In his darkness. And while I believe the world would be a much safer place without the likes of you, I also see that you have a purpose. Kill Halm of Zhiberia, and I will have my man talk with you again, under more agreeable conditions. And don't consider murdering him outside the arena."

"You have... my word."

"I do?" There was a smile to the words. "Like this poor dog over here? The reason for the perfume?"

The light shone in a direction Vadrian could not see, but he knew what it revealed.

"Who was he?"

"I don't know."

"You just went and twisted his head around like that and hung him off a hook for amusement?"

Vadrian winced. "He tried to speak with me."

"He did?" Another smile around the words. "About what?"

"He wanted... me to join his master's school."

"And you killed him for that?"

"Aye."

"Which school?"

"I did not ask."

The ghost paused. "Did you happen to kill another? I sent two men to you, and one has gone missing."

Vadrian knew the second man but, thankfully, he had possessed the sense to bury the body outside in an old grave. "No."

The ghost thought for a moment, then exhaled harshly. "You're a special one, Vadrian. I'll give you that. My men will release you upon my word. If you rise up in arms, they will hang you by your guts from the rafters overhead and leave you swinging. Do you understand?"

"I do."

"Kill Halm."

"I will."

"Good." A reflective silence. "Sleep well, then."

The silence stretched on, as if the ghost had paused to consider something, but then he was gone.

Tense heartbeats later, the knife at Vadrian's throat left. Hands released his limbs. He didn't rise straight away, so he lay there, listening as his visitors departed, the sound of their passing receding.

Only when they had gone did he move.

With a trembling hand, Vadrian wiped the cold sweat from his brow. His stomach knotted. Never had he come so close to dying. Never had he felt so helpless. He took a deep breath and got to his feet. The gloom of the church's interior never seemed deeper.

Kill Halm, the voice said.

Vadrian rubbed the stubble of his throat.

Praise Seddon, he silently prayed.

*

In another part of the great city of Sunja, across a bridge and river, three men made their way toward the innermost parts. The leader was man called Bojen, of average height and build, in his early forties, with a head of clean white hair. Bojen didn't like being in this shadowy part of the city. His master had given him a task to do, however, and he dared not disappoint him, not even if it ultimately meant traveling to this filthy place. Bojen didn't know he was going to be sent into the sewers, however. If he had, he would have dressed for it. Expensive leather sandals meticulously stitched and fashioned covered his feet, while soft silk leggings and a white shirt dressed the rest of him. His cloak was one of rich fox fur, and he found himself hitching it further up by the fistful, not wanting the hem to make contact with the ground.

The three men quietly made their way off the main road, down a stone stairway which slipped below the bridge and waterline. Foul vegetative matter crusted the stonework. To their left, behind a thick brick wall ran the inner river and moat surrounding Sunja's palaces. To their right was another solid barrier, red and scratched in places, but otherwise remarkably well kept. Sewage percolated the air, causing Bojen to cover his mouth and nose with a cloth. He released his cloak, allowing it to drop to his ankles. Cursing, he stopped and inspected the length and saw that it didn't touch the wet steps. Not yet, anyway. It would sooner or later, he knew, and that made him swear again.

Behind him, his guards said nothing.

The little group halted at the bottom of the stairway, before a brick tunnel brimming with darkness. The smell became far more potent, threatening to gag Bojen, and he knew he'd have to bathe soon after this meeting. If he was truly unfortunate, he would have to burn all of his clothes.

"This way," he muttered miserably, hoping the passageway remained dry.

They entered that black maw, feeling their way along the wall. Bojen's fingers dredged up damp sludge that had collected on the brick, and he fluttered his hand to dislodge the filth.

A torch came into view near the end, the glow appearing damn near magically. The visitors paused at the sight. A figured dressed in black robes stepped around a corner, his face partially concealed by a deep cowl, his torch lifted to the ceiling.

"Only one of you may come closer," the figure spoke.

Hesitantly, Bojen signaled his guards to remain.

The robed man beckoned the Bojen closer and led him around the corner, down a surprisingly long length of brick and mortar. Bojen sidestepped puddles and ducked under strands of filth hanging from the ceiling, often taking second glances at the pitfalls.

The mysterious guide didn't slow in the least.

The guide's torch disappeared around a corner, becoming a glow. Bojen barely caught a whimper as he scurried to catch up, wincing as his right foot splashed through an unseen puddle. Water soaked his toes, the touch sickening.

Muttering curses, Bojen proceeded carefully. He wasn't fit to such dealings under the earth, in the smelly damp and wet. He should have sent another in his place.

Turning the corner with a bump and a grimace, Bojen saw that the torch had stopped just up ahead. He closed the distance, seeing that the light had been placed in a sconce but the guide had vanished, perhaps continued ahead in the dark. The air thickened with moisture and the puddles widened into pools. The sewage smell became much stronger. Bojen stopped in the light, peered deep into that blackness beyond, and wondered if he was supposed to proceed. Keeping the cloth firm against his mouth and nose, he reached for the torch set into a sconce.

"Come no further," spoke the voice in the dark.

That stopped the agent.

"I cannot see you." Bojen said, the words muffled by his cloth.

Silence. "What did you say?"

Sighing, Bojen lowered his cloth and winced at the stench. "I said, I can't see you."

"No one looks upon the faces of the Khas-Jantos. If you did, you would die. You were told to come alone."

"The streets are a dangerous place after dark," Bojen answered, quickly covering his mouth.

"State your business."

"My master wishes a man dead."

"Who?"

Bojen lowered the cloth. "A gladiator. Free Trained. Shouldn't be a problem for you."

"What's this dead man's name?"

Bojen said it with a gasp, knowing full well he'd have to burn his clothes later, and that he was no longer sure it was just water seeping between his toes.

"Describe him," commanded the voice.

Bojen did so, coughing at times.

"You know our fee?" the voice asked.

"I have it here."

"Show us."

Fuming, Bojen reached for a small sack hidden beneath his cloak. He held it up to the light and shook it. Coins jingled.

"Stand where you are and hold it at arm's length."

The sack was heavy, but Bojen did as he was told, stretching his arm further into the darkness as thick and fragrant as sewage water. He jumped, startled by two white hands appearing and plucking the payment away from him. They vanished back into the gloom.

Coins rustled. "When do you want the gladiator dead?"

Bojen composed himself. "He fights tomorrow. The first match of the day. We want him killed then. In the Pit. And we do not want to be connected to his death."

A pause. "His death will not come back to you."

Eyes watering, Bojen nodded vigorously while all but smothering himself with his handcloth.

"Take the torch and leave us. Tell your master this man will die. Tomorrow, during his match, as instructed."

Bojen dropped his cloth. "Do not fail."

That summoned an ominous silence.

A different voice whispered from the dark. "Do not threaten us… lest you be given a stronger warning."

Those haunting words raised the hair on Bojen's scrubbed neck. He held the cloth to his face again, fearful he'd said too much. The moments stretched, and he tensed, ready to shout for his guards if anything should rush him from the dark. Nothing did, however, and time stretched on.

"Hello?" he called tentatively.

No answer.

"Are you there?" Bojen tried again, and heard only the dripping of water. *Tsking* to himself, yet relieved the encounter was concluded, he sighed. He plucked the torch from its sconce, the flame flickering low, and considered venturing deeper into the tunnel.

That brought on a scowl. Bojen scolded himself for such a foolish thought. It was time to vacate this miserable place.

He made his way back through the tunnel, the smell receding as he went, and remembered the words of the killers in the dark. They spoke of warning. Bojen wondered what they meant by that.

He slowed, detecting a new smell on the air, one that brought him close to retching.

The torchlight revealed the corpses of his two guards lying dead on the brick stairway, their throats cut, their blood flowing over the stairs.

Bojen stopped and gazed upon the dead men, his torch hand trembling. Panic rose in his chest, and he quickly looked behind him.

Then ahead.

Then the two dead men again.

"Seddon above," he whispered.

He stooped to study the pair, cringing at their opened throats. Both men had been taken from behind. Bojen straightened and regarded the narrow staircase, wondering how they could have been killed in such place. It was much too small for a killer to take them by surprise. Bojen hadn't even heard a thing. Not a single squawk of terror, and he hadn't gone on that far ahead.

Sorcery! flashed through his mind.

That was all the impetus he needed.

Bojen quickly edged past the dead men and ascended to the streets.

He ran back to his employer, fur cloak blowing in the wind.

· 12 ·
Day 4

On the morning of the fourth day, Halm awoke in his rented room. He breathed deeply and yawned. The straw bed was too comfortable to leave, so he lay there and gazed at the bare timbers of the ceiling. Here and there, a cobweb could be seen, and Halm even thought he spied the makers. Outside the wooden-shuttered window, the world was coming alive, and there was a sleepy goodness on the air.

Halm's eyes narrowed.

He had to kill a man this afternoon.

Blood match. Blood fight. Blood feud. They all meant the same thing. For whatever reason, two men had agreed to fight to the death. It happened all the time in the games. That didn't bother Halm. The Zhiberian had no qualms about sending a man on his way, especially a noisy ass-licker like Vadrian, but the unpleasant business of what was to happen later that afternoon crept into the purity of the morning, ruining it, like spilled blood touching a piece of parchment.

He then remembered the words of the Kree, Goll.

Halm knew he was good enough to fight a few men and

win some coin. He could win enough to make it through a winter or until some other work came along, if he was wise with his money—and he rarely was. Then it would be a struggle to find something to take him to the next set of games. Truth be known, Halm wasn't much good at anything else besides fighting. He couldn't work wood, and he was clumsy around a forge. He couldn't read or write, except to scrawl his name. Farming was too boring, and handcrafts of any kind were laughable for his rough fingers.

There was only one thing he was good at.

One thing, Seddon save his soul, he enjoyed doing.

And that was smashing heads.

A mighty sigh left him. There wasn't anything else for him to do, and do well. The sad thing was he fully understood he couldn't do it forever. These games might be the last for him. *Today* might even be the last day for him. It would be merciful if it was, but what if it wasn't? If he survived this day and even the next, he wondered what then.

He was getting older. Slower.

Perhaps that was reason he found Goll's idea appealing. He'd have to give the notion greater thought. After this day.

He got out of bed, *bare-arsed and brazen*, as his mother used to say, and wandered to a table where a pitcher of water and a clay basin waited. He drank and poured the rest into the basin. Then he plunged his head into the water, wet his face and hair, and snapped everything back out. Water flew. He massaged his scalp with one hand, considered cutting his hair as he disliked having it too long.

Perhaps after the fight.

He had no shirt as it was too warm this time of year, and he had no qualms about walking about with his gut hanging out. He pulled on his breeches and slapped the bare flesh of his belly. Then came the sandals, which he slipped his feet into. He checked his leather purse—still quite full—and made his way to the door. *Today would be a serious day*, he thought, and removed the timber barring the door from the inside.

Halm exited the alehouse alone, leaving his companions. They'd talked the night before, and the Zhiberian informed them all he would see them at the arena. He wanted to collect his thoughts and not speak to anyone if he could manage it. Halm knew himself, and while he enjoyed company and conversation, he equally enjoyed solitude and quiet. This time, he preferred not speaking to anyone.

Trouble was, there were a lot of people in the city of Sunja.

The morning sun warmed the stone tiles of the street, but overhead clouds threatened to blanket the sky. That wasn't a bad thing in Halm's mind. He liked the idea of fighting in the shade.

The streets weren't too crowded this morning but that would soon change. Halm walked against the growing current of people. Merchants took boards down off their street side stalls as Halm strolled by, while others worked at unpacking their goods. Livestock were led down alleys. Workers climbed ladders to where other men hammered repairs into old rooftops. Under wide canopies to shield them from the sun and rain, leatherworkers with awls and strings settled in at tables. Two men coaxed a forge to life, while a handful of women scrubbed clothing in wide washtubs. Halm caught a whiff of sewage, which didn't bother his senses.

He spotted a stall with an old woman cooking eggs and fresh bread, and he stopped for breakfast. Others gathered around the old woman's offerings, making purchases and either walking away with the food or standing and eating it right there. When Halm finished his meal, he headed to the arena.

It was early, but he had decided on something.

He found the closed booths of the *Domis* and plopped down beside one, content to wait until it opened. There was nowhere else to go and waiting was as good an idea as any. Halm placed his back against a wall, squinted at the sun, and relaxed.

The open area surrounding Sunja's Pit gradually filled with people waiting for the day's games. Merchants set up their food stalls. Some of them recognized the Zhiberian and nodded. Others watched him warily. None dared approach.

That suited Halm just fine.

Later in the morning, a handful of Skarrs arrived. They stopped and positioned themselves around the small buildings, and Halm moved farther away so as not to bother them. All he needed was the attention of the city guard.

The shuttered windows of the Domis opened shortly after the Skarrs' appearance. The coin keepers sat behind bars and busied themselves with coin matters.

When he felt ready, Halm stood, dusted himself off, and went to one of the windows.

He produced his leather purse. "I wish to place a wager."

"On who?" the middle-age keeper said, squinting.

"Halm of Zhiberia."

The keeper consulted a list. "First fight of the day. How much?"

Halm slid his purse through the slot beneath the bars. The keeper took it without comment. He emptied the leather and counted. Upon finishing, he reached underneath the counter and brought up a white marker.

"We take one gold piece for the wager. Agreed?"

Halm already knew it. He nodded.

"Place your scrawl on this marker," the keeper instructed.

Halm did so with a quill and ink from a small container.

"Do not lose this, understand?" the keeper admonished.

"I understand."

"Off with you, then,"

A pensive Halm walked away.

The wager was everything he had. If he won, the riches would be enough to… to do what? *Well*, he thought, *it would be enough to keep busy, anyway.*

He entered Sunja's Pit by way of the Entryway of the Sun. He didn't immediately go to general quarters, but wandered over to the arena stands. He made his way up a stairway and stood at the bottom line of seats ringing the arena. Thousands would be there later but, at the moment, only handfuls sat here and there. Tanned men in loincloths and sandals groomed the sands with wide straw brooms.

Halm watched them for a bit.

The pissers were old and probably doing the work for a few silver coins, or even a copper. The more the Zhiberian watched, the more he disliked the thought of having to do such work at such an age, if he lived to see it. Then he wondered what they thought of their lot in this life.

Halm thought for a long time on that. He wasn't one to think too deeply into such matters, but there he was.

All because of Goll and what he'd said.

Shaking his head, Halm left the arena and made his way to the gateway of the sun, to the lower levels of general quarters. Once below, he waded through pit fighters of all shapes, sizes, and health, holding a hand to his nose. The chambers stunk with the night's air, open latrines, and the faint stink of blood.

Eventually, Halm located his bag of equipment, waiting for him at the base of a wall. He pulled out the old leather sleeve, waving a hand at the odor. When he reached for his shield, he noted that his sword was missing.

Sweet Seddon. Halm straightened and shook his head.

Had someone actually stolen his sword? He'd never heard of anyone stealing swords from general quarters since there were plenty of blades in the armory. It was considered bad luck to steal the sword of a living gladiator.

Halm wondered if someone had mistaken him as dead. He glanced around and decided to visit the armory.

"I need a blade," he said to the quartermaster behind a barred window. The armory man was hunched over, perhaps stricken with some unknown sickness, and possessed a large nose that appeared to have been broken at least once.

"Come around, then," the quartermaster said. "Choose what you like."

Halm entered the large room and gazed upon dusty aisles filled with racks of all manner of weapons and armor, all free to the gladiators in the games. He meandered along a rack and studied the selection. All the weapons were serviceable, usually taken from the dead and repaired if necessary. He skipped the assortment of axes and mauls, passed on the spears and maces, and began hefting and swinging swords. Once blade in particular, a short sword, got his approval.

"I'll have this," Halm rumbled.

"When do you fight?" the quartermaster asked.

"I'm the first."

"Where are you?"

"Just out there," Halm pointed to where he had left his bag.

The quartermaster frowned. "I'll put an edge on it, put it in a scabbard, and bring it over to you before it's your time."

"My thanks." Halm said and walked back into the greater chamber. Pig Knot wandered into view.

"I'm here," The Zhiberian called out.

Pig Knot turned around. "Didn't run after all, hm?" He smiled.

Halm frowned. "Placed my wager as well."

"Did you now? Everything?"

"Aye that."

"So you'll either be well off or dead." Pig Knot seemed pleased. "Not a bad idea, really. Need help getting ready?"

"The day I need any help from you is the day I find myself wounded, near death, and surrounded by Paw Savages."

"So you need help, then?"

"Aye that."

After they had finished, Muluk appeared with Goll limping behind on his crutches. Muluk handed Halm the previously damaged greave. Halm took it, inspected the repair, and nodded his thanks.

"How do you feel?" Muluk asked, sizing up the big man in his leather sleeve, studded leather skirt, and newly applied greaves.

Halm gave him a tight-lipped smile. "I'll feel better when I collect from the *Domis*."

"We've placed our wagers as well," Goll told him.

"How much?"

"Almost everything," Muluk said.

"Everything." Goll watched for a reaction from the Zhiberian.

Halm exchanged looks with Pig Knot.

The Sunjan smiled. "I could have shown you better gambles than this dog here."

"Do you think so, Halm?" Goll asked.

The Zhiberian didn't reply, but stared across the chamber, through pockets of shadow and torchlight and men.

The three companions followed his gaze.

Vadrian the Fire appeared in the general quarters. Dressed in his leather armor and sporting bared weapons, the blond man strutted to the *Madea*. The warrior turned in the Zhiberian's direction. Vadrian's face twisted into hate. He fitted his winged helm to his skull and gave it a shake.

"This day you die, Zhiberian!" Vadrian shouted. "This day you greet Saimon himself, you heathen shite!"

Pig Knot grunted. "The man's a punce."

Halm grunted agreement.

"Kill him just so we can have some quiet in here," Muluk said, eyeing Vadrian in distaste.

"I will try, friend Muluk."

Overhead, a roar shook the dark ceiling as the Orator whipped the eager crowds into a frenzy for the first fight of the day. A blood match. No other contest demanded the same level of interest as when the two warriors fighting possessed a dislike for each other.

Across the way, the *Madea* called out to Halm, informing him it was time.

The Zhiberian donned his conical helm and hefted his square shield.

"Where's your—" Pig Knot began, impatience in his voice.

The quartermaster appeared almost instantly. "Here you are. Apologies for being late."

"Late?" Halm grumbled. "I could've forged a new blade myself in that time."

He looked at the smaller man, noting the broken nose again, and took the sword in its scabbard. Pig Knot helped him strap the weapon to his waist. The quartermaster retreated into the masses of pit fighters and disappeared.

Halm watched him, however, and noticed the man didn't return to the armory.

"Halm of Zhiberia!" the *Madea* roared.

"It's time." Pig Knot held out his fist.

*

Sweat traveled down his back as Halm stood in armor at the base of the stairs. Light shone through the lowered portcullis above him. The same old bastard from before stood across from the Zhiberian, his hand on a lever. The gatekeeper eyed him evilly while chewing on something.

Overhead, the Orator introduced Vadrian.

"I wagered against you," The gatekeeper smirked, revealing a crenellated row of blackened teeth.

"Daresay you'd wager against the sheep you call sons, old topper."

The older man grimaced as if he'd just swallowed poison. "May Saimon take you to his hell."

He yanked down on the lever.

Halm remained silent and supposed Saimon just might. And soon. He jogged up the steps.

The time for talking was done.

*

Dark Curge clenched his jaw and looked upon the sands. The Orator had finished introducing Vadrian the Fire, and now he focused on the Zhiberian. Curge rubbed a rough hand over his bald head and struck the stump of his left arm against a stone wall.

"You seem anxious this afternoon," Gastillo said, lifting his mask and dabbing at his mouth.

"What would you know about it?" Curge snipped and stroked his jaw. Vadrian the Fire, he mulled, had better kill the Free Trained bastard that had robbed him of his house's finest prospect for this year's games. The time and energy invested in priming a warrior for the season was immense, and to have such a fighter taken away from him by the likes of the unfit pisser entering the arena was almost too much for Curge to bear. He intended to see the man killed, if not by Vadrian's hand then by someone's else's, and then send whispers into the city that *he* was responsible.

It would all serve the greater glory of the House of Curge.

*

The introductions finished, the spectators screamed and cheered in anticipation. No one doubted Vadrian's skill, and the crowds were equally aware of the Zhiberian's. Both gladiators had the potential to deliver one of the most exciting fights of the games thus far. Word of the gladiators' dislike for each other had also spread amongst the onlookers.

The best fights often erupted from those with the taint of hate on the air.

Below on groomed sands, Halm looked across the way and took in the huge form of Vadrian the Fire. The man's bronze helm gleamed in the afternoon sun, and he threw his arms wide, accepting the thunderous applause.

"Good people of Sunja, this fight *is* a blood match," the Orator reminded them from above. "Only one man will walk away this day, and may the Lords watch over the dead. And now, good people, a moment of silence for Vadrian's prayer of the Pit."

Halm snorted. *Prayer of the Pit?*

Such gurry.

A suddenly solemn Vadrian pulled forth his sword, the blade flashing.

Halm remembered the Mademian blade then, once belonging to the hellpup whose name he didn't remember. He remembered the dead man's face, however, along with the image of him allowing Pig Knot to hold and swing that sword.

Vadrian sank to one knee and, bowing his head, began to pray.

"Sweet Seddon above—"

To hear the words spoken by such a person annoyed the Zhiberian.

"Jigger that," Halm muttered, and decided he wouldn't allow such gurry. He brought up his sword, gripped his shield and advanced.

He was tired of the punce's theatrics.

Cries of warning flew up from the crowd, loud enough to cause Vadrian to look up in mid-prayer.

Halm increased his stride.

The Orator observed to the sand and saw the Zhiberian about to charge.

"Good people of Sunja! On behalf of the Gladiatorial Chamber and King Juhn's best wishes-for-you-to-be-entertained—let the fight *begin!*"

Vadrian stood just as Halm's sword flashed for his head. He deflected it off the small buckler strapped to his left arm and whipped his spiked fist across the Zhiberian's visor.

Missing by a finger.

Halm stabbed and stabbed again, driving the Sunjan back toward the arena wall. The Zhiberian cracked his square shield toward a head, thrusting with his sword underneath, but the Fire jerked himself out of harm's way.

Vadrian circled to his right, placing Halm's shield between both of them. "Heathen shite, interrupting my prayer so. I was right about you. You're unfit to live."

Halm smirked. "And you are?"

"I have—"

Halm lunged, thrusting for the man's stomach, wanting to punch his sword's tip through to the man's back.

Vadrian dodged the blow.

The Zhiberian wouldn't let him catch his breath, however, and rained a storm of sword chops and shield punches, one after the other, grunting with the effort.

Vadrian the Fire darted left, slipped right, backing away from the onslaught, until coming close to a wall.

The people voiced their approval.

"You run well enough," Halm shouted, loud enough for the masses to hear.

From behind his visor, Vadrian's eyes narrowed in anger. "I'll cut your—"

Halm didn't want to listen. He unleashed a combination of strikes and slashes, robbing the wind from Vadrian's words. Yet the Fire got out of harm's way every time, avoiding the more dangerous attacks and ultimately evading the Zhiberian.

"Saimon take your soul, you—"

Again, Halm came in swinging, sweat flying from his person. He aimed for his adversary's winged helm but sliced only air. He cut for an arm but had his blade knocked aside by Vadrian's buckler. He feinted, intending to thrust for a chest, but the opening didn't happen.

Worse, Halm realized he was getting tired.

"Godless cur," Vadrian taunted, looking still fresh. "You're no warrior at all. You're a poor excuse for a shite pile. A cow kiss. How did you ever get this far?"

The Zhiberian lunged for a leg.

The Sunjan was ready, however, and Halm caught the twinkle in Vadrian's eye as he went by—missing the leg— and immediately had his helm rocked by a spiked fist.

Halm crashed into the sand, his helm shifting and blinding him. He rolled onto his back, then his knees, and lashed out.

Striking nothing.

The Zhiberian hurried to correct his helm.

When he did, he saw the Vadrian standing before him, waiting.

"Get to your feet, you unholy cur, and stop mucking about in the sand," Vadrian bellowed for the people to hear. "I've heard you Zhiberians like to prance about in shite, but this is Sunja. Our streets are made of stone!"

Halm grimaced.

"See how he plays in the sand, good countrymen?" Vadrian shouted. "See? I'm not certain the savage knows our tongue! Come here, fat man. Come here and take the blessing of Seddon's steel. I'll make it painless. One quick thrust through your black heathen heart."

Taking a deep breath, Halm got to his feet.

*

From where he watched, Curge smiled. He had to commend this Vadrian. The man did indeed have talent. He played to the masses, making them laugh while making the Zhiberian look stupid. Curge might not trust the Sunjan, and he certainly wouldn't turn his back on him, but the man knew how to play to an audience. He even knew how to enrage a foe. That was an art form in itself.

The golden face of Gastillo remained impassive, the owner sitting beside Curge in the box.

"Free Trained idiot," Nexus snapped on the other side of the box, shaking his head in disgust. "Get up, damn you. Get to your feet, you unfit sheep shagger. At least die like a man. Lords above! See how he drags his fat ass up from the ground? Dying Seddon. *Dying* Seddon!"

Curge frowned and then remembered Nexus had lost one of his young fighters to the Sunjan below. *Unfortunate*, he thought without truly meaning it, and focused once again on the match. Any fight that would grant him revenge, win him gold, and infuriate Nexus all at the same time was a good fight indeed.

*

From the gladiator-only viewing boxes built into the base of the arena walls, Pig Knot, Muluk, and Goll watched through open archways at ground level. Pig Knot didn't understand what the Zhiberian was doing. He swung at every word the Sunjan threw at him.

And not only was he missing, he was becoming *weary*. That much was clear.

"What's he doing out there?" Muluk asked.

"I have no idea," Pig Knot answered.

But Goll suspected.

*

"See how slowly he rises from the sand?" Vadrian shouted at the crowds. "Like one—"

Halm stabbed, sword shooting from his shoulder like a crossbow bolt.

And as before, Vadrian stepped aside and chopped downward, aiming for the Zhiberian's outstretched arm...

But it wasn't there.

For most of the fight, Halm had let his foe think that his prattling was urging him on, that each verbal outburst would be answered with a flurry of cuts and jabs. Vadrian would evade the attacks and counter with his own strikes. Halm also knew Vadrian was becoming overconfident, fighting a clearly inferior Zhiberian, and would never suspect that a trap.

Thus, when Vadrian lashed out with his counter, Halm was already pulling his sword arm back, his feint completely fooling his opponent.

The Zhiberian flicked his sword in a wide sweeping arc, drawing a red line across his foe's upper right shoulder. He charged then, seeking to take advantage of first blood, but Vadrian recovered and nimbly retreated several steps, nowhere near hurt.

Unfortunate, Halm thought.

He was nearing his endurance's end.

"You tricky bastard." The Sunjan growled as he glanced at his wound. "Well now, he has first blood! Seddon above, I fight a Godless dog that resorts to trickery! I knew you

Zhiberians to be savages! I swear, I…"

The warrior paused and considered his shoulder a second time.

Taking deep breaths behind his guard, Halm was almost set to charge his foe one again, but his sword caught his attention.

And the faint green sheen at the blade's base of the blade, as slick as a lamp oil.

Halm's breath caught in his throat.

Poisoned.

His blade had been poisoned somehow.

A poison that was already coursing for Vadrian's black heart.

The Sunjan's eyes flashed outrage, fixing upon the Zhiberian with the very same realization. Vadrian drew breath to shout, to announce the wicked treachery to the arena, and Halm knew if the man uttered those words, it would mean his own death.

A desperate energy took hold of the portly Zhiberian then.

Halm attacked, throwing all of his remaining energy into a combination of slashes and thrusts.

Vadrian's words never past his lips as defended himself. The Sunjan parried and blocked, turning aside blow after blow. Then he countered, swinging for Halm's head and grimacing with the effort.

The poison slowed Vadrian.

Halm's knew it instinctively as he ducked under the wide cut, pivoted, and hacked the Sunjan's sword arm off at the wrist. Blade and hand flew from the Son of Seddon, and the fanatic turned as if unaffected, studying his ruined arm.

Halm reset himself, struggling for air, but Vadrian lunged

with a speed that caught the Zhiberian off-guard. A heavily muscular arm—the stump still spewing blood—clamped around the Zhiberian's neck and pulled him close.

"Not yet, treacherous son." Vadrian squeezed Halm's head to his chest. "Oh, I'm not done—"

Yet.

The close contact shifted Halm's helm once more, blinding him, just as a spiked fist crashed into his gut. Fat iron needles stabbed deep and robbed him of his breath, twisted, and withdraw. Halm slumped, almost fell to his knees, but the Vadrian held him upright with a strength belonging to the vengeful righteous.

And he continued to talk.

"I feel, I *feel...*" the fanatic shouted over the building cheering from the crowds.

Halm tried to twist away, but Vadrian fastened onto his head even tighter, squeezing the air from his throat.

"The *fire...*" Vadrian barked to harsh applause.

Spikes slammed into Halm's belly a second time, hard enough to cause black stars to appear.

"In *me...*" Vadrian shouted.

A third punch to Halm's stomach and something *ripped* down there. His legs buckled. "But before I die…"

A fourth punch broke Halm's ribs like frail kindle.

"*People!*" Vadrian gasped, still holding the wounded Zhiberian to his chest. "*This maggot ha–*"

With his last remaining strength, Halm brought his sword up and sawed at the underflesh of Son of Seddon's right armpit, drawing his weapon's razor edge back like a bow to a fiddle, before plunging it deep into bare, unprotected flesh.

He shoved deep, cutting for the insane man's heart.

Vadrian shivered with violence and his mighty strength disappeared all at once. He sputtered, blood flecking his lips, and regarded his killer with jerky movements.

Then he collapsed on his back.

Vadrian's severed stump wavered upright for a heartbeat, before falling and thumping the sand. Blood pooled about the fallen warrior. He shuddered once more and became still.

Not quite believing he was still alive, Halm bent over on unsteady legs, grasped his sword and shoved the weapon deeper. Blood gushed over the hilt, hiding any trace of the blade's poison. Halm's stayed that way until his head cleared, though his lower ribs sparkled with pain. The sand became a scarlet stew under the dead man, hiding any evidence of the poison. At least as far as Halm could tell.

And he knew the day's bodies would be burned.

Just to be sure, however, he straightened, took a quick gulp of air, and kicked sand over the corpse's torso.

He stepped away from the corpse, the full weight of his wounds hitting him, and distantly realized that, for the first time, people were cheering his name.

*

Dark Curge's back stiffened so quickly that Gastillo initially thought someone had rammed a length of steel up his arse. The old gladiator stood, pounded his stump against the nearby stone wall, and shoved a servant aside as he stomped out of the box. Gastillo watched him go, surprised, but far from disappointed.

"I suppose he had coin wagered on that match." Gastillo said and wiped at the drool hanging from his mangled lips.

"I suppose so," a cool Nexus replied.

Gastillo glanced at the man out of the corner of his eye. The wine producer seemed unusually smug, an abrupt change to his earlier mood. It was a strange contrast, and Gastillo made note to think about it at greater length when he was alone.

He sensed something afoot.

*

Holding a hand to his belly wound, Halm half-turned and squinted at the people cheering his name. The sword Vadrian had used then stole his attention.

The Mademian sword.

Cringing with discomfort, Halm walked over to the weapon and pried the blade from Vadrian's severed hand. He hefted it, looked at the characters stamped on the metal, and slipped it into his scabbard. Halm had no intention of allowing such a fine weapon go to the Pit's armory. The scabbard wasn't the right length for the blade, but that could be fixed with a new one, which he intended to purchase with his considerable winnings.

That put a smile on the Zhiberian's face.

He applied pressure to his wound and his smile disappeared. The brutal blows had hurt badly, perhaps a couple of broken ribs or more. Halm sighed. Even though he'd won his fight, the games might very well be over for him.

Ignoring the crowds, the Zhiberian trudged to the open tunnel.

Thoughts of poison and gold dimmed the pain of his side.

· 13 ·

Musings

"You're damn lucky," the gray-haired healer said, as he wrapped bandages around the Zhiberian's midsection. "Your fat saved you."

"Really?"

"Like a big pillow." The healer squinted, narrowing intelligent blue eyes. "If it was any of those other bastards, with nary a shred of fat on their bones, I daresay I'd be putting their guts back in."

The healer drew the bandages tight, drawing a hiss from his patient, and tied them off. "Off with you, then. I'd tell you to only drink water and to rest until mended but I don't think you'd listen."

Halm slid off the table and moved through the empty infirmary. He paused at the door. "Thank you for that."

"It's my job," the healer remarked.

"You do it well."

"Hm." The healer turned away from him.

Halm walked down a torch-lit hall, toward the general quarters. Pig Knot, Muluk, and Goll had left him for the

Domis to collect their sizeable winnings. Halm had his own marker to cash in, and he wondered how much it would amount to. Probably enough for a woman or twenty. And definitely enough to keep a man in fine spirits until he had to fight again. Halm didn't know when that would be. He wasn't eliminated from the tournament, but he had to return when called upon, else be removed from contention.

A ghostly roar of the crowds reached him through the ceiling. The fight on the sands was an entertaining one.

"Good Halm?" a voice from an alcove reached his ears.

The Zhiberian stopped and turned. A man of medium height and dressed in well-made robes stepped from the shadows. The stranger raised a hand in greeting.

"What is it you want?" Halm asked.

"A moment of your time, good sir."

He thought about it, his hand resting on the pommel of the Mademian blade jutting from an ill-fitting scabbard.

The gesture didn't go unnoticed.

"I assure you, sir," the stranger said, "that's not needed. I have some very good news, if you are inclined to listen."

"Lead on, then," Halm said, wondering if this person was responsible for the poisoned blade.

The stranger led Halm to a wooden door and ushered him inside. The room was empty, illuminated by torches. Halm knew they were on the level underneath the general quarters, and he wondered why the room was bare. Not a chair and table lay within it. Only warm air.

Halm turned to the stranger. "What is it, then?"

"I won't keep you any longer than necessary, good Halm."

The Zhiberian didn't like the way the man called him *good*. Halm knew Vadrian had been poisoned and it was that reason alone he'd managed to defeat the screaming hellpup. That knowledge tainted his victory over the Sunjan. It also didn't make Halm feel particularly *good*. At least, not in the way the stranger meant it.

"My name is Varno." The man's blue eyes were steady. "I represent the School of Gastillo. Perhaps you've heard of him?"

"I have."

"Excellent, excellent." The other smiled, displaying fine white teeth. "My master, Gastillo himself, has noted your skill in the arena, and would like to extend to you an invitation to join his school, to further your training, and prepare you for the day you might very well fight for the arena title."

"I see."

The response drew a perplexed expression from the man. "Well, I might add that it's a great honour to receive such an invitation. From one of the top gladiator schools in Sunja, no less. To be chosen is a compliment to your skills at arms."

"Hm. That so?"

Varno paused. He cleared his throat. "To be chosen to—"

"Yes, you've explained it all well enough."

"But I have not explained the benefits of being a gladiator."

"I already *am* a gladiator."

Varno smiled. "Of course. I meant a *recognized* gladiator, belonging to a prestigious school or house. The value of such—"

"I daresay," Halm interrupted, already bored, "I'll be plenty recognized after today."

"Where are you going?" Varno asked, suddenly alarmed.

"To collect my gold," Halm replied. "Then to get drunk. Mead and ale are the best killers of pain I know of."

"What about my master's offer?"

"What about it?"

A confused Varno blinked. "Are you refusing his generosity?"

Halm smiled. "His generosity? I would have to pay him for my learning, would I not?"

"Yes, that's correct but—"

"And you think I have to be a part of a school? Just to be recognized? Maybe to even have a chance?"

"That is correct."

Halm shook his head. "Not for me."

"What do you mean 'not for you'? Good—" Varno smiled again.

Halm didn't like the smug expression. "I will do this on my own."

"But... you cannot."

"Why can't I?"

"You are a Free Trained," Varno explained as if talking to a child. "No Free Trained warrior has ever won the games."

"That so?"

"Yes. In fact, there has never been a Free Trained warrior in any of the *later* rounds."

Halm grunted."We'll have to change that."

"We'll have to...?" Varno sputtered. "You don't understand. None of the gladiatorial schools will *let* a Free Trained warrior progress. Even if you manage to win a few matches, they'll single you out, in or *out* of the arena, and do whatever it takes to... to... "

"Kill me?" Halm cocked an eyebrow.

"I never said that." Varno held up his hands. "But they will not allow you to advance in the games."

"Let them try, then," the Zhiberian growled.

Varno appeared to be at a loss. "You simply don't understand. They will stop you by any means. They don't *recognize* Free Trained warriors—"

"Gladiators."

"For you to even *fight* amongst them," Varno continued, offering no apologies for the slight, "is seen as a slap across their bare kog and bells! You're an affront—"

"A what?"

"An affront! An *insult* to their profession. If you say no to me and to any other offers, they will eventually find out. And when they learn you actually *refused* an invitation, they…" Varno trailed off, shaking his head. "They'll punish you."

"I see." Halm stepped to the door. "I still say no. Go back to your master and tell him that."

"You'll be a hunted man," Varno warned. "One against hundreds."

"I'm that now, you punce," Halm growled.

With that, he left the stunned messenger alone in the room. Halm smirked as he closed the door. What did he care about joining a group of pampered warriors? The games were always suspect for being underhanded, and the poison he had detected on his own blade soured his own beliefs. This invitation business and warning ruined it all the more. He wondered if he should just take his winnings and run?

His shadow appeared and disappeared on the wall as he walked through pockets of torchlight. Halm decided to not head to the surface right away. Instead, he made his way back to the armory, holding his side as he did so. He pushed through the masses housed in general quarters and stopped before the barred window of the armory

The quartermaster within looked up from inspecting a dagger.

"What do you want?" he asked.

He was a taller man, gaunt, with his hair shaved close to the skull. A different man entirely than the one who handed Halm the poisoned blade.

"Where is the other man?" the Zhiberian inquired, keep his voice calm.

"What other man?" the quartermaster stated.

"The other man."

"There is no one here but me."

"What about the short one here earlier."

"The short one?"

"Yes, he allowed me to..." Halm trailed off and shut his mouth. He could tell by the quartermaster's puzzled expression he knew nothing of what had happened. Saying anything more might incriminate the Zhiberian in ways unknown to him. Without another word, he patted the iron bars and left the armory, deciding it best to put the entire event behind him. Vadrian was dead and Halm was due some coin.

He found a stairway leading to the surface. It was time to collect his gold.

Thoughts of listening to Goll entered Halm's mind. That house idea of his wasn't an entirely bad thing. Perhaps being drunk would help him think more on the subject.

It certainly couldn't hurt.

But the poisoning of Vadrian remained at the back of his skull, scratching at bone.

Not as happy as he would have liked to be, Halm of Zhiberia climbed the stairs to daylight.

*

Later that night, after the day's fights were done, a content Nexus lounged on a bed of fine pillows and sipped wine from a goblet of polished silver. He relaxed in his private chambers, with shuttered windows curtained by long flowing drapes of dark satin. The smell of rosemary hung in the air, heavy and choking to anyone unaccustomed to it. Nexus, however, breathed it in deeply and loved its heady scent. Wine, incense, and perhaps a woman or two was his way of celebrating good fortune. The day at Sunja's Pit had seen his wagers bring in gold aplenty, and he had watched the death of the Sunjan responsible for the slaying of one of his own at the start of the games. The Khas-Jantos were expensive, but they were always reliable. When the time was right, he would allow a whisper of the revenge to circulate into the populace, and that would cause people to fear the name of Nexus.

He lay back on a hill of cushions, careful not to spill any wine. *The games.* He'd only been part of the games for a short while, but in that time he'd learned much. Nexus was a quick study of the sport and its attention to strategy. It was certainly much more exciting than haggling with merchants. The only thing he didn't like, but saw as a necessity, was feigning ignorance in front of his fellow, more experienced, owners of older houses and schools. Gastillo wasn't so bad, and malleable, but Curge was a barbarous swine dressed in expensive clothing and calling himself otherwise. *No*, Nexus corrected. That description better fit Gastillo. Curge was a dolt in thinking Nexus was inexperienced in matters of the games. The games were *business*, in reality, and Nexus excelled in business. It was easy to play the ignorant newcomer around Curge and Gastillo, even going so far as to throw exaggerated fits in their presence.

Nexus supposed they would eventually see through his ruse, but the wine merchant hoped it didn't happen this season. Eventually, yes, but not too soon.

He wanted his slyness to be recognized and appreciated.

His thoughts returned to the day when he'd first seen Vadrian the Fire fight his man. The Sunjan had killed his gladiator, but that wasn't really the knife in his craw at all.

Nexus sipped his wine.

The killing had only mildly put him off, as he recognized Vadrian's skill straight away. He used the guise of being infuriated, however, to leave and give instructions to one of his agents, charging him to find Vadrian, extend the offer to join the School of Nexus, and fight under that banner.

It was an offer that scant few Free Trained fighters would decline.

Vadrian had, however.

Even further insulting, Nexus believed the savage had murdered the agent sent; another slap in the face. If Vadrian had been a rival merchant, Nexus would've made it so that the fanatical Sunjan would suddenly discover it exceedingly difficult to purchase goods from other producers. Nexus had done it in the past, exerting all of his considerable influence upon lesser merchants to break them or drive them out of business entirely. There were plenty of ways to deal with slights in matters of moving goods. Some more deadly than others.

In *this* business, if a gladiator died, no one cared in the least. It was all part of the games.

Well, the venerable business man thought as he drank and smacked his lips, *see how you like rotting in your grave.*

Vadrian the Fire was the first Free Trained warrior to

cross Nexus. Sipping on his wine, he wondered if there would be others.

Seddon above as his witness, he hoped there would be.

Part II:

TEN

1

Chipped pitchers rose up in the middle of the table, creating an empty fortress that towered over a surface worn with pockmarks, gouges, and lettering of unknown meaning. Wooden cups surrounded all this, long abandoned in favour of drinking straight from the pitchers. When one was as numb as the present company, it was important to get as much down as possible with the least amount of refilling. Halm held on to his pitcher for dear life and blinked slowly at the curved container. *Wine.* It was half-filled with the shite. Somewhere during the night, he'd stopped drinking ale and switched over to this particular poison. Not that it was bad. He'd learned long ago that, if one started out drinking one kind of slop, one should finish the night drinking that *same* slop. It was in one's guts' best interest. Changing halfway through the evening was a guarantee that he was going to regret the dawn—if he lived to see it.

One good thing about the wine's magic was how it suppressed the ache in his ribs and belly. Halm gazed at the white bandages covering his wounds and noted that they weren't bloody at all. "Keep them clean; change them often," the healer had told him, saying nothing about drinking until blind. Still, the Pit's healer had trussed him up damned fine. Halm would have to thank him again sometime.

Halm leaned back, thudded against the wall, and knew it was going to hurt that much more in the morning. He and his three companions sat and drank in the same alcove of the same alehouse they'd come to occupy a couple of times. The air boomed with laughter. Bar wenches squealed while nuzzling into their men. Slurred insults cut across the smoky interior. Halm picked up smells of sweat, foul body odour, and spilled drink. Muluk sat next to him, partially concealed in shadow, whispering in a woman's ear and making her smile. Pig Knot roamed about the main floor, appearing and disappearing amongst the glistening mob of flesh occupying it. Two wenches clung to him as if he were a broken spar keeping them alive in a sea of drowning men. Pig Knot's eyes, dark and unsettling as a crazy rat's, seemed to Halm to have swelled three times their size, giving his smile an unsettling, predatory gleam in the gauzy air.

"Are you still with us?" Goll's voice. From across the table.

"Aye that," Halm said after a moment, blinking dreamily.

"You look dead."

"Really?" Halm cocked a curious brow. "Feel good. Can't even feel this." He touched his bandages.

Goll stood up, stumbled, and inspected his companion's dressings. Frowning, he reached across the table with his own heavily bandaged arms and pulled Halm's hands away from his belly. He dropped them on the table, across a moat of wine that had somehow collected before the pitchers. Halm made a face. Nodding to himself, the Kree plopped back into his seat, landing hard and mussing up his sandy hair, which fell into his eyes. The swollen part of his jaw and face pulsed like a fat vein. Like Pig Knot's, the Kree's eyes appeared dark and soulless and seemed to bulge out of his skull. Halm regarded him as he would some sort of curious bug undergoing a strange, yet-undecided metamorphosis. He looked from Goll to the wine, back to Goll, and back to the wine once more.

Not bad. Halm's mind buzzed, and he belched hard enough that he thought he might've just pissed himself. Then he paused and wondered if he only *thought* he just had or if he'd actually done it. Seddon above. The wine was getting better. He'd be buying more. Saimon's hell, he'd buy them *all* more of the swill.

"Don't pick at those," Goll ordered him, meaning the bandages. The Kree's mantis eyes swivelled in their sockets, and Halm wasn't sure if he was looking at him or someplace else. "All right? Good. We have to talk, you know."

"Huh?"

"We have to talk about what to do tomorrow."

"Ah." Muluk sighed with exasperation and lapsed into Kree speech, none of which Halm could understand. Sometimes he wished he could hear his native Zhiberian tongue being spoken, but tonight wasn't one of those nights. Muluk turned back to him. As with the others, his eyes were damn near popping out of his face. The frightful things appeared the size of white saucers. Even worse, the Kree's yellow teeth jutted out of his jaw at irregular angles and lengths, and his scraggly features shrank underneath the expanding eyes, which were blackening like a spider's. Halm didn't feel any fear, however. If anything, he was genuinely amused by his companions' interesting new looks.

"I told him to leave you alone." Muluk leaned over and

smiled, his teeth springing forth from his mouth like great fence pickets.

Halm chuckled, remained calm, and took another pull from his pitcher. "I don't... don't mind," Halm replied. "What is it we have... to talk about? Anyway?"

"See," Goll said accusingly to Muluk. "Go back to her."

On cue, the woman next to Muluk, a blond-haired girl of perhaps twenty, pulled him closer. Muluk said something that sounded like a curse, but then he was in his companion's arms, half-smothered in limbs gleaming like wet pearls in the overhead lamp.

"The guild." Goll leaned forward, his eyes now ogling different points of the alcove. It was difficult to meet his gaze.

"Are you drinking this?" Halm held out his wine.

Both of Goll's eyes lined up to peer inside the pitcher. He shook his head. Halm observed that when Goll leaned forward, parts of the man's scalp rose and swelled as if plums were about to pop forth.

"Where'd you get this?" Goll asked.

Halm pointed at the throng of people. In the middle of the men and women, Pig Knot crowed and grinned like a hyena.

"Him?" Goll's swollen face split into a hideous smile that might have reached the back of his ears. It fascinated Halm while the table stretched out in all directions at once.

"Pig Knot!" Goll motioned for the Sunjan to come forward. He did, grin blazing as if it were pitch on fire, with two women still clinging to his muscular arms.

"What?" He looked from Goll to Halm and then blinked again at Halm. Seeing those mighty eyes close and open made Halm smile in delighted wonder.

"You poisoned him!" Goll shouted.

"Did no such thing, you punce."

"Look at the man! He's pickled!"

Halm did indeed feel pickled. Not that it was a bad thing. Pig Knot zoomed in closer, his face a black moon of eyes and concerned smiles. He *tsked*, and the sound crackled like ocean rocks tumbling over each other.

"Hm," Pig Knot remarked. "If he's in there, he's feeling no pain, I wager."

"What is this?" Goll demanded, indicating the pitcher.

"Sunjan Gold," Pig Knot answered. "The finest I could buy in this pisshole. He deserved a little taste of the good stuff after putting that screamer into the ground."

"Wine couldn't have done this to him."

"Well," Pig Knot said slyly, "maybe I bought a little something more. And maybe he ate it."

"You…" Goll trailed off, shaking his head and appearing horrified.

"He's not going to perish or anything," Pig Knot countered.

"I'd say he's perished and come back," Muluk added from the depths of his woman's arms.

"Didn't ask *you*," Pig Knot said.

"I'll remember that when he's pissed himself."

Pig Knot frowned and shook his head. "He's not going to piss himself." Then to Halm, "*Don't* piss yourself."

"I wanted to talk to him this night," Goll said, his voice cutting through the momentary darkness of Halm closing his eyes.

"About what?" Pig Knot asked. Both his and Goll's faces resembled suns now.

"Starting a house of our own."

"Did you take a sip of that?" Pig Knot wanted to know, sending his clinging women into giggles.

"What do you mean?"

"Now's not the time to speak of starting houses. I'll get a woman for you."

"I don't want a woman."

"What do you mean, you don't want a woman? Look at these! You should—wait, you're not a daisy, are you?"

Goll looked mortified. "No, I'm not a—look. Off with you. Get a room."

"Who needs a room?" Pig Knot exclaimed. "The next alcove over has the table cleared."

Goll had no response to that.

"Right, we're off." Pig Knot suddenly swooped both women off their feet and squeezed them to squeals. With a roar, he spun out of sight.

"Doesn't he fight in the morning?" Muluk asked.

"I'm not sure he knows," Goll replied, "or cares."

A slow-blinking Halm watched the Sunjan disappear around a corner. Even though it was only a corner, the simple completion of the movement fascinated him. He scratched at his belly and regarded Goll across the table. "Start a house?"

"A house." Goll nodded, taking the lead, and leaned in. "I've been thinking more on it."

"Been thinking, too." Halm grunted and took a dangerous-sounding breath.

"You see the wisdom in it?"

Halm grunted again. "Can't keep doing this." He patted his bandages. "Getting old. Sooner. Or later. A screamer like Vadrian the pisser is going to fishhook me dead. So aye that, a house seems a... a good reckoning. I figure."

He exhaled hard enough to rattle his lips, wrinkling up his face, and spittle flew.

"This is pickled talk," Muluk said and rattled off a burst of Kree.

Goll erupted in a louder burst of Kree, silencing him with a harsh look. For a moment, they glared at each other across the table.

"Not fit in the head," Halm mumbled, getting both the men's attention. "Gastillo talked to me this day."

"Who?" Goll pressed.

"Gastillo."

"Gastillo talked to you?"

"Aye that. Wait…" Halm had to think hard on that count. "No. No, no, not Gastillo. A *man* for Gastillo. Wanted me… to join his school."

"Gastillo did?" Muluk asked, quiet awe in his voice.

"Did. I said no."

Goll sank back against his wall and gazed heavenward. "Thank the Lords for that. You don't want to be with them."

Halm screwed up his jowls and shook his head in distasteful agreement.

"But the idea that they noticed you is heartening. They *noticed* you, Halm. They could even have eyes on you this very moment."

"Doubt that," Muluk said. "This place is only for Free Trained and Farmers. The *real* gladiators are in better holes than this."

This summoned from Goll another verbal lashing in Kree. Muluk countered with an equally heated retort, but Goll's voice rode above it in a crash of angry sound, drowning the other. A sour Muluk gave a lingering, dirty look to his countryman and turned back to the woman at his side.

"Hope not," Halm said after that spent charge of anger.

"You hope not?" Goll composed himself.

"Feel like… about to piss meself."

Goll's hands fluttered in warning. "Don't piss yourself. Don't. Hear me out first. All right?"

"All right, friend Goll."

"Gastillo sent someone to speak with you. That means they want you with them, but you'll be just another face in their stable. Not an owner."

"Not?" Halm croaked. "Who?"

"An *owner*. Not at all. With what I have in mind, you'd be an owner. We'd *all* be owners." His eyes shifted to Muluk.

"They won't let us," the other Kree warned.

"If we establish a house, a school, they'd have to."

"The only thing they'd have to do is kill the lot of us," Muluk grumped. "I've heard stories. We're meat to them. All the Free Trained is meat. Just waiting to be cut up. To be bled. They don't take any of us serious."

"They took him serious." Goll pointed at Halm.

"And he said no," Muluk cut in again. "I wouldn't be surprised if there's a pack of men waiting for him outside this night. They do that to the ones who turn down such invitations, you know. They beat them into maggot shite. We'll have to watch him, you know."

This time, a pensive Goll stared at Muluk.

"Muluk's right," he finally let out, his eyes shifting to Halm. "We'll have to be careful with you this night. And any others. All the more reason to band together now."

"Band?" both Halm and Muluk asked.

"Yes, the Free Trained. As many as we can get to our

banner. There are hundreds of us. *Hundreds*. All fighting over scraps. I believe if we establish a Free Trained house, the other houses and schools won't dare touch any of us. Not like before. Even better if we can find ourselves a taskmaster and trainers."

Muluk sputtered and struggled out of his woman's grasp. "Taskmasters? The tournament's already begun! You're talking about shite that rightfully should have been done a year ago! *Two* years ago. Are you certain you're not drinking the same piss he is?"

"No one's to say when we set up a house, only that we do. The sooner the better. The very notion would hide our ability and ambitions from the major and minor houses. I'm thinking their asses would fall off from laughing, and we can use that to our advantage."

Muluk shook his head, speechless.

"Look. They went after Halm. He refused them. That's an insult that will bring about punishment the likes I doubt even bathing in Sunjan Gold will fend off. We need to group together for the protection alone. If anything, think of the coin that could be ours."

"It costs gold to even get the Chamber to recognize us. And then the taskmasters and trainers will need to be paid. Where's all that coming from?"

"We'll get it."

"What about a place to train then, hmm? They won't allow us in the Pit. In fact, the idea of house fighters *living* in the Pit is a joke. Using their weapons and armor. I can hear it now."

"We'll get our own."

"You're unfit in the head." Muluk's eyes narrowed. "I thought you'd be smarter than this."

"I am." Goll fumed, staring back hard. "Oh, I am."

"No one will join us."

"They will."

"Do you even *know* how much it'll all cost to do this during the season?"

"I'll find out."

Muluk stared at him as if he'd grown two more faces. "Madness. You're unfit. *Unfit.* Never thought I say that. You." He jabbed a finger at Goll. "Unfit. Here." And he tapped his own temple.

Goll didn't answer him. For a while, from beyond the confines of the alcove, the sounds of drinking and talking and making merry filled the air. Goll looked at the revellers for a long sobering moment before turning back.

"What do you think, Halm?"

Halm shrugged. It took everything he had.

Goll smiled in spite of himself. "Tomorrow, I'm going to the Gladiatorial Chamber. I'm going to ask to see them. You"—indicating both Halm and Muluk—"can decide for yourselves if you want to join me or hear about it later. But I tell you this now: I was trained by the Weapon Masters of Kree, and I'm not about to give up anything I set my mind to. And I've set my mind to this."

Halm noted the stiffening of Muluk's hairy jawline. The Zhiberian had to ask, "These… Weapon Masters any good?"

Muluk smiled at his companion. "They are."

"Hmm," Halm said in a drunken tone of *Oh, really?*

He passed out then, the darkness rising up in the shape of the table's surface. When he hit, it was a distant, solid thud, like a fist being driven into a slab of heavy meat.

A moment later, he was snoring.

2

The city lights, oil lamps, and open torches dipped in pitch, flickered across a dark canvas of knobs and points underneath a darkening skyline. A draft pushed the smells of the city to Curge, and he wrinkled his nose upon getting a whiff of sewers. He took a drink from a clay wine bottle, swallowing three times before letting it drop, and wiped his mouth with the stump of his left arm. If his house had been built a little higher, he would have a fine view of Sunja's glittering wares. As it was, he could see only a fraction of what he might have otherwise. That little thought poisoned him and turned his innards a hot vengeful red.

After the loss of Samarhead and the defeat of Vadrian and knowing Halm of Zhiberia still drew breath, it didn't take too much to have pleasant thoughts turn into something dangerous. *Easy to hate*, he thought, and he hated the Zhiberian now. Somewhere out beyond his compound's walls, Halm was probably drinking himself into a stupor. That knowledge alone rankled the old warrior. Free Trained were mostly inexperienced, undisciplined, and uncivilized hellpups in the games, and when one got lucky enough to kill one of his investments, Curge took it personally. He took it *very* personally.

He drank again, savouring the dry yet tart burn of the grape and wondering if it might have come from one of Nexus's vineyards. If it did, he couldn't wait to piss it out. *Hate. So very easy to hate.* He scoured the dark tops of the city, shadowed peaks and roof tiles below higher burning points of lights, and thought evil thoughts. Just under him were the courtyard and training area where his twenty-nine—*eight!*—gladiators prepared themselves under the watchful eye of Curge's taskmasters and trainers. High torches affixed to posts in four corners burned low now and transformed the sandy ground into a grim mire.

The bottle emptied, and Curge held it before him, contemplating hurling it over the balcony and watching it smash beneath. It stayed in his fist and trembled under the pressure Curge directed around the neck. Unable to crush it, he sighed and half-turned around, holding it at arm's length.

A servant, a young, shapely woman dressed only in the barest of robes, came forward and took it away from him. She provided another bottle, and Curge didn't bother looking at her as he removed the cork with his teeth. The wine gushed down his throat, more fuel for the murderous thoughts smouldering within him, and when he finally lowered the drink, he bared teeth and hissed, savouring the smooth taste of berries.

"Bezange," the large man growled, speckling the air with wine. "I'm in a foul mood this night. Foul mood."

Curge turned around and met the gaze of his baby-faced agent. The much smaller man stood before a bare wall, underneath a flickering torch. The room was minimalist, with nothing more than a few lounging chairs made of cherry wood and cushioned with soft squares of red satin. It was enough for a meeting room where Curge could entertain his guests or motivate his servants. The once-gladiator knew that Bezange's innocuous features served them both well, for the man was a weasel of the deadliest kind. Bezange used words to get what he wanted, and Curge mentally patted himself on the back for finding him and bringing him onto his side.

"I want that Zhiberian dead."

The space between Bezange's eyes furrowed for a moment. "I will make the arrangements if you wish."

"Arrangements?" Curge slurred. "I want the man killed in the arena, not butchered in the street. I haven't gone that far, you shite-speckled idiot."

"My apologies, Lord. I misunderstood."

"Aye, you did. Anyone can hire a killer to stab a man in his sleep or the main square. I want the man killed in the Pit. On the sands. In front of thousands. I want a damned *spectacle* made of that foreign bastard."

Curge walked over to one of the chairs and sat down heavily. The servant moved to place cushions at his back, but he shooed her away with a drunken frown. "I'm getting as soft as these things. There was once a time when my *name* would make children shite white about their ankles."

"It still does, my Lord," Bezange added quickly. "There isn't anyone in Sunja that doesn't fear and respect the House of Curge. Even those that don't attend the Pit know and talk about your matches from long ago. Wars you fought and won in spectacular fashion. If we were to go and walk along the streets right now and listen to the people talk in their hovels, you'd hear your name mentioned a score of times, and all would be in awe."

Curge studied Bezange with all the grace of a lion tired of the sun. He waved his stump in his agent's direction, cutting off the stream of shite that would have continued if Curge allowed it. Bezange was a weasel, but he could be too *obvious* about it at times.

"Shut up," Curge told him. "What I was thinking, if you would take your tongue out of my ass for a moment, is for you to pay greater attention to the bastard's whereabouts. He was hurt in that fight with that lunatic Vadrian. I want to know how badly. It might stop him from coming back to fight. I'm well and truly jiggered if he doesn't."

Bezange appeared to think. "As you wish, my Lord."

"And issue the blood challenge. Get it out there. Tell the Madea to post it on his bloody board. If that flick of maggot shite is hurting, I want him to know that when he returns, he'll be facing another one of my hellpups. He may have pulled a rag of fortune out of Seddon's crack to put Samarhead and then Vadrian into the ground, but I want him to regret every passing moment for yanking it out and leaving a burn. If he's suspicious enough, he'll be looking over his shoulder at shadows anyway, not that I'd have anyone cut him like that. Unprofessional. The Free Trained might be a pack of unfit, whinging whelps, but they are taking up the steel. And be clear on this. No one is to lay a hand on that walking shite sack unless it's in the arena."

"No one has in the past, my Lord."

"I know that, you brazen tit. I'm making certain *you* know that so that you won't be going about doing something without my knowledge, thinking it's what I wanted in the first place. As for my dogs, I'll warn those he-bitches in the morning. Lords know they'll be tempted this time around. Never has a Free Trained struck down one of my own. Never. And now this. If I don't ward them off, they'd eventually find him in the streets and lure him down some alley, and *then* that fat topper would sing. I can guarantee you that."

Curge stopped then and gazed towards a dark wall, shaking his head in dangerous reflection. "Zhiberians. More trouble than they're worth. Thank Seddon that only a few ever venture this far southwest."

"It is rare to have them in Sunja."

Curge sized up the curves of the woman serving him and looked away in mounting annoyance. "How goes the wagering?" he finally asked.

Bezange's face revealed nothing. "Poorly, my lord. But we've only had the one victory, that belonging to Samarhead. It's still early."

That got Curge thinking black thoughts once more. A pinch of pain, sharp and lingering, took him in the belly, and caused him to fume all the more. If he got any angrier and didn't release it soon, he imagined he'd burn a hole in his very flesh.

That made him rise. He walked over to a wall covered in the weapons he used when he was a gladiator fighting in Sunja's Pit. He chose to keep them like old, venerable friends in the meeting room, as he knew such a collection both impressed and unnerved his guests. And rightly so. Curge stopped and beheld the shortswords, daggers, maces, and spiked bucklers that gleamed in the torchlight, spread over the wall to maximum effect. The decorated face cages and helms stared back, their surfaces polished but still dented and scratched from blows that Curge remembered as if they had happened yesterday. He was proud of his collection, and his one known weakness was prattling on at length about each weapon and each story that came with it. Curge remembered every fight he'd ever bled in and the weapons he'd used at the time.

He studied his old but still-serviceable tools of the trade before finally reaching up and wrapping his fingers around the grip of one. The mace came down from its perch with a rasp of metal on metal. The shaft stretched as long as a man's arm, while the head was nothing more than a heavy block of wrought iron with ruts covering its surface. Curge looked at another mace, one with spikes covering a head the size of a small child's, but there was a menace about that solid wrecking block of iron with the ruts. Many a time, he'd heard men talk about it in fear, as if Curge were about to stamp his mark upon their flesh in the same manner a face might be pressed into gold or some other soft metal. It was easy to cut or stab, but Curge found he greatly enjoyed *smashing* things with the weapon. There was no greater feeling than splitting flesh from the sheer force of impact, not from edge or point, but simply from power. He knew no better rush than feeling bones snap with one heavy blow, seeing the blackening of a man's bare skin and muscle as the mace tenderized it with every dense kiss.

He hefted the weapon with his good arm, appreciating its weight and studying its face.

"Come with me," he commanded Bezange. He left the room with mace in hand and the female servant following. He didn't look to see if that composed little bastard was on his heels. Bezange would be. Curge had to get rid of the energy building in him, and he couldn't think of a better way than hitting something.

He descended to the ground floor and made his way to the empty training area. Racks of wooden and metal swords, all weighted, greeted him, as did the heavy timbers the men tossed around as part of their strength and conditioning training. At one end were the long upright logs, each as tall as a man. Their trunks were chipped, splintered, and battered from countless strikes. It was a goal and honor to be the gladiator who finally toppled the wooden practice marks. In his life, Curge had chopped down five from repeated blows with swords and axes.

Curge walked to one heavy timber, feeling the sand get into the spaces between his toes. The log was a new one, replaced after the day's exercises. He leaned the mace against it and ran his hand over the wood's rough skin, keeping it there for a moment. Curge rubbed his forehead with the stump of his left arm and stepped away from the practice target. He picked up the mace, not choking it, and let the weapon's weight pull it towards the ground until Curge caught it at the end of its leather-bound shaft.

Lifting the mace with his right hand, he waved it at the target and looked about until he found Bezange. "Have you ever used one of these?" Curge asked.

"No, my lord."

With his one arm, Curge whipped the mace into the base of the wooden pillar, the connection ringing out. Wood chips scattered to the sands. Dark Curge bared teeth and brought the mace to his shoulder. He let it rest there for a moment then whipped it once more into the target.

The sound made Bezange involuntarily jump. The woman stood off to one side, no doubt hoping that the partial darkness cloaked her from her master's attention.

Curge struck again and again in a merciless rhythm. Particles of bark and fibers sprang from the wood and sprinkled the ground. Though in his sixties and using one arm, Curge channeled the angst he was feeling into each swing, meaning to topple the log this very night. The mace left a white spot where the bark had been smashed away. The old warrior swung repeatedly until his sweat beaded and fell, and the strokes began losing their power. He didn't care if he woke up his fighters. He didn't care if he woke up the dead and gone. He just needed to hit something, and it was best no one interrupted him.

And no one did.

In time, Curge stopped swinging and stood back from the pounded spot on the midsection of the timber. Wilting fibers hung off the point of impact. Curge lazily swung the weapon through the night air for a moment. His shoulder ached from the exertion, but it was a comfortable ache and not something serious.

He glanced at Bezange. The little man stood at attention, and Curge had to hand it to him. He didn't seem uneasy at all with the display.

"Are you listening?" Curge asked.

Bezange swallowed then, and that one motion sent a stab of satisfaction through Curge's heart. "I am, my lord."

"Keep an eye on that punce Zhiberian. Let it be known that the House of Curge has unfinished business with him… when he's ready."

"And if he flees from the city?"

That quieted Curge. It was a good question. He looked back to the post and hefted his mace.

"Seddon help him if he does."

He swung with all of his remaining might.

3

When morning found Pig Knot, he was in bed, tangled under a pile of expensive limbs and cheap blankets. With a sniff, he stared at the white arms holding him down before taking in the high, bare plank ceiling and the thick beams supporting it. His insides felt ravaged, and a deep, deep thirst seized his attention. He wanted water this morning, and he studied the arms and legs on top of him for a moment, searching for the best way out of the fleshy puzzle.

The women he'd slept with the night before did not move as he extracted himself. One moaned in protest before burying her dark head in a pillow. Pig Knot got both arms free and sat up. A mistake, as he felt the room whirl. Cold sweat broke out on his face and skin, and he knew if he saw his own face, he'd probably find that he looked like something shat out of a dead man's hole.

Worse, he had to fight this day. And he didn't know what time it was. Sounds of activity from a closed, shuttered window reached him, and he figured it was late in the morning. Feeling his stomach sink all the more, he struggled to get his legs free from his two darlings, both of whom were naked underneath the blankets. It took a few moments longer than he wanted, but he untangled himself from the ladies. He got to his feet and shook his head at the sight of both of them on the bed, their bare, ripe asses pointed at the ceiling.

He was a fool to leave that.

The clothes he'd worn the night before were scattered around the room as if a windstorm had ripped them from his person, and it took a while—time interspersed with moments of physical weakness—to pick them up. Getting into his pants, shirt, and boots required more effort and focus, and he almost fell getting out the door. A thick wooden rail stopped him from going over the edge of the second floor, and he stopped there, feeling sick from the height.

Before him, the alehouse's main floor stretched out, lit by wide beams of sunlight from open windows. A barkeep moved about, humming as he cleaned up the garbage and vomit from the night before. Pig Knot's frame shuddered at the smell of spilt wine and ale, and he opened his mouth for a settling breath of fresh air. There was no such thing in the place, however, and what he took over his tongue, what he tasted, was the foulness of the night before.

But the windows are open. He blinked in confusion and held onto the railing for dear life as he eased himself down the stairs. Each step shook him just enough to give him pause, for fear of voiding right there.

"You all right?" a gruff voice asked.

Pig Knot felt the sweat drip from his face as he regarded the mopping barkeep.

"No."

"Don't heave up in here. Do it outside."

"Fine."

Grunting, the barkeep moved away, continuing to clean.

"Any water about?" Pig Knot asked.

"The pitcher on the counter, if you like."

"How much?"

"Coin, you mean?"

"Aye that."

"Drink what you like. I'll not charge a man thirsty for water."

Thank Seddon. That motivated him down the last few steps and to the bar. He picked up the brass pitcher, took a quick peek to make sure it actually contained water, and then downed the liquid in large gulps. He felt life come back into his body, and when he placed the pitcher back on the counter, it was almost empty.

Pig Knot palm-wiped his face and gazed about the cave that was the alehouse, feeling himself shiver. He looked towards the alcove where his boys, as he now thought of them, were and saw that they were scattered over the table and long chairs as if slaughtered to a man. Every step he took towards the alcove warned him not to move too fast or sudden. Then his bladder suddenly awoke and demanded attention.

Sighing, Pig Knot hurried to the adjoining latrine and unsheathed his manhood just as he thought he wasn't going to make it. The foul smells from the small, open room disgusted him and almost tipped his stomach. Emptying his bladder weakened him, and he leaned heavily against a wall, something he would never do in the right frame of mind. That movement made him miss the trough with his stream, and he pissed everywhere before he realized what had happened.

Groaning in sick frustration, Pig Knot got himself back

under control and finished. He banged through the doorways back into the alehouse and staggered to a stop at the alcove's edge, ignoring the hard looks from the barkeep. Muluk snored while sitting upright, a woman facedown in his lap. Goll was nowhere to be seen, but the cripple couldn't have gotten far. Halm was on the opposite seat, stretched out as though it were a narrow bed. His bare gut pressed up against the edge of the table was the only thing keeping him in place. The man's face was pointed at the ceiling, and his mouth was open to allow a view of his terrible teeth. Light snores ripped the air, which seemed fresher down here.

"Hey," Pig Knot called weakly. "Wake up."

No one heard.

"Hey." Pig Knot reached out and tousled the Zhiberian's short hair, not liking the greasy touch of it at all.

"Wake up." He wiped his fingers on his leg.

One of Halm's eyes cracked open, rolled around sleepily, and focused on Pig Knot. He smacked his lips once before the eyelid closed, and he fell back to sleep.

"Wake up, you git." Pig Knot slapped the top of the man's skull.

"Ughhhh huh?" Halm lurched and peered once more at the Sunjan standing over him.

"I have to go."

"Huh?"

"I have… to…" The strength almost left his legs then as a new wave of nausea overtook him. Another sheen of cold sweat glazed his face, and he leaned against the alcove's corner, thankful for it.

"Go?" Halm suggested softly.

"Yes, go. I have to… to fight this day."

"You?" The Zhiberian blinked in confusion. "You can't fight like that. You'll piss yourself first. Then you'll piss on the one you're fighting."

Pig Knot chuckled. "We'll both be fortunate if it's only piss."

Halm struggled to get into a sitting position, casting concerned looks at both Pig Knot and the toppled fortress of empty pitchers littering the table. Muluk and his companion didn't interest him, but he regarded Pig Knot from head to toe.

"Dying Seddon, have you looked at yourself? I've seen cow kisses in finer shape."

Pig Knot didn't need this. "Are you coming?"

"With you?" Halm balked and winced as if in pain. "You're joking. Look at me. I'll be lucky to get to a piss trough. Doubly lucky to get to a shite pot. And if I do, I doubt if I'll make it back."

Across from them both, Muluk *snorked* a loud, startling snore that almost brought him back to consciousness. His head rolled to one side, and he started a slow slide, stopping gently on the motionless woman in his lap.

Halm directed his attention back to Pig Knot. "You can't fight this day. You'll be killed."

"I have to. Or I'll be heaved out of the tournament."

"What do you think you'll do on the sands? You won't have that corner to hold you up."

Pig Knot scowled and moved away from the wooden arch, standing on his own power and trying to project an air of defiance. He felt very close to dropping to his knees, however, and just letting his bowels run empty in one spine-shivering gush. "I'm going." He turned to leave.

"Wait…"

But Pig Knot was already moving for the door, ignoring the Zhiberian's pleas for sense. Pig Knot couldn't afford to miss his fight. He needed to win. He needed the coin. The money would help him pay back what he already owed and keep him in food, drink, and women until the next fight. If he didn't make it to the Pit, life would be worse than what it currently was. That thought didn't give him any extra strength, however, and when he entered the brightness of the streets and the streams of people, the light and bodies struck him as solidly as any maul tap to the head. The nearby wall of the alehouse caught and supported him for the moment it took to compose himself. The sun overhead was almost at its apex, and that caused another cold bolt to surge through his frame.

Pig Knot set his jaw.

He was going to make it to the Pit.

Travelling the city and entering the arena's gate was a torturous blur. Bodies bumped against him, and once, he even shoved back. As big as he was, Pig Knot was a handful even when he was as sick as a dog. He pissed often, never near a latrine. Somehow, he managed to sign in with the Madea and later find the Pit's armoury and its quartermaster. He selected a leather cuirass that was tight enough to make him see stars and squeeze more cold sweat out of him. Then he took a helm that seemed to grip his brain with a sensation he couldn't decide was cold or hot. The first sword that he chose felt too heavy, and the second one wasn't much better. Pig Knot finally decided on a blade so thin the quartermaster cocked an eyebrow in mild amusement. One sick glare from the pit fighter wiped the look off the man's face.

Then, somehow, he was in the white tunnel.

And everything caught up to him.

Pig Knot leaned against the tunnel wall, guts churning. Whatever was in his stomach wanted out, and he had to push his visor up over his forehead before it all came up for real. A moment later, it did, heaving up his throat and out of his wide-open mouth in a soupy torrent of a roar. Pig Knot squeezed his eyes shut as he voided, seized by a terrible, shaking energy he only wished he could use in the upcoming fight. Madness—it was madness to be doing this in his condition. He remembered Halm's expression of disbelief.

At the time, Pig Knot had laughed it off. At the time, he'd still been drunk.

His stomach had soured with the intake of water. He remembered pissing, each time the stream hot and gushing, until the sourness had become rotten and threatened him with worse consequences. Pig Knot moaned and placed a hand over his mouth, wiping off dark drops and screwing up his face upon realizing what he'd done. He straightened and stepped back from the wide pool, fresh from his guts. The sight of it almost made him vomit again. He lurched and moaned once more, caught himself, and took perhaps the deepest breath ever. That *almost* helped. He squeezed his eyes shut, but the darkness spun so sharply he could've sworn it had him by the ankles, so he opened them back up.

There, not ten strides from him, stood the gatekeeper. A hardwood bench stood across from the old man, and its worn surface struck Pig Knot as being incredibly comfortable.

"You done?" the gatekeeper asked without sympathy and placed a hand on the lever that would open the portcullis. Steps lay beyond the man, wide and leading up to the arena where another man lingered, his body crossed in the portcullis's shadows. Pig Knot knew he waited for the signal from the orator outside, which he would in turn relay to the gatekeeper below, who would raise the gates.

Pig Knot focused on the steps and felt his stomach growl a question. The steps alone would make him piss himself.

Seddon above.

He was going to *die* on those damned cuts of stone.

Pig Knot gazed imploringly at the white ceiling of the tunnel and took another gulping breath as if it would float him above the tide of nausea coursing through his body. It was an immediate mistake. His stomach rebelled once again, and he found himself suppressing juice, which persisted until he could resist no more, and the flow burst from his lips, spattering down his front. Once finished, Pig Knot drew a forearm across his face and regarded the old topper with his hand still on the lever.

The gatekeeper wasn't a helpful sort at all. His expression asked *well?* as if the fight might not happen at all. That thought had merit. Pig Knot couldn't remember if a match had ever been cancelled. He bent over and drew in air, which seemed to help a little.

"Not sure I can go out there," he admitted.

The gatekeeper scowled and motioned with two fingers.

That made Pig Knot look back the way he'd come. Fright seized him.

Skarrs, Sunja's keepers of the peace, guardians of the populace, and all-around killers were leaving their spots along the white tunnel and closing in. Pig Knot couldn't remember seeing them there, nor was he exactly certain what they were going to do, but at least eight of them were coming towards him, and eight of them might as well have been an army. Their mail vests gleamed mystically in the glare of the tunnel, but they didn't draw their shortswords. Yet.

"I'm fine." Pig Knot raised his hands. "I'm fine. Really. See. I'm—"

His stomach bent him over, and he had to make a conscious effort not to soil himself. Hands found him. They slammed Pig Knot against the wall. A knife was placed to his throat, and one pair of angry eyes sized him up. More hands moved over him. They clamped his visor down over his face. His shield got fixed to his arm. Someone pulled the sword from his scabbard and slapped it into his hand, wrapping his fingers around it and squeezing until Pig Knot held it with his own strength. He doubted if he could swing the thing.

But he wasn't about to say anything to the Skarrs.

"Ready?" the gatekeeper asked without remorse. The old bastard sounded anxious to be rid of him.

"Aye that," Pig Knot rumbled.

An instant later, the Skarrs stepped back from him, but they didn't go far. He realized some of them had tracked through the vomit on the floor, not that he would point that out to them. Skarrs were dangerous—not to mention humourless.

"May Seddon take pity on you." The gatekeeper yanked down on the lever. A rumbling sounded from above. Pig Knot's eyes rolled in their sockets, and his head thrummed. He did not want to go out there.

Two Skarrs noticed his hesitation and went for their swords.

Pig Knot got moving, realizing why there weren't any cancelled fights. *Bastard Skarrs*. When he reached the steps, he relied on momentum and the nearby wall to keep him moving upward. He paused at the halfway point, feeling the sun's heat. His stomach curled up like a snake nailed into the dirt and left thrashing. He caught a pungent whiff of his own stomach juice coating the front of his armour. The Skarrs had moved up to the base of the steps, barring any retreat and appearing more than willing to cut him up if he didn't go through the open entryway at the top of the stairs. Pig Knot tipped his helmet towards them and regretted even *that* little movement.

He shuffled forward, feeling the uncontained wall of sound that battered his senses, feeling it grow as he neared the opening. The voices of *thousands* were out there, drawing him into that hateful, hot sunlight, twisting his guts like a sailor's wet, dripping knot.

The sheer volume of noise almost dropped him right there on the threshold as he stepped out into the light. He swooned, feeling the might of the sun on his helmet and having an image of his very brain stewing inside his skull. The heat and noise of the midday punished him like a god's hammer to his body. Once more, he thought about turning around.

But the portcullis dropped behind him.

Across the way, a monster of a man came into view, making Pig Knot wince in hungover exasperation. It was bad enough that he was unfit to fight, but looking at his brutish opponent made him feel like dying on the spot. The man wore heavy armor with spikes decorating the shoulders. A grinning, jawless skull was somehow tacked to the visor, which did nothing for Pig Knot's confidence, nor did the hellpup's long-shafted mace and wide shield.

The Orator's voice rose above the crowds, calling for silence and introducing them both. Pig Knot caught the name Darcevo and thought it sounded as if it might belong to a daisy.

Then the Orator stopped speaking, and the noise of the crowd intensified. *Lords above*, Pig Knot thought with cold clarity. *I'm going to die this day.*

"Is this to the death?" Pig Knot croaked, burning precious energy just to do that.

The gladiator across from him, Darcevo, didn't show any sign of having heard.

Wonderful. Pig Knot shook his head. He didn't have the strength to repeat himself.

Darcevo shrugged his big shoulders and made no move to raise his mace or shield, keeping them both at his sides. Pig Knot couldn't see the brute's face, but he still had the mind to sense all was not well. The sun beat down on them, and Pig Knot got a whiff of his own skin cooking in the heat.

"Is this," Pig Knot shouted to be heard over the crowd, "to the death?"

No answer, but the monster moved towards him. Darcevo came on in a slow, almost off-balance stagger, as if all wasn't well with him either. He was as tall as Pig Knot and perhaps even a few fingers taller with the helmet. The black eyes of the jawless skull fixed on him, then the stands, then back to him, and so on. He came onward, and the ripe stench of sweet sweat perfumed with the overpowering odour of a man who had drunk himself silly some time before, made Pig Knot blink with realization.

Darcevo was drunk.

Even better, Darcevo appeared *insanely* drunk.

And this wasted form of meat and metal lurched towards Pig Knot, bringing his mace up to his shoulder and his shield to guard. It wasn't uncommon for Free Trained fighters, as Darcevo clearly was, to combat their nerves by drinking something before their matches. Pig Knot never did it for any of his fights, though he was guilty of it the night before at times. Such was the risk when a person came to see a Free Trained battle. The houses and schools would string a man by his kog and bells if he did such a thing, but the Free Trained had no such worries. A part of Pig Knot swore upon having drawn Darcevo this day, as fighting a drunkard wasn't anyone's idea of a good time. It was just bad form. Anything was possible in a Free Trained match.

Sputtering inarticulate sounds Pig Knot didn't understand, Darcevo grunted as he closed with the Sunjan and swung for his head.

Despite being hung over, Pig Knot's reflexes got him out of the way of the mace's arc. Darcevo staggered to his right, carried in that direction by the momentum of the swing, and came close to falling. But at the last moment, he stomped both feet into the sand and firmed up.

Pig Knot regarded the man over the edge of his own shield, his arms suddenly finding the energy to maintain a guard. Darcevo turned and actually started, as if surprised Pig Knot was still standing.

"That's right, you drunk bastard, I'm—"

Darcevo came at him with a roar made metallic by his bony visor. Pig Knot dodged one swipe of the mace then another. He ducked and moved around the man's shield, hearing another grunt as Darcevo swung once more and missed. Pig Knot circled to his foe's shield arm, and the movement made him dizzy. He stabbed with his sword and missed, attempting wildly to regain his own balance before his opponent. Darcevo got his bearings first, however, and charged in, swinging and missing badly.

Pig Knot's equally clumsy counterstrikes and graceless dodging were just as sad. He swung at the man's head and rang his sword off Darcevo's helm with a *gong*, causing the brute to shriek and then moan like a boy.

For long moments, the two men attacked each other in poorly executed attempts. They waved their weapons before each other's faces, coming nowhere close to making contact, before staggering away as if engaged in an awkward dance. Pig Knot lunged, missed, and skidded face first in the sand. Darcevo tried to smash his head in, but lost grip of his mace and sent it flying twenty paces behind him. He drew the rage of crowds when he turned about unsteadily and walked over to pick it up, allowing Pig Knot time to get to his feet.

Pig Knot allowed him and took the time to just sit on the sand, basking in the growing insults and taunts. The Sunjan didn't blame them. He'd do the same.

From his place on the arena wall, high above the combat, the Orator looked at the audience watching the battle and shook his head in barely concealed contempt.

The people, incredulous at the display of arms, jeered at the fighters, spiking the hot air with insults.

"What shite gurry is this?"

"Fight, he-bitches, *fight*!"

"Unfit!"

"How did the Chamber allow you two tits onto the sand?"

And on and on. Pig Knot's mental anguish now matched his physical state.

Darcevo walked back towards his foe, perhaps having had enough of being goaded or having sobered enough to do something. Pig Knot stood up heartbeats before his opponent lashed out with the mace and cracked it off his shield, driving him backwards. The heavily armoured fighter whipped his mace into the Sunjan's shield once more, ringing it like a dinner bell and numbing Pig Knot's arm. He retreated, wanting a breath of air. But Darcevo came forward, snapping his mace out and making Pig Knot duck. The crowd cheered the attacker on, quite happy that one of them had finally taken the initiative. Darcevo stepped up his pace, swinging at every part of Pig Knot within reach—an arm, the head, a shoulder, a knee. The Sunjan deflected strike after strike with his shield, steadily retreating and not daring to look to see where the arena wall might be. Drunk as he was, Darcevo was strong, and each blow had the full might of his arm behind it.

Pig Knot's shield, a wooden barrier ringed with a thin band of iron, abruptly split down the middle. He felt his guts go cold as the iron head of the mace punched though the wood just above his forearm in a burst of splinters. Darcevo stepped into him and smashed his shield into Pig Knot's weapon arm, pinning it, pushing him back, and creating room for another swing.

The mace flew at Pig Knot's helm and clipped his metal cheek, spinning him around. He stumbled and fell in a spray of sand. Darcevo slammed his mace down, missing the Sunjan's weapon arm by a finger.

Pig Knot drove his feet into the sand, pushing himself away, but Darcevo matched him and swung his weapon. The mace barely missed Pig Knot's head. The Sunjan kicked out and struck the greave protecting his opponent's left leg.

Again and again Darcevo rained down punishing blows with his mace. Pig Knot rolled away, avoiding each attack by hair widths, horrified as his shield fell away from his arm in a crumpled wreck of splinters and shards.

Then Darcevo backed up. He staggered, his arms hanging at his sides as if completely spent. Metallic coughs and hoarking issued from the skull helmet, and for a moment, Pig Knot realized just how quiet it had become in the Pit. The big man straightened and then stumbled forward, as if uncertain as to how to proceed. Then he stunned the crowd completely when he retreated two more shuffling steps and fell on his arse in the sand.

Pig Knot couldn't believe his luck. He got up, hearing the growing chorus of insults and disbelief from the audience. Some screamed at Darcevo to haul his carcass to his feet, and Pig Knot thought those men had placed wagers on the pit fighter. Darcevo moved slowly however, the skull visor studying the sand about him as if suddenly curious about it.

Pig Knot brushed off the remaining ruined fragments of his shield and freed his arm. He held his sword with two hands and moved in on the fallen man.

Darcevo saw him but made no move to defend himself. The crowds begged the gladiator to get back up.

Pig Knot raised his sword. Someone cried out something about doing the honorable thing, to give the fallen man a chance to get up. The Sunjan almost barked a laugh. Just as the topper had done for him?

Darcevo seemed to realize the danger just as Pig Knot's sword came down. He threw up his mace in an attempt to parry but misjudged badly as the edged steel lopped off two of his fingers. The digits disappeared in the sand, and Darcevo took the moment to simply study his gurgling stumps, as the weight of the weapon slowly wrenched itself free of his ruined grip.

Pig Knot thought his foe was trying to say something.

"Mercy," Darcevo finally garbled out but got stabbed through the shoulder instead. Pig Knot fell on the wounded man, laying him flat with one well-placed knee. He placed another knee on Darcevo's chest and poised the tip of his sword at the warrior's throat.

Pig Knot might have felt merciful any other day of the week, but it was Darcevo's misfortune to catch him in foul spirits.

The Sunjan punched his sword through the white throat of his foe. Darcevo's legs didn't even kick as his life was taken. Pig Knot twisted the steel, managing to hear the gristle crinkle over the roar of the people and left the weapon in the dead man's neck. It was, perhaps, the only thing he'd done correctly all morning.

Sweating, choking on dust, and suddenly feeling miserable, Pig Knot distanced himself from the body, crawling away on hands and knees. Insults fell about him, every bit as stinging as edged steel. He stood up, swayed on his feet, and walked as slowly as he could to the entryway. As he neared it, the portcullis creaked upwards, and somewhere behind him, Pig Knot heard the Orator declare him the winner.

The people lavished him with more verbal barbs, making him want to find a very deep hole and drown himself with drink.

Once inside the tunnel, Pig Knot ripped the helm from his head and threw it at a wall. It rebounded off the stone with a clatter and a spark, earning the attention of the old gatekeeper below. Pig Knot leaned against the tunnel for moments, while outside, the crowd still taunted and voiced their disapproval of the finished fight.

"What?" he barked at the still-staring gatekeeper.

"Get down from there before I call the guards."

His face flushed, Pig Knot shook his head in derision and

straightened. He walked down the stairs, not once meeting the weathered look of the gatekeeper.

"You fought like shite out there," the old man grumped.

"I won, didn't I?"

To that, the gatekeeper had no reply.

Pig Knot walked past the impassive visors of the Skarrs lining the white tunnel. The crowd became less bothersome the farther he walked. Even half-drunk and sick to his stomach, he'd still managed to win his fight and kill a topper. He realized he'd forgotten to place a wager on himself, but that was fine. A small purse of gold was coming to him, and he was still alive to enjoy it. That thought made him smile.

In the end, that was all that mattered.

*

All around him, the crowds continued talking about Pig Knot's fight. They flung insults at the Gladiatorial Chamber for allowing such men to participate in the games, and for once, Goll had to agree. What he had seen on the sands was a disgrace to the sport and the spirit of the event. Even though he'd won his wager, having placed gold on Pig Knot, he was far from pleased with the Sunjan's sloppy victory. The only reason Pig Knot was alive, Goll realized, was because the other idiot had been even more inebriated. And even then, the dog had still managed to put up a fight, unlike Pig Knot, who merely took advantage of an exhausted opponent, killing the man.

The Weapon Masters of Kree would not approve.

Glowering in dark thoughts, Goll sat in the stands and mulled amongst the still-livid crowd. When they settled down, he intended to make his way to the Domis and collect his winnings. He'd wait until the people watched the next match, not wanting anyone to know he'd wagered coin on the sick dog known as Pig Knot.

The embarrassment would be too great.

4

They called him Crowhead, although his real name was Brozz. He preferred his earned name, mostly because it was intimidating. There was a simple delight in disturbing people, Crowhead found, and he discovered that people were much more honest with him because he *was* frightening. It would probably damn him to Saimon's Hell—of that he had little doubt—but he still enjoyed scaring people. He relished staring fighters in their eyes and projecting that fear.

And the fear was justified.

He was tall, perhaps the tallest he had ever encountered in his own travels. A great, long moustache flowed down the edges of his mouth, as black as pitch. The ends were actually longer than his beard, which was short and non-existent compared to his forked whiskers. His complexion was dark and moody. He wore his hair short but not spiky, just enough to keep it out of his eyes, which were just as black as his beard and gleamed with malevolence. But the thing that got most people's attention, the thing that started people whispering as he walked through a crowd, was the chilling necklace of severed crow heads hanging from his neck. There were five dried heads, their black beaks as sharp as claws, dangling from his necklace and separated by knots. All were threaded through the eyes, as if the last thing they had felt was the knife tip.

In the depths of Sunja's Pit, amongst the rest of the Free Trained, he stayed in one corner and removed the nearby torches, claiming the ensuing void as his own. He'd been one of the first to enter the general quarters at the beginning, and he'd gotten no argument from any of the others when he settled on the corner. Outside the arena, he usually wore an open leather vest, which showed off his washboard stomach and muscular chest. His physique was chiseled but not heavy, with lanky limbs.

When he was in general quarters, inside the dark he claimed as his own, he sat with his back against a wall and watched whoever was closest. He studied how the men interacted with each other and made note of the friends, the fake friends, and the potential enemies. The fake friends, the ones who stood and joked and listened to their companions but smirked when backs were turned, were snakes in Brozz's opinion. They couldn't be trusted. The men who outright hissed at one another... well, he didn't mind them. At least one knew where one stood with them.

There were very few *real* friends in the Pit, which didn't really surprise him.

The air was hot and unpleasant with so many men in the bowels of the arena, but Brozz didn't mind. He gathered his weapons and armor in the dark and prepared for his fight. A part of him figured he'd have to kill a man this day. He didn't want to, as killing a man in the arena invited retribution from other quarters—friends, or worse, even more proficient gladiators if the victim was part of a house or school.

But if he had to kill, he'd do it. With no hesitation.

When he emerged from the corner, conversations dribbled into silence. Men stepped out of the way of the tall man with a thick shortsword and handaxe and the necklace of screaming crows about his neck. Droves parted for the warrior heading to the Madea as if he were a hellion about to snatch one of them up. And so they should.

Brozz—Crowhead—was terrifying.

In places, the corners of the white tunnel were draped in cobwebs, which made Kade reflect on pit fighting. It was all one big web, sticky strands crossing over each over, spiraling downwards towards a center that would ultimately eat you alive. He wasn't about to be devoured by the rabble around him. Though he was Free Trained, he considered himself better than most and certainly better than the two drunkards staggering about on the sands in the first match of the day. No wonder people had such low opinions of the Free Trained. Kade didn't blame them for their curses and howls when they were offered such utter shite. Unprofessional louts. Thinking back on the fight filled him with contempt for the pair of so-called warriors. The dead one was lucky, in his mind, and the victor would be ridiculed long before he set foot on the sand again.

Kade had worked with his weapons long and hard enough to think he could fight for a House, but they only selected the cream. This day, he intended to put forth the best show he could manage, even if he had to crush a few heads in the process. He had fought in the Pit last year, for the two months the fighting season had gone then, and he had won three of four matches before a brute from Osgar broke his right arm with a mace. Even now, Kade's forearm ached during the winter as if remembering the blow.

It wasn't as though he needed the money. He got paid for his work and service to the crown and the men he killed upon their command.

He did this simply for the fun.

Kade was an executioner and a fine one at that. With his axe in hand, he could take the head off a man with one fell chop, forty in a line if need be before he had to stop for rest. He'd seen plenty of fear and death in his time. Signing up for the fights in Sunja's Pit was almost like another day of work. It didn't bother him as it did a few of the newer, self-declared gladiators. Kade had to roll his eyes at some of the noisy bastards. He was thankful he had a hovel in the city to return to, for if he had to stay just one night in general quarters listening to those braying animals, he'd start swinging steel before the sun rose. He knew he would.

Thinking these thoughts, he made his way past the Skarrs standing at attention and to the gatekeeper at the end. A sword was in his hand, and a large, square shield hung off his arm. He would have preferred to take a battle axe to the men on the sand these days, but an axe wasn't the best of weapons for such reaving. Not like a good broadsword. And with an executioner's attention to edges, Kade had sharpened his blade by himself.

He was a big, burly man, well-protected under a suit of mail that gleamed. Heavy for most, but Kade didn't notice it. He wasn't as fast as some, but he was strong in both endurance and limbs. As a greeting to the gatekeeper, he tapped the flat of his sword against the visor he wore, the grill poked with holes that gave the iron helm a grin.

Already, the people were warming up to the next fight.

"They're looking for blood after the last one," the gatekeeper informed him. Kade recognized the man from last season. He was one of a pair the Chamber seemed to keep on. Old, with no chin to speak of and a flab of flesh that jiggled like something hooked and freshly landed from a river, the gatekeeper regarded Kade with a pair of eyes that could have been mistaken for a dungeon rat's.

"They're always looking for blood," Kade rumbled. "Their nature."

"S'pose it is. Fight hard then."

"I will," Kade promised and meant it, studying the steps leading up to daylight and barred by thick portcullis.

He intended to take the arms and legs off whoever was waiting for him on the sands.

The gatekeeper nodded and pulled the lever.

The Orator's real name was Qualtus, and he was thankful this afternoon that the king wasn't about to see the pile of cow shite that he would forever curse himself for calling the first fight of the day. Still, he glanced to the raised viewing box situated high on the south wall, just to make certain it was still empty. *Sweet Seddon above,* he thought darkly, squinting from the sun's glare on the arena sands and feeling the dainty beads of sweat making their way down his back towards the crack of his ass. If there ever was an argument to stop the Free Trained from entering the Pit, those last two toppers were it.

He looked towards the north end of the arena, directly across from the king's viewing box, to the stand where nobles and the owners of some of the top-ranked houses sat and watched the games. That particular construction towered above the sands, with a high wall dividing the two groups. Rumour had it the wall split the viewing box so the nobility wouldn't have to look upon the sometimes-changing owners sitting in the section. Six men sat on that side this day, and Qualtus wondered what they had thought of the first show. Nexus, Curge, and golden-faced Gastillo occupied the other side, and he could almost hear the swearing, from the wine merchant in particular. Curge probably didn't care for him in the least. Gastillo, however, was hard to read due to the mask he wore. Who really knew what that one thought? As for the Chamber members on the other side of the wall, Qualtus hoped they hadn't eaten heavily beforehand.

Qualtus consulted the scroll that outlined the day's fights, given to him by a messenger sent from the Madea, who organized and oversaw everything. The Orator didn't envy that position in the least. A person would have to think about what he was doing, and Qualtus knew very well he wasn't cut out for such tasks.

He was merely the voice of the Pit.

He was the thunder above the sand.

And right now, he had to sway the audience back to more favorable grounds and wash away the memory of the first fight. Qualtus had learned long ago it was best not to even acknowledge such a piss-poor showing. It was better simply to move on.

Clearing his throat, he lifted his arms, the white sleeves of his Orator's gown slipping to reveal his skinny limbs. The people, several thousand this day but nowhere near the Pit's capacity, took longer than usual to quiet.

"Men and women of the Pit." The Orator elected to go with the traditional introduction in an attempt to reset the entire day. "You are honored guests to these blood games, games which have been a granite mast of our civilization for hundreds of years. Listen for a moment. Can you hear it, as I do? The hushed cries of champions dead and gone yet whose spectres gather still to witness these new games. Time after time. When the season grows cold, dead, then awakens and becomes hot, those warriors are here. Now. Where once they stood... we *stand*. Where once they fought... men *fight*. And where once they died..."

Qualtus let that hang in the air for a moment.

"We *watch*. And we applaud skills of arms. And the rousing beat of death. For in these games, fought by men risking all for your entertainment and their own desire to be the best, in Sunja's Pit, the only things that are certain are life, combat... and sands red with blood. On behalf of the Gladiatorial Chamber, dear guests, I present to you, for our mutual entertainment, a battle fought by two men who will stir the very sands and lift the earthy grains into the air. A fight that will make Saimon's hellions rise up to bear witness and a fight that will have Seddon's heralds descend from the heavens and bless the best. I present to you a *war* that will have you talking well into the evening."

Qualtus paused, allowing his words time to be absorbed. If that didn't get their juices going, he didn't know what might.

Then he chopped a hand towards the taller of the two Pit warriors. "From Sarland. He is the caul ripped from Death's face. A walking plague in man's form that kills all conversation in a busy street. He is a hunter. A collector. And he sets to make his mark known in Sunja's Pit for the first time this season. He. Is. *Crowhead!*"

The man draped in leather armor, with the exception of

his helmet and face cage, stood still upon the arena sands, showing no indication of having heard anything from the Orator. At the ends of seemingly lifeless arms hung a shortsword and hand axe. The crowds did not quite know what to make of such a tall wraith partially hunched at the shoulders, as if the very heat of the sun sought to melt him. Some of the people cheered, but it was a small few of the thousands watching.

The Orator liked that. He quickly switched to the other and started once more in a voice that commanded attention.

"Facing this hellpup is one of our own. A son of Sunjan and a wall of a man. Prisoners fear this brute like no other, and if your name is on his breath, you are certain his axe will find your neck. Born on the plains of Sunja and bronzed in the heat of her sun, he was a beast as a lad, and this day, he carries with him the experience of one already well wise to the ways of the Pit. You asked for a champion for these games? I give you *Kade... the executioner.*"

Upon hearing the name of Kade, the arena exploded in thunderous applause. The mass of onlookers pulsated in the stands like fat veins about to gush. Kade stood motionless, a beach rock of armour, quietly appraising his opponent.

Qualtus dropped his hands to his sides. As far as he was concerned, he had done his job and, as always, done it well. Now it was time for the chop.

"Let this contest... *begin!*"

The howls and cheers of thousands drowned out the Orator's final word. The two fighters raised their guards like wary veterans of the Pit and circled each other while closing the distance between them. Crowhead let his arms dangle before him, his weapons swinging gently as if caught in a breeze, while Kade lifted his shield and held it in front of his body like a heavy door. Kade eyed the shadowy shape of Crowhead as he approached, keeping his broadsword just above his right shoulder like a cocked catapult. The first chance that showed itself, he would swing that blade for all he was worth and let the Pit's servants clean up the mess.

Crowhead got close enough for Kade to see the necklace of heads around his neck, and that set his head shaking in disbelief.

"You're a grim one, aren't you?" the executioner asked the man looming before him.

Crowhead said nothing in return.

Not that Kade wanted him to say anything. In his line of work, more than half of the prisoners he killed begged him not to take their lives, as though it were up to him. No, he preferred it when they were quiet.

"Come on then, you black bastard," he whispered.

And he got his request.

Like a huge net flung into the sea, Crowhead lunged forward, swinging with both arms, his shortsword and handaxe flashing in a flurry of strikes. He attacked the squat head of his foe, then his shoulders, and then suddenly dropped down to make a swipe at an extended leg. Planting his feet, Kade stopped all thrusts and chops with his shield, moving the iron-and-wood door on his arm where needed, placing his body behind it at all times. The crowd became quiet with each impact, until Crowhead suddenly broke off and took a few steps back.

The speed of the other man's attack impressed Kade. The larger man was fast. He shifted to his left, keeping his shield in place and his sword ready, tightly wound like a loaded catapult ready to snap.

The Orator was also taken aback by the initial flurry of

strikes flying at the shorter Kade. He thought about the armour on Kade and wondered if perhaps it was a hindrance to him.

Crowhead went at the heavily armoured man again, cutting and slashing and stabbing at the end. Kade's shield absorbed every blow, and he counterstruck with his broadsword when Crowhead stopped. His hunk of edged metal scythed out and split the air once occupied by his adversary's skull.

But the taller man ducked under the slash, surprising everyone.

Crowhead jerked to Kade's left, prodding with his shortsword and forcing the man to match him. Kade kept his shield before him and his sword set once more just above his shoulder, waiting for the opportunity to separate head from torso. Metallic *whacks* punctuated the air, as Crowhead didn't stop circling or swinging as he went, turning both men around in a complete circle and a half before breaking off to catch his breath.

Kade countered with a straight-arm, over-the-shield chop, missing his foe's helm and shoulder by the barest hair. Crowhead moved away then, placing a few strides between them while defensively weaving his long arms. Kade did not pursue.

Qualtus believed the executioner was either tired or conserving his strength. The crowds were cheering the Sunjan, which was to be expected. The darker fellow had the feel of evil about him, and these games sometimes depended on a hero and a villain.

Crowhead rushed in and again whipped his blades at the steely form of the executioner. Sounds of each connection with the shield rang out, and the crowd collectively gasped at the onslaught. Crowhead's weapons chewed at the iron-bound shield. Sparks flared. Kade backed up, relenting against the intensity of the attack. Sword and handaxe chopped and slashed, and with every new swipe, the onlookers expected blood to fly.

Then Crowhead broke away to catch his breath once more, and Kade jumped at him, unleashing his sword arm in a vicious counterstrike and connecting with his opponent's head with a loud *krang!* that brought several cheering spectators to their feet. Crowhead moved backwards, placing room between him and his adversary, his axe hand going to his helmet.

He ripped it from his head, and the crowd roared.

Kade allowed him that, once again readying himself for a flurry of blows, wearing the Sarlander out and waiting for that one moment to strike, the one cut that would drop a very dark head rolling into the sands.

Crowhead shook himself, and blood from a scalp cut dappled the ground. Hunched over and wary of the other man, he tossed the helmet away and pressed a forearm against his wound. It came away red. Taking fresh grips on his weapons, Crowhead slowly moved towards the wall that was Kade.

The executioner watched him come forwards and smiled behind his visor. He knew what was about to come. And he knew with no helmet to protect his foe, now was the time to go headhunting. His grin growing just a little more confident,

Kade readied himself for the storm and saw himself taking Crowhead's grim skull with one almighty chop.

True to form, Crowhead charged in. Kade tensed. And the violent clash of metal on metal filled the air until the Pit's audience roared approval, drowning out the noise…

Until they collectively gasped.

Crowhead charged in and swung, almost wild with his strikes this time. His sword struck Kade's shield while his handaxe sought his foe's sword arm and helmet. Kade turtled up, moving the barrier almost impossibly fast, stopping Crowhead's attacks even as his long arms looped around the shield. Kade stood firm and absorbed it all, parried everything, waiting for that break in the squall of edged steel he knew would come.

And when it finally did, Crowhead stepped away, his weapons slipping down.

Kade lashed out with his sword, stabbing for his foe's black eyes.

Crowhead ducked under the arm, stepped in as if he knew the attack was coming, and uppercut with his sword. The blade sank halfway into Kade's chest, piercing metal links and flesh alike. Blood burst from the wound. Kade's eyes went wide with pain a split second before Crowhead's handaxe cleaved the side of his neck, splitting armor and flesh and driving the larger man to one knee. Crowhead left his sword in his prey, but he placed a hand on the fallen warrior's shoulder and wrenched his axe free in a torrent of red. Kade's sword dropped from his fingers. In the abrupt silence, there were only a few who didn't hear the executioner's haunting moan.

Crowhead hacked at the neckline three times, driving the edge of his handaxe deeper into his dying opponent and opening him up enough to allow the blood to truly spray. It splashed up against his leather armour like a newfound spring. Crowhead pushed the dead man forward.

Kade landed facedown in the sand.

Crowhead studied the corpse at his feet for a moment before stooping and retrieving his sword. He flicked both of his weapons, sending black beads of blood into the air. He found his helmet and picked that up as well before turning and focusing on the Orator.

Qualtus remembered he had a voice. "Your victor! Crowhead!"

Some of the audience cheered. Some of them cursed. The majority sat, puzzled over how the match had gone and how it should have been.

Crowhead didn't appear to care. With his weapons in hand, he turned and headed back to the portcullis creaking open, retreating to the more comfortable shadows.

The Orator watched him and nodded in approval.

He appreciated a good surprise.

5

The sun beat down with a heat that sought to sizzle sweat on bare skin. Halm sat outside the alehouse he'd woken up in, feeling as if his innards had been roped and tethered to the flanks of a horse that was then slapped on the rump and made to run. He sat with his back against the foundation, a few strides away from the open entryway so not to offend the owner. A river of people with two distinct currents ran by him, but he paid them no heed. With his face lifted to the sun as if that glowing ball of heat could somehow purify him, Halm tried not to move at all and kept one arm around an alehouse pitcher filled with water from a nearby well. His Mademian sword lay on his other side, in the ill-fitting scabbard.

"Ugh," he muttered. The dark of his closed eyes was orange-black from the sun. He knew he should find some shade and rest, but his legs didn't want to support him just yet. On the other hand, just sitting there and stewing in his own sweat didn't appeal to him either. The decision to refill the pitcher came to him, and then the notion to perhaps find and sit in some shade in the city's centre where high trees were allowed to flourish. That seemed like a promising idea.

"You look like shite," someone said.

Halm opened his eyes to see the shady figure of Goll supported by a pair of crutches. He raised a hand to shield his eyes, peering at the Kree with his mouth half-open in an ugly grimace.

"Good thing you're you; I might've said something," Halm croaked.

"Like what?"

"Dunno. Something. What do you want?"

Goll smiled and stood with the crutches jammed into his armpits. He squinted at the sun. "You. Actually."

Halm studied the man. He wore a short skirt that stopped mid-thigh, befitting the style of the season. A white tunic, loose, covered his body, but bandages were visible along the shoulder where the cloth stopped.

"Where're the others?" Halm asked.

"Who? Pig Knot?"

"Aye."

"He fought earlier this day. Won his match in perhaps the worst way possible."

"He got cut up?"

Goll paused and thought about it. "I don't think so."

"Then any win is a good one."

Standing there, balanced on his crutches, Goll seemed to think even more. Halm found that refreshing.

"How well do you know that man? Is he a friend?" the Kree finally asked.

Halm considered it. Pig Knot a friend? "Well, yes. He is. Sort of. He… he's pretty much the only one who's been around as long as I have in these games, although I have a couple of years on him."

"I see." Goll threw his head back and inhaled sharply

through his nose. "You didn't accompany him to his fight this morning."

"Pig Knot needs no nursemaid. And I was still unconscious. I don't even know where Muluk is off to."

Someone jostled Goll from behind, and he had to stamp his left foot into the ground to stop himself falling over. The offender disappeared into the crowd, but Halm saw how Goll's arms had been cut up and bandaged by the Butcher of Balgotha. He remembered the Kree saying that his right shoulder might have been broken as well, so just using the crutches would probably be an agonizing challenge. The old champion had danced a jig on his flesh before Goll had killed him.

"You want something to drink?" Halm asked him.

"Me? Now?" Goll frowned and shook his head. "Too much drinking going on around here. No, thank you."

More for me then, Halm thought.

"You and I have to talk." Goll stared straight into his eyes. "We have some work before us. Or at least I have work to do. You have a decision to make."

Halm squinted in the sun's glare. "Sounds serious."

"I'm going to meet with the Gladiatorial Chamber this day. I'm going there now, in fact."

"What? Why?"

"To see what must be done to set up my own house."

Halm felt his mouth go dry, and he wasn't sure if it was from the drinking the night before or something else. He kept his eyes on the man before him as he lifted his nearby pitcher and took a drink from it. When the water was gone, Halm got to his feet, his great belly quivering, and tucked the pitcher under one arm. He didn't bother to brush the dust from his black breeches or bandages.

"You really want to do this?" he asked.

"I do."

Halm shrugged. "Let's go then. At the very least, I'll be interested to see where it all leads. Which way? It's next to the Pit, isn't it?"

"It is. Part of the Pit, really. This way, but walk slowly. I can barely stay on these things"—he indicated the crutches—"as it is with my arms and shoulder. The healer said I only need to keep off my toes for a few weeks. And I don't think my shoulder's broken like before. I can still move it."

"Hard to take a piss?" Halm joked gruffly.

Goll regarded him with a mildly distasteful look.

"Only asking," the Zhiberian muttered. The Kree wasn't Pig Knot; that was for certain. He placed a hand to his own covered wounds, the bandages stained with dust and dirt. "You think the Chamber will see us?"

"They will."

Halm looked at his companion and saw the determination on his battered face.

"They *must*," the Kree said simply.

The Zhiberian grunted and idly adjusted the sword at his waist. They walked through the crowds, keeping to one side and away from most of the traffic in the middle. The smell of the city could always be improved upon as every so often even Halm wrinkled up his nose at an old man who smelled as if he hadn't washed in months. Also, the merchants were guiding strings of horses, goats, or cows, not in the least concerned with the heaps of dung—collectively and colloquially known as cow kisses—their animals left behind. The Zhiberian had no trouble passing through the mob. Big and ugly as he knew himself to be, all he had to do was keep a hard face about him, and the masses parted like wheat. It was even easier this day than most since he looked as though he'd been in a fight. Goll fell in step behind him, moving along as best as he could on his crutches. Bare clotheslines spanned the main street, but down the smaller alleyways, more lines hung and drooped with washed clothes, some colourful, some grey in the shade.

As they walked, Halm noticed a leather worker and stopped in his tracks.

"What is it?" Goll asked from behind.

"I need a new scabbard," Halm told him. "Wait here, would you?"

"Don't be too long."

Halm didn't respond to that, letting his silence do the talking. He would take as long as he needed to get what he wanted done. The leather maker, a middle-aged man with a chin full of rusty stubble, sat in the middle of a wooden stall that ran far back and ended in a wall of curtains. On tables, fine leather scabbards for all manner of blades were on display, and the merchant paused for a moment, looking up from his stitching as Halm closed with one table.

"Ho, leather worker." Halm's voice carried over the bustle of the people. "Can you make me a sheath for this?"

With that, he removed the scabbard from his waist and handed it over.

The merchant took it from him and turned it about, extracting the sword and nodding favourably. "Mademian. Very nice. I can put something together, but it will cost you. Too bad I can't adjust one of the scabbards already made."

"When can you have it done?"

"Come back tomorrow. I'm not that busy. What's your name?"

"Halm of Zhiberia. And best be careful with that piece. It has… memories attached to it."

"Sentimental, are you?" The man smirked.

Halm scowled. "What did you call me?"

The leather maker cleared his throat. "Nothing. Have no worries. It'll be here when you come back tomorrow. You can pay me then."

Mulling over whether or not he'd just been insulted and whether he should slap the punce in front of him, Halm eventually turned and left. He rejoined a waiting Goll.

"Buying a scabbard?" Goll asked him.

"I am. When one has coin, it's best to spend it."

Goll didn't say anything to that, and Halm wondered if he had misjudged the man somehow. The Kree was becoming increasingly more serious as the day went on. Halm really didn't know anything about him other than he was from Kree and he had killed Baylus, who had spared Goll in their fight only to lose his life to him.

"Let's be off then." Goll swung away on his crutches, pushing back into the crowds and leaving Halm to catch up. The Zhiberian soon stepped around the Kree and resumed his place as a divider of people.

"You're a serious one, aren't you?" Halm asked, splitting his attention between the masses and Goll.

"What?"

"I said, 'You're a serious one, aren't you?'"

"You're not?"

"Seddon, no." Halm chuckled. "Not since birth. Too much going on around me to be that way. I try to just live and make my way through it all."

"I see," Goll said pointedly. "And how has that worked out for you?"

"Not bad thus far."

"This is not bad?"

"Er… yes." But Halm wasn't so sure anymore.

"When I look at you, do you know what I see?"

Halm wasn't certain he wanted to hear this. It sounded far too serious, and him still partially hung over. It was a wonder his headache was gone, but his innards still ached.

"What?" he finally asked, deciding it would be good for a chuckle.

"I see a man with little push and motivation but fat with potential. A man with little, if that, to his name, who deals in life or death games for the amusement of the people, while there is a war on, and ignoring the gathering dangers beyond Sunja's walls. Living in ignorance as you are, I see you dead perhaps by year's end. If not sooner."

Halm slowed in his tracks at the mention of Sunja's walls and turned around to appraise the man as he prattled on.

And Goll did. "I see a man who would jump at the chance to better himself if the opportunity arises, for he's smart enough to know this life will be the death of him, but by Seddon above, he has no idea of how to better his lot. So he placates himself by getting drunk when he has the coin. Comforts himself with hired wenches if need be. Tells himself life isn't something to be taken seriously while searching for that very thing that will save him—though he doesn't know what it is. And who jokes about his life as if it's no more than cow kisses dotting the road."

Goll stopped then, locking eyes with the bigger Zhiberian and not backing down in the least.

"*That's* what I see."

Halm stared into the depths of the Kree's brown eyes and saw, even felt, a man who would start swinging the very crutches he walked with if Halm took a swing at him. And he believed that Goll *expected* him to swing at him. He had the sense to see that, but why would the Kree say such a thing to him?

"Why are you saying this to me?" Halm finally asked without a shred of humour in his voice. "I've done nothing to you."

"Sometimes, the hardest hits come with words," Goll said, barely heard over the din of the crowds milling around them, "and they also do the most good."

With that, Goll moved back a step and went around Halm, leaving him to stare after the smaller man. He thought for a moment, weighing the Kree's stinging words. Not too many men had the balls to say such a thing to his face, and in the middle of the street, no less, before simply walking away.

"Saucy bastard," Halm said. He hurried to catch up.

To the north of Sunja's Pit, placed seamlessly up against the wall of the arena, stood the building that housed the Gladiatorial Chamber. Like the arena, it was built of brick, stone, and heavy timbers, but it rose far above the highest seats and the walls of the Pit, and it was rumoured that the members of the Chamber could actually see the matches from the highest points. Grey and white rock composed the outer shell of the five-story building. A row of six white marble columns, their bases too wide to embrace, rose up from street level to an overhang, offering protection from harsh summer rains if needed. Near the bottom, their surfaces were chiselled into scenes depicting small battling figures and ferocious animals. A pair of great oak doors fashioned to fit an archway lay just beyond the marble giants. Six Skarrs stood on either side of the entryway, their backs against a wall cut with a scattering of windows fixed with closed wooden shutters. Each warrior carried sword, shield, and spear. Their visors remained fixed ahead, watching the pair of battered men as they drew closer and entered the shadow of the Gladiatorial Chamber.

6

Goll hobbled straight for the main doors, and Halm expected the Skarrs to bar the Kree's way at any moment. Where it went from there, Halm only hoped they would be able to walk away. The city guard remained motionless even as Goll stopped and jerked his head towards the doors, indicating that Halm open it. The Zhiberian did so, pushing them inwards and holding them open until Goll hopped past on his crutches.

Even as Halm followed his companion inside the building, he expected someone to shout orders to throw them out.

On the walls inside, intricate scratchings of arena battles adorned gleaming sheets of copper. The pictures faded into the height of the ceiling. Despite the shutters being closed, some of the higher windows allowed thin shafts of light to spear down and mark the walls at steep angles. Torches burned from wall sconces, and a black iron brazier dominated the middle of the foyer, burning some exotic incense that Halm didn't expect at all. It felt out of place. The area seemed more like a temple of sorts. Benches made from heavy wood with cracked surfaces spotted the floor in places while six doors, some opened and some closed, ringed the walls at even intervals.

A group of four men, two of whom sat on the benches, turned and eyed the newcomers. The two standing men, who faced Halm and Goll as they entered, watched them with expressions of disdain. They were well built and casually dressed in light clothing, but there was no mistaking the ominous strength in their limbs. One of the sitting men, an older one, regarded them over his shoulder and then turned and took a closer look before smiling smugly and showing his back once more. He spoke something to his companions, which caused the two standing to break into leers.

Halm didn't like them from the start.

Goll drew up on his crutches and studied the six doors. Officials moved past the open ones like pictures leaving their frames, carrying scrolls in and out of view or undertaking some unknown organizational tasks.

Goll started for the nearest one, his crutches echoing in the vast foyer. Halm followed him.

"Where one goes, the other follows."

Halm heard quite clearly that time and cast a frown in the direction of the foursome. The pair standing continued to eye him like meat gone bad while the older one, wearing a light beard of grey, caught Halm's eye and winked at him. The Zhiberian frowned once more, no longer liking the feel of the room.

"You there," Goll asked of a robed official as he passed from one room to the next, "where might I find the Chamber members? I wish to speak with them."

Halm heard the four men chuckle behind him.

The official, a middle-aged man losing his hair, stopped

in his tracks and blinked at Goll. "Are you supposed to be here this day?"

"No."

This brought more chuckling from the men near the brazier. Halm half-turned towards them and eased his hands to his hips in warning.

"Oh ho, that one seems upset now." Grey Beard smiled slyly, his eyes cruel. He didn't look away from the Zhiberian. "Imagine that."

"You have to have an appointment to see the Chamber," the official said dourly, not hearing the men beyond.

Goll didn't seem to hear him. "I wish to see them this day, if possible."

Another rash of snarky giggles came, with one man even snorting and shaking his head. Halm felt his blood rise, wondering what was so damned funny. Then it struck him like a thrown spear. The four were gladiators, gladiators that belonged to a house or school. They all wore swords, with the exception of Grey Beard. The realization made Halm chew on one corner of his mouth, mulling dark thoughts.

"That's impossible," the official said.

"Please ask," Goll kept on.

"I just said it's impossible."

"I'm asking you to ask."

"You cannot simply enter and ask to see the Chamber. There are rules, you know."

"Really? And what are those?"

The official let out an exasperated sigh. "You need to schedule a meeting. I've just told you that. The Chamber is very busy during the season."

Goll screwed up his face as he took in the almost-empty foyer. "Well, I'm asking for a meeting now."

"You can't have a meeting on the same day."

"Why not?"

The official rolled his eyes. "It isn't done that way."

"Perhaps it should be done that way."

More scalding snickers came from behind. The evil smile on Grey Beard stretched even farther, and he leaned in the direction of Goll, finding great amusement in the conversation and sadly shaking his head. He nodded to Goll but directed his words to Halm.

"Your man is persistent; I'll give him that."

Halm wanly smiled back. He was tired of these bastards already. "In your hole, old tit."

The startled look on Grey Beard's once-smug features pleased Halm immensely.

"Look—" Goll struggled forwards on his crutches, speaking in a low voice. Halm's attention became wholly centered on Grey Beard and his men.

"You've got a smart mouth, dog." Grey Beard's unpleasant smile returned. "The last man to speak to me in such a tone disappeared."

"Probably went looking for your mother." Halm bared his own unpleasant smile. "If she shat out a pup like you, best for all concerned to sew the hole shut before anything else dropped out."

The men about Grey Beard became visibly tense, but the old one—their leader, Halm assumed—smiled on.

"At least I know my mother," Grey Beard came back, leering.

"You're a right happy topper, aren't you?" Halm immediately fired. "Why is that, I wonder? Unfit in the head, are you? Simple-minded?"

"Simple enough to—"

"Because," Halm spoke over Grey Beard, seeing the man's mouth quivering at the corners. "I pity simple-minded idiots like yourself. Truly. I see you have three punces to walk you around. That's a good thing. Which one cleans your ass? Hmm? Or do you just leave it in the street when the urge takes you—just like a cow kiss?"

Grey Beard's face twisted in on itself. His companions were all ready to pounce now, and for the first time, Halm saw just *how* large they were, and powerful looking. The brute that had been sitting next to Grey Beard even had an eye-patch draped across his left socket.

Though he didn't show it, Halm winced at the fact that he had left his blade with the leather maker.

"You've got a sharp tongue, youngster." Grey Beard seethed.

"Not as sharp as yours, I wager, to service the ass cracks of those three around you. You must pull it out once in a while. Why else are they just standing there? Hm? How much do you charge them a go? Or is it free all round?"

Grey Beard stood up, a storm cloud rising amongst thick hills. Halm smirked. He knew bare bones when he fastened onto them, and he had riled these men but good.

"You have a problem," Grey Beard said, suppressed anger in his voice. "I know you. I watched you fight just yesterday. I know you very well. And with that gut and that ugly mouth, it won't be much trouble for me to find out your name. And when I do—"

"Halm of Zhiberia," Halm blurted with a genuine chuckle. "And here I am."

He threw his arms wide.

Goll suddenly appeared on his right and edged around him, a dark look on his features, yet curious as to what was going on.

"Halm of Zhiberia." Grey Beard cackled, throwing back his head. "That's right, now I remember. You're Zhiberian. You Zhiberians know all about tonguing asses. And here I was almost getting annoyed with you. You there, cripple. Why don't you place your *animal* on a leash? Eh? And drag him back to the forest you found him in."

Goll said nothing, but his scowl was a step away from what Halm thought was something very dangerous.

"Nothing to say? Your boy speaks for you?"

Goll kept silent, releasing his pent-up air in a huff. With it, his expression relaxed.

"Ah, the *intelligent* one," Grey Beard nodded. "I'll be watching for you. It'll cost you more than a gold coin to avert my eye elsewhere. I'm not as easy to persuade as that one you paid just a moment ago."

Ignoring him, Goll limped to a nearby bench and sat on it. Once comfortable, he gazed at Grey Beard and then back to Halm as if wondering how far this exchange was going to go.

Halm wondered the same thing. Then he noticed the officials standing in their respective doorways with their pensive expressions. Grey Beard abruptly saw them as well and shook his head. He wagged a finger at Goll, quietly appreciating the man's tact and understanding him for the first time.

"You *are* the smart one," Grey Beard said in a sly tone and looked back and forth between the two. "I'll keep an eye on you both. Especially you, Zhiberian."

"I'll guard my ass." Halm smiled back with a flick of his chin. With that, he showed them his broad back and stepped in front of Goll. Confident he couldn't be seen, Halm lapsed into an expression of amazement and rolled his eyes.

Goll showed no indication of having noticed.

And together, they waited in the simmering silence of the room, broken once and again by the soft murmurs and giggling of Grey Beard and his men.

"Well?" Halm asked Goll softly.

"We wait." The Kree stared off at a copper wall.

Halm paused for more, and when it didn't come, he sat on a bench with his back to the others and resigned himself to getting comfortable. Grey Beard and his boys continued muttering, deep mewlings that Halm found as evil sounding as axe heads being dragged over quarried stone.

*

Much later, an official appeared and called the four men. They rose and entered the room just ahead of them, disappearing behind a set of double doors. Broken from his trance of boredom, Halm glanced over his shoulder just as the doors were closing. As soon as the men were gone, he leaned towards Goll.

"Those were gladiators."

"I saw that."

"A right proper unpleasant bunch at that."

Goll's head dipped to one shoulder in an *I suppose so* reply.

"Why didn't you say anything back there?" Halm asked.

"And add more wood to the fire?" Goll challenged. "Do you really want to be forever looking over your back from this day forth? These are my first games, but even *I've* heard stories of house fighters hunting down Free Trained outside of the Pit and pounding them into the dirt. I'd say you might have to be careful from here on."

Halm reflected on that. It was just his nature to throw back insults and give as good as he got or at least to try his damnedest to piss off the offenders. "I wasn't about to hold my tongue and say nothing to that brazen topper. Not here. And not with him."

"Well, you got his attention," Goll assured him. "I'm pretty certain I'm fine—being seen as a cripple and all. But I think *you* are well and truly fish hooked. I mean *truly* fish hooked. No sense in me being brutalized as well. Or outright killed."

Halm became pensive, thinking on the three brutes accompanying Grey Beard. "Well… perhaps."

Another head dip from Goll. *Just perhaps?*

They lapsed into silence then and waited some more.

"Why are you fighting in these games?" Goll eventually asked him, his voice respectful of the place they were in.

Halm had been sizing up the pictures on the wall, the lines almost indistinct from where he sat. "Coin."

"Nothing else?"

"Well… no. Not really. Was always good with a blade. Didn't take to anything else. Every season, I could count on fighting in one or three matches. Win some gold. Not good enough to carry on through. But I'd win enough to get me over to something else. Or win enough to get me through to the next season of fights. I'd train here and there, practice my swing and shield work on wooden posts or whatever. If I got put out early, I'd get into a bit of mercenary business but stay away from wars. I was always able to find work body-guarding merchants. That sort of thing."

Halm stopped then and thought.

"Not counting on getting old is what I mean."

In the copper gleam of the room, Goll's profile tightened.

"Why did you enter?" Halm asked.

"To win," the Kree replied simply, yet all business. "All of it."

The stark truth of the answer made Halm shift uncomfortably.

Time dragged then, until the perfumed air from the burning incense became much too sweet and made Halm clear his throat or cough every so often. Officials sometimes appeared in doorways and crossed the floor, only to vanish behind other doors. Sometimes, the balding man appeared and eyed them as if they were a nuisance. The others did not, or at least they had the sense to ignore the two fighters.

They sat and waited. Halm continued his dreary appraisal of the pictures on the walls while Goll hardly moved at all.

Finally, the double doors before them clicked and opened, and the four men walked out. Grey Beard looked straight at Goll and then Halm. To the Zhiberian, he lifted a finger to his eye and tapped it, smiling tightly and giving him a wink. That one gesture rankled Halm, and he scowled at the lot as they walked by him. If Halm and Goll had sat any closer to the outside of the benches, no doubt a kick or a shove would have been delivered by one or all of the four men. As it was, dirty looks flashed in their direction, and the glare of the one-eyed guard in particular needled Halm. An unspoken threat if ever the Zhiberian had seen one.

They walked past and exited the building.

"Pricks," Halm said under his breath.

"I agree," Goll threw in.

"That one-eyed bastard gave me the look."

"Did he?"

"Aye that. Have to be on the watch for him now."

"Well, no surprise there. Not after the words from earlier."

"No. Suppose not."

There was nothing else to talk about from then on as Halm chewed on the inside of his mouth and saw Grey Beard's smiling face and the one-eyed fighter in his mind's eye. He reluctantly admitted he might have a problem there.

"How long do think we'll have to wait?" Halm whispered.

"Until they see us?"

"Did you really slip a coin to that topper?"

Goll nodded.

"That might not work."

"I think it will." Goll's hands strayed to his crutches. "Because if it doesn't, we'll find that very same man who took my money and get it back. What do you say to that?"

It was something Halm could understand. "I can help with that."

"Good."

Halm hoped they would see the Chamber members soon. Pressure was building in his bladder, and there were fights to make money off.

He couldn't ignore either for long.

7

Men called him Sapo, which in Sunjan, meant "hill." He didn't think it a good name but recognized it as readily as his real name these days. He'd grown up swinging an axe and lugging fallen timbers over his shoulder. As he grew, the bigger the tree trunks he carried and the more power he got behind his axe. Somewhere along the expanding border of Nordun, he got into a fight with a lone Nordish warrior and split open his head with one swipe of his axe. Delighted with the kill of an invader, he ran home to inform his parents, only to find they had already been killed by three other Nordish soldiers. What happened after that was something he could no longer exactly recall, but he remembered coming out of a frenzy and standing amongst the hacked and unmoving bodies of the Nords.

He was sixteen at the time.

He traded in his wood axe for one properly suited for battle. His frame grew and expanded, and more muscle clung to his bones. He found work as a private killer of animals and men alike for Sunja's merchants, realizing early on that fighting the Nords, while satisfying, wouldn't be as profitable. A mercenary captain by the name of Bassu took him under his wing for a while, training him in the basics of sword and axe fighting, until an arrow from a Dezer horseman took his life. Seeing as the wilds surrounding Sunja could be an unpredictable place at best, yet not wanting to give up the skills he was sharpening, he had decided to do something a little more controlled.

Now twenty, he entered his first season in the games as a Free Trained. Standing before the portcullis and hearing the swelling energy of the crowd above, he was aware of the gatekeeper nearby but paid the old man little attention. Slabs of plate armor hung off his person. Heavy armor, but he wore it just as easily as a man wearing leather. His arms were bare as he couldn't find anything to cover them other than the spiked metal gauntlets, and those only came halfway down his forearms. His biceps were also mostly bare except for leather tiles worn as short sleeves that hung off his shoulders and protected only the upper part. His breathing sounded like the gasp of bellows, and he stared out at the world through a helmet that protected his cheeks and the rest of his head but left his mouth, nose, and eyes uncovered in a T.

He thought of his dying parents and just about any bad thing that had ever happened to him. Hate. Fear. Anger. Faces of men and women who had been stupid enough to challenge or taunt him. Sometimes, the drunkest people sought to fight him for no other reason than he was the biggest around at the time. The anger welled up inside him, bursting from a nugget deep inside, and powered his limbs until his very chest seemed to burst with it.

He heard the Orator call his name, and the portcullis opened to a slow cadence, sunlight dappling his mighty form.

Gripping his battle axe, the enraged Sapo rushed up the steps and outside, seeking to smash whoever was before him.

His fingers flexed on his broadsword, and he rolled the shoulder and arm carrying his shield. Vuille Ghor took a deep, calming breath and opened his mouth as wide as possible, feeling his jaw pop. Tall and muscular, with a deep chest and meaty shoulders, he carried the armor like a second skin and didn't feel the pot helm at all. It was his third season in the games, and he hoped to go farther than last year. Last year, he'd only made it to the second round when he was knocked out and spared by a club-wielding countryman from Northern Sunja, somewhere on the border with Marrn. A troll hunter by profession, Vuille had the opinion that his trade was becoming increasingly dangerous. There weren't too many men who wanted to see a troll these days, let alone hunt one down and slay it. It was work for Vuille, something he'd spent four years doing in between fighting in the Pit. The money was better in the games as he could wager on himself in addition to any gold won, and he was beginning to prefer seeing who he fought on open sands instead of dark, unknown terrain of any type, where a troll's claw might take one's head off in one quick swipe.

With his group of hunters, he'd killed six trolls total. He didn't fear the beasts, but it was wise to maintain a healthy dose of respect. The monsters were huge, towering over men, and immensely powerful. In the arena, he'd run up a record of five victories and three losses. The losses didn't bother him, but they had prevented him from advancing further in the tournament and thus earning more money. Gold was everything to him. To his family. His wife wanted him home more often, becoming increasingly worried about him risking his life in the troll-hunting trade. The games didn't suit her tastes either, but as Vuille reasoned, at least he could plead mercy with a pit fighter. His two daughters wanted him home as well. Only four and three, they were as pretty as their mother, and Vuille adored them. All he needed was perhaps two more seasons in the games and at the hunting. He'd have enough then to purchase a parcel of farmland. Thereafter, he intended to switch from trolls to something a little more manageable. Wild boars or rabbits perhaps. If times became tough, he might be persuaded to do a little bounty hunting for the occasional escaped prisoner.

He just needed two more seasons and the potential gold that came with it.

As the portcullis came up, Vuille looked up and saw blue framed in a stone archway at the end of the white tunnel. The Orator cried out his name, and he inspected his shiny mail shirt and tapped his pot helm with his sword. As always, before any fight or confrontation with a troll, he took a deep breath, wiping away any fear as effectively as a rag dusting off a tabletop. After years of hunting down trolls, not much bothered him anymore.

His thoughts on cutting down whoever opposed him on the arena sands, Vuille Ghor strode towards the light.

The sound of the crowds raked over him like beach rocks rattled by a retreating surf. He didn't look at the people but listened for the order to begin while sizing up the brute across the way from him. Vuille saw a man the height of himself but larger. Plate armor covered most of his body, with the exception of parts of his arms. Greaves protected his legs. The battle axe was different, however. Not many used the heavy weapon. And Vuille could see that the man's gauntlets were spiked. He'd have to be wary of those.

The thing that caught Vuille's attention was the shaking of his opponent. The pit fighter *quivered* in place, head trembling, shoulders heaving. He was even stomping on the sands like a bull about to charge. The crowds took notice as well and cheered. They sensed blood in the air.

Vuille sensed it too. He'd left the wilds and hunting trolls only to find one in the arena. Bright Seddon obviously had a plan, but Vuille had no idea what it might be.

"Let the match… begin!"

Vuille brought up his sword and shield, settling into a guard position as he moved forwards across the sands. The one called Sapo came head on, walking briskly and soon reaching the middle of the arena. Some trainers urged their fighters to take the middle ground quickly, in order to maintain a wide range of movement from the centre and to prevent their foes from trapping them against a wall.

Sapo broke into a jog now. The crowd's cheers grew louder. Vuille shook his head. A troll indeed. Armoured and swinging an axe. Seddon above. He got behind his shield and tensed to move, already anticipating cutting the legs out from the oncoming brute.

The last few feet separating them, Sapo roared and charged, sweeping his axe up over his shoulder.

But Vuille wasn't standing in the same place.

With practiced ease, the troll hunter stepped out of the way of the oncoming mass. With deadly intent, he sliced his sword across both knees of Sapo, feeling the clang of metal on metal. Vuille spun as he felt his blade rasp across the greaves, knowing he'd missed.

What he didn't expect was Sapo's speed.

Vuille saw the battle axe, blurred and double bladed, slicing for his head. He ducked reflexively, but Sapo's fist slammed into his head, torqueing it to the left and bringing black motes before his eyes. Sapo bellowed and thrust with the head of his axe, punching the off-balanced Vuille square in the chest and knocking him to the ground.

After that, nothing really mattered.

The one called Sapo hacked at the fallen Vuille and the crumpled metal of his helm, squashing the flesh still inside, all to the delight of the watching crowds. Grunting as if unhinged, Sapo continued hewing at the body in bloody arcs. A sword arm was taken off above the elbow. A foot jumped into the air. Then a leg. The head sprang from the man's shoulders with one mighty chop after Sapo realized he hadn't completed the job the first time around. Three startling strikes to the armoured torso of Vuille mashed the dead pit fighter into the sands. Only then did Sapo step back from his work and spread his arms in a V above his head. A scream of unbridled fury exploded from the man's throat, stabbing through the noise made by the onlookers. Men and women applauded in awe of the short but blood-drenched spectacle.

Then, realizing there was no one to fight, Sapo caught his axe mid-shaft and marched back to the opening portcullis, leaving the people marveling over the almost elemental power the man possessed. The storm that was Sapo appeared, killed his opponent, and having done that, wanted out of the Pit as soon as possible.

It was over much too quickly. But only after Sapo disappeared did the crowds wish for more.

High above it all, the Orator approved.

The day had started out piss poor, but it was shaping up nicely all the same.

8

After winning his fight, Pig Knot went and unloaded his weapons and armor at the feet of the quartermaster, either letting items drop or stripping them off as if they were diseased. He didn't impress the quartermaster, who took the equipment with a frown. Pig Knot knew he couldn't have seen the match, so he just believed the man was being a dog blossom. Pig Knot wanted nothing more to do with the Pit and only wanted to be free of it. Fighting was over for him. There were better things for him to do.

His clothes stained and smelling of sweat, sour wine, and even fear, Pig Knot pawed at them as he made his way from the general quarters of the Pit, avoiding the stares of the fighters there. From the corner of his eye, he saw three men pulling the body cart, which he knew was full by his hand. He stopped for a moment, watching the cart turn to wheel away from him, heading down a side tunnel to the fire pit, which would make short work of the remains.

Pig Knot stared until they were out of sight.

Later, he collected his winnings—twenty gold coins— from the paymaster, who eyed him distastefully from behind a barred window. Four Skarrs stood ready on either side, their backs to the wall and facing the fighter or any rising threat. In the disgusted mood he was in, Pig Knot actually considered starting a fight just to see if one of them might kill him, ending it all. He'd take it as a favour.

Snatching his money from the paymaster, Pig Knot walked away from the window and climbed the stairs back into the light. The sun struck him with its heat when he exited the Gate of the Moon, and for a moment, Pig Knot thought about what it must be like to perish in a fire. He pushed for the Domis, got caught up in the crowds pressing into the arena, and remembered he had never wagered on himself in the first place. That stopped him in his tracks, and he stood there, a rock in a river of people, with his hands on his hips and staring at the dusty ground between his feet.

It wasn't proving to be a good day.

It was his fault he had still been half-drunk when he fought, but he hadn't expected to face *another* drunkard. He didn't mean to kill him either, but what was done was done. He made a fist about the small leather pouch full of gold and decided that if he'd won it, he might as well make use of it, no matter how foul it felt.

But that was just now. Pig Knot knew that after a few pitchers of Sunjan gold, the mire he felt he wallowed in would fall away.

Mire.

Bathhouse. That was a right proper thought.

Not wanting company in the least, Pig Knot wandered past an open stall where a merchant sold wine by the clay bottle.

"Give me two of those," he told the merchant, a much smaller man than himself, escaping the sun by selling his wares underneath a wide canopy. He handed over two bottles as asked.

"How much?" Pig Knot asked.

"Two gold."

"Two gold. Gold," Pig Knot spat as he dug out the coins. "That's what I dislike about Sunja. These"—he held up the coins—"are only *pieces* here. The lands to the north call them *talons*. Something, eh? Sounds respectable. Valuable. And to the south, they're called *cutaros*. Hmm? Strikes me as something cultured. Here, what do we call them? The most uninspired, boring, *laziest* thing we could think of. Pieces. *Shite* comes in pieces. Seddon above. Here."

He slapped the coins down into the merchant's waiting hand. No sooner had he done that than he placed one bottle on the counter between them. The cork came out with a twist, and Pig Knot took a deep, mind-numbing pull of the bottle, holding it up and letting it empty into him as if it were the best thing in his life.

Or in his day, at least.

The merchant watched him with unimpressed eyes.

Pig Knot finished the wine with a gasp and left the bottle on the counter. He snatched the other one, popped the cork, and walked towards the bathhouse. For two gold pieces, he knew he could lounge in a public bath and relax until the sun dropped from the sky. He meant to drink as well and get his clothes washed and aired. If one could find a bench near the pool, sleeping was perfectly acceptable. The more he thought of the warm waters, the more he wanted them.

They might even wash away what he was feeling. They certainly couldn't do any wrong.

People crowded over the flat and rectangular quarried stone paving the streets. Pig Knot got through them all with the help of the second bottle and a forced smile. By the time he reached the bathhouse, the second bottle was gone, and he deposited the empty container into the hands of the attendant who took his gold in the main foyer. Two levels of carefully wrought stone, brick, and marble, with belowground piping and heating systems, Sunja's public bathhouses were a relaxing delight for anyone who had the coin. Thick coils of steam issued from the archway and floated through cracked-open windows constructed in regular intervals in the outer stonework. Long grey bandages of mortar, freshly applied, gummed up cracks in the building's shell.

"Any wine here?" Pig Knot asked gruffly, staring at one long tributary running almost the height of the wall.

The attendant, a younger man with a stick-like physique, blinked. "Some."

"Bring me two bottles of anything, and I'll pay you extra."

The fellow nodded, summoned yet another man from a side room, informed him of what to do, and sent him off. The first attendant then handed Pig Knot some rough towels. He took them without comment and proceeded into the steam.

The bathhouse. For a fee, any commoner could lavish in coarse opulence. Just breathing the hot air lifted his weary and sickened spirits. Pig Knot kicked off his boots in a side chamber lined with tiers of open lockers containing the outer wear of the current bathers. He chose a locker, stripped, and proceeded to the baths through veils of billowing steam, holding his towels. The marble flooring was moist and warm to his bare feet as he made his way to the bathing chambers.

There, he chose one of many large barrels filled with hot water and climbed in, submerging himself to his armpits. He scrubbed away the stink of the previous night and early afternoon with a washcloth and a cheap bar of scented soap. An attendant asked him if he wanted a woman or a man to massage him, but he turned down both. Anything beyond washing up would cost extra, and Pig Knot felt he should be try to be conservative, even though he knew he would spend his winnings before they burned through the bottom of his pouch. Once clean, he left the bathing chamber and its smells of soap and water and padded into the main heated pool. Overhead, a white ceiling was topped off with a glass dome that seemed in need of a scrubbing itself. Frolicking dolphins decorated the glass, while near the corners of the ceiling were dark, shuttered vents, which could be opened if needed. Flat white rock, chipped and fashioned into irregular shapes and wet from footprints, ringed a huge oval pool lined with marble that turned the water into a pleasant shade of turquoise. Steam rose from waters that rippled and lapped up against the pool's edges. Men relaxed in the water up to their chins, some appearing as mossy rocks while others' bald heads glistened. Pig Knot made his way to the steps and waded in, the depths hot enough to make him wince. He found a spot near the far end of the pool and caused ripples as he forded towards it. He didn't care who he pissed off by making waves—it was that kind of day.

He reached his spot and sat down, feeling his backside touch a smooth marble ledge. Heat. Heat soaked into his frame and took away his aches. He sputtered water, laid his head against the pool's edge, and closed his eyes. An attendant found him moments later and placed two bottles of wine near his head, informing him they were there in a whisper, so as to not disturb the other bathers. Pig Knot grunted, and that was that.

His skin tingling and adapting to the heat engulfing him, Pig Knot sighed contentedly and let the subtle lapping of water rock him into a doze. The wine waited for him, and he thirsted for it, but the pool was a seductive decadence that slowed time. Steaming water rose just above his chin, summoning sweat from his opening pores.

He was only distantly aware of someone sloshing down nearby, the ripples pushing the waterline above his lips. Voices just a touch louder than a whisper made him wrinkle his face at the intrusion. Public pools. If he could afford it, he would have paid to have one of the private tubs, away from the main one.

"Ah… good…" a voice rasped. "Just the thing."

The sound of it disturbed Pig Knot, and he mulled moving.

"Don't be sloshing the water about, you punce. There are other people about," the same voice said.

"Apologies, Toffer," said another.

"Just be glad Bar Bar isn't here. Can you imagine him? Dying Seddon. He'd be like a sick horse thrashing."

"Aye that."

The wrinkles about Pig Knot's closed eyes deepened. It seemed there would be no peace for him at all this day.

"Do you remember the time Bar Bar—"

"Why don't you boys be quiet?" Pig Knot asked, not bothering to open his eyes. "Or at least try to whisper."

The silence that answered him made him feel better. He'd gotten his point across.

"The punce wants quiet," a low voice growled to his right, the one belonging to Toffer.

"Maybe we should make it quiet for him?" another asked.

"Sounds like an idea," yet *another* voice said, this one coming from his left.

Three of them, all surly sounding. That made Pig Knot open his eyes.

Then he saw the fourth man, and all of them, two on either side, appeared none too friendly. They hunched forward like a band of crocodiles about to snap and drag him under the surface.

Pig Knot took in the threatening faces to his right, then his left. Perhaps one was as large as he, but the four of them all at once was far from favourable odds.

Still, he was having that kind of day, so he decided to try hard to not show any fear. Amongst dogs like these, fear would be deadly.

"Just the four of you? Thought there were more."

"Enough to slap you about some," one snarled. He had a mouth full of broken teeth.

As if I haven't been slapped around enough already, Pig Knot thought. "You want to fight me? Sign up at the Pit as a Free Trained, and we'll have at it. At least there we'll get some coin out of it. One of us will anyway."

That quieted them all.

"You a pit fighter?" the one called Toffer asked. Flecks of grey coloured his temples while the rest of his hair was short cropped and black. His eyes looked ancient, however.

"Aye that."

"Any good?"

Pig Knot frowned. "I can fight."

"But are you any good, I asked."

"I won my match this afternoon."

"Which one was that?"

"The first one."

The men exchanged glances. "You were the ball licker that killed that other pisser?" asked the one with the broken fangs.

That hurt. "Aye that," Pig Knot groaned quietly.

"That was a disgrace of a fight," said another. "Saw it. You both were begging to be ball slapped. Should've both died, in my eyes. Terrible."

"It was a bad fight," Pig Knot agreed.

"It wasn't bad; it was *shite*," said the brute with the teeth.

"Seen worse," mumbled the quietest of the four.

"The boys are right," Toffer said, eyeing Pig Knot. "I don't know what you were thinking, but that was a poor performance, and every last soul in the Pit knew it. I'm not so angry myself. I had coin on you, so I'm happy. But you…" He smiled evilly and indicated the wine. "I guess I'd be doing the same. Only more."

"A lot more," said the largest of the four.

"Enough to go blind," said Broken Teeth.

"How long you been doing this?" Toffer asked.

"Too long."

That admission made Toffer smirk. "What's your name?"

Pig Knot groaned inwardly. He should never have come to this place. He didn't have to give his name to these men, but he certainly didn't want the fight that would probably start otherwise.

"Pig Knot," he muttered in the end.

"Well, Pig Knot, I'll tell you what. Just because you made me some coin this morning, and only because of that, I'll let you go about your day as though it were any other. Let you drink as much wine or ale or whatever as you want to see if you can't wash away that taste of shite in your mouth, which you're no doubt tasting."

"My thanks," Pig Knot said drily.

Toffer spread his hands in a *don't mention it* gesture and then spoke to the others. "There it is, lads, to the other end of the pool. Let the man relax."

Like famished animals denied a meal, the three other warriors eyed Pig Knot reproachfully, making it very clear what they wanted to do to him.

But Pig Knot closed his eyes and tried hard to appear unbothered.

The sounds of them wading away, making waves, diminished in his darkness. Toffer's voice cut through when he ordered someone at the other end of the bath to move. Pig Knot didn't hear any protest. He cracked an eye and saw the steam made the far-off figures appear smoky, and that suited him just fine.

With one hand, he carefully reached up behind him and felt the curve of a bottle. He brought it back down, chewed out the cork, and drank until a third of the wine was gone.

Toffer sat and thought about the name of the fighter at the other end of the pool. He silenced the killers about him with a glance, not wanting their prattle to disturb him. There was opportunity here, and perhaps more than what Clades had given. All that was needed was to think of a way to go about it. He always did when it mattered the most.

9

The light in the foyer dimmed at an eternally torturous pace. When the bench became too much, Halm got up and walked around the room, sizing up the pictures etched upon the copper walls. Most were fights from the earlier days of the Pit, a time he didn't know. Some scenes depicted warriors battling beasts of war. One picture in particular caught his attention, that of a single fighter standing alone on a field awash in ruins of flesh, armor, and weapons. A grim feeling of satisfaction seized Halm. For him, that one image encapsulated the spirit of the games.

When he tired of the images, he tried to engage Goll in conversation. The man from Kree didn't feel the same way, only responding directly to questions, keeping his answers short if longer than a grunt, and never offering an opinion. After a while, Halm simply gave up. Goll had things on his mind and couldn't be bothered. The Zhiberian then wondered if Goll's ass was getting sore from sitting on the bench for so long. He didn't dare ask him. He was still just learning what was acceptable to the Kree. Pig Knot was different. Halm and the Sunjan joked all the time, and he knew what he could say to the man and what he couldn't.

Pig Knot knew him as well. Muluk, Halm thought, also had a sense of humor, which was good.

Goll didn't appear to have much of a sense of humor. If he did, he kept it choked off like a pisser's flow.

They waited long enough to see attendants come and go, as well as other well-dressed individuals, some of which Halm thought to be owners of lesser gladiatorial houses. They all entered and exited the inner doors, which led to the Chamber members. At times, the doors would open, and Halm looked up expectantly, knowing that *this* would be time to leave the foyer. The attendants leaving the room paid them no heed, however, and left both men to continue simmering like forgotten pots over a fire pit.

It was only when Halm thought about suggesting they leave and come back the next day that the door opened, and the attendant Goll had spoken with earlier motioned them to enter.

Goll struggled to his feet. Halm waited until he was ready and followed him in. He had no desire to speak with anyone of note. He had no tongue for it.

The Gladiatorial Chamber was uninspiring. After such a long wait, the drab stone walls set behind a semi-circular panel of red wood and raised above a cream-colour marble floor disappointed Halm, especially after the rousing ambiance of the entry foyer. The Chamber members sat behind the elevated panel and gazed down at them, appearing just as weary and hard as Halm's ass. Goll moved along on his crutches to a waist-high table where visitors stopped and addressed the Chamber members. There, he stood and regarded the nine men in turn. They were clothed in robes of gold and white and appeared quite regal. Some of them were balding while some had full heads of hair or beards leaking grey. Halm stepped up behind the Kree and stayed off to one side, within arm's reach in case Goll fell over. Not that he expected the slayer of Baylus to do so. He turned halfway around and eyed the attendant standing near the doors behind them all. He also made note of the six Skarrs against the walls. He always made a point to know where everyone was in a room.

"Chamber members." Goll spoke in Sunjan with a slight accent. "Thank you for granting me this moment to speak with you. I will not take much of your time. My companion and I have business to discuss with you all."

This was answered with silence and eyes that glowered back. Halm secretly prayed to Seddon that the Kree *would* be brief. The Chamber members possessed a venerable fierceness about them. If Goll did take too much time, they'd probably give the Skarrs the word to remove them both from the room. Forcefully, if needed.

Don't prattle on, Halm willed into Goll, hoping he picked up the thought.

"I am from Kree, and I have trained with the Weapon Masters there to compete in Sunja's tournament of arms. I'm with no house in Sunja. My companion also belongs to no such house. In your eyes, we are Free Trained gladiators, trained by unrecognized men, and have freely chosen to enter the games. Our skill is questionable, as are our reasons for being in the arena, but our hearts are strong. What I wish to do this day is create my own house. My own stable. Made up of Free Trained pit fighters who wish to rise above their station, their class, and become fully backed fighters seeking the ring of the arena. The title of champion. To do this, I must have your approval, and I'm willing to do what is necessary for my vision to become reality. What is it I have to do?"

Silence. Long, *uncomfortable* silence, as the men sat above them regarded them as talking oddities.

Halm looked from Goll to the Chamber members and craned his neck to check on the Skarrs.

"You say your name is Goll?" the voice of one of the men finally rumbled, startlingly loud in the stillness.

"I am."

"And you're from the Weapon Masters of Kree?"

"I am."

The speaker leaned back in his chair. His hair and beard were cut short but grey, and Halm suspected him to be the oldest. He also saw the man's right ear was missing. The Zhiberian wondered if he ever got the sensation it was still there.

"I visited the Weapon Masters of Kree several years ago," the speaker said. "Watched them train about thirty of their whelps. I wasn't impressed."

Goll's back stiffened ever so slightly.

"But I'm not surprised one of their hellpups has made to it our games to participate. To try their luck. I wonder what your... *masters* would say if they knew you were here? Bowing down to us. Asking for permission to establish a foothold in great Sunja. That amuses me. You've put a smile on my face this day and given my companions quite the subject for conversation once you're gone."

Halm didn't think that sounded so good.

One Ear paused for a moment and sized up the Kree before him. The other members leaned in like jackals waiting for a bite of something taken down by the pack leader.

"I know what they would say. The Weapon Masters of Kree would choke if they saw you now. Here. Asking for such a thing. It's not their way to do things." One Ear cleared his throat with effort, his face turning somewhat red. He smirked then, baring teeth that lit up half of his grizzled features in a sour light. "Yes, they would paddle your balls, I imagine, if they knew you intended to do such a thing. You see, I *know* those men. I know their arrogance. If you were sent here, you were probably sent with their blessings of war. Expected to… *dazzle* us all with your skills. No doubt expected to win it all. Looks to me that you had the shite pounded out of you on the first try. Imagine that, a disciple of the Weapon Masters of Kree being beaten, being punished, so soundly."

The rest of the Chamber members smiled in contempt.

"I wasn't defeated," Goll said quietly.

"From here," One Ear stretched out an arm, "it looks you were."

"I killed Baylus the Butcher."

"Ah. I saw that match. Yes, I did. Well fought." The sarcasm dripped and scalded. "Well, with the fighting season only lasting two months, I think it's safe to say you're eliminated from champion contention. Weapon Master."

Halm raised his chin. Old One Ear did not think much of the fabled group of taskmasters and trainers from Kree.

"What is it you're taught? Hmm?" One Ear cleared his throat once more. "When faced with defeat, do the unexpected? Well, this certainly is the unexpected. Rousing the rabble underfoot. Inciting the gurry. What is it you hope to achieve by doing this?"

"To offer a place for any Free Trained to ply their skills, like a regular school."

One Ear smirked and shook his head. "I don't think so. That's what you're telling me and that brute next to you, but I don't believe you. You see, I learned a bit about the

Weapon Masters' art of deception."

One Ear held up an open hand and fluttered it. "See, this is dangerous, this one here. Pay no mind to this," he said as he raised his left fist. "The trouble with the Weapon Masters is that they *believe* their tricks are still new. Still magic. They're *not*. The world has moved on. Learned."

One Ear leaned back and studied Goll then, searching his face and thinking deeply.

"No matter to me," he finally said. "You wish to establish a house here? A stable? I'll recommend to my esteemed companions here to accept your request."

One by one, the other Chamber members nodded.

One Ear cleared his throat again, making a horrible noise that even made Halm feel a twinge of disgust. "I see it's unanimous. You have the Gladiatorial Chamber's permission to start your house."

Goll smiled.

"On condition…" One Ear raised his rattling voice as if he badly wanted to cough. "On condition that you pay the fee to register your house. Pay the fee, and you may hang your flag, so to speak. Whoever you have under your name may continue fighting as a gladiator representing your house, provided he has not been eliminated. If he has, well, any additional fights taken are non-tournament matches. Good practice, but just as deadly. Those are the terms. Though it's quite unusual to set up a school during a season. Quite unusual."

"How much do you want?" Goll asked stoically.

"A thousand gold," One Ear said, saying it as if it were no great sum. It was great enough to make Halm widen his eyes in disbelief.

"A thousand," Goll repeated. "Anything else?"

One Ear shook his head, suppressing a cough.

"I may bring it to you anytime?"

"Anytime. I doubt your Weapon Masters are so lenient."

Goll appeared to think it over. "Then we are done. Thank you for hearing us."

One Ear dismissed them with a hand as if it were nothing. Halm felt as if he had been paddled by a maul. A *thousand* gold to enter the games as a house? Games that had already started? That amount of coin would give him a new life anywhere but here. All that money just to be recognized as a—

Goll turned about and briefly met his eyes, indicating it was time to leave.

Halm kept quiet, but he swore he heard the low rumblings of laughter on their way out, and the doors were closed behind them. Not even the Chamber thought it possible to get that amount of coin. Not amongst Free Trained warriors. By the time they got outside, Halm couldn't believe he'd kept his dismay suppressed. Every step away from the Chamber seemed to increase the disbelief of what had to be done just to be *recognized* amongst the other houses.

The nearby arena was silent, the fights done for the day, yet some people still hung about the walls. Goll said nothing to Halm, seemingly content to just lead him into the milling crowds of the streets. Halm waited for something from the man, feeling it wasn't prudent to speak while still so close to the Chamber building, but as they walked deeper into the crowds, away from general quarters, Halm's impatience swelled until it nearly burst.

"Wait." He made Goll stop on his crutches. "What are you going to do now?"

Goll studied him for a moment. "We have work to do."

"What?"

"We have to get that coin for the Chamber."

"You can't do it."

Goll's eyes narrowed. "I can do anything. You heard them. They don't expect anything from a group of Free Trained fighters. They certainly don't expect much from me. We're all beneath them. Nothing more than children playing at something meant for men. Well, we're going to prove them wrong. So *very* wrong. We're going to get what they want and *more*, and you'll be there to see their faces drop."

"You're unfit." Halm was horrified by what he was hearing. "In the head."

"Not at all. I'm *determined*. I'm going to bring back that fee and watch that one-eared bastard choke on his tongue. I've already told you what I intended to do. Why are you doubting me now?"

Halm stood and stared. "It's the gold."

"The gold is nothing. I can have that in…" He thought about it. "One or two weeks. No more than two."

"You *are* unfit. Where are you going to get it?"

"Where do you think? Come now, Halm. Think for a moment. Where can I get that amount of coin? Certainly not from winning my matches. And I won't steal it. So where?"

Halm thought about it. The only place that came to mind… "You mean to gamble," he muttered in disbelief. "The juice of Saimon's balls, I'll have no part of that."

"Listen to me," Goll insisted, leaning in close and glancing around. "Listen. I'm going to gamble with *my* coin. Not yours, so rest easy on that. If you want to throw in, that's your decision. I'm already working on building up our pot. There's no magic involved. It's just a study of the fighters before they step out onto the sands, knowing their history, their opponents, and their strengths and weaknesses. Know all of that, and a wager is as good as won. The gold is already yours."

"Not always."

"Not always," Goll granted him that. "No. But I'm not going to throw all of my coin into one single wager either. I'm more careful than that. Any loss will be absorbed. But you don't have to worry about any of that. If you want to be a part of this, you only have to do three things. Fight, win, and guard my back. Can you do that?"

Halm thought about it. "I think I can do two of those."

"Really? I need to know now if you are with me or not. This is what we both want. You want more than just fighting from season to season, and this is it. A chance to be a part of something grander without having to bend your knee to any of the toppers ruling their own houses. You would be a founder of a house just by doing those things I asked. After that, anything more you can give is up to you. Chances like these don't often appear. They aren't commonplace."

"I just turned down one of those chances."

"To fight for *another's* house? To further *their* name? You're smarter than that, Halm. *We're* smarter than that. Not only that, think of the stab to the guts we will give them all if we do it. No one considers any Free Trained to be of worth to anyone, but they secretly think *some* of us are worth something. Think of how *rankled* the houses will be if we rise above them and prove them wrong. Just establishing a new house that will take in Free Trained and train them even further. Into champions. It can be done. That picture alone is enough to make me do whatever I can. I want the dogs to rise, Halm. To *rise*. And to latch on to the hands feeding them bloody scraps."

Halm stood before the Kree, thoughts swirling in his skull and settling on none. He rubbed his jaw and mouth, glaring at Goll, who returned it and waited. People passed them.

"Can you do this?" Goll asked him. "If you don't think you can, I will find others who will."

Feeling the heat rise up his neck and into his face, the Zhiberian screwed up his face and looked around. Could he do such a thing? It seemed insane, and to start on this road while the games were in progress… Then thoughts from another time entered his head: he was getting older, and after the games, he had nowhere else to go. No trade to fall back on. Like it or not, he was nothing outside of the arena. Just another brute with a blade going through the days like pitchers of cheap wine… until he died.

Or until he tossed a spear into the crowds and got dragged out of the arena on meat hooks.

Halm sighed and locked gazes with the Kree. "All right."

To his surprise, Goll gave him a little, satisfied smile. "Good."

He held out a closed fist. Halm considered the gesture and eventually pressed the hand with his own, almost pushing Goll over. The Kree righted himself on his crutches.

"We have work to do," Goll told him. And with that, he swung past Halm's bulky frame and got walking. Halm watched him for a moment, and then he followed.

The pair of men walked off then, cutting through the masses and heading deeper into the city while sunset burned the sky orange and the smells of cooking meats and spices hung in the air, thick enough to make them both long for just a taste.

And from one side of the busy street, a man watched them go.

And eventually followed.

10

Grey Beard's name was Borl Grisholt, of the Stable of Grisholt, and after leaving the Gladiatorial Chamber, he quietly fumed all the way back to his residence outside the walls of Sunja. He rode in the back of a brown koch pulled by a team of four horses. Fancy red cloth decorated the cabin's interior, and Grisholt idly picked at cushioning worn with age while looking out at the passing landscape. In his other hand was a bottle of Sunjan mead, and the drink did little to placate him. He measured the passing country with sips and glares, wanting it all to go up in flame. It wasn't often than Grisholt got into such a fury, but that fat Free Trained lout had gotten the best of him—in front of his lads, no less. And a Zhiberian, at that. Barbarians all, hardly worth his time, but the insolence of the bastard stuck in his craw like a meat hook. It was enough to brand the face of the one called Halm in his mind's eye. He'd instructed one of his men to stay behind and find out where the man slept, but Grisholt guessed the wretch probably slept in the Pit's general quarters with the rest of the stray dogs.

Still, he was going to make it his hobby to find out more about Halm of Zhiberia.

Try as hard as he might, Grisholt didn't have a great selection of fighters in his stable this year. In fact, for three years now, Grisholt had struggled to keep his house in order and pay off his debts, all while cultivating what he hoped would be champion stock, or at least fashion a fighter notable enough to elevate his name in the arena circles. His father had much more success back in his day, yet times had changed. The competition had grown, become fiercer. His father's greatest fear when he was alive was actually living long enough to see what Borl would do with the stable. During some of their heated exchanges on the future of the family business, Borl had challenged the older man, vowing that he'd "see." In the end, however, the older Grisholt died of a fever at sixty-eight. And he died quite right about his worries.

Grisholt had taken over the stable, keeping the name intact when all others were changing theirs to "houses." The first year was a good one. He didn't win an arena championship, yet he placed high enough that he didn't lose his standing in the rankings and almost got invited into the owners' viewing box, the place held in high esteem for all in the business. An average showing saw him slip in the rankings the following year, and from then on, it seemed Grisholt only barely managed to hold on. His fighters were average, the victories balanced by an equal number of losses, and his fortune dwindled. His taskmasters tried to prepare the fighters as best they could, but only so much could be done with the stock they possessed. Prized warriors got killed unexpectedly when Grisholt thought they would be the names with talent to win it all. He placed wagers on his own and others, consistently winning and losing enough to make him wonder enviously at how other managers did so well. What was he missing? There was coin to be had wagering on the Free Trained, but their mettle was spotty, unknown most times, and carried a high risk. It was better to wage coin on the house gladiators whose abilities, weaknesses, and strengths were known or could be learned.

The coach bumped its way along the main road until it made a short turn. It rattled towards a walled compound with its stony hide reared up against a small forest. Creepers veined the wall, almost completely hiding the red brick, while apple trees stood in front with crooked majesty. The weathered gates opened, and the hinges squealed, for Grisholt was unable to spare the grease. He knew two of his own gladiators manned the gates as he could no longer afford the extra servants. The cook was a necessity, so Grisholt still employed one, but the rest were gone. He didn't even have any women serving him. The thought of Dark Curge having his way with the veritable harem at his beck made Grisholt's bile bubble. Then there was half-faced Gastillo with his golden mask and womanly hand towels; the image of him dabbing at that wreck of a mouth made Grisholt shake his head. After that came Nexus the wine maker, lowering himself to the level of the games just so he could see a bit of blood. Grisholt really didn't know much about the man personally, other than that he'd made all of his coin being a shrewd merchant of wine and other valuables, unlike Curge and Gastillo, who were both former gladiators. It wasn't so unbearable that a merchant owned a house of pit fighters, but what rankled him the most was that the man was rumoured to press his beliefs that Curge and Gastillo *didn't* know what they were doing and that it would only take a merchant with an astute sense of value and proven business skills to rule the games. Grisholt even heard from his spies that what truly annoyed the old guard was that Nexus was actually proving himself to be *right*.

The koch door opened, and his one-eyed henchman, Brakuss, stood waiting. Grisholt regarded the man for a moment. Powerfully built, he'd been one of the stable's prime fighters until one stroke from a blade robbed him of his left eye, ending his career. Though still as menacing as one of Saimon's underworld hellions, to send him into the Pit crippled as he was would result in a loss. Still, the man stayed for merely lodgings and food and, in turn, served as a bodyguard, for which Grisholt could do no better. Brakuss had no problem slapping someone if ordered or of his own volition. In fact, it wasn't a problem at all for him to *start* brutalizing someone; the problem lay in getting him to *stop*.

Grisholt sighed and finished his Sunjan mead, gnashing his teeth as the last swallow went down. He got up, swayed slightly before grabbing the frame, and stepped down.

Home again.

"When that weasel Caro arrives, bring him to me right away." Grisholt stroked his beard and moved inside his house. He considering walking about the open grounds and seeing how training was progressing, but at this point in time, with a bottle of mead in his system, he decided not to. If only he could afford the firewater… yet the fabled alcohol was far too rich for him these desperate days.

He ignored the places in his walls where the mortar crumbled, the dust collecting on the floors, and the cobwebs hanging in the corners, and proceeded to the wine cellar. Though he barely had enough gold to keep his head afloat, he did have the foresight to make certain that Marrok, his cook, was also versed in wine and ale making. Marrok didn't have time to cultivate grapes, but ale was a different matter.

And while apples grew about his property and could be pressed and fermented into cider, Grisholt could not afford the labour to harvest the fruit. Still simmering with dark thoughts, he went into the larder, found three sealed bottles on the shelves where Marrok kept the finished drink, and took them all.

From there, he wove his way through his household, knowing that the roof overhead leaked in places when it rained. He arrived at his study, which had once been his father's before him. Tomes of history and poetry filled the shelves covering three walls, not that he read any of it. History was depressing to recall, and poetry was simply painful. He wandered behind his desk and dropped into in a large padded chair, the green cloth material every bit as frayed as everything else in the room. There he stayed, directly across from an oil painting depicting a small warship on a flat sea, steering into a sun being swallowed by the horizon. Grisholt knew he was drinking far more than he could afford and staring at that painting far more than he should, as if it might reveal some sorcerous path to profits. Though his window, between a set of shelves, was shuttered closed, he could still hear the calls of the trainers as they carried out the taskmaster's overseeing will, honing the warriors to the best of their ability.

But it wasn't enough, Grisholt's mind whispered. That made him pop the cork on the bottle and drain a third of it. He thought back to his exchange with the Zhiberian. That one had balls, to be sure. It was unfortunate that he was a Free Trained bastard and also unfortunate he'd gotten on Grisholt's bad side, adding further poison to a venomous day. He'd gone to petition the Chamber for funds, willing to agree to any interest, just to keep his stable going until he could get a few victories this season. That they refused him was really no surprise. The Chamber was as reputable and sly as bankers, but only for awarding and collecting—not loaning. And Grisholt was at the end of his credit.

Halm was only a fart in a summer storm, yet he drifted across Grisholt's nose at the very worst time.

Zhiberian shite.

And to actually insult him in front of his men! The memory of the exchange cut him freshly again. That was something he couldn't allow. His conscience would not permit the slight to go unanswered. Grisholt's very *name* depended on him doing something to the Zhiberian. The question was… *what?*

There, in the receding light, Grisholt sat and simmered and drank. Marrok brought him his supper, and the servant gave him a hard eye for taking all of the ale. Grisholt ate the stew, which seemed mostly juice and gristle with a few chopped vegetables tossed in. He left the empty bowl on the desk, pushed aside as though a dog had slopped it up. Back in his father's day, women flaunting exquisite figures would have been serving him. Not now.

Grisholt sighed. Now he had shite, and he was on the verge of losing even that.

He became aware of how much time had passed when he heard the shades come through the door, one carrying a torch. Their entry alerted him that it was night and he'd been mulling in the growing dark.

Grisholt didn't even have the coin to buy oil for the lamps anymore.

"Yes?" He despised the drunken slur in his own voice.

"Caro is here," Brakuss announced, his face orange from the flame.

Caro edged past the bigger man and slipped into sight. He'd been a fighter himself at one time, but unlike Brakuss, age had slowed him. His skills were still there, but against a younger opponent, he'd be sliced up the middle and garnished with his own guts.

"Master Grisholt," Caro greeted.

Grisholt reached for a bottle of ale but knocked it over. It clattered on his desk, but nothing came out. Grisholt frowned. He'd forgotten he drank it all a moment ago, but at least he didn't lose any.

"What did you find out?" he croaked.

"Their names are Halm of Zhiberia and Goll of Kree. The Kree was the same one who killed the Butcher of Balgotha. The pair is looking to establish their own house. It seems the Chamber asked for a thousand gold pieces as a fee to do so, and if they pay it, they can introduce whoever they have with them as belonging to their house. This I learned from one of the attendants who was there, listening in on it all."

Grisholt winced. "How much did that cost?"

"Nothing," Caro said with a stony air. "It saved him from having both his arms broken."

"Excellent. You certainly have a style about you. Doesn't he, Brakuss?"

"He does," the once-gladiator said.

"Go on." Grisholt tugged on his beard.

"They went into the city afterwards and stopped at an alehouse. The cripple did most of the talking, it seemed. The fat man did little except stand there and scowl."

"The Zhiberian."

Caro nodded. "I followed and eventually got close enough to hear they'll be looking for a taskmaster. And trainers. And a place to work from. Seems they want to get out of general quarters."

"Don't blame them for that," Brakuss muttered and earned a hard silencing look from Grisholt.

"The one named Goll already knows of two names," Caro continued, "Thaimondus and Clavellus."

"Thaimondus and Clavellus," Grisholt repeated. "Thaimondus won't be bothered with them. They're beneath him. And he's retired. Clavellus is also retired. That one had a falling out with Curge of all people. Was practically run out of the city for crossing him. He won't go back for fear of that bastard's wrath."

Grisholt leaned back in his chair. "Thaimondus. He *might* be bought though, for the right price. If this pair can afford to establish a house…"

That notion made him sit up. "How can they afford a thousand gold? Where are they getting it? Or better yet, where are they keeping it?"

The pair of men before him had no answers.

"What else did you learn?" Grisholt asked anxiously, tugging firmly on his whiskers.

"That was all. I had to go back to question the attendant before he left for home. Then I rode here. Practically killed my horse."

"Good man, good man." Grisholt sat and mulled, trying to fight off the ale numbing his brain. *A thousand gold.* "They wouldn't be asking for taskmasters if they couldn't afford one. That means they have something somewhere. They have coin. Coin, lads. Those Free Trained bloods o' bitches have *coin* hidden somewhere. Not a bank. Too cumbersome to leave it in a bank, especially if they're wagering. So the question is…"

Caro looked at Brakuss.

"Where could they be hoarding it, I wonder?" Grisholt gazed at the painting draped in shadows. "Where could they? They're probably confined to general quarters, and I can't see a pot like that being kept secret amongst those dogs for long. So where is it?"

Neither Caro nor Brakuss answered.

Taking a deep breath, Grisholt pointed at Caro. "In the morning, I want you to find exactly where these toppers are and follow them. If they stop at a shite trough, I want you to hand them the scrub brush for their cracks. Understood?"

Caro nodded.

"Find out where they go and where they are staying if they aren't in the bowels of the Pit, and keep me informed of the situation, especially if they go to either Clavellus or Thaimondus. Use any other contacts or scum if you have to. A thousand gold would make... a very large difference in the existence of our stable. If you find anything and need extra arms, let Brakuss know. He'll take a few of the lads out to deal with any situation. Stay away from the Skarrs, and..." Grisholt paused, releasing his beard.

"We might be able to profit from this information. Just might... Seddon's black hanging fruit, this is excellent news. Well done, Caro. Very well done. Keep at them. Sniff them out and stay in the shadows. Don't move on anything unless I say."

"I understand."

"Brakuss. Do we have any lads who might be up for a little blood work if needed? And it probably will be needed. Those dogs won't let any funds go for nothing. They'll fight. Pick six or seven who aren't concerned with spilling blood outside of the Pit, and keep them close."

Brakuss nodded.

"Wonderful news boys, wonderful news." Grisholt beamed. "I can almost feel the tides of fortune swinging in our favour. There isn't anything quite like pounding a pair of dog blossoms into the dirt and taking what's theirs. A *thousand* gold pieces."

In the torchlight, Grisholt's wet smile glittered.

11

In the alehouse alcove that had become their meeting place and den, Halm, Goll, and Muluk, only now recovering from the night before, sat and talked. The night deepened outside, and the air within the building warmed up as farmers, merchants, drinkers, and even a few warrior types filled up the space and tables. Laughter, shrill and low, pierced the low din of conversation, but the three men sitting around the table barely heard it.

"You're both insane." Muluk shook his head. The thickening stubble about his chin only made him appear meaner, darker. "That's a thousand gold you're talking about. A *thousand*. You can't just yank that out of your ass."

"Maybe his ass." Halm indicated Goll. "He seems to think it isn't much at all."

"I understand it's a lot of coin." Goll's voice grated. "And I didn't say I'd get it tomorrow. But if we gather what we have, I'll start wagering it—"

"That's the fishhook I was waiting for," Muluk interrupted his countryman. "You want me to put into this?"

Goll regarded him, visibly checking his growing annoyance. "You were quick to throw in with us a moment ago. Any venture is a gamble. This one is no less. Don't worry about your money. Just give me what you can afford, even if it's just a piece, and I'll make it work. I know how to gauge fighters."

Muluk winced. "This puts me out. I'm not even in the regular tournament now. Been put out by this one here." He chopped a hand at Halm. "Best I find something else."

"Didn't you once say you could hammer out armour?" Goll asked.

Muluk blinked at him. "Aye, but—"

"But what? Can you repair armour?"

Muluk shrugged. "I can, but—"

"And you certainly can put an edge to a blade."

"Yes, but—"

"But what?"

"But if you'll let me get the words out, you cut-up he-bitch, I'll answer you." Muluk snapped, glowered, and shook his head in exasperation at Halm. The Kree took a moment to compose himself. "I grew up around an armourer, yes, but that was a long time ago, and I've only done the easy work. Nothing like actually fashioning a chainmail shirt— which is damned *boring*, I'll have you know—or fitting a man for armour. And it all takes time. I'd need a smithy and then a person or two to help."

"You'll have them."

"What?"

Even Halm blinked at Goll.

"You'll have them. Once I've set the House up, we'd need to have a proper weapon smith and armourer. Can't use the weapons of the Pit after that. Most only take them from the armory because they don't have their own. We can use them in the *meantime*, until we can afford our own, but not for long. All other house fighters have their own weapons, and so shall we. We won't be any different."

"I can't make weapons."

"You can still put an edge to a sword?"

Muluk closed his eyes in resignation and gave the barest of nods.

"Then you have a place amongst us. Until we can find someone better. You can even fight in the matches that aren't in the tournament if you like. Not something I'd want you to do. You'd be as useless as a rock to us if you lost a limb or were killed outright. You're more valuable now, unhurt. So are you with us?"

Appearing as if in agony, Muluk rubbed the side of his face and nodded.

"You give your word?" Goll persisted.

"I don't want to give you my word."

"I'd feel better if you did."

"I'm *not* giving my word. I want to be able to leave if I have to."

That didn't impress Goll. "Are you sure you're from Kree? I'm starting to have suspicions."

"As am I."

"Look," Halm broke in, "this is all well and fine, but we do have one problem. We still don't have a place to do all this. We can't use general quarters. We'll be laughed out of the Pit."

"I have a few ideas on that," Goll said. "We'll take the trip to this Clavellus tomorrow. I've been told he's the closest. His land is east of here, within a day, and I have directions to get there. If he'll be our taskmaster, we'll take him. If not, we'll go southwest the next day and visit Thaimondus. Either one of them may have an idea of where we might set up the training area, if not on his property itself."

"And if they both turn you down?" Muluk asked skeptically. "I'm not so sure about a couple of names thrown at you for a coin by some half-drunk bastard in a tavern."

"I don't like this damn attitude of yours," Goll informed him.

"Well, let me have a little more Sunjan Gold and see me later."

Goll ignored that. "My information is correct. Halm was there when I double-checked it with other patrons. And if the taskmasters both turn us down, then we'll have to find property for ourselves. That's when it'll get difficult as it'll probably be outside the city and beyond the bluff. We'll have to stake it or buy it, which doesn't please me either way, as it'll take away time we could be using for other things like training and wagering on fights. If we're truly unlucky, we'll have to build it from the bottom up. But we'll have to be prepared to do so, even if it means not competing in the games any further."

"That's more sensible," Halm stated. "Next year might be the right idea. I think there's just too much to be done in such a short time. The season's only about sixty days, you know."

"Next year?" Muluk repeated. "You've never held a hammer before, have you? If we have to build it, it'll take longer than a year. It's no house we're talking about. And what about the others?"

"Who?" Goll asked back.

"The *others*. Right now, it's only you, me and him."

"And Pig Knot," Halm added.

"Did you ask him about this?"

"Not yet. Waiting to see where he is."

"Well, he won his fight this day," Goll reported pensively.

"He could be anywhere then. Probably drunk. And with a woman in each arm as well." Halm smiled. "Pig Knot knows how to celebrate."

"I'm not so certain I want him with us on this." Goll eyed Halm frankly.

"What? Why?"

"I saw his fight. Granted, he won, but it wasn't anything to be proud of. Both fighters looked to be drunk at the time. It was, in fact, the worst fight I've ever witnessed. It was *that* bad. He didn't impress me in the least."

"He was probably hung over." Halm's smile withered when he saw the seriousness on Goll's features.

"Hung over. That proves my suspicion right there. He was drinking the night before his match. What kind of man does that?"

"I do," Halm answered.

"I do too," said Muluk. "Or did."

Goll was momentarily speechless. "Well, no longer. You won't see any of the house fighters doing such a thing because the taskmaster and trainers would kill them for it. That's one part of your lives you'll both have to give up. Not you, Muluk, so you can shut your hole now, unless you do happen to try for one of the non-tournament fights. But you, Halm, you're still in the tournament. No more drinking the week of your fight."

"Sometimes we don't know if we're to fight from day to day."

"Rarely happens, I expect. And even then, it's probably because someone else can't fight. The Madea, if he's professional, is supposed to check his matches the day before, but he should be planning fights a week in advance. We'll check with him and the schedule every morning. I'm certain the other houses do it, and so will we."

"They get advance warning," Muluk said.

"And why is that?"

Muluk paused for a moment, thinking. "Because they're houses."

Goll nodded in satisfaction. "Good. Nice to see you can think."

That made the other Kree scowl.

"Pig Knot'll want to be with us," Halm said. "I know he will."

"I'm not so sure."

"He will. Guaranteed."

Goll didn't answer right away. "I'll think about it, but I don't care for the idea. That man's reckless. Sloppy. Unless he can offer something off the sands perhaps."

"I'll talk to him." Halm scratched his bare belly.

"Perhaps it's best you do…" Goll trailed off.

In another part of the city, Pig Knot staggered along back alleyways, kept upright only by the wall pressing against his right shoulder. His reality swam and lurched up and down and side to side. The quarried flat stones seemed to warp and ripple like the waters of an open bay on a moon-bright night. Voices swirled about him, sounding like gibberish, and for a moment, he placed his cheek against the surface of the wall and just breathed in the sour air of the city.

Drank too much. *Much* too much. He should be dead. *Wished* for death. Or at least a place to piss. He remembered the men in the pool. They'd left him alone for the rest of his time there, but he was certain they were keeping an eye on him, lurking in the dark. Even when he got up to leave, they talked to him, watched him, which bothered him more than he cared to admit, even with the spirits steeling him.

He had gold left on him but not as much as when he started. Two gold coins were in the right pocket on his trousers and one in his left. The trousers felt damp, for a bathhouse attendant had cleaned and hung them out to partially dry while Pig Knot became progressively drunker. His white shirt had been washed and cleaned as well, but that would probably change sooner or later this night. Pig Knot planned on throwing up at least twice more before the dawn, and in his experience, when it happened, *wherever* it happened, a few drops were bound to splash him somewhere.

He stood there, cheek seemingly fastened to the brick, gasping like a fish and enjoying the coolness of the wall. It grounded him, and he became aware of people going by, shadows in a shadowy place, and laughter echoing and sounding as if he were several feet underwater. Dying Seddon, he'd drunk *far* too much this night.

But he had two coins in his pocket to buy more. The left coin, when he was ready, would afford him a room for the night somewhere. He liked to save a little just for that exact thing.

"Can't stay here," Pig Knot mumbled to himself, gasped for air, and pushed away from the wall. He felt as if he was falling for a moment, and his hand flashed out to catch something.

Missed.

He hit the road with a bone-jarring thud, his jaw

snapping and biting his own tongue hard enough to draw blood. He got his arms out in time, so he didn't break his face, which would only have added more insult to injury. Pig Knot grunted and just lay there, thinking himself unhurt but drunk enough to lie in the alley and feel the pulse of the flat stones covering the road. Someone kicked his shin.

"Move on," Pig Knot slurred, warning his attacker. More laughter, more voices, but he ignored them, and tasted grit and blood. He spat and breathed in, feeling more dust go up his nose.

"Errrg," Pig Knot twisted his face up and rolled onto his back. He sat up slowly, baring his teeth at the end, and sat in the street for another moment. The grit and dust in his mouth made him spit and wipe his face, and he grimaced when he saw his palm was darker than usual. It took him a moment to realize he'd bitten his tongue, but at least he didn't piss himself. That was all he needed. The final touch and insult.

Someone nudged his shoulder with a knee and got a grumble from him. That contact got him moving. He stood unsteadily and took in a deep lungful of air. That helped him a bit, and he stepped forward, seeking more drink.

He didn't stagger far.

Lanterns lit the entryway to an alehouse, and the sounds of laughter and conversation pulled Pig Knot in. The building seemed to have only two levels, and garish green-and-orange banners hung from the eaves overhead. He walked up a short series of steps to a worn landing and stopped on the threshold, placing his shoulder against the frame and peering inside. Men and women stood and sat, mingled and drank. Smells of fresh breads and meat caught his attention, as did several people drinking at what looked to be a very long bar. Women tossed their heads back and flaunted striking figures while the men crowded them with lecherous smiles and conversations. People drank deeply of flagons and bottles while more such containers jigged behind a fence of heads and shoulders, being carried off somewhere. A platter of roasted pork steamed by, and Pig Knot felt his stomach come to attention.

The room sucked him onto the main floor. Good times were being had here.

And he was all for having good times.

Some of the people parted for him, and he smiled back with a drunkard's politeness, not recognizing the puzzlement on their faces. In Pig Knot's wine-soaked mind, they were in awe of him, as they should be. He could be damned handsome when he had clothes on. The mass of people continued to get out of his way until the bar revealed itself to him. He reached it like a swimmer who'd gone a very, very long distance. He placed his elbows on the dark wooden surface, swung his head about, and rapped knuckles to get the barkeeps' attention. All three of them seemed to notice him, as did some of the patrons standing around.

Pig Knot forced his best smile at them all to ease their minds. Aimed the same smile at a few lovely women nearby and even winked at a comely one with dark hair. She frowned and whispered in another woman's ear.

Unfazed, Pig Knot thought to greet his neighbours.

"Fine night," he slurred to a man nearby, who shook his head and showed his back.

"Fine then," Pig Knot said simply. He had better things to do as well, but he wasn't about to do them if he couldn't catch the attention of the barkeeps. Across the way, brass flagons and pitchers filled with goodness only Seddon knew about gleamed and teased and were handed to others. Just watching the exchanges made him all the more thirsty.

"You there," Pig Knot called out to the nearest barkeep. "I've got coin here. Help me spend it, would you?"

The barkeep, a young man with a gap in his front teeth and a long face, glanced to and away from the Sunjan. He didn't appear to be the happiest, not in Pig Knot's mind.

"Lad's deaf," he slurred to another man nearby, who moved a bit away from him. Pig Knot shrugged and looked around. Two more women caught his attention, attractive and wearing tight, dark dresses that lifted their white breasts. It was like an overripe orchard around here, he mulled.

"Ladies," Pig Knot greeted them. The women's once-pleasant expressions soured, and they huddled closer together before moving away.

"Tarts," Pig Knot declared. The lot of them appeared to be right unfriendly. And the barkeeps were slower than frozen cow kisses sliding uphill. He dug into his trouser pocket and dug out the two coins. He rubbed them together, making that metallic grinding that he and Halm often joked would hook the attention of a barkeep the next country over.

Here, it drew only annoyed faces.

"This is unfit." Pig Knot grunted and rapped the coins off the countertop. Hard.

They noticed him now. In fact, several around him noticed the burly man. Pig Knot didn't care. He wanted a drink. He wanted one *now*.

He rapped the coins on the surface again. "Come on, you see me here. What damn gurry is this about? Look!" He held up his gold and rubbed them together once more, for perhaps a longer period than he intended, but he didn't care.

The wine and beer he'd consumed earlier armored him.

"You hear that? Listen." He scrubbed the coins together, clenching his teeth as he did so. "First alehouse I've been in where the keepers stay away from that sound. How does one get a pitcher around here? Should I drop my trousers?" He guffawed in inebriated jest, glancing around and finding only the backs of heads.

"You there." He poked the nearest man in the spine. The fellow only half-turned, enough to reveal a none-too-happy profile.

But Pig Knot was drunk. "How does one… go about get—*erp*, excuse me—getting a drink in this place? Pardon me, my lady," he directed at the disgusted face of an otherwise pretty blond woman standing in front of the man he was talking to. Or talking at.

They both moved away, leaving Pig Knot puzzled. "Right unfriendly bunch," he muttered and clashed the coins off the bar once more.

"Wake up there," *you punces*, he was about to say, but a part of him stopped those last words. Drunk and brazen though he'd become, he was still conscious of causing an uproar. No wench would have him if that happened.

"This fellow wants a drink here." A man stepped in beside him, smiling at Pig Knot, and put his elbow on the counter, facing him and properly studying him. Pig Knot sized him up back, swaying as he did despite being anchored by the bar. The stranger was a few fingers shorter than Pig Knot, with white hair, of all things, and a youthful face. His blue eyes were dull yet filled with amusement. The man wore a sleeveless shirt as well, showing off meaty arms.

"Thank you," Pig Knot said to him. The stranger nodded it was *quite all right*. A barkeep approached and snatched the coin with a dark frown.

Pig Knot scowled back. "No need for that. A pitcher of wine is all I want. Please."

The barkeep turned away almost immediately.

"Unfit," Pig Knot said. "Did you see that? Right unfit."

"I saw," agreed the smiling man.

"They like this with everyone?"

"Only you, I think."

"Why is that?"

The man's smile widened. "You don't belong here. Obviously don't belong."

Pig Knot grinned back. "I don't below... *belong* in a lot of places. Heard that all my life, it seems. Well, I like this place. Could be a bit more *friendly* is all."

He directed the word at the returning barkeep, who set a brass pitcher down in front of him hard enough to make the contents jump.

"Argh!" Pig Knot let out and got to sucking up the drops spilled over the curves of the pitcher. "Too good to waste," he remarked between noisy slurps.

"It is that," the stranger agreed. "What's your name?"

Pig Knot straightened up, glad to have finally met a decent fellow to share a conversation. He held out his fist to tap. "Pig Knot. Yours?"

"Prajus." He ignored the offered fist and pursed his lips. "You're Sunjan?"

"Aye that."

Prajus smiled at something over Pig Knot's shoulder. "What is it you do, Pig Knot? Interesting name that."

"It is... it is. Presently, I fight in the games." Pig Knot realized his fist wasn't about to be tapped and so let it drop. He took a long pull at the wine. It was sweet and strong and to his liking.

"Oh, you fight in the games?" Prajus repeated with mild fascination. "I see… I see. Have you fought yet?"

"I have. You?"

"Have you won any?" Prajus asked, ignoring the question put to him.

And Pig Knot was drunk enough to let it go. "I have," he replied, but when Prajus smiled at something over his shoulder again, Pig Knot turned. There stood three hard-looking men shadowing him, the biggest being able to glare directly into Pig Knot's eyes. None of them appeared too pleased with him, for whatever reason.

"Don't mind them." Prajus pulled Pig Knot's attention back. "So"—Prajus's brow crunched in thought—"did you happen to fight this day?"

"I did. Won it as well."

"Oh, you won it?" Prajus's expression lit up with interest. "Your stable master must have been happy about that."

Pig Knot shrugged. "Don't have one."

"Why is that?" Prajus asked amicably.

"Just in the games by myself."

"Free Trained?"

"Aye that."

"He's *Free* Trained. Seddon above." Prajus seemed genuinely amused and looked at the counter. "You hear that, lads?" he asked the other three men.

"Enough of this gurry," someone said behind Pig Knot as he took another swallow of wine.

But Prajus shook his head. "I'm a gladiator myself."

"You are?" Pig Knot brightened.

"I am. House of Gastillo."

"House of Gastillo? Heard of him."

"Oh, you have?"

"Aye that. Isn't he the one with the gold mask?"

"He *is*. He *is*. I see you know something of the houses. The ones that matter, that is."

Pig Knot noticed that Prajus's smile hardened, his eyes narrowed, as if a great joke was about to be revealed.

"I know a bit. He's quite nice to let you out for a drink."

"Ah Lords, I *know*." Prajus agreed again. "But then, I don't have to fight tomorrow. Or for the next few days, for that matter. None of us do. Not yet. Unlike you Free Trained shite. You can just about drink whenever you like. Isn't that right?"

"Something like that." Pig Knot nodded guardedly, wondering if he'd just properly heard himself being called shite.

"Fought in the games before?"

"End this now, Prajus," someone said behind Pig Knot, and that caused warning tingles to course up the back of his neck. He turned about and placed his back against the bar, noting the men behind now surrounded him.

"I have."

"How many seasons?" Prajus held up a hand to the other three men.

"Don't remember."

"You don't remember." Prajus chuckled.

"Aye that."

"And you're Sunjan!"

"I am."

The smile drained from Prajus's face. "You must truly have a head full of shite then, to come in here and drink with us. Or you're looking for another fight."

Pig Knot blinked.

"Let me make this clear." Prajus's face became exceedingly

understanding as he took away the pitcher of wine. Pig Knot made to protest, but Prajus shook his head as though admonishing a child. When he had it in his hand, he made to drink it then stopped. "Seddon above. I forgot this dog blossom was drinking from this." He smiled quite cruelly.

Prajus splashed the wine into Pig Knot's face, sending him into sputters. So much for his shirt.

The House of Gastillo warrior brightly smirked as Pig Knot cleared his eyes and face.

"You Free Trained ass-packers don't have enough brains to rub together, let alone two Saimon-damned coins. You even know where you are, maggot shite? Hmm? This part of the city is far and away from the green shite troughs you sleep in, and with good reason. You lot are an embarrassment to the profession. *Our* profession. Galls me black to even see you in the same city. So you'll understand if we toss you out. Lads…"

Arms looped over Pig Knot's while one powerful limb lashed around his throat, choking the life from him.

"Take this ass-licker outside."

They manhandled him towards the door, and Pig Knot could not resist. Prajus followed them, grinning at other patrons as if to say *Did you hear that?* The crowd erupted into cheers, loud whoops, and whistles, startling Pig Knot as the darkness of the open doorway loomed ahead. Curses rained down, scalding his drunken senses. All he'd wanted was a damn drink, perhaps something to eat, and most definitely a woman. Was that too much to ask?

They hauled him out into the streets, where they twisted him towards an alleyway.

"Over here." The one holding his neck grunted the words into Pig Knot's ear.

The darkness of that alley set off an alarm in Pig Knot's

drunken head, and he struggled with growing ferocity. He didn't want to be taken into the shadows. Memories of stories of Free Trained warriors being found dead or savagely brutalized in the dawn's heat filled his mind and added even more strength to his struggles. He dug his boots in but felt them slide over the smooth stones paving the road. The alley drew closer until his legs disappeared into the blackness.

"Easy, you tit," one said from the side.

"He's like an eel," said another.

"Get his… his legs there."

Then Prajus's voice, sounding as if he had another smile on his face: "Grab him by the kog and bells. That'll take the fight out of him."

No sooner was it said than Pig Knot felt a hand enter between his legs from behind, brushing against his inner thighs, and he knew very well that if he didn't do something, something right *then*, that he'd be another alehouse story of horror, another tale of how a Free Trained man, drunk out of his skull, wandered into a nest of house gladiators, *angry* house gladiators, who proceeded to remove him from the premises and drag him, kicking, into the night, where they did unspeakable things.

Pig Knot felt the hand rise further, twisting, searching, about to grab his plums.

He went crazy.

He snapped his head back while kicking upwards, evading the hand between his thighs and surprising them all. They shoved him towards a wall. Pig Knot slammed his feet against the surface and walked briskly up the side, twisting his limbs in his captors' grasps. He pushed off, breaking the grip about his neck amid straining grunts.

Pig Knot landed, set his feet, and rammed a shoulder into the brute holding his right arm, slamming him into the wall. He stomped on another's foot and got one arm loose, smashing a fist into the throat of the lout holding his other arm.

Suddenly, Pig Knot was free.

He spun around in time to have a fist crack across his cheek, whipping his face to the side. Another punched him in the gut, making Pig Knot wheeze in pain. He dropped to a knee. Something crashed down on his back while a fist smashed into the side of his head with teeth-rattling force. Whispers laced the shadows, threatening as the hiss of snakes. A knee smacked into his forehead, spinning his senses.

"Hold him!" someone insisted, and hands grabbed his shoulders.

Pig Knot reached up and grabbed two different sets of kogs and bells. He clenched the genitals as if they were bad grapes, and two voices became shocked squeaks. The hands on him fell away, and two figures crumpled to the road.

"You brazen topper!"

Prajus.

Pig Knot surged upwards and tackled a shape, driving Prajus against the opposite alley wall. He hit hard. Fingers covered Pig Knot's face, feeling for eyes. Pig Knot lifted the man off his feet and hurled him to the road. Prajus crashed with an angry gasp and scrambled halfway to his feet before Pig Knot kicked him squarely in the face, snapping his head back and dropping him again. The Free Trained twisted to one side then, barely evading the knife slicing the space he once occupied. He punched the knifeman twice, solid blows to the face and gut, backing the attacker up on his heels, but he recovered quickly. The steel flashed in the night, and Pig Knot blocked it with his forearm. He cracked the knifeman a third time, across the jaw, twisting him against the wall.

"Knives," Pig Knot hissed. "Four on one and still—"

The knifeman sprang off the bricks. His blade lashed out and licked the Sunjan across his brow, dropping a sheet of blood into his eyes. Pig Knot cried out, grabbed the weapon arm, and smashed the midsection of his attacker, pummelling him until he slumped to the road like a broken sack of meat. Pig Knot continued pounding his head, driving his knuckles behind his foe's ears. He pulled back a boot to finish him off.

An arm whipped about his throat, immediately robbing him of air.

"Not yet, pig shite."

Prajus again.

The man's vice-like arms clamped down on Pig Knot's throat with enough force to make the alley spin. Pig Knot clawed at him, feeling skin shred under his nails. He reached up and tore at eyes. Prajus screamed. Pig Knot screamed back. He slammed the house pit fighter against the wall, loosening the grip on his throat. Pig Knot crushed him there once more, then again. Blood bubbled and sputtered on his lips as the alley elongated and pressed in all at once. Prajus's grip tightened, tightened more, until bones creaked.

Pig Knot staggered from the wall and heaved himself into the air, taking the man latched onto him all the way.

And landed flat on the stone road in a brutal impact of mass flattening mass.

A dazed Pig Knot untangled himself from the stunned gladiator's limbs. He got to a knee, wiped the blood still oozing over his face, and took a quick look around. Prajus didn't move. People watched from the mouth of the alleyway, and when Pig Knot tensed up, the lot of them bolted out of sight, squealing.

"Not finished," Pig Knot breathed, clearing his eyes of blood yet again. He looked down at the stunned and gasping form of Prajus, desperately trying to pull air back into his frame. Pig Knot cupped the man's head with one hand, yanked it from where it rested on the stones and pistoned a fist into it twice, knocking the lout unconscious. Pig Knot stood, swayed, and regarded the other three men down. Shouts were coming from the alehouse. Time was running out. He had to get away.

But something made Pig Knot stop for a moment. "What odds," he muttered. He'd only wanted a drink in the first place.

He kicked the knifeman twice, buckling him up like a length of broken wood, before delivering equally powerful and savage kicks to the pair still clutching at their fruits.

Only after he finished the fight he hadn't started did Pig Knot turn and flee into the deepest part of the alley, into the night, clutching at his bleeding forehead.

Back at the mouth of the alley, the man called Toffer watched with his handful of warriors as Pig Knot disappeared into the murky gloom. Men from the alehouse streamed into the alley. Toffer shook his head at the fallen pit fighters. Four of them against one. He and his boys had followed Pig Knot all the way from the bathhouse, and Toffer was almost of a mind to stop the drunken bastard before he set foot into what was known as a drinking place for the elite. He was glad he didn't, however. He hadn't seen all of the fight, as it was in the shadows, but he had seen enough. Beating four gladiators to a finger of their lives impressed Toffer, and he could tell from the silence of his lads that they'd been impressed as well.

Toffer rubbed at his chin. It was something to keep in mind for the future. He eyed the men now fussing with the fallen gladiators, lifting them from the blood spatters on the road's cut and fitted stones.

Pig Knot, despite being drunk, had the goods, and Toffer sensed an opportunity to make coin.

12

After talking of their plans and lesser matters, Halm, Muluk, and Goll retired early for the night. Halm and Muluk decided to split the price of an upstairs room to spare them the trek back to the Pit and the crowded general quarters. Goll elected to stay in a room of his own.

In the morning after a brief breakfast, the three of them got walking, intent on visiting the one called Clavellus. Goll believed that if they walked fast enough, they should reach his property by noon. Halm hadn't drunk much at all the night before, so he believed it was possible to cover the distance in short time.

By late morning, it was a different story.

"Saimon's crack." Muluk panted and wiped at the sweat on his face while his white shirt and black trousers were saturated. "Who thought of doing this?"

A shirtless Halm cleared his own face of sweat and dried his palms off on his own black pants. A heavy sheen of perspiration covered his shoulders drizzled with dark hair. He pointed at Goll, who swung himself along on his crutches and, though sweating, didn't seem nearly as tired as his companions.

"Dying Seddon," Muluk muttered. "Easy to figure. Even on crutches, he outpaces us."

"I'm fine." Halm eyed the twisting road, dusty and full of ruts. It cut through a field of wild grass. Thickets of woods sprouted up in places, blotting out the horizon. "Good to get out of the city."

Muluk drew his hand over his face and neck and again wiped it off on his trousers. "We didn't ever take the time to look at the matchboard."

"No need," Goll answered from ahead.

"Why's that?"

"You're not fighting this day."

"I *know* I'm not fighting this day, you git. What about Halm here? He's still in the tournament."

"Never thought about checking it," Halm admitted.

"Halm isn't fighting this day or tomorrow. He just fought a few days ago." Goll focused on the road. "Besides, he'll need the time to heal."

The Zhiberian touched the soaked bandages covering his belly and frowned. He had to take shallow breaths as well, for deeper ones made his ribs ache. *Vadrian the Fire*, he thought grimly. *I'm glad the maggot's dead.* His hand strayed to where his sword would be hanging, the only possession he had these days, besides his purse of gold coins.

"*I'll* need time to heal after this walk." Muluk's voice grated.

"I think I like you better when you're drunk," Goll said.

"*I* like me better when I'm drunk. We don't even have weapons. Sweet Seddon above."

"I'll have my sword back later this day, with a new scabbard," Halm said.

"Well, if any Dezer are about, I'm sure they'll wait for

you to go get it and then return here."

Halm regarded Muluk. "You *are* cranky this morning."

"Just can't believe I'm here doing this."

"What else would you be doing?" Halm's voice boomed.

"Women," Muluk answered.

"They'll still be there when you get back. This is for you," Halm said. "Once things come into place, you'll be happy you did this."

"You'd be doing nothing," Goll said reproachfully. "You need coin for women or drinking or eating. Unless you can pull gold out of your arse."

Muluk scowled at the sun overhead. "Nice morning for it, anyway."

"More like it." Halm smiled, showing terrible teeth. "I'll say one thing about this country. The scenery is nice."

"That might change if we travel far enough. There're marshlands to the east."

"Far to the east," Goll cut in. "Clavellus is nowhere near that. We'll be there by noon. You'll see."

"This road's terrible," Halm observed. "Needs to be filled in. Widened too. We wouldn't have roads like this in Zhiberia."

"Never been," Muluk said.

"We'll have to go sometime, once this is all done."

"I hear it's full of barbarians. Visigar roam its plains, riding down any weak enough to steal from."

Halm looked at him. "Where did you hear that?"

"Around. You listen to people's conversations, hear things here and there."

"Well, there are Visigar, but they aren't ones to start a fight. You'd have to cross them first. Unlike the Dezer. Those are right evil bastards. They'll ride anyone down for coin or fun. Even the standing army is wary about areas where the Dezer might be."

"Heard they were gathering up tribes. Starting an army."

Halm shrugged his hairy shoulders. "Heard that one for years. The trouble with that is the land is so damn big, and the Dezer are divided, scattered, and untrusting of each other. Oh, they might form up one of these days, but I doubt I'll be alive to see it. Anyway, we should be more concerned with what happens in this part of the world. Sunja has Nordun to worry about." Halm looked at Goll's back. "What do you think of the war?"

"Not mine," the Kree answered.

"Deep thoughts now, is it?" Halm chuckled. "I suppose I was asking the wrong one. Never was one for mass land wars or politics or such gurry. If Sunja falls, well… we'll just have to see what happens under Nordun rule. Or leave."

"I've heard they're pressing into the Paw Savages' tribal lands," Muluk said.

"Paw Savages?" Halm's brow furrowed. "Who are they?"

"You call them Pak Savages, but they're rightfully called Paw."

"Pig Knot called them Pak Savages as well."

"Pig Knot was probably chuckling at you when he did."

That wouldn't have surprised Halm. "Where are they about?"

"Timberlands to the west. Far over there, in places where it's said civilization hasn't touched yet," Muluk informed him.

"Ah, I've heard about those forests. Well, anyway, Nords are greedy bastards then to open up a two-front war."

"Right greedy," Muluk added. "And from what I hear, *Paw* Savages have nothing against forming up to butcher an invader. That's a terrible place to wage war though. Their forests are… are…"

"Big?" Halm supplied.

"Big and—"

"Vast," Goll said from ahead. "Dense. Places where the sun doesn't sun because of whole canopies formed from thick branches. Haunted, too, if you believe the stories."

"I believe them," Muluk said solemnly.

Goll didn't look back. "When her borders touched the Paw tribal lands, huge expeditions from Sunja went into those forests and never came out. I hear the king sent three before giving up on establishing relations."

"Three?" Muluk asked. "Never heard of that."

"Three. Before the Nordish war and on the command of King Juhn's father. Don't know why, but you ask any of the Sunjans. Say what you will of them, they know their history."

Halm realized there weren't any Sunjans in their little group. Pig Knot hadn't returned to the alehouse where they'd slept the night before. He thought of the room he and Muluk had shared. It had been a luxury compared to sleeping in general quarters. Goll surprised them both by paying for his own. *That* Kree, Halm believed, had his tastes.

"Any idea of who might win the war?" Halm asked.

"Sunja, I hope," Muluk replied. "At least while I'm still within her borders."

"Goll?"

The other Kree didn't answer right away, so consumed he was with forging ahead and watching where he placed his crutches. "Doesn't matter what I think. I said already. Not my war. It's beyond me."

The conversation lagged then as the three men placed their remaining energy into walking.

"Thought you said this place was close," Muluk griped.

"Shaddup," Goll griped right back.

The walls rose up and over the fields like a small fortress, stamping the top of a small rise and giving anyone looking a far view of the surrounding grassy sea. The gates hung open, and dark shapes moved about the wall while the midafternoon sun fell from the sky. That it took longer than Goll had expected to reach their destination gave fuel to weary griping from his companions. Halm and Muluk were almost spent. Goll, however, marched on towards the structure. He paused every now and again to mop the sweat from his brow and face but was soon swinging on his crutches. Halm had to admire the Kree and his Weapon Master training. The bastards obviously stressed endurance.

The wall's wrought-iron gates abruptly closed, pushed by three men behind the bars.

"See that?" Goll asked the others. "They know we're coming."

"They'd have to be blind not to see us." Muluk glanced around. "You could see anyone from up there. They built that place well. Right on a rise in the land."

An old bridge came into view, crossing a shallow trench. They thumped over it, listening to the hollow sounds of their crossing. White rocks in the moat were bone dry, and a cloud of insects lifted into the air and snaked away from the men.

"Mind yourselves now," Goll told them as they drew closer. "Let me talk. Neither of you look fit enough to do anything anyway."

"I could piss right here," Halm huffed, red-cheeked and

feeling as if he were about to melt.

That brought a look of alarm from Goll.

"Far enough," yelled one of the figures behind the gate, distant enough that his features could not be seen. "What is it you want?"

The three travelers stopped well within bow range of the walls.

"We want to speak with Clavellus if this is his house," Goll shouted back, recovering from what Halm had said.

"It is," came the reply. "What do you want to speak to him about?"

"The gladiator games of Sunja and whether he would be interested in being a taskmaster again."

Silence.

"Wait there then. I'll see if he's taking visitors."

One man walked out of sight, leaving his two companions to mind the walls. Four torsos carrying spears and bows appeared along the top and lingered.

"How tall are those walls?" Muluk asked quietly. "Ten feet?"

"At least. No more, I think." Halm kept his own voice low.

"High enough to keep the likes of us out then."

"Aye that. Like we're about to climb anything," Halm muttered. He wanted a drink very badly, and he wasn't kidding about the piss either. "How far does it go around, I wonder?"

"Shut up," Goll whispered. "You'd think we were about to lay siege to the place."

That quieted both men for a few moments.

"Farther than I'm willing to walk," Muluk commented to Halm in an even lower whisper, eyeing Goll's back warily.

"The old bastard must be rich though, to have all of this."

Moments later, the man returned.

"Approach the gates," the voice shouted. "Mind yourselves. Do you have any weapons?"

"None," Goll answered for them all.

"Dangerous to be travelling without something."

"We don't have much," Goll yelled back.

Except the gold in my purse and no doubt what friend Goll is carrying under his shirt, Halm thought.

They approached the walls, seeing the whitewashed stone and the grey lines of fresh mortar. The men at the gates pulled them open just enough to allow entry and closed them right after. A tall brute of a man walked over to the three newcomers and inspected their persons for weapons. Broad of shoulder, the man had no hair to speak of, while a gruesome scar stretched up the left side of his face. The ear was missing on that side as well. Halm frowned slightly. It wasn't the first time he'd seen scars or missing ears, but this one wore them with a sinister air—as if he were one word away from beating the three of them senseless.

"Careful, aren't you?" the Zhiberian asked the bald man, noting the old scabbard hanging off his hip.

For a moment, green eyes held his attention, judging him a troublemaker or simply harmless. Halm kept his mouth shut and studied the other men inside the walls. All of them wore assorted clothes of a modest make, suited for hard work in the countryside. As the green-eyed brute checked Goll and Muluk in turn, Halm took in the rest of the enclosed courtyard. White sands covered much of the ground, but he saw walkways made of fitted brick curving in a ring that encompassed the whole area. He recognized it as the training grounds for pit fighters, saw the crossed practice timbers with the simple shape of a man's height and outstretched arms, all for working strikes. A pile of thicker timbers for strength training lay piled up neatly against a far wall. More bare walls built underneath and holding up the ramparts were divided up into several equally spaced doorways, some closed, some open. To Halm's left lay an open smithy, dead and empty to the world. He spotted two anvils, a slake tub for cooling hot metal, and a fire pot. Tongs hung down from unseen hooks set into overhead timbers. Two fresh piles of plum-sized shite dotted the sand just beyond the smithy, making a trail between it and the master's residence, perhaps leading to a stable. The master's residence was situated across from the main gate. A second-floor balcony fenced with stumpy columns leaned out over the training area, potentially offering a place for archers if the gate was ever breached. Under this and within the shade was a set of heavy-looking wooden doors.

As Halm sized it all up, a figure opened the balcony doors and walked through. He stopped and leaned on the fat stone railing and studied them curiously.

A shorter man waved the three of them forward while the guards kept watch on the ramparts. The tall, one-eared ogre stayed three quick strides away from Halm's left as he and Muluk walked behind Goll.

Goll swung forward on his crutches, stopping directly below the balcony. "Are you Clavellus?"

"I am," was all he said. Clavellus's skin was deeply tanned, which made his bushy white beard all the more memorable. Light trousers and white shirt were all he wore, and he scratched at a bald head. He didn't appear heavy with muscle or fat. "What is it?"

"I'm Goll of Kree. These are my companions, Halm of

Zhiberia and Muluk of Kree. We're here this day to ask you if you would consider training us for the gladiator games of Sunja, as our taskmaster."

Clavellus took his time answering, meeting the eyes of all three visitors before settling back on Goll. "The games have already started."

"We know this," Goll said. "We're already participating in the games, but we wish to establish our own house, and we request that you consider being a part of it."

"You want to have a house?" Clavellus leaned forward. "You're Free Trained?"

Goll hesitated a moment. "We are."

This struck Clavellus speechless for seconds before he cut loose. "Free Trained. What are you punces thinking? Who put you up to this? Do you know who I *am*? I've trained warriors for years. I've trained *animals* with more skill than you lot. Seddon above knows I've cursed you masterless Pit dogs when, by whatever luck or trickery, you spoiled a run at greatness by one of my own fighters. Sweet Seddon. You ass lickers turn my guts! And to think you came here to ask me face to face. I only wish I lived days away from the city. The balls on you all. And to do this while the games are already in progress! *Unfit*. Train you? The likes of *you* and those like you? You lot truly belong out there with the gurry. Let me tell you this—you don't have a hope in the games, and the sooner you perish the better."

"We can pay you," Goll said when he had the opening.

"*Pay* me?"

"Yes. Handsomely."

"*Handsomely* is it? You'll pay me handsomely? And if I did take your money, where is it you think we'll train you? Where should I transform you into killers? You have a training area?

Equipment? Practice weapons? Where are your own weapons? Where are you intending to sleep at nights or eat during the day? Or were you going to pay me *handsomely* to use everything I have?"

Goll did not answer, appearing increasingly chagrined.

"Yes, I see now. You expect me to bow and offer up my ass at the mention of coin. Wave gold about and expect me to throw open my arms and mind you as though you were sons. Do you see how shortsighted that is? Clearly this wasn't your plan before you stepped through my gates. Probably even figured you'd build your own house if I said no, am I right? Defy us all."

Goll looked at the ground and pursed his lips as if he were about to give someone a very hard kiss. Muluk cleared his throat, and even Halm felt heat rush into his face. Things weren't looking so rosy after all.

"Who *are* you?" Clavellus finished from above.

Not even Goll had the mind to answer.

"Get out of my sight." With that, Clavellus motioned to the men standing about Halm and the others.

"Master Clavellus—" Goll started suddenly.

"Get them out of my sight!" Clavellus shouted, disappearing through a doorway.

One Ear moved in, scowling, with his hand on his sword. The archers and spearmen on the ramparts took aim while five more men surrounded the Kree men and the Zhiberian and closed in.

"We're going," Goll said calmly. "We're going."

Moments later, the gate rattled and clicked closed behind them. The men behind it and on the ramparts carefully watched the three. With Goll leading, they marched away from the House of Clavellus and did not look back.

"Well, that was a cow kiss," Muluk said quietly, studying the grass.

"Aye that," Halm said. "I feel terrible."

"Don't mind them," Goll said, peering ahead. "We go to Thaimondus now."

"And if he says no?" Muluk asked.

"He won't."

And that was all Goll had to say on the matter.

*

Clavellus collapsed on a divan and crossed one leg over the other. He idly stroked his beard, pausing only to sip from the bottle of mead he had gathered. It had been a fine day to drink, and he'd done enough of it in the morning that when those three punces visited, he had been feeling little to no pain. From the courtyard, he heard the squeal and clack of the gate being shut, and he shook his head at the balls of his visitors. Free Trained wanting to be trained by him, as though he would do such a thing. He might have fallen out of grace with the other houses and schools of Sunja, but he still had some pride.

"What was that about?" Nala asked him from their bedroom, her voice sounding only half-interested. However, as his wife, she felt she should be privy to everything.

"Nothing."

"You were shouting."

"I'm drunk."

"I heard only a part of it."

"Everything's fine, Nala. I've taken care of it."

"All right."

He took another drink and beheld the purple bottle at arm's length. It reminded him of royalty. He was royalty once—hailed like a king. Still had a few followers who had chosen to stay with him even after his fall from grace. *Fall from grace.* The thought both amused and galled him. Evidently, he'd fallen far enough to be courted by Free Trained.

Oh, how he'd fallen.

Free Trained.

Clavellus eyed the mouth of the bottle, dark and fragrant with mead, and took another, exceptionally long pull of its contents.

13

They had called him a weapon enough times for him to believe it. His given name was Junger, from far-off Pericia, and he was in the games to be respected, to be feared, and to punish any who faced him. He'd trained with schools in his homeland and done some soldiering with the army there, and when the opportunity came to leave, he did so with an eye on the great games of Sunja. Coin was only an afterthought in his mind. He wanted to prove to them all that he was the best.

And as far as he was concerned, he was Free Trained.

When his name was called, he came forth wearing a plain helmet, brass bracers, greaves, a stiff vest of leather, and his sword hanging off his waist in a scabbard.

The Madea stopped the fighter in front of his wooden desk, which rose above the grounds of general quarters so that he looked down on all of the Free Trained fighters. He was slim of build and dressed in white robes identifying his station in the games. Like other men of his age, he had his thin white hair cut almost perfectly down the middle. A row of Skarrs lined the front of the platform while six others stood at guard behind the Madea himself, three on each end of the massive matchboard designating the fights for the day, as well as a week ahead.

"You there. Your name. Are you from Pericia?"

Greatness recognized, Junger thought. "I am."

"Why aren't you listed with a house then?"

"I represent myself."

That put a smirk on the Madea's wizened face, and he momentarily scratched at the finely parted crease that ran down the middle of his fine white hair. "Off you go then."

Junger stared at the arena official with an air that might have blown down from the Lands of Great Ice. He didn't like that condescending slant to the man's face. The Madea cocked an eyebrow at him in return, as if daring him to say anything while several Skarrs stood before and behind his station. The line of the older man's mouth was a borderline sneer.

"Off you go, Free Trained." The Madea dismissed him and went back to consulting his lists.

Junger gave him no further thought, thinking the official undeserving of the effort. The next time they would meet, he was certain the Madea would treat him differently. He meandered down the white tunnel, past the Skarrs standing guard at marked intervals, eyeing them with only a distant curiosity of how their training might have differed from his own. His mind then filled with images of what he had gone through to reach this point. Above, the ceiling vibrated with sound, reminding him of waterfalls in the winter. He stopped in his tracks at the noise and studied the stone above him for signs of cracking. When he saw none, he continued on his way. Junger wasn't a large man, but he knew he was fast and well-built as well, like most of the fighters in general quarters, although he'd spotted a few who were grossly out of shape. Still, looks could be deceiving as he very well knew—as he hoped *his* would.

He stopped at the gatekeeper and regarded his own boots.

"See anything of note back there?" the old man asked him. "Saw you stop."

"Just listening," Junger replied, uninterested.

"Only wearing the leather, eh?" the gatekeeper croaked and flexed woolly jowls.

Junger exhaled and squinted at the portcullis above. "Only the leather."

"You'll be nimble out there."

"Hm."

"Going to pull that sword out?"

"Eventually." Junger went back to studying his boots. The gatekeeper grunted, thinking the young pup was going to be bleeding meat in only moments, and pulled the lever.

Junger took his time and purposefully climbed the steps to the waiting daylight.

He emerged from the tunnel and felt the hot sun on what skin was exposed. The audience cheered and cursed, the sound falling on him like rough winter surf. He only glanced in their direction, glimpsing faces and torsos mashed together like a writhing collage of sun-bronzed flesh. In a detached moment, he thumbed the pommel of his undrawn sword and wondered who'd placed coin on his head to win. They'd be happy after the fight. He intended to make them remember. To make them *all* remember.

The Orator introduced him, but he was only halfway listening. The sun blazed overhead, and he felt sweat bead uncomfortably on his forehead. It was too hot to fight this day, even with the little armour he wore. He could smell the heat and the ripe sweat of the spectators. Across the sands, another Free Trained warrior waited, holding a sword and shield and dressed in chainmail. A helmet sporting a single fin down the middle nodded in his direction. Junger didn't hear the fighter's name. Junger frowned and wondered how hot the heavy armor must feel.

"Begin!" shouted the Orator.

Too hot, Junger thought. He wouldn't make this mistake a second time.

It was then he decided to make a spectacle of himself.

With a gasp of relief, he pulled off his helmet and let it drop to the sand, taking all the time in the world. He swiped his hand over his bristly hair, disturbing a mist of sweat. His right bracer followed, dropping into the sand where the sun flashed angrily off their worn surfaces. The crowd's deafening drone became one of hushed disbelief, but Junger paid them little heed. He doubted they knew what it was like to wear armor under this sun.

His opponent halted in his tracks, watching with peculiar puzzlement. It wasn't every day a pit fighter stepped onto the sands and stripped.

Junger checked on him when his left bracer fell, making sure the man behaved. When he stooped to a knee to unlace the leather binding of a greave, the crowd's muttering of wonder became as loud as a field of locusts. He tossed the slab of metal away, checked once more on where his opponent stood, and took his time unlacing the second.

By this time, the jeers from sections of the audience grew louder. Laughter rang out from both men and women.

"Take it all off, you stupid punce!"

"This is the kind of show I want more of!" cried a female.

"Stupid ass! What in Saimon's hell are you *doing?*"

"The lad's unfit!"

Junger stood up, took a breath, and grimaced with the heat. Even the Orator was looking from side to side now, gauging the reaction of the crowds and his own confusion at what was happening on the sands. Junger squinted and slowly unlaced his leather vest at the side, appreciating the time his opponent allowed him. He nodded in the direction of the heavily armoured man, who shook his helmed head in reply.

No doubt thinks I'm unfit, Junger thought and mentally shrugged as he lifted the vest away. He pulled off his shirt then, receiving screams of delight from the female onlookers and even a few of the men. Inspecting himself while placing a hand to his chiselled stomach, Junger saw that he was free of everything that could come off except for his trousers. He wasn't about to remove them.

"Gut him!" someone shouted, urging the other warrior on. He didn't think that was called for in the least.

"Take his head!"

"Carve his heart out!"

Junger cocked his head, puzzled at such hatred. He didn't understand what he'd done to deserve such venom. He undid the belt holding his scabbard and took it away from his waist. There was no need to take out the blade. The Free Trained across from him didn't pounce while he was stripping down, and Junger intended to repay that small gesture. Bringing his sword up before him, the belt wrapped around one wrist so the scabbard wouldn't fly off, Junger swished the weapon from left to right while the audience got even more impatient.

In the end, it was probably them who got Junger's opponent moving.

The warrior crunched over and came on, peeking up over the lip of his shield. The sun made his mail look all the hotter.

Junger stopped in his tracks and kept his sword close.

More howls. The warrior picked up speed, shifting into a slow jog. His sword came up to his shoulder. The *chuff chuff chuff* of his boots in the sand rose above the voices.

Junger took one shallow step backwards, turning his body to one side, and stretched his free hand towards the approaching pit fighter.

The warrior closed in, his eyes glaring from the depths of his helmet, slits of concentration that saw only an easy kill. His sword lifted off his shoulder, and the shield, a rounded thing of metal and wood, aimed for Junger's chest. The audience screamed ever louder. The pit fighter closed in, almost there…

And swung with a yell, looking to take off Junger's head with one swipe.

Except Junger was no longer standing before him.

The Perician swooped under the powerful swing of the Free Trained man and darted behind him. The pit fighter pivoted on his heel, sweeping his sword back as he turned to face his Perician foe.

Junger ducked under that as well.

Then he struck.

His sword—still in its scabbard—snapped out and stuck the side of the helm with a great *gong*. The impact staggered the warrior back on his heels but did not drop him. Junger stepped into him and struck him six more times about the head, his sword whirling about his foe's skull like a wooden plank caught in a windstorm, crashing into the metal helm with loud clangs that silenced the crowd.

And on the last strike, Junger switched targets and jammed the sword in between the legs of his opponent, uprooting him from his spot. The warrior fell hard on his back and did not get back up. Junger plopped atop his chest and bared half of his blade, the metal flashing in the sun. He placed its edge underneath the chin of the fallen pit fighter.

Stunned, the audience watched on.

The warrior didn't raise an arm to surrender. Puzzled, Junger leaned in and saw through the eye slits of the helm that his foe was already unconscious, his eyes almost rolled entirely into the upper part of his sockets.

Heat shimmering off the sand, Junger stepped up and away from the fallen man, well out of reach in case trickery was afoot. When the fighter remained motionless, Junger looked expectantly to the Orator at his podium.

"Your victor!" the old man blurted, every bit as surprised as the crowd.

At his feet, the Free Trained man propped himself up onto an elbow and held his face in his hand. Junger backed away from him, until he deemed it was safe to turn his back. The crowds were no longer so hostile towards him, and some even screamed praise on his name. He'd heard the masses would be easy to sway. With nothing else to do but collect his winnings and get a bath, he entered the shade of the tunnel, not bothering to pick up his armour. There was no way he was going to wear any of it ever again.

It was just too hot for the Perician Weapon.

14

The three companions made it back to the city just as the sky turned orange around the edges. Exhaustion kept both Muluk and Halm from talking much, so they simply followed Goll, hopping along to what they now considered their alehouse and navigating the crowd-filled streets with weary patience. The smell of suppers clung to the air— roasts, breads, soups, and sweet things that made their stomachs rumble.

"Seddon take me, we've landed in Saimon's hell." Halm looked around, hoping he might catch a glimpse of whatever was cooking.

"I smell it too," Muluk said. "And it's the best thing I've come across all day."

Goll stopped in the street and waited for the pair to catch up to him. Even after walking all day, he still seemed more than ready to do another march. He sweated, but nowhere near the amount Halm and Muluk did. Halm believed that a good chunk of him had wasted away on the journey back from Clavellus's residence and that soon, very soon, his stomach would start gnawing away on his ribs.

"I took you out there this day, so I'll pay for your meals

this night," Goll informed them both. "I'll even pay for your room—if you don't mind sharing one. It's better than sleeping on the floor of general quarters."

That brightened the two men considerably.

They reached the alehouse and saw only a handful of people were inside. A group of men lounged in their usual alcove, so they took the one nearby. Muluk and Halm collapsed on the benches, their foreheads flat on the surface of the table. Goll slid in behind them, taking up the remaining side. He placed his crutches upright nearby and signaled for a serving wench.

The young woman, not unpleasant to gaze upon, brought over three pitchers of water.

"Agg." Muluk grimaced when he took a mouthful. "Never sweeter."

Halm gulped down half of his own before dropping the pitcher to the table with a gasp.

Goll ordered roasts for the three of them and a pitcher of mead for the table. The woman went off with the order, and for moments each of them sat and recovered his strength.

"So…" Halm sat back and laid a hand on his belly. "What's next for us?"

Goll studied him, his dark eyes sharp. "Thaimondus. Tomorrow. Be ready to get up at dawn and walk again. His residence is once more out towards Plagur's Reach, but to the southwest this time. Another good day of exercise, at least."

"Exercise," Muluk hissed. "We're… *spent* here."

"So you are."

"What about the day after?"

Goll frowned. "Never expected to hear a Kree putting things off."

"I put a lot of things off. Something I probably should have let you know about, but I put it off. Maybe I'm not the person you're looking for."

"Then I suppose you can pay for your own food."

Muluk blinked. "Right evil bastard," he said under his breath.

"Your own room as well, for that matter," Goll added.

"You're not doing me a favour there. This one snores." Muluk jabbed a thumb at the Zhiberian sitting next to him.

Halm smiled gently. "Just a little. So I've been told."

"Just a little." Muluk shook his head and looked at Goll. "This man sounds worse than a… a thundercloud crashing down on your skull. A maul smashing an egg. Like a whole beach of rocks rattling over each other in a surf. No wonder I'm exhausted. I hardly slept last night."

"You can always sleep in the Pit," Goll pointed out, stoically.

Muluk rolled his eyes. "Oh that's *much* better. It comes out of all ends down there. Saimon's black, hanging fruit. I don't know how the Madea summons the nerve to go down there in the morning to do his job. The smell could knock down a whole army of Dezer. Breath, shite, piss, vomit… am I forgetting anything?" he asked of Halm.

"No, you have it all."

Muluk turned back to Goll. "And you *know* this. You've slept down there before. One eye open and the other on your belongings."

"That's one thing a person *doesn't* have to worry about, I've found," Halm threw in. "No one tries to take another's possessions."

"No one *has* any possessions to take; that's why," Muluk countered.

"There are Skarrs posted throughout," Goll said. "I've seen them at night, in and around the infirmary. They're there."

"A handful," Muluk added.

Halm glanced about the room.

"Who are you looking for?" Muluk asked.

"Pig Knot."

"You seem to worry about him a lot."

"Not worried. Just want him a part of this." Halm returned his attention to his company. "He'll want to," he directed at Goll, who said nothing. Halm was beginning to feel the Kree truly didn't like the Sunjan at all.

"He'll show up eventually, in the Pit at the very least," Muluk said.

"Hmm. So what of tomorrow?" Halm asked of Goll.

"I already told you. We get up, and we walk out to Thaimondus," Goll repeated hotly, clearly becoming annoyed. "Just like this day. We ask if he's interested and go from there."

"Just thought of this… who's going to pay him to train us?"

"We will."

That surprised both Halm and Muluk. Goll frowned at their faces. "Where did you think the coin was coming from? We have to pay on top of the Chamber's fee. They aren't going to train any of us for nothing."

"How is that going to work?" Halm asked.

"From our winnings. All gladiators pay a sum from their winnings to their houses, for their training, food, and lodgings. Wagers as well. The Domis will be seeing my face quite a bit in the days to come. Those are the main ways to make coin in this business."

"Where do you keep all of this?" Muluk asked.

Goll didn't seem to like the question. "I'll keep that to myself, for reasons best unsaid. And if you don't like it, you can cast off now."

"Sensitive." Muluk scoffed, but he didn't pursue the matter.

Halm cleared his throat, wanting to get the conversation back on safer ground. "And if Thaimondus rejects us?"

Goll didn't immediately have an answer to that. "We'll continue on. Do things the hard way. I'm committed to this, and I'll tell you now—you both have to make peace with yourselves on whether you truly want to be founders of a house. I'm not going to keep checking to see if you are both with me. This is just the beginning. Just the beginning."

Halm held up his palms, submitting. Muluk grunted and kept his eyes downcast.

"That a yes?" Goll asked him.

"Aye that, it's a yes. Leave me alone about it now. Seddon above, I hope that food gets here soon. I'm famished. We haven't eaten or drunk anything all day. Do you realize that?"

They did.

"Just thinking about that one big bastard with the missing ear," Halm said. "That's two men I've seen in as many days with the same injury."

"Who was the first?" Muluk asked.

"One of the Gladiatorial Chamber Members. Older man. Right ear sliced off."

"That one we saw this day had his left shorn off. And that scar."

"*That* was a scar," Halm agreed. "He didn't have it stitched together, and the flesh never came to on its own.

Looked like a pair of lips running up the side of his face. Or petals half bloomed."

Muluk made a face. "Ugly thing."

"Be hard to sleep with that picture in my mind. Or eat."

"It didn't bother me *that* much."

"Well, get what you can into yourselves this night, and sleep," Goll told them. "Tomorrow is going to be more of the same but with a different ending."

The Kree swept his hands over the worn knots in the table's surface.

"I guarantee you."

*

Later that same evening, Grisholt sat and stared at the painting on his wall, the colours cast in a darkly orange hue from a torch sputtering in its sconce. The warship's course held steady, charging the sun, with just a touch of white froth around the prow where it cut the sea. Grisholt had never been at sea, and it occurred to him that he was getting too old for any kind of lengthy travel. Any ocean might very well kill him. It didn't bother him much. Other matters of concern pressed him. Marrok had just informed him that the pantry and larder were running low and that he'd have to go to market soon, within two days at least, else the men would be eating fried-up flour sprinkled with a little sugar. Grisholt told him to make do until he could get him the coin to buy food. Then it was Sarkus, the smithy, wanting new iron to fashion and leather to be bought for straps and bindings. More coin that Grisholt didn't have. He ordered the smithy to make do. He didn't even want to think about the coming fall when the cold winds would start blowing. They rattled the roof last year and this year; who knew what damage might be done? This season had to pay off handsomely for Grisholt.

Coin.

It all came down to coin. And he needed a sizeable sum from the games. A fat pot of gold.

He sighed and hefted the bottle of mead. Even though times were difficult, he still managed to have a bottle for himself. One of the few remaining pleasures granted him, and even *that* needed coin.

Grisholt had a lad fighting in the tournament tomorrow, a brute by the name of Gunjar with a good chance at winning. Even better, he was marked to fight a Free Trained lad. The odds would be high in his favour, but the problem was there weren't many who would take a wager on a Free Trained facing a house fighter. Regardless, Grisholt would play with what little money he had left and wager all of it on that match. He *needed* that gold. He needed a winning season. The notion made him run a hand over his brow. Grisholt was glad his father wasn't alive to see how low the stable had sunk under his management. The shame would kill him on the spot.

The rattling of a door and the sound of approaching footsteps prodded the master, and he diverted his attention to the study entrance.

"Master Grisholt?"

"Hmm?"

Brakuss stepped into the room with a torch, which made Grisholt think of the need to purchase oil for the lamps.

"Caro is here."

Grisholt perked up. "Show him in."

Keeping to the shadows, Caro eased around Brakuss and stopped before the desk. Grisholt had gotten used to reading the body language of his spy, something he never revealed to the man, and Caro's suggested that all was well—which was good. Grisholt needed some good news for a change.

"Yes?"

"Master Grisholt, I have some news."

"Out with it."

"I have at least one man following them at all times. If I had coin, I'd be able to—"

"There is no more coin. Out with this news," Grisholt said impatiently.

Caro gave a curt dip of his head. "One of my lads followed Halm of Zhiberia, Goll of Kree, and a third man outside the city this day. To the residence of Clavellus. He couldn't proceed any further for fear of being spotted by the guards on the wall, so he waited, and they left the residence not long after."

"So they've made contact with Clavellus."

"Yes, but I have no idea to what end. They appeared to be downcast, so the meeting may not have gone in their favour."

"Maybe." Grisholt stroked his beard. "Maybe. Regardless, tomorrow morning, as early as you can, you go to Dark Curge and tell him you have information for him. I'm sure he'll be interested to learn about the visit to his old taskmaster's hole. Tell him only about the visit. Get paid as well, and use it to keep our lads on our three friends. And who is the third?"

Caro shook his head. "I'll find out."

"Any word on the gold?"

"Nothing yet."

"When you do, even if it's just a sniff of something, you let me know. Find out where they're keeping it. Don't do anything else until I know what the situation is and decide on a plan. Understood? And no killing."

Caro nodded.

Grisholt leaned back in his chair. "They'll probably be heading to Thaimondus soon. Perhaps even tomorrow. This *Goll* is the intelligent one. Watch him above the others. Everywhere he goes and anything he does. He leads the Zhiberian pisser. That one probably has to be instructed on where to leave a cow kiss."

That made both henchmen smirk.

"I'll have a man follow them right from the alehouse," Caro said.

"Get back there this night. Sleep in an alley if you have to, but keep me aware of what's happening. I'll be at the Pit tomorrow as well. See if I can't win us some coin," he ended with a knowing smile.

"Who is fighting?" Caro asked.

"Gunjar." Grisholt stretched the name ominously. "Odds are on him and rightly so. And truth be told, the money can't come fast enough. Oh yes, be there as well, to place the wager after me."

"Hmm," Caro grunted thoughtfully. "I'll leave for the city this night."

"Yes, do that," Grisholt said and waved, dismissing his head spy. Caro slunk back into the dark, leaving him and Brakuss in the study, their features made hellish by the torchlight. "Our fortunes haven't been the best lately, but I smell change on the wind. Do you have your boys picked?"

"I do."

"Now, I want to you be careful about this. Anything we do might come back on the stable. Obviously, I don't want that. My name's in the shite enough these days without having thievery added to it. What I want is a faceless wraith to descend from the night, do my bidding, and leave with nary a sign of passage. If there's anything to be discovered, Caro is the weasel to discover it. I'll have your lads do the striking when the time is right. Understood?"

"Clearly."

"Excellent." Grisholt eyed his once-gladiator. "Our hard times are about to come to an end, Brakuss. Oh, I can *feel* it."

15

Long, lazy streamers of cloud smeared the early morning light of the sky, and the temperature was already warm. By noon, the sands would be scalding. A harsh day for pit fighting, but then Dark Curge supposed most days were. Facing the training grounds of his house, he bent over a table and ate the flesh of a red melon, swallowing the seeds and heedless of the juice covering his jowls. From his balcony, he watched the activity below. His trainers put his pit fighters through an early-morning hell to the steady beat of blunted, weighted swords being smashed against practice men—thick crosses of wood that would be chipped away until broken. He eyed each one of his fighters in turn as he devoured his breakfast, lingering, studying, making mental notes of a swing or a stab, the posture or placing of the feet. The taskmaster and trainers walked amongst the men, snapping whips when needed, taking gladiators aside and correcting them if they spotted something amiss.

After the loss of Samarhead, Curge wondered who might fill the place of his prized fighter. All of his lads were animals in the more flattering sense, and after Halm of Zhiberia killed Samarhead rather decisively, his trainers had reported that there were several lads wanting a cut at the fat man. That kind of desire placed a warm tingling in Curge's black heart. All he had to do was choose one, and he mulled that very question. Even the unfit Vadrian had been unable to kill the Zhiberian, and Curge still felt the lingering burn of that one. He should have kept it in his house from the beginning, as custom went, and selected one of his own to challenge Halm. As it was, he still had time to seek bloody retribution against the Free Trained piece of shite, but truth be known, seeing the Zhiberian hack down his best man concerned him.

Curge sat and chewed, periodically drinking water from a silver cup filled by one of his female servants, raking his attention from one pit fighter to the next. Something whispered to let this one killing go, to not do anything. He had the sour feeling the Zhiberian was more trouble than he was worth, but the old warrior in Curge refused to let him take Samarhead's scalp without a blood match.

But *who* could challenge the Zhiberian?

"Master Curge?" said someone behind him.

Naturally, Curge didn't turn right away. Instead, he gnawed at the melon, right down to the white of the rind, and dumped it on a juice-wet plate before him. A servant gave him a hand towel to paw at his hands and face.

"Didn't I once tell you not to disturb me this early in the morning, Bezange?"

A fearful pause, ripe as a blister.

"You did, Master Curge."

"And what time is it?"

"Morning."

"And what am I doing?"

"Eating?"

"So you have good reason—dare I say *very* good reason—to come into my private quarters? Hmm?"

Another pause. Saimon below, things were getting bleak.

"I believe so."

Dark Curge sighed and looked at his baby-faced agent. Bezange was dressed in his usual plain clothing, so as not to draw attention, and was trying very hard to not tremble in his black boots.

"What is it?" Curge finally asked, his throat thick with breakfast and making him sound harsher than usual.

"You have a visitor."

That made Curge frown. "A visitor? This early in the morning? Who?"

"He says his name is Caro and that he has information for you he's willing to sell."

Curge's frown deepened. "Why wouldn't he give it to you?"

"He wanted to see you."

A growl came from the owner then, and he glanced back at his gladiators' morning paces.

"He wanted to see me?"

Bezange stood there, looking every bit the messenger bearing annoying news.

"Who's his employer?"

"He wouldn't say."

"A real mystery this morning," Curge rumbled. "Little bastard has balls to see the lion in his den." He sat and stewed. "Have Demasta and a few of the guards escort this Caro to the meeting room in the lower level. See to it he's uncomfortable. I'll be down in a bit."

Bezange dipped at the waist and disappeared through the inner curtains of the house. Curge watched him go for a moment before directing his attention back to the training pit fighters. He scrutinized them for a bit longer, losing himself in the very same thoughts that troubled him during breakfast.

Eventually, he remembered he had a visitor waiting for him in what he called the meeting room. Curge had two such chambers. One was a regular audience hall, a smaller room and undeserving of its title, where he met visitors. The meeting room, however, lay beneath his house's cool stone floors, only accessible by descending two flights of stairs. He kept cells down there as well, off from the main corridor of the lower level and behind an iron door, and he wondered for a moment if anyone occupied any of them.

Curge stood, his left stump rubbing his ribs, and stretched. He was a noisy stretcher, yawning like a bear. One of his women came forward to wipe his hairy chest with a cloth, and he kept still long enough for her to complete her job. Once done, he left the balcony, wearing only his trousers, and proceeded to the meeting room. He passed the plants and tapestries decorating his home, in no mood to appreciate them. The door to the lower level lay half open, and he descended with heavy steps, feeling his knees each time. Getting old did not set well with Curge. He supposed it didn't with most people, but for him, after a life of pushing his body to physical extremes, feeling and watching his strength slowly diminish galled him.

Lamplight illuminated a long corridor walled with slabs of flat rock, and the ceiling was mere fingers above his hairless head. The air was much cooler, and Curge liked its damp feel. He walked past the door leading to the cells and went to the half-opened entryway at the end. The sounds of people moving reached his ears, then a curse, drawing a thin line of satisfaction on his face.

Dark Curge entered the room with a threatening grace, immediately quieting the visitor lashed to a heavy wooden chair. He stopped and simply studied his prisoner for a moment, not saying a word. Strips of leather bound his captive's neck, waist, wrists, upper thighs, and ankles, keeping him as firmly in place as possible. Curge knew from experience that once he got cutting, nothing really kept a body still. The man's hands rested on thick chopping blocks attached to the ends of the chair's arms, his fingers knotted up into protective fists. Bezange stood off to one side, fidgeting with his belt, while thick-bodied Demasta, the head of Curge's household guard, stood to the right of the chair. A thick X of studded leather crossed his chest while another leather slab protected his midsection. The warrior's blue eyes flashed almost angrily at his employer, but upon recognizing him, he smoothed over his short black beard, nodded a greeting, and backed off. Three more household guards stood about the chambers, dressed in the same intimidating armor, carrying assorted weapons, and glaring at the prisoner. Curge took on hard men who could follow orders and had no qualms about taking a life. He didn't care what manner of weapon they used, but he demanded they wear the armor.

Curge looked at each of his lads before settling on the worried expression of his restrained guest, noting the torn front of his shirt and the heaving of a hairy chest underneath. With a menacing air, Curge stared, sizing the bound man up and down as if he were gauging an expensive cut of steak.

"What is this?" Caro asked, barely keeping the fright from his voice. "I came here to sell information! I have information, and your dogs grabbed and lashed me to this chair. Let me go! Let me go this instant!"

Curge glowered at the man, mildly piqued that he'd spoken at all.

"What?" Caro demanded, becoming more unnerved. "What is it? I only want to sell you some *information*! That's *all*. A few gold pieces for what I know. Why all of this? There's no need of it."

Curge kept his face unreadable.

Caro chuckled nervously. "Do you greet all informants the same way?"

No one answered. Not even Bezange dared to move, his fingers now firmly plunged into his belt leather. The household guard stood like trunks of timber, ready to fall on the captive's skull upon command.

Caro gawked at Curge with bulging eyes. His lower lip quivered before he finally lost control. "What? Release me, damn you! Release me this instant!"

Caro screamed then. He emptied his lungs like a wild rabbit caught in a snare and seeing the hunter's axe. He howled and raved to be released, rocked against his bonds. He threw out threats, and when he saw they held no power, he changed his tune and begged.

A stoic Curge listened and watched, masking his thoughts expertly, until he'd had enough. He had no fear of the man's yowling reaching the surface, and even if it did, he didn't care.

But a man could only take so much noise.

As if remembering something, Curge turned his bulk towards an area behind him. There, on a table, rested an assortment of heavy iron tongs, dull knives, and well-used meat cleavers. Curge stepped over to the table and picked up a cleaver, turning over the fat blade in his hand so the light flashed along its girth. He flicked a calloused thumb across its edge, testing it, and then considered Demasta. Grim approval sparkled in his head guard's eyes. Curge slowly revealed the instrument to Caro… who, not surprisingly, stopped screeching upon seeing the weapon.

Curge reflected that damned near everyone who'd been strapped to the chair shut up when he revealed the steel.

"Dear Seddon above," Caro said in a much more sensible tone of voice, his red eyes blinking. "What do you… do you intend to do with that?"

Curge did not answer him.

Instead he took a step closer.

"I'll tell you everything! I don't want the gold anymore. It was a mistake. It was *all* a mistake!"

Curge gripped the cleaver and closed with the man. With practiced care, he placed the blade's edge against Caro's right forearm and stroked it, sliding the blade over his skin as if stropping it.

"Open your fist," Curge instructed him quietly.

"What?" Caro burst out, expelling breath and snot. Tears gushed over his cheeks.

Curge did not repeat himself. Instead, the cleaver stopped just below the leather that kept Caro's forearm in place, its edge pressing into skin.

"Yes, yes!" Caro burst out and spread his fingers on the chopping block.

"Spread your fingers wide."

Caro hesitated long enough to make Curge screw up his face and then did as he was told.

The old owner placed the tip of the cleaver to Caro's last finger, barely touching it, before moving to the next one and the one after that. In a question, his eyes flicked up to the messenger's sweating face.

Caro took the hint and sang. "Ah, I… Clavellus was visited yesterday by three men—three Free Trained men. They weren't there long and walked back to the city afterwards, but they were there. One of them was Halm of Zhiberia."

Curge dipped his head to the left, his ear almost touching to his shoulder.

"That's all!" Caro yelled.

Dark Curge straightened up. "Who do you work for?"

"Stable of Grisholt!"

"Grisholt? That old punce still alive?"

"He is! He told me to come here!"

Appearing unconcerned, Curge gouged out gnarls of wood between his prisoner's fingers, stilling the terrified man. Sweat beaded on Caro's face. Curge stopped after a moment and rubbed his forehead with his stump.

"He told you to come here just to let me know of Clavellus's visitors? A waste of my time. Clavellus does very little that interests me these days. Your name is Caro?"

"It is!"

"Caro, I don't think you are a particularly *smart* person. I don't think Grisholt is particularly smart either, sending you here by yourself puzzles me too early in the morning. I think both you and your master should be more concerned with this season's games rather than picking up scraps of information and then begging for coins. Dangerous business begging for coins, don't you think?"

"I do!"

"Hmm. I should teach you a lesson as to why they call me *Dark* Curge. Would you like to learn it?"

Caro blinked, clearly caught between not wanting to risk harm to himself and not wanting to anger the ogre with the cleaver. He gasped, eyelids fluttering as if struck soundly in the head, yet could not summon the words.

"Yes?" Curge asked, his glare intensifying.

A terrified Caro gave the barest of nods.

And Curge gently smiled.

He brought the cleaver up and over his shoulder then whipped it down into the chopping block between his captive's index and middle fingers with a bowel-loosening *thunk*. Caro sucked in his wind in a breathless shriek and sat gawking at the blade thrumming between that sliver of a gap, his fingers still in place. Veins as thick as rope protruded from his neck, enough for Curge to strum several at once if he desired. He released the cleaver and left it shivering in the wood.

A wide-eyed Caro slumped in his seat and panted, trying to calm his nerves.

"Go back to your master," Curge growled with contempt, "and don't come back here ever again. Understood?"

"Yes," Caro managed, emotionally spent.

With a glare at his household guard, Curge showed his back and stepped away from the chair, allowing Demasta and his men to get to work on the leather bindings. A moment later, they pulled the weeping figure of Caro from the bindings and hustled him into the corridor.

"*Thank you!*" was the last thing Curge heard before he gestured to Bezange to close the door.

"Smell that?" he asked his agent.

Bezange inhaled and shook his head.

"That little maggot's bowels didn't let loose," Curge

informed him. "Must be losing my touch. Ten years ago, I was much more frightening. A real terror."

"I thought you were going to take his head off," Bezange said truthfully.

"Might've. Keep a watch out for that one. He might feel some resentment towards you or me although he'd be truly stupid to do anything after this. Still, I know about Grisholt. That one's a whinging little shagger if there ever was one. Just like the shriveled-up hole sucker he called his father. One old bastard who never really did anything other than dreaming about days of glory that never were. Can you think of anything more hellish? The only thing he ever did was pass on a drying-up estate and stable to the bastard he knew was his son."

"I recall they once had a man in a champion's match," Bezange said.

"Oh that." Curge's expression eased. "They *almost* did. And almost ranked high enough to sit in the viewing box of the three houses. I think some other house had gathered up enough victories to beat them out. Tilo, I believe. Or Vorish. Well before Gastillo and Nexus took their seats. I liked *their* company a damn shade better than the two pissers I share the box with now. But I was glad that old bastard Grisholt never saw in. A lot of owners were. He had this… *air* about him, as if his shite didn't stink even though he wallowed in it."

Curge shook his head. "Grisholt is a one-legged dog amongst wolves now, and he'd rather lap at his own balls than fight over my scraps. Probably delights at my expense as well—any loss I incur during the games. Spiteful, you see. Just like the others. Sparing his topper here this day sends him a message. That punce will rather chew off his own plums than come around here anymore. Willing to sell *me* information. *Pah.*"

With that, Curge uprooted the cleaver and returned it to the table. "Three Free Trained pricks visited Clavellus. Where is the information there? He's nowhere near the Pit. Stupid, stupid man-child."

He paused, mulling and staring at the stone wall, his fingers drumming on a bare spot in an otherwise cluttered table. Nexus had only just informed him the other day that he'd hired the man to train his men, which Bezange later investigated and revealed as false. The old drunkard of a taskmaster remained secluded at his villa not a half a day's ride from the city. As long as he stayed there, Curge would let him live.

Still…

"Do you have anyone watching Halm of Zhiberia?"

"Not at the moment."

"Then start. Find out what he's doing and with whom. Just that. Anything more will be settled in the Pit. He still owes us a blood match. For the death of Samarhead."

"Master Curge."

Curge dismissed his agent with a wave of his stump and listened as he scuffled away. Once he was gone from the lower levels, Curge brooded and remembered his promise to his long-dead father, also named Curge, concerning Clavellus.

Old teacher. Old dragon. Old drunkard.

Why *were* three Free Trained warriors visiting an almost-dead taskmaster? That Clavellus was still alive surprised Curge even more. The man had once been regarded as the best in Sunja. The only trouble was he'd started believing it himself, even when his fighters lost. Then came the addiction to drink and the stormy comfort in the depths of the firewater bottle. Clavellus had even trained young Curge how to fight in the Pit long ago, back when his father ruled the affairs of the house. The taskmaster had broken many a gladiator's will in and beyond the arena. It was only after an exceptionally blustery exchange between old Curge and Clavellus that the man was cast out entirely.

Back then, his father had been just as monstrous as Curge was now, and he'd made it clear to all other potential courters that Clavellus was banished from the games and that he was to *remain* banished. But that wasn't enough, not for elder Curge. He started rumors about the taskmaster, effectively destroying his reputation. He also made it known that any house seeking to employ the man would instantly earn the enmity of the House of Curge, the strongest and most influential house of the day.

That was a hatred no owner in his right mind wanted.

When Curge's father took ill and became too sickly too move, sensing his time was near, he made his son swear to uphold his decree and keep Clavellus from the games. In his father's eyes, Clavellus had betrayed him, refusing to do as commanded, so he took away the one thing he was meant to do.

Train pit fighters.

At the time, many felt that aging Clavellus would die on his walled estate outside the city, living out his last years with the reputation for being too fond of wine and too hard on his fighters. His dying father made young Curge swear to keep Clavellus from the arena, to uphold his threat.

But Clavellus stayed away from Sunja and built a home just half a day away from the city, like an abandoned dog whimpering to be allowed inside the gates. Even he understood the consequences of the old man's venom.

Curge had never really believed much would come of it.

Until this day.

Clavellus. Curge's mind seethed. The young warriors didn't know about the taskmaster at all, and that, unquestionably, was pure salt in the old bastard's wounds—he was being *forgotten*. His father had held just enough sway over the Gladiatorial Chamber members to see Clavellus's name struck from any and all records with their halls. No one would ever see the old man's name associated with any champion or ruling house.

Old Curge could be a right vengeful bastard at times, a man who remembered old scores. It had rubbed off on his boy.

Dark Curge straightened and felt his spine crack. It seemed that Caro and Grisholt possessed some information of interest after all.

In memory of his father, he would honor his vow. Clavellus would not be allowed back into the games of Sunja.

Not if he had anything to do with it.

16

"I was wondering when you'd be coming back."

Though only mid-morning, the sun was well out of its gate and already cooking Halm. Sweat oozed from his face, shoulders, and back and ran earthwards in rivulets. Standing in the shade offered by the leather worker's overhead canopy, he regarded his new leather scabbard in wide-eyed delight.

"This is beautiful," Halm breathed, examining the piece at arm's length and turning it this way and that. The leather was soft to the touch, and strips of intricate hide strings latticed both ends. "I'm almost afraid to strap this on. I'll be marked by every thief in the city."

The leather maker rubbed at his rusty chin stubble, grown just a bit longer since last time. "I'm glad you approve."

"Approve?" Halm smiled mightily, unashamed of his terrible teeth. "With this, you just helped me with the ladies. How much?"

"Five gold pieces."

A sigh escaped the Zhiberian but only partially slowed him from untying his purse from his belt. "Costly, but well worth it. Here. If I ever have more work, I'll be back."

The merchant smiled, revealing a mouth with half of his own teeth missing. "Please do so."

Nodding that he would indeed, Halm tied up his purse and left it dangling from his belt. He gripped the hilt and pulled a quarter of the Mademian's length free, admiring the dull shine of the broadsword. He turned to the street.

Goll stood before him on his crutches, watching impatiently.

"Look at this," Halm exclaimed.

"I see a scabbard," Goll said drily.

"An exceptionally well-*made* scabbard."

"How much did it cost you?"

"Five gold."

Goll winced. "An exceptionally *expensive* scabbard."

"One has to take pleasure in the little things." Halm was disappointed that his companion didn't share his good feelings about the purchase. "Can't drink and whore all my winnings away."

"Surprised you have any left after that."

"A few coins, but getting low."

"Hmm." Goll watched as he strapped the scabbard onto his belt and adjusted it to his left side.

"There." Halm held his hips. His great brazen belly, bandaged and black with hair, hung over his belt and partially obscured it. He turned to the side to show off the scabbard. "What do you think?"

"I think you should have spent the coin on a shirt."

"Next purchase I make," Halm said good-naturedly. "It'll be cut from the cloth just for me."

"No other way, I imagine?"

"No other way!" Halm declared, not upset in the least at

the verbal jabs from his companion. He stood before the man on the crutches and swiveled at the hips to the left and right, studying the people moving along streets just beginning to strain at the seams. "No sign of Muluk."

Goll glanced about. "Not yet. At least you're tall enough to look over most of these heads."

"Mm. Don't see him."

"He'll be along."

"Not looking forward to another day of walking, I'll tell you that for nothing," Halm said.

Goll screwed up his face at the comment, enough to draw Halm's attention.

"What?"

"Nothing."

"I don't believe that. You're hiding something. How far is it to this Thaimondus?"

Goll looked at the rising sun, the brightness making him squint uncomfortably. "Two days."

"Two days?" Halm's jaw dropped. "My boots were about to split after a half day's march to Clavellus's! I'll wither up like a dead snake's skin on a two-day trip."

"You've got a few days of living on you." Goll still looked at the sky.

"That's…" Halm glared at him. "That's not the point. Two days, Goll. Is that on two working legs or two crutches?"

Goll's gaze dropped to his feet. "Working legs."

"So really you mean three days on the road?"

"Possibly."

"Goll…" Halm said with a tight-lipped expression of disbelief, "you… punce."

The two men stood in the gathering swell of people

making their ways through the street. The sounds and smells of the early morning activity only made the air hotter. Halm kept glaring at the crippled man.

"All right, I'll pay for a koch or something," Goll said.

"Or something?" Halm repeated. "What else is there? We can't buy horses. At least I can't. And even if I could, I don't have anywhere to stable it. Certainly can't *afford* to stable it. And did you happen to think about the tournament? Hmm? That *thing* going on? The one that just so happens is making us some coin?"

"That's why I sent Muluk off to the Pit this morning."

"Ah, and I wager it's also why you paid for the room last night. And breakfast this morning, am I right?"

"That's right," Goll said without humour.

"That's... *low,*" Halm said with a scalding look.

"Well, I'll just go by myself then. It'll be cheaper if I do. Spending two days aboard a koch in this heat with both of you wasn't something I was looking forward to anyway. That space might be taken up by a few good-looking ladies. I can hope anyway."

"Oh, you're hopeful," Halm countered. "I'll say that for you."

"What do you mean?" Goll's eyes narrowed.

"Nothing."

"Are you saying I can't find a woman?"

"You mean a good-looking one?"

Goll's expression darkened.

Halm pointed a finger. "You're the one who said I should buy myself a shirt just a moment ago. And now *you're* offended by a few harmless jabs? Sensitive topper, aren't you? If you sling shite, be ready to have it slung back."

Goll looked away, fuming.

"Sun's hot this morning, isn't it?" Halm smirked at his victory over the serious Kree.

A few moments later, Muluk joined them. "Lads." He took a second look at the red-faced Goll. "Sun's powerful this morning, I see."

"Did you see the matchboard?" Goll said testily, making Muluk frown.

"I did. Seems you'll be fighting in two days. Both of you."

"We won't make it," Halm said.

"Well, he's in no shape to fight," Muluk said of Goll. "But you're fine to go."

"I am. But our leader here has other ideas."

Muluk looked at Goll, who sighed. "The trip to Thaimondus will take a day and a bit. I think I can convince the Madea to hold off if we miss a fight. As you say, I'm in no condition to do anything. But you could," he said to Halm. "Easily."

"A day and a bit?" Muluk repeated, clearly not liking the idea.

"I'll hire a coach for the trip."

"Even then…"

"What're you worried about?" Goll asked him. "You're no longer fighting. Where do you have to be?"

"He's harsh this morning," Muluk said to Halm.

"He is, he is."

"Look," Goll growled. "Are you part of this house or not?"

Both men exchanged looks.

"Well?" Goll demanded.

"This is why he bought us breakfast this morning, isn't it?" Muluk asked Halm. The Zhiberian winked back.

"I'm going to hire a koch," Goll fired at both men. "See you in a couple of days."

With that, he got moving on his crutches and left them both in the street.

"Harsh this morning," Muluk repeated, watching him go.

"He is. He is."

"What're you going to do?"

"Well, I've got a fight in two days. I should get ready for that."

"You're not going to get ready for that. You're just going to sit and get drunk. Maybe even a rutting. I'm surprised you have the coin for it."

In such a short time, Muluk was reading him quite well. Halm was mildly surprised.

"If he goes, we'll be sleeping in general quarters," Muluk said.

That was true. That revelation caused Halm's expression to wilt. Even though he'd only had a room for a very short time, he'd gotten used to it, despite sharing it with Muluk and having to put up with his snoring. The Kree sounded like an avalanche of boulders.

"Best go after him then." Halm huffed, divided on the matter.

"He did say he'd talk to the Madea."

"Best get him to do it now. A ride in the country might be just the thing to speed up the righting of cuts and bones."

With that, they started off after Goll.

"New scabbard?" Muluk asked approvingly as they walked along.

They caught up with Goll halfway down the street and continued with him to a koch bay, the largest located conveniently next to the legendary main merchant's square of Sunja. It was a great wooden structure three levels high. Great yellow and green banners hung in sleepy, festive loops from its heights, prompting Halm to wonder why Sunjans hung so many of them off their buildings. Goll proceeded inside the bay, charging his two companions to wait outside until he was done, something which Muluk and Halm had no issue with.

"Did you happen to see Pig Knot about?" Halm asked.

Muluk shook his head. "Wasn't looking for him, to be truthful."

Goll emerged moments later, his crutches rattling as he hopped down the steps. "That's done. Nine gold pieces, I'll have you know. Another expense I'm bearing. I'd best learn to piss silver before all this is done. We'll leave when we get back from the Madea."

"We're heading to the Pit?" Muluk asked.

"Aye, the Pit. Have to speak with the Madea and let him know. Maybe he can push Halm's fight back a bit."

"Right nice of you, Goll." Halm beamed.

"Right nothing. I'll be wagering on your bulbous black hide once we get back. You can repay me by winning your match. If I can reschedule it, that is."

"You almost sound like a house master," Muluk said.

"I'm certainly spending *coin* like a house master," Goll grumped. "Or house lord, whatever pleases you. Unless either of you intend to throw in some gold."

Neither man moved or said a word, carefully staying quiet so as to not draw attention to themselves.

"Thought so." Goll made a face. "Come on then, you wretched bastards. My luck the first founders of the house are without coin."

Bearing the heat of the day, they arrived at the Pit,

entering its depths through a brick archway. Above were wavy lines etched into the stone surface, depicting a rolling ocean and marking the Gate of the Sea. Halm had once heard it was named such because it faced south and the great ocean that lay weeks away. Once inside, they located an entrance to the general quarters and quickly descended steps lit by the barest of daylight. The light died a dozen steps down, giving way to bare torchlight bathing the stairs in baleful orange. The men quickly caught a whiff of the bad air they had been breathing only nights before. General quarters was a hole for the Free Trained, and returning to it now, just for a visit, made all three thankful for rented rooms at an alehouse. Talking, swearing, and laughing mingled with the crash of weapons as Free Trained gladiators practiced as best they could in the cramped space. When the stairway opened up into the general quarters, the full power of the stench hit them—a mixture of bad breath, urine, shite, blood, and vomit. Torchlight flickered at various points around the massive chamber, giving those men who were without shirts a gleam as slick as ripe maggots. Armour and weapons appeared dull and shiny in the meagre light, and men passed in and out of shadows. Even the dark places of the underground chamber writhed with motion. Neither Goll, Halm, nor Muluk commented, knowing full well they had been a part of this only days ago.

Halm stopped at the base and craned his neck, unconsciously tightening his grip on the hilt of his sword.

"What are you looking for?" Goll asked.

"Pig Knot."

"Do you see him?" Muluk asked.

"No, not directly. He might be passed out in one of the dark patches."

He caught the shaking of Goll's head. The Zhiberian was getting the distinct impression that the Kree wasn't fond of the Sunjan. He couldn't really blame him. Pig Knot was a free soul, and as much as Halm liked the man, he knew one shouldn't expect much from him. Thoughts formed in Halm's head of whether or not Pig Knot would join their pursuit of a taskmaster and the establishing of a house. He had to admit, he was beginning to have his doubts.

Goll continued on, walking through the throngs of men, and Halm relinquished his search to follow. They moved towards the matchboard, careful not to step on the legs of still-sleeping men sprawled in the middle of the floor without any semblance of order. It was the way of the quarters—one slept where one could. Only the latrines, the armoury, and the Madea's matchboard were in designated areas. All else was fair game.

The arena official stood behind his wooden desk, on a stage raised above the floor of general quarters, pursing his lips as if it were dry land above a seeping marsh of fluid and flesh. He scratched at the almost perfect part in his haircut. A row of Skarrs lined the front of the platform while six others stood at guard behind the Madea, flanking the huge matchboard displaying the fights of the day as well as the week ahead. When Goll stopped before him, the Madea looked down as if sniffing the air. Dark eyes scrunched up in a question.

"Madea," Goll greeted. "I wish to talk to you about my upcoming match."

"Name?" the older man grunted.

"Goll of Kree."

"You got cut up there pretty well, Goll of Kree."

"I know."

"Won't be able to fight?"

"Daresay I'm out of it entirely."

"Hm." The Madea grunted and consulted his charts on his desk. "I'll make note of it."

"And this man here." Goll gestured at Halm. "He's Halm of Zhiberia."

"Ah yes, the Zhiberian," the Madea said, offering neither favour or dislike.

"He'll be accompanying me on a trip outside of the city."

"Hm."

"I hope it's possible to move the time of his fight."

"To when?" the Madea grumbled.

"Perhaps later in the week?"

The older man frowned at his charts. "It's possible."

"Then make it so."

"It'll cost you a gold piece," the Madea rattled off in an administrative huff, not looking at Goll at all. "Organizational fee."

The Kree regarded Halm with a dirty look. He fished out a coin from his purse and slipped it onto the Madea's desk. The older man did not acknowledge it.

"Be here later in the week. Understood?"

"Understood," Goll repeated and glanced at Halm.

"Understood," Halm blurted. "And thank you."

The Madea muttered something none of the three men could understand and went back to consulting his matchboard as well as the charts on his desk.

"A moment." Halm gazed up at the board. "Do you see Pig Knot's name anywhere?"

Goll squinted at the matchboard. "No."

"Nor I."

Halm nodded. In truth, he couldn't read a single word in

his own language, let alone Sunjan. He wasn't proud of the fact that he was illiterate and kept it to himself. After a moment, Goll limped away, and Halm and Muluk followed.

"Where now?" Halm asked.

"Karashipa," Goll answered.

"What's that?"

"The name of the village we'll be travelling to. Where the great Thaimondus lives. That's where we're going."

"So back to the koch bay?"

"Yes. Unless you want to walk?"

Muluk mouthed a soundless *no* while Halm scoured the shadows.

Searching for Pig Knot.

17

Looking out over the courtyard, a pensive air about him, Clavellus sat on a wooden chair and drank. It was only late morning, and he was already halfway through his bottle of Sunjan black—the dark, bitter beer he favoured over the sweetness of ale any day. Another mouthful and he leaned back in his chair, feeling the trembling in his left hand— never his right for some strange reason. The healer who came to visit had examined him thoroughly and agreed that the shaking was "quite interesting" but could offer no other advice on the matter. Nothing else was hurting, so the healer had left the estate, asking Clavellus to contact him if anything got worse.

Healers. Clavellus scoffed and took another pull of his drink. The beer was his medicine of choice these days, and Nala, his wife of forty years, didn't argue with him about it. He wondered why she had stayed with him during the younger years, as there had been plenty of other suitors flittering about her like bees drawn to sun-ripe petals, and in his opinion, better looking and richer. She married him in the end, and with each passing year, his insecurities about having such a striking woman lessened. He loved her with the same passion he'd been smitten with so many years ago, and after being expelled from the games, he believed it was she who truly kept him alive.

He'd been that close to going insane.

Old Curge had nailed his topper to a plank when it came to plying his trade in the games. Disagreeing with the man in front of his pit fighters was bloody sedition. Clavellus knew why he was cast out, and he knew he was still in the right. The fact that he had outlived the old bastard proved it. The only price he paid was never to be able to train fighters for any of the established houses in Sunja. He had trained a few warriors in the past, some from Vathia and one or two from Pericia, but even that had dried up like sap from a chopped tree. Curge's influence was so great that even the mere mention of a connection to Clavellus would result in that fighter being targeted in the arena and killed in violent fashion. Eventually, no one sought out the taskmaster, and no one in their right mind would hire Clavellus to train their fighters. Not when it meant living with a death mark in the arena.

Old Curge *had* died, however.

And time might have brushed away most memories of the outcast taskmaster.

Some, but not all, a pensive Clavellus supposed as he sipped his Sunjan black. And the ones that *did* remember… Free Trained. The slop of the entire pack. The rogues, the murderers, the butchers. Oh, there were some who genuinely had talent, but the majority of them were classless brutes quick to fight—undisciplined and easy to put down in the Pit. Clavellus even chastised old Curge's lads if any of them actually fought and lost to a Free Trained hellpup. Encouraged them to take their own blades and spike their brains and have done with it, for if they lost to such filth, their very names would be forgotten in a grey vat of maggot shite.

Free Trained.

And yet, years after being made a pariah to the sport, the very ones he had ridiculed and held in such very low contempt had approached him, asking for his expertise, asking him to *train* them.

Clavellus palm-wiped his face and drained his beer. He placed the mug on a nearby table, a pretty piece when Nala had bought it years ago but now every bit as worn as himself. Sturdy, chipped in places, but old. He was seventy-five years into his life, his skin tanned by the sun and made leathery. His hair had all but deserted his head, gathering in a silver bush at his neck and chin. All told, his health seemed still good, despite dull aches flaring in his joints, which he muted with medicinal quantities of alcohol. Then there were the nights when he rose to piss in the dark as often as three or four times—another mystery befuddling the healer. Yet he felt he still had fight left in him, despite the shaking of his left hand and the aches of his joints. He looked at the ball of fire in the sky, scorching the land beyond his walls. To the west, ghostly Sunja rose up on her high plateau like a crown set upon a cushion of gold.

And the games were in progress.

Just that knowledge set his mind to simmering.

"Ananda," Clavellus called, peering down into the courtyard and recalling better days. In his mind's eye, he could see the field alive with men going through their paces as trainers walked amongst them, transforming ordinary fighters into gladiators, instilling the knowledge and confidence needed to dominate the arena sands. He could almost smell the blood and sweat and that mystical spent-lightning sense of warriors finally becoming *aware* of their potential.

Free Trained.

Why did they have to be Free Trained?

"Lord Clavellus?"

Clavellus barely turned his head as he held out his cup. "Fill this again. And bring the bottle this time. Don't tell Nala."

Ananda was Sunjan, born in one of the smaller villages that had no games. An orphan Nala had taken as a servant and paid a few coins to at the end of each month, she was a pretty little thing, blond of hair with skin naturally darker than most. The lads who stayed in his employ, guards he and Koba trained and positioned around the estate just in case *young* Curge ever attempted to hurry along Clavellus's death, all snuck peeks at Ananda when they could. Clavellus didn't forbid them to gaze upon the woman, but he did warn them about making unwanted or awkward attempts to court her. Such distractions were all he needed under his roof.

She returned shortly with a large clay bottle. Without a word, she filled his cup, and Clavellus glanced at her clothes. Nothing revealing in the least. That was Nala. Ananda was an attractive young woman, and he hoped that the man that won her heart would treat her well.

He didn't thank her when she finished, nor did he watch her go. He drank a mouthful of the beer and eyed the guards on the ramparts. An insect buzzed by loudly. Somewhere in the direction of the stables, he caught the snort of a horse. Men talked in low tones, some chuckling, then nothing.

Just the sullen drone of silence, like a throat robbed of its voice.

"Shite." Clavellus burped and rubbed his bald head. He didn't want to think about how many years he'd been away from the roar and energy of the games. To do so meant remembering how long he'd been in this grave.

Free Trained.

Nala drifted onto the balcony. "You're starting earlier and earlier." The scent of her perfume, light and smelling of wild flowers, distracted him from his gloomy thoughts. She wore robes of white silk, old ones she'd bought for herself years ago when the material was overabundant and cheap. She had her grey hair tied back, and her hazel eyes twinkled at him.

Clavellus grunted.

Nala leaned on the railing. "What is it?"

He scratched at his nose before answering. "Those damn Free Trained."

"What about them?"

"Can't get my mind away from them."

Nala studied her husband. "You're thinking about going back?"

"I am." He met her gaze. "Would that disappoint you?"

"Isn't it dangerous?"

"Possibly."

"But you still want to do it?"

Clavellus nodded, suddenly very interested in the beer remaining in his cup. "I do. I do. What do you think?"

"Aren't they Free Trained?"

The older man frowned into his drink. "They are."

"Didn't you once say they were shite? Or maggot shite? I forget now, exactly."

Clavellus pinched the bridge of his nose. "I did."

"And didn't you once say that they were the rot festering

around… what was that you said? Saimon's shite trough? Or something like that?"

Clavellus exhaled mightily, chewed on the inside of one cheek, and squinted at the hot sun. Seeing no reply was forthcoming, Nala grunted, pleased she'd won that exchange, and studied her husband for a moment. A bee bungled its way past the balcony and zigzagged out of sight.

"Well," she began, "it isn't my choice. If you *want* to do it…"

"You won't be disappointed in me?"

Nala frowned then smiled gently. "When have you ever disappointed me? Perhaps *confused* me at times…"

Clavellus couldn't answer that. Even though his insecurities had lessened over the years of marriage, they weren't entirely gone. Every now and again, he wondered why she stayed.

"You… you'll go to the city then?" Nala asked, concern lacing her voice.

"Maybe. But not as much as you might think. I would like to see the games again, however. I think that's the biggest attraction for me. To see them as a taskmaster once more. Not as a mere spectator."

"I'll never understand that."

Clavellus could have guessed that response. "But I'm thinking that these men don't have a place to train. They're from the general quarters. That's the rat nest underneath the Pit. I'm thinking, with your permission, I'd move them here. Train them on the estate."

"An army of men around?" Nala thought about it. "The place won't have that sleepy air anymore."

"All depends on how many there are. Only three came here."

"You think there might be more?"

"Yes." Clavellus gnashed his teeth on the brim of his cup before sipping.

Nala moved closer, gently took his beer, and sipped it. She made a face. "Still tastes horrible."

"You saw what it was before you drank it."

"I prefer the sweet wine." She handed the cup back to her husband.

Clavellus hefted it and frowned, discovering it was empty. "I thought you didn't like it."

"I was thirsty."

Shaking his head, he reached for the bottle. "If I do this—train them—it might mean extra money coming into the house."

"Do we need it?"

"No... not really." His face was long and drawn like that of a cat pulled out of the ocean.

"You don't have to make imaginary reasons for doing this. If you really want to train these men, I'll not stop you. Just be honest with me. You'd be doing this because you miss it?"

He filled his cup, nodded, and peered into the courtyard below, hearing something metal clatter on stones.

"Koba will be happy," Nala said.

"I suppose he might." He placed the bottle back on the table.

"I'm sure he will. He's eager to crack the whip now. It's a good thing we don't let him near the horses."

Clavellus chuckled gently. "So you don't mind?"

Nala shook her head. "Just be careful. I'd like to have a few more years with you, you know. If you can manage it."

And with that, she slipped away, through the curtains and beyond.

I'd like to have a few more years with you—she'd said those words to him more times than he could count, and every time, he wondered how he'd ever won her heart in the first place. She knew it too; thus, the constant reminders. She didn't have to say it, but Clavellus suspected she knew how much he loved it when she did.

Just then, the tall, bulky form of Koba came into view, walking in almost a swagger across the courtyard and heading towards the smithy, his bald head glistening in the sun.

"Koba," Clavellus called out.

The man stopped in his tracks and gazed up, the horrific scar on the left side of his face glistening with sweat.

"Come up. We have something to talk about."

The big man blinked for a moment, his teeth shining in the brightness of the sun, and turned towards the front door of the main house.

18

Rolling away from the capital city of Sunja, the koch bounced over the pitted road, and the forest framed in the open windows jumped with it. The pleasant smell of country air, trees, and fresh water enticed the men to take deep breaths, comfortably filling their lungs and marvelling at how good it tasted. They stared out at the passing scenery, wistful at times, almost forgetting the rough road. Houses and barns, few and far between, drifted in and out of sight like dark islands in a swaying sea of yellow against a wall of jagged green. They passed the open fields known as Plagur's Reach, which were used as farmland. The driver had assured his passengers they would be in Karashipa before nightfall. That suited Goll fine as long as his arse didn't drop off from the rattling of the koch. They would find lodgings for the night in town, perhaps with a hot bath if he had his way. After such a lengthy run, he'd need a good hot soak.

Halm took up one side of the koch, at one point smoothing a hand over the blue cloth covering the worn cushions, while Goll and Muluk shared the opposite seat.

They were the only ones aboard the vehicle, which Goll had reminded them twice already, was fortunate. "As some of us are larger than others," he'd said without a smile, keeping a hand on his crutches where he'd laid them across the floor, pinning them to the wall.

"Was that a jab, friend Goll?" Halm asked. "Because if it was, I can sling it back, I'll have you know."

"Wasn't a jab," Goll said. "You're fat. I've no idea how you ever managed to survive a fight when you are carrying all that weight."

Halm placed a hand against his protruding gut. "This is nothing. It's armour."

"Armour that bleeds."

"Only if I get hit," Halm said. "See, men look at me and think what you're thinking, and then I go and prove them wrong. I'd be *too* fast if I were thinner. Fights would be finished too quickly."

Goll stared at the Zhiberian in disbelief, his head resting in a hand propped up by his elbow sticking out the window. "It's not amusing. We *need* to take some of that off you. If you were back in Kree—"

"Nice country, I've heard."

Caught off guard, Goll stopped, frowned, and continued. "If you were back in Kree, my trainers would punish you for being such a size."

"Would your trainers allow me to fight with them?"

"Not if you looked like that."

"Well then, I wouldn't have that problem, would I?" Halm said through a straight line of a smile.

His frown deepening, Goll averted his gaze out the window.

"Big forest coming." Muluk craned his head half out his window. Halm twisted around and did the same on his and Goll's side, knowing full well he blocked the Kree's view.

"So there is." Halm settled back. "These copses grow together. You know the name of this area?"

"No," Muluk said.

Goll shook his head, clearly not in a mood to talk with the Zhiberian.

"Damn being a foreigner, eh?" Halm smiled.

"Plenty of farmland." Muluk squinted in the breeze.

"Sunja grew itself up out of these lands."

"I thought it was livestock."

"That as well. Furs. Cloth. Silk." Halm became thoughtful. "Do you know what they make the silk from?"

"No."

"Worm shite."

Muluk's face crunched in disbelief. "What? That's not true."

"It is. It is." Halm grinned. "Worm shite."

Goll clenched his forehead in his hand, an action that didn't go unnoticed by Muluk. "Is it true?"

"No, it's not true."

"It *is*," Halm insisted.

"I'll ask one of the guards there once we stop again." Muluk bounced as the wheels rolled over a pothole.

"We already stopped once for a piss," Halm said. "Unless you mean when we reach the town itself."

"That's what I meant," Muluk replied with a chop of his hand.

"We'll have to stop for a piss again. Or just to get out for a bit. Stretch the legs," Goll added.

"Or the crutches," Halm said.

"Don't start anything," Muluk warned him. "I'm starting to fall asleep here."

"Too rough to fall asleep," the Zhiberian said.

"After general quarters, this suits me well enough."

Goll went back to watching the passing landscape, causing Halm to break into a grin. Daylight gradually darkened as the tall elm trees formed a natural canopy above. Wild grass rose up perhaps as high as a person's knee but stopped and drooped at the edge of the travelled road. The ride started to smooth out in Halm's mind, and by late evening, sleep tugged at him. He sniffed and wiped his face, feeling sweat there. As nice as it was to have a breeze blow through the koch, the temperatures were still high. Across from him, Goll had already gone under, his forehead pressed against one side of the interior. Next to him, his Kree countryman also struggled with staying awake. Muluk's mouth hung open as his head tapped the back wood in a warped beat. His unshaven beard appeared even blacker in the shadowy light. Halm felt the hellion's urge to scream right then and frighten the shite out of both men, but that would only cause him to sleep with one eye open later on. Krees could be right vengeful bastards.

Muluk crossed his arms, and his head slumped forward, bouncing lightly with the koch. Only a moment later, a thin line of drool slinked from his lips to his lap. Halm made a face and closed his eyes.

He hoped he didn't have nightmares.

The koch came to a stop with a gentle shake, rousing Halm from his sleep. It was night, and from where he sat, he couldn't see any moon. He yawned and made a face, glancing out the window and seeing torchlight in a few homesteads' open windows. Woodsy air carried a hint of smoke, cooking roasts, and something else that was certainly food but unidentifiable. The koch rocked as the drivers and guardsmen hopped to the ground, their groans piquing

Halm's interest all the more. He scratched his belly and kicked at his sleeping companions.

Goll woke in an instant, gasping and whipping his head about as if he'd been underwater for some time.

"We're here?" Muluk straightened, wiping his mouth with an open palm.

"We are." Halm eyed the homesteads. "Earlier than expected. But it doesn't seem like much though."

The door opened, and one of the drivers—a portly man wearing a white shirt—bade them step out. "Karashipa," he announced.

"Is there an inn nearby?" Goll asked.

"An inn? Not here. Too small." Darkness veiled the driver's face. "There's a small alehouse down by the water, however. But no rooms if that's what you're looking for."

"It is."

"Well, you're in luck. The night's a good one, and there's no rain on the air. A good time to sleep outside."

"Outside?" Goll did not sound impressed in the least.

"We sleep under the koch all the time during fair weather. Over there are a few more trees. It's quiet enough. And safe. We've pulled up into a little waiting area near the village. We'll be heading back at noon, by the way."

"Should be plenty of time. We'll be here." Goll slipped out the open door. "You said village. I heard it was a town."

"A town?" The amusement in the driver's voice was unmistakable. "Who told you that gurry? Not enough people to be a town. You'll see."

"Not much to look at, is it?" Halm commented.

"There's a lake that way." The driver pointed west as he walked towards the horses. "That's where the alehouse is. You'll find both. Easy enough."

The driver left the three companions to the darkness of the trees.

"Well?" Muluk asked.

Goll swung himself to a nearby tree trunk and settled down. "Not the first time I've slept outside."

"Sounded like the first time."

"Yes, well, you weren't listening right."

"Hungry." Halm touched his belly.

"It'll be easier to find things in the morning," Goll said. "This isn't Sunja. Barely a village by the looks of it."

He was right on that point. The road twisted off, but in the sparse light, Halm couldn't see exactly where. He liked the smell of the place, however. After the city's brick, stone, and sewage, the country air was almost as potent as mead. Sounds of distant conversation, ghostly in the night, perked his ears.

"What're you waiting for?" Muluk was already stretched out on the earth with his upper half leaning against a dark trunk.

"Not that tired."

"Not a *point* of being tired," Goll explained from where he settled down. "It's waiting until the morning. Can't seek out Thaimondus after dark. The man could be sleeping or anything. We'll find him in the morning. At least then he'll be able to see our faces."

"I'm going to find this alehouse," Halm muttered and didn't wait for a reply though he did heard Goll say something in Kree. He didn't want to hear the translation. It would probably be a warning about not spending any coin.

A small glade surrounded the parked koch, and he spotted the driver and one guard settling down for the night. Halm waved to them both. One of the shadows raised his hand in reply, and Halm walked off, following the road, which led deeper into the village of Karashipa. The houses, their hewn timbers fitted together with the seams filled with clay or some such material, lay on either side of the bare road. Huge plots of land divided each dwelling. Trees grew between the structures, and as Halm walked on in the night, listening to the soft sounds of voices coming from within, he found himself smiling at the sleepy quiet. He wondered if the villagers living here were famers or other tradespeople.

Farther down the road he trotted, expecting to strike the edge of the lake at any moment. Though the night was moonless, he could make out the vast black surface of the water and a few indistinct lumps. Conversation and laughter drew him towards a small building on his right. A doorway briefly opened, and a figure trekked to the corner, heavy footsteps clapping on the bare planks. The shadow winked out of sight.

Halm peered at the open windows glowing with firelight.

Probably the only business in the whole village, he thought and proceeded, thinking about buying a drink and seeing what was what.

He stepped up to the door, noting the wispy sheets of netting over the windows to keep the biting bugs out. The thick logs appeared old and fibrous, long since dried out and bereft of scent. The door itself was ill-fitting in the frame and looked more like an archery target as several splintery grooves and holes scarred the surface. The alehouse wasn't anything fine, not like the ones in the city, but "serviceable" came to mind. All was fine in Halm's opinion as long as it did what it was supposed to do. Patting his belly in fond anticipation, he took hold of the door's latch and pulled it open.

Some smoke drifted out, and seven faces turned in his direction. Five men sat divided amongst two of four tables in the place, while a pair of rough-looking characters swayed at the bar. They paused, bleary eyed, with their pipes. A rough-looking stone fireplace dominated one wall, with the remnants of a few wooden junks smouldering within, while above it, stretched out and nailed in place, was a rough canvas painting of rolling hills and a sun. A woman minded the place from behind the counter, like a fresh soldier standing guard behind battlements, and gave him the only nod as he crossed the threshold. Halm greeted them all with what he felt was a friendly wink and grin while very much aware that the conversation had died away into nothing.

Still, he was inside now, and thirsty.

"What do you have?" he asked the bar wench, putting on his pleasant best of a smile.

"Just ale and Sunjan black." The woman studied him and made no qualms about it, as did the rest.

"Nothing to eat?"

"You came in too late."

"Then a pitcher of ale."

"A pitcher?" She smiled in a dubious way. "Five silver."

"Five silver?" That impressed Halm. "Half price of anything in Sunja."

The woman, with her sable hair tied back and her narrow face, regarded him for a moment as she took a pitcher and went to one of five raised barrels behind the counter. She wore a plain green dress buttoned to the neck, with a white apron tied around her waist. Halm thought there was nothing special about her looks, certainly not like the dishes in the city, but his eyes ran over her form out of habit. There was, just perhaps, a figure well hidden beneath her unflattering clothing.

He felt his smile widen when he realized that the two men standing at the bar had steadied themselves and watched him with stoic expressions. They were farmer types, smaller than the Zhiberian but solid looking. Halm knew it only took one wrong look to set off a protective husband, and a blade was always an equalizer. Clearing his throat, he nodded to the pair. They didn't return it, and he knew then they'd seen him sizing up the bar wench. Behind him, someone laughed, perhaps a little too loudly, but Halm didn't turn around.

The woman plopped a wooden pitcher and cup down in front of Halm as he fiddled with his purse. He still had a few coins left, and he placed one of the gold ones on the counter. The expression on the woman's face softened just a little as she took it.

"Won't be needing the cup." Halm nudged it back towards her.

She made it disappear without a word and then avoided his gaze by looking at the counter as she counted out his change. She left the few coins on the counter before moving away. Frowning at his failed attempt, Halm scooped up the silver and deposited it in his waist purse. He hoisted the pitcher in one fist and saluted the nearby men. Halm took a great draining sip from it, downing a third before placing it on the counter. *Good*, he thought and rubbed his face. The trip had been lengthy, and he was growing increasingly tired of travelling distances without anything to eat or drink.

Scratching at his belly, Halm belched loudly enough to startle the pair of smokers and took a moment to study the cozy interior of the little alehouse. The men sitting at the table still stared at him—he could feel it—but he wouldn't turn around. The long cut logs of the place put Halm in mind of the homesteads back in his native land and a longing for the coolness of short summers.

"He's a fat one, isn't he?" someone croaked from behind him.

That made Halm cock an eyebrow.

"Thick around the neck, too."

He took another swallow straight from the pitcher before turning. The speaker was a shrivelled-up thing—an ancient-looking topper, his jaw hanging low as if panting for breath, with one gleaming tooth jutting up from the lower lip like a forgotten fang. Grey hair was slicked back, keeping clear of a face that hadn't aged gracefully. His clothing, perhaps once well made, were three sizes too large for him.

"Aye, you see me now, don't you?" The man wheezed, his glaring, rheumy eyes locking on the Zhiberian. "You fat bastard."

Halm looked from this unpleasant old punce to the younger one sitting beside him. Dark of complexion, hair, and eyes, he observed Halm with a lethal air, his chin unshaven. Well-built and broad of shoulder, his tunic displayed arms that were coated with a sheen of fat but powerful looking all the same.

"My apologies." Halm pleasantly saluted them both with the pitcher. "I'll leave shortly."

"Not soon enough." The old man puffed the words as if their very utterance pained him. He grinned, displaying yellow nubs that passed for teeth. His jaw rolled as though he chewed on something, but his sickly eyes remained on Halm, making him uneasy. "Not soon enough, fat bastard. You *fat*…" The attacker seethed the word to its fullest, making the sound snap. "*Bastard.* There was a time when, if a man had that much meat on his bones, it was considered hoarding food while others starved. Gluttony is a *crime*. A *crime*, you unfit ball licker."

Halm regarded the thick man sitting next to the old bastard. "I think he's had enough."

The one with the dark complexion and eyes said nothing, but the corner of his mouth hitched ever so slightly in a sneer. "He hasn't had a drop."

"You wish I did." The old man cackled and broke into a cough that made his sloped shoulders jump. "You *wish* I did. No, I see you with these old, sick eyes of mine, and I can tell you, you filthy, wet dog blossom, you shite eater, that the pitcher of horse piss you're quaffing down is worth more than twenty of the likes of you."

Halm frowned. "Well, that's rude of you."

"You speak funny, too." The old man drew back in curious abhorrence. "Well enough, mind you. Probably can't quite wrap that foreign tongue around a civilized one, but you make a go of it. Keep just enough of an accent to believe you're charming. Probably figure it's endearing, somehow. Those snake charms are lost upon me." He chuckled then, a rattling noise that ended in a heavy cough. He leaned to one side and hoarked, spitting up lengths of yellow phlegm. The old man allowed two thick strands to hang off his lip.

Halm straightened, the feeling of unease giving away to revulsion. That was a sight he could well have done without.

But the sickly speaker wasn't finished.

"Sunja's been too damned accepting of other races. Too damn welcoming. Tainted her blood. Made her weak. Now, we have…" A pallid hand groped and pulled at the mess dangling from his weathered face and retreated under the table to wipe it on his leg. "We have *breeds*. Breeeeeds…" He hissed to the point of coughing again. "*Fat* breeds like you."

Halm exhaled and took a quick pull of his pitcher. He didn't have to drink it at all. He could leave it on the counter as it was, but he'd paid money for the ale. He glanced to the serving wench and noted she wasn't taking too kindly to the jabbing either but wasn't about to do anything. Halm didn't expect her to; she was only a barkeep. A wench.

"Breeds walking about and packing the asses off anything lying still enough. Making *more* breeds. Unending cycle of impurity. An ever-fattening cloud of flies over a pile of shite. Maggot shite. Dropped out of Saimon's rosy ass itself and left to spatter decent folks like ourselves."

"Well." Halm finished his last bit of ale in a painful gulp. He nodded affably to the woman, slapped his belly lightly, and made to leave.

Just then the door opened, and a man stepped in, a few fingers taller than the Zhiberian, huge, and heavily muscled. This one wore no tunic, and his bare chest, slicked with black, heavy curls, heaved as if he had downed more than his fair share of drink. He ducked slightly to fit inside the room, and when he did, Halm felt the temperature drop and the tension rise.

"I'm not finished with you," the old man sneered as if sampling venom. On those words alone, the giant's eyes squinted with violent apprehension, and he blocked the Zhiberian's exit. Halm didn't like that. He didn't like getting into fights while drinking, and he never liked being cursed at by a corpse of an old man.

"When I'm done lecturing, *boy*, I'll let my *man* allow you to go, unless…" The contrary pisser stuck his head out as he leaned forward with dawning delight. "Unless you wish to *fight*. Hm? Wish to fight? You… you great, greasy prick? He'll kill you where you stand. Put a blade through that fat neck of yours and let your… breed blood bubble up."

Halm remembered his sword then and thought perhaps he could frighten them all. From what he could see, no one else in the place had any weapons. With that, he casually placed his left hand to his pommel, making his intentions clear.

"Now, you listen to me, you hollowed piece of horseshite," Halm said, steel in his voice. "I'm leaving now. Right out that door. If your boy tries to stop me, I'll put this blade up his ass and make him sing like a castrated dog. And when I've done that, I'll do the same to that pretty little girl beside you making eyes at me."

The old man's companion bristled at the insult, his dark eyes suddenly flaring to life.

"And after I've done painting the walls here, in true *breed* form, I'll slap *you* around like the brazen he-bitch you are. Knock that one pearl of a tooth out of your hole so people will really have to think about which end the shite drops from."

If looks could start a fire, the old man's indignant glare would have illuminated the whole of the night. "No one speaks to me in such—"

Halm didn't need to listen to more. He took his sword out and scowled at the brute blocking the door. Checking on the rest of the patrons, he stopped at the barkeep. "My apologies," he said and meant it.

Her expression said the same.

Then he brought the blade up, torchlight flickering along the steel.

"I'll find you, you sack of pig-ready gurry. I'll find you," the wretched man sputtered from behind his table. "When my… my lads are better prepared. I'll find you and… and skin that filthy colour off your hide. I'll take days to do it and let your blood run—"

But Halm had had enough. He walked towards the door, weapon ready. He'd learned long ago that when bluffing, it was best to be fully prepared to do as you promised and to make it known through the eyes. Halm stared at the big man as if he were a piece of meat ready for the butcher. The lout backed off, actually hissing at the Zhiberian, half-daring him to *take* that swing and let Saimon sort out the mess afterwards. Halm then heard a screech of wood on wood and knew it was the other one, the dark-eyed one, getting to his feet.

"I'll find you, *breed*, I'll find you and slice your balls off." The old man cackled, every third word punctuated with a rattle of loose phlegm and a brutal cough that almost made Halm sick. *"I'll find you!"*

The Zhiberian edged around the large brute and backed out of the alehouse, his sword bright with deadly intent, reflecting the way his mind was warming to the notion of a little bloodletting. He stepped off the front step and moved away, concentrating on the path ahead and still hearing the old man cackling. *"I'll find you. I'll fiiiiiind youuuuuu."*

Halm glanced over his shoulder to see two shadows, one taller than the other, standing outside the alehouse and watching where he went.

"Right rude old punce," Halm muttered, keeping his blade unsheathed. He wandered back up the road until the alehouse was out of sight. The two henchmen didn't appear to be following, so he relaxed a little but decided on sleeping somewhere away from the koch site, just in case. By the time he reached his companions, their snores made the tension slip from his features. He wandered through some trees and found a place where he could see both the koch and anyone attempting to sneak up on him in the night.

Breeds, insisted the hoarse voice of his tormenter, still lingering in his head.

Halm ground his teeth, applauding his own restraint. It wasn't often he had to stop himself, but it wasn't often he was so pigheadedly insulted by old men who should rightfully be dead.

His last thought before sleep took him was of the apologetic expression of the woman behind the bar.

19

When he opened his eyes, Pig Knot felt the sting of the knife wound on his forehead. A grimace twisted up his face as he felt the cut, tracing the stitches with two fingers. *Stitches.* He had stitches in his head. Where had he gotten those? And when? Above him, thick planks lay across dark timbers coloured with shadow. Light lanced into the room through an open window, and Pig Knot could hear the daily commotion of the masses outside.

Groaning as he pulled himself into a sitting position, Pig Knot felt the blood rush from his head, replaced by a dull pounding in his temples.

"Never drink again," he breathed, knowing he'd be on the grape before the day was done. He'd lied to himself many a time before and gotten used to it. There were two more opened windows in the walls and another three cots filled besides the one he lay upon. A desk and work area was next to one of the windows, and an impressive collection of knives, saws, tongs, and things he knew not the purpose of, hung from pegs or were laid out with professional grace, all redolent of medicinal herbs.

Healer's house. He recognized it now and winced again.

How in Saimon's hell was he going to pay for this? A quick feel of his pockets—not minding the quiver in his hands—told him they were empty. He couldn't remember if he spent it all or lost it or was robbed the night before.

"Alive, I see," a voice said, and Pig Knot looked upon a middle-aged man emerged from a stairway, his hands gripping the edges of the door as he hauled himself up. The newcomer wasn't overly tall and possessed blond hair an argument away from light brown. Under this were eyes of smoky grey. Upon climbing to the top of the steps, he straightened out the white tunic he wore and walked over to his patient.

"You'll want this, I believe." The man handed Pig Knot a pitcher filled with water.

He could smell the goodness before he tasted it. "Thank you," he muttered before downing most of water, lowering the vessel with a gasp and wiping his mouth with a hand. "Seddon above, that was needed."

"There's a chamber pot underneath the cot as well. If you need it."

"I need it." Pig Knot handed the pitcher back and bent over to see the clay pot, its surface etched with fancy writing. Why people crafted such pretty work for shitting and pissing in was beyond him. He dragged it out and fumbled with the front of his trousers. The healer turned away. A moment later, Pig Knot groaned with release, and the sound of a healthy stream cut the air.

"Ahhh, that's good. Almost as good as the water. Easy in, easy out, eh?" Pig Knot chuckled and sighed. Once finished, he wrung out one last shivering dollop before returning the pot under the bed. A moment later, he tucked himself away and took a breath.

"Lords above, I got dizzy towards the end. How much does one have to drink to get dizzy when he pisses?"

The healer shrugged. "Quite a lot, I imagine."

"I suppose so." Pig Knot smiled faintly and indicated his scalp. "Thank you for this."

"You're welcome," the other replied pleasantly.

"How much do I owe you?"

"Nothing. You gave me your last coin last night."

"I came in last night?"

"You did. Some men brought you in. Soldiers by the looks of them."

"Soldiers, eh?" Pig Knot became thoughtful, trying to remember what had happened the night before. His shirt was missing, and he took in the scrunched hardness of his otherwise fatless midsection, presently mottled with purple and yellow bruises he couldn't remember receiving. Then he remembered the fight and the man called Prajus. "Where am I, in regards to the Pit?"

"North."

"Hmm. What's your name?"

"Bindon."

"You've been working at this for long?"

"Had my infirmary for a few years, I suppose," Bindon replied. "There are quite a few older ones about. But I expect to gather more patients as time goes on."

"The way of it. Um, where's my shirt?"

"Oh, I had to throw that away. Blood covered it. Ruined." Bindon frowned. "You cut yourself to the bone last night, by the way. A right frightful gash."

"They're all right frightful. But thanks for sewing it together. I don't owe you anything?" he asked again.

Bindon shook his head.

"May I stay here for a bit?" Pig Knot asked quietly. "Get back my strength? Perhaps a little more water?"

"Certainly. There's room, as you can see. Just be mindful of your..." Bindon touched his own forehead to get his meaning across.

"Feels like I had the top of my head taken off."

"It actually *looks* as if you had the top of your head taken off. You could pass for a Sujin returning from the front if you wanted."

"No, wouldn't want to sully their name."

Bindon shrugged and, as if a thought took him, handed back the pitcher and turned to leave. "I'll return," he promised.

Pig Knot watched him go then sipped on the water remaining in the pitcher until it was all gone. Dust motes bounced dreamily off sunbeams cutting through the open windows, and the heat informed him that the day was already a warm one. Best to stay low if he could. He felt the straw-stuffed mattress of the cot and drew his calloused palm over its pointed lumps, unable to remember exactly when he had owned a bed he called his own. Not even when he was a boy did he have one, having been an orphan and living off the streets with others of his kind.

Bindon returned as promised, carrying another pitcher and a loaf of bread. He handed both over to Pig Knot.

"The bread's a day old, what my wife made yesterday. But it's good."

"Thank you," Pig Knot said with genuine delight. "Ah, might I eat it later? Gut's a little..."

"You may." Bindon appeared both puzzled and pleased.

"You took my last bit of money, as well. I mean... I can't pay you for this."

"Ah, don't worry about that. You have a day here to recover at least. Anything after that, I'll make a list, and you can pay me later."

"Kind of you."

Bindon shrugged, as if it were simply business.

"You live here?"

The healer nodded. "Just down the steps there and through a short hallway. My house is behind the infirmary. From my father. We live here now."

"Ah. Father's passed on?"

"He is. As is my mother. Five years now."

"Sorry to hear that."

Bindon waved a hand. "No matter. He taught me what he could. What I do from here on in is my choice now. We'll do fine, I imagine."

Pig Knot found himself hoping this young man and his wife would indeed prosper. He seemed a right friendly sort, he thought, just as Prajus's leering face shimmered in his mind's eye.

"You're a soldier?" Bindon asked.

"What? No. Just a pit fighter. Free Trained. In and out of trouble as you can see."

Bindon nodded, keeping his thoughts.

"You're a big man. Ever do any soldiering?"

"Worked as a hand with builders. And ate my wages pretty much. Took up the steel when I was old enough. Probably should have stayed with the builders. Damn sight better. Easier on the clothing as well."

They chuckled at that.

Bindon glanced away for a moment before clearing his throat. "Well, I'll be in and out of here for most of the day. Stay in the shade and sleep. Close the shutters if the noise from the street becomes too much, but rest easy. You're fine here."

"Thank you again."

Again, the hand waved as if dispelling evil spirits. "You take your time and stay on that cot. It's not the best, but it's yours for the time you need to get your bearings back."

With that, Bindon departed the room. Pig Knot listened to the healer's softly receding steps on the bare wooden stairs, guessing the man wore slippers inside. He took a sip from the new pitcher of water and relished the feeling of it going into him, bringing life back to his person.

Putting the pitcher on the floor, Pig Knot lay back down and gazed at the woodwork of the ceiling. Dust motes wandered through his vision at times, and the sounds of the city in the street below sometimes caught his attention—but never for long. He stopped thinking about Prajus and the other men who had attacked him.

And they didn't follow him into his sleep.

The day started hot and became almost unbearable, waking Pig Knot from his slumber. He didn't care about losing his shirt when the sweat ran off his skin and soaked into the cloth covering the cot. He wandered about the upper room, peering out at the heads milling up and down the side street, people passing the healer's house and carrying on with their business. Bindon came up twice more during the day, bringing more bread and two apples, which Pig Knot devoured almost as soon as he took them. They didn't have time to converse then as someone from the street wandered into the healer's house and called for the healer. For the remainder of the day however, Pig Knot didn't have to share the upper quarters with anyone else, and for that he was thankful.

The day's heat lessened with the evening, and a light, wonderful breeze blew into the upstairs room. Pig Knot went to sleep staring at the darkness of the ceiling and listening to the murmurs of people outside.

The next morning, he got up and made ready to leave. He hauled on his boots and haltingly made his way down to the ground floor of the house, feeling things ache as he moved, and passing the hallway which led to Bindon's house.

"Leaving?" Bindon startled the pit fighter. Pig Knot located him behind an old desk, with a worn-looking book open before him. The healer sipped on something in a cup, peering at him through wisps of steam. Pig Knot took a breath before answering, smelling ointments that reminded him of deep forests.

"Leaving. Do I owe you anything?"

"No. But if you need anything more done, please return."

"If I ever get my head gashed open again, you mean." Pig Knot saw the first floor had a number of shelves along the walls, full of vials and jars containing items pertinent to a healer's trade. Some held fibrous white roots preserved in juices the colour of piss, while others held unknown, organic-looking baubles that sat and stewed. All a mystery to him.

"Well, yes. Or anything else but nothing life-threatening." Bindon lowered his cup.

"I will."

"Here, take this."

Pig Knot chuckled. "More bread? Just how much of it does your wife make?"

"Enough to give away."

"Or you just don't like bread."

Bindon smiled. "I like it well enough."

"Tell her she's a fine baker."

"I will. Good luck to you in the Pit."

Pig Knot waved at the healer and passed through the front door. With the sun rising and the streets practically deserted, he headed east, squinting at in the morning light and intending to strike north once he reached a main road. He reached around and gave a tug on his long war braid for the luck to find his way back to the Pit.

He didn't see the man detaching from the shadows of an alley and following from a safe distance.

General quarters smelled like shite.

After spending the night in the nest of the healer, the underground felt more like a rumbling, musty sewer reeking of gas than a place to sleep. Or perhaps that was the problem with the place. It was being used for too many things by too many people. The air rankled his nose the deeper he went until he got to the lower level and looked about in the dark. Torches burned from sconces set into walls, fighting a losing battle against the gloom. He stepped carefully around snoring bodies that lay scattered throughout, searching for the spot where Halm usually slept. Moments later, he found it and discovered a trio of men sleeping there, all unknown to him. The pair of Krees were nowhere to be seen either. The matchboard, large and prophetic, loomed up, and Pig Knot wandered over to it, whispering the names aloud.

He didn't see Halm's. Or anyone else's he knew for that matter.

Rubbing his face, he wandered to another spot where he and Halm and the others had once stayed. That area was still bare, but the large cloth sack containing Halm's armor and helm was missing. Pig Knot shook his head. Someone hadn't actually *stolen* that garbage, had they? The thought gouged him. He gazed about the immense underground chamber, finding shadows that moved and those that did not. Huffing, he gave up and hunkered down, got comfortable, and listened to the dull, rattling snores that seemingly shook the Pit's foundations.

He tried hard not to think about a clean cot and fresh bread.

20

The rickety gates of the Stable of Grisholt opened early in the morning as men finished preparing a wagon and a koch for departure. With a greasy saunter, Grisholt made his way from the entryway of his house and climbed into his transport. There, he shifted his ass upon the cushions until just so and waited with an air of indifference as Brakuss closed the door behind him. The stable owner truly hated travelling at such a time, not appreciating the fresh country air or dew moistening the courtyard grass. But travel he must, for on this day, his fortunes would change. In anticipation of this change, he wore his finest clothes that hadn't been wasted by time, a rosy vest of satin over a black shirt and beige breeches befitting a man of his position, complemented by high leather boots of worn but distinguished-looking leather. The perfumed water he wore was the last to his name, and he promised himself that after this day he'd replenish his supply.

He heard the drivers snap the horses into movement, and the two vehicles rattled through the gates, eventually turning towards the grey heights of Sunja. Inside his private koch, Grisholt tugged on his beard and thought about the day and the first fight of the season for his stable of warriors. He'd already spoken with Gunjar, and though he could see the young man was disappointed with the order to lose his first match of the season, Grisholt assured him there would be other seasons for him to perform well. The fighter could certainly make a name for himself cutting up Free Trained warriors in other matches outside of the regular tournament, which would be practice all the same and opportunity to make a little extra gold. In addition, losing the match would endear him to the Stable of Grisholt, even place him in Grisholt's favour, and that was something that couldn't be measured in gold alone. His loss would extend life not only to the stable but also to his fellow pit fighters as well.

Gunjar accepted it, but Grisholt could see he wasn't happy. The old owner didn't care in the least about the man's feelings on the matter. In the end, Gunjar did what he was *told* to do.

They made the short journey to the city and entered the main gate with no questions from the Skarrs. Grisholt took the time to gaze out his window and studied peasants, farmers leading livestock, and the shoddy merchants in their open stalls. He gathered a fine hand cloth and placed it to his nose and mouth. After the clean air of the countryside, smelling the shite of thousands of people pent up within city walls wasn't something he could endure for long periods. And to think they thought it fresh! Even as the koch's ride smoothed out, a farmer stopped in front of the horses with a string of cows. Grisholt leaned out to see what the delay was just in time to glimpse of one of the beasts defecating right there in the street. He drew back, but the image remained in his mind. And who knew how long the offensive pile would remain there, and the countless number of feet, bare and booted, that would trek right through it. He thanked Seddon above he wasn't born to a farmer's life.

The koch rolled past the scene and made good time until it stopped once more.

A question on his face, Grisholt again looked out his window. People of all their shapes and colours milled about, but nothing held his attention for long. He leaned to the other side in time to spy Caro pass by the window and rap on the door. Grumbling, Grisholt quickly closed all of the shutters, encasing the interior in mid-morning gloom. Assured that people outside could no longer see in, he gripped the handle and cracked the door open, screwing up his face at his agent.

"Get in, quickly."

Caro did so and deposited himself on the cushion opposite his employer, his face veiled in shadow. Grisholt closed the door and eyed the man with contempt. He detested stopping in the middle of a street. It drew unwanted attention.

"What is it? And it had best be something, to catch me on the way to the arena."

Caro fidgeted, not at all comfortable. Grisholt thought the man looked terrible. His shirt had been torn open to reveal hairy, sweltering parts of him the stable owner didn't wish to see. Sweat dribbled down the agent's face, and there was something about him that just seemed unwell.

"Well?"

"I saw Curge early this morning." Caro glanced at the shutters as if suddenly aware of where he was.

"No one can see you in here," Grisholt blurted impatiently. "Well? Why aren't you at the Pit?"

"Curge…" Caro faltered. "He tortured me!"

That made Grisholt cock an eyebrow. It didn't really surprise him. Not really. "Did he pay you for the information?"

Caro shook his head. "He… he was going to chop off my fingers."

Grisholt looked at his henchman's hands. All digits were in place and accounted for, which *did* surprise him. "But he didn't?"

"He didn't. Instead, he… held his hand, and I told him about the Free Trained visiting Clavellus."

"You didn't mention anything about the gold?" Grisholt leaned in, his temper rising. By Saimon's blue pisspot, he'd strangle this idiot right here in the koch if he so much as—

"No, not that. Just everything else."

"Everything else? What everything else?"

Caro hesitated. "He knows I work for you."

Grisholt shrugged impatiently before forcing himself to assume a veneer of indifference. "As if I care what that ogre thinks. Curge is elemental at best. Now then, did he harm you in any other way?"

Caro shook his head so violently he might have just been pulled from a winter river's icy depths. Not that Grisholt particularly cared. Spies weren't too difficult to come by. But he could plainly see his man was somewhat unhinged, and unhinged agents could be damaging.

"All right. Now think. Did you…" Grisholt paused for a moment, for the next part was quite serious. "Tell him anything else?"

Sensing the danger he was in, Caro again shook his head and exclaimed, "No, nothing! I swear!" His hands clenched the ragged ends of his shirt.

Grisholt made the conscious effort to appear relieved. "I

have to be certain, you understand. You said nothing about my plans this day?"

"Nothing, I swear!" Caro's eyes widened in fright.

Grisholt stared into those terrified orbs.

"I believe you," he stated after a short, considering silence. Then the owner gave his agent a wink. "You can relax now, Caro, you survived your encounter with Curge. I won't ask you to do something like that again. It was a mistake on my part. Here…"

Grisholt pawed at a cushion and slipped if off the seat, revealing a sliding panel. He removed this as well and reached inside the hole meant for long journeys when he didn't wish to step outside to use a latrine. Reaching just under the lip of the hole and grimacing, realizing full well where he had his hand, he brought forth a leather purse. He handed it over to his man.

"Take this. You know what to do with it. I'll have a few lads around to ensure no one robs you later."

Blinking and making the effort to relax, Caro reached out with two functioning hands and took the small leather bag from his employer.

"Yes," Grisholt went on, convinced that his agent hadn't compromised anything else to Curge, and thankful he didn't have to dispose of him. Even though the interior of the koch was frayed, it was still clean and quite comfortable. Killing a man inside of it would only bring about bad luck on this day. Instead, he went about replacing the panel and cushion, smoothing it when done. "We won't do that again. Not if he's going to be *that* way. I should have realized it was Dark Curge we were dealing with. My mistake, good Caro. Have no worries. Now then. Can you do the task at hand?"

Caro nodded, finding his backbone.

"Excellent. Then we're done here. Bring the gold to my viewing chamber once you have it."

With that, he leaned over and opened the door for Caro, shooing him out.

When the spy was gone, Grisholt closed the door and tugged on his beard unconsciously, swearing at himself and Curge. The gall of the brute to terrorize his messenger. Caro had gotten off lucky this time around, and so had Grisholt. It would be the last time he approached Curge with any information. Scowling, he rapped the wood behind his head. A second later, the koch laboured onwards.

As they approached the inner city and Sunja's Pit, Grisholt opened his shutters and recognized the wagon carrying Gunjar and a handful of his other fighters steering towards the entrance of the sun, while his koch veered towards the stone and timber booths of the Domis, where wagers were placed. The driver got as close as possible to the four booths, as Grisholt ordered him to before they left the estate, and he waited until Brakuss opened the door. Then Grisholt stepped out into the sun with a snarl of a squint on his face.

"Miserable heat." Grisholt switched from the hateful ball overhead to the lines of peasants waiting for their turn with the Domis. Skarrs could be seen in menacing full armor, watching the crowds for any sign of trouble. Four lines of people stretched back from the open windows where one placed wagers, and Grisholt had no intention of waiting at the end of any of them.

With the intimidating form of Brakuss behind him, glaring at the world with his one working eye and a hand on the pommel of his sword, Grisholt summoned a smile and made his way to the front of the nearest line. He didn't excuse himself, and the gathered people took note of him with indignation quickly suppressed when Brakuss came into view. The seven or eight Skarrs standing about did nothing to stop the stable owner, which added even more insult to the people waiting in line. Grisholt detected the repressed sputters, and his smile widened. He knew the Skarrs recognized him, and he knew they would only act if a fight started. Unlikely with Brakuss on his heel.

The second peasant in line frowned and relinquished his place without a word when he saw Grisholt and then Brakuss. When the owner reached his selected window, he stared at the back of the head of a man who hadn't noticed him and continued making his wager.

Brakuss stepped in and shoved the peasant aside, pushing him away from the window and surprising the Domis within. A glare from the henchman silenced any protest from both men. Grisholt stepped up with an unruffled sigh and a pleasant demeanor.

"Ten gold on Gunjar, Stable of Grisholt," he announced just loud enough so that those nearby would hear the princely sum. He only needed a few ears, and the reaction would be swift. No one placed that amount of coin on a fighter without knowing something, and the peasants behind him would be quick to choose Gunjar themselves. Already he sensed eyes on his back and felt a greedy energy building in the air.

The Domis, a shorter man who squinted, made the wager and handed over the marker.

Grisholt snatched it away without a word of thanks.

With a glowering Brakuss securing his back, Grisholt returned to his koch, ignoring the wary looks from those he passed. He pulled to all the shutters once inside his transport. It wouldn't keep the smell of unwashed bodies out, but at least he didn't have to see the populace. He leaned towards one window and, after a moment, opened it just a crack. There, he spotted Caro at the back of the nearest line. Smiling to himself, Grisholt rapped on the wall behind him, prompting the koch to lurch forward. He twirled the ends of his beard. Caro would quietly place a fifty gold bet on Gunjar's opponent, whoever he was—Caro knew, and that was all that mattered. Fifty gold coins was, in fact, almost the last of Grisholt's existing treasury, but it was worth it. The winnings would give Grisholt's stable breathing room once more. This year, he wanted to be more aggressive in his wagering. He didn't want to ever reach his current financial state ever again.

The koch stopped once more, and Grisholt waited until Brakuss opened the door.

"I feel lucky." The stable owner smiled at his bodyguard before pointing beyond him. Brakuss then became a meaty knife cutting a path between the crowds entering the Gate of the Sea. Grisholt followed with three more of his lads guarding his back. Brakuss led the little band to the private entryway allowed only for owners and other important figures. Grisholt was glad for the entrance as it bypassed the Free Trained nest completely. They had to pass the stairs that descended into the general quarters, and the stench that rose from that black throat made Grisholt want to heave up whatever was left in his stomach.

Once off the public walkways and descending another set of stairs, Brakuss steered them towards a private room, one of several that allowed owners or house gladiators to look out at the arena sands at foot level. Once inside, the door was closed behind the party. It wasn't the most comfortable of rooms, bare except for a few benches, and built out of the same brick, mortar, and timber as the rest of the arena. But it afforded a certain amount of privacy to the owners. Sand sometimes blew in from the arched window flush with the arena floor, but this particular day, Grisholt was glad to see that it hadn't happened yet. He waited until Brakuss got out of his way and proceeded to the archway, stopping a foot before the window and peering outside. If he leaned forward, he could very well rest his elbows on the chest-high ledge—not that he would do such a thing. He didn't want to get any closer and risk ruining his appearance or scent. After this day, he would have the coin to place more wagers, as well as to purchase much-needed goods for both the stable and himself.

Beyond the arched window, the sand glowed, almost blinding, while rising heat distorted the very air.

Miserable heat, Grisholt scoffed, dabbing a hand cloth at his neck.

The benches in the room were hard to the ass and not at all to his liking, but he sat on the cleanest-looking one and waited for the first fight to begin. Brakuss stood, eyes flickering towards the sand and no doubt remembering his own short but violent career in the Pit.

"Do you miss it?" Grisholt asked him.

Brakuss took a moment before answering. "No."

Liar, the owner thought smugly, kneading the end of his beard with two fingers.

"This is going to be a very good day." He looked expectantly at the arched window. "Lucky, lucky, lucky."

It was at that precise moment the door to the private chamber opened.

And in walked Dark Curge himself.

Curge regarded them all with a black countenance, like a venomous butcher working his blade through a stubborn piece of gristle. He stood in the center of the room, challenging any who dared take a swing, wearing black trousers and a tunic the colour of sand. A single hand axe hung off a wide black belt, and Grisholt was quick to notice that it was well within reach of Curge's right hand if he needed it quickly.

Grisholt did not think he would need it. At all. He had to consciously let his breath out.

Curge stared out the archway, taking in the sand of the arena as though seeing it for the first time. Then he centered on a tense Brakuss, who like the other three guards, stood with his hand on his sword.

Curge eyed him with malice, his lips curling in a silent challenge to pull steel.

Behind the ogre dominating the room lurked a bear of a man, not as tall as Curge himself, but as wide as the door. A thick X of studded leather crossed his chest while a paw of a hand gripped a scabbarded broadsword. Curge's fearsome killer, black of hair and beard, closed the door and stood with his broad back against it. He glared at Grisholt as well, delivering the unspoken message that he was quite willing to spill blood if commanded.

"Grisholt," Curge rumbled, not taking his eyes off Brakuss. "I wanted to thank you for this morning's message."

Curge then turned his murderous gaze upon Grisholt with all the scorching heat of a midday sun.

"Ah…" Grisholt started. He made to stand, but Curge *tsked* no. The killer that the one-armed owner brought along glared at Grisholt's four guards, and Grisholt suspected that the man could butcher the lot if given the command.

"Ah, you're welcome, good Curge. Glad to be of service. I had hoped to make a few gold coins with the information, but my man said he caught you perhaps a little too *early* in the morning?"

"He did."

"My apologies."

Curge didn't blink. "I wasn't overly offended. I left him his fingers. And his balls."

This set Grisholt's eyes to flutter for a moment, as if a horse had kicked in his skull. He cleared his throat, composing himself. "Ah, well, I appreciate that."

"What do you care if the topper has balls or not? Not a daisy, are you?"

This struck Grisholt speechless. "Uh, no, I'm not," he finally managed.

"This place." Curge took his eyes off the man for a moment and gestured with his stump, which disturbed Grisholt for some reason he could not quite identity. "Feels like a grave. You really can't see much down here, can you?"

"We see enough."

"Hm. This is only my first—no—second time at this level. I was fortunate enough to inherit my father's run of luck when I assumed command of his house. Never stepped beyond the view box of the top three. One sees everything up there. Everything. All the feints and strikes. The tactics and strategy."

"We see that down here as well," Grisholt said quietly, trying hard to not look at Dark Curge's stump. Lords above, the man was well over sixty, yet the aura he projected was as menacing as a full complement of battle-hardened Sujins. "As a matter of—"

"Down here," Curge cut him off, "you are limited. You have no idea *how* limited until you are up there, looking down. Do you get my meaning?"

"Yes."

"Good. I wish to say two things, and I'll be off. One, thank you for the information. To be honest, I haven't thought of Clavellus in an age. What the Free Trained want with him, I have no idea, nor do I truthfully care as long as he stays away. And two, don't ever send your man to visit me at such a damn early hour ever again. Not if you wish him back."

Grisholt nodded his understanding. "I apologize for—"

Curge's chilling smile killed the sentence. "Saimon's unholy ass crack, I can't keep this up." He shook his head wearily and glanced back at his killer. "Demasta, what's the best way of dealing with a weasel?"

"Kill it," the brute answered, glowering.

"Kill it. My father warned me of men such as you, Grisholt. 'There's only one thing worse than a house with a vengeance,' my father would say, 'and that is a house *wanting* your place.' So I'll be blunt and not mince words. Don't cross me, you grey-haired *prick*. Nor toy with me. And Saimon take you now if you actually think to outwit me. If you do, I'll start a house war and see your shack crushed like balls under my boot. I'll make it my hobby to see that every one of your maggots is matched against my killers each and every time they set foot on the arena sand and hacked to pieces in the most horrific way possible. I'll *destroy* whatever you have beyond these walls, Grisholt, whatever few planks nailed together that your father had such high hopes for. I'd even make the argument for bringing back the old custom of master fights and challenge you personally. I'd take great pleasure in splitting that skull of yours, just to see how unfit it is inside."

At this, Brakuss bristled and visibly restrained himself.

And, unfortunately, drew attention.

Curge glared at Grisholt's one-eyed bodyguard. "Something bothering you? Maggot-shite?"

Tension, the likes of which Grisholt had never experienced, lashed at his heart and senses, causing him to stroke his beard with brisk flicks of his hand. Brakuss didn't like being talked to in such a manner, only because Grisholt was certain his bodyguard wasn't entirely aware of Dark Curge's reputation. Grisholt was *very* much aware. His father had also been exceptionally wary and had taken time to ensure his son understood the dangers of any contact with the Curges. Dangers that never seemed more imminent than this exact moment.

When his one-eyed guard looked at the floor, Grisholt almost expired with relief.

"No, I thought not," Curge rumbled, his attention lingering on Brakuss for a few moments more. "I don't wish to see you again, Grisholt. I certainly don't wish to see that messenger of yours again. And I certainly never want to smell this lavender shite you must have bathed in for a year to smell so damned ripe. Do you understand?"

"I think you and I—"

Curge waved his stump as if clearing the air. "Do you really think there is a 'you and I' here? Does this look like a meeting of equals? Hm?"

"No."

"Good. You understand then?"

"I understand," he whispered.

"Excellent. Thank you for the winnings, by the way."

Grisholt didn't get the man's meaning, and his expression said as much.

"Ten gold on Gunjar." Curge screwed up his mouth. "Bit obvious, don't you think? Especially when my lads know your man's face now. Caro is his name, I believe. I don't suppose Caro was wagering all that coin *against* Gunjar, do you?"

Grisholt blinked, suddenly unable to muster his voice.

"Oh, he placed your wager, have no fear," Curge hissed. "*This* time."

"Thank you," Grisholt managed, trying unsuccessfully to regain his dignity.

Curge made a face. "And I tell you. Perfumed shite is still shite." The one-armed beast locked eyes with him for a moment, and Grisholt blinked, fighting down the urge to look anywhere else but into those steely blue chips of ice.

Then Curge gestured with his stump, and the bear behind him threw the door open. Curge left then, his bald head glistening with sweat. The one called Demasta followed, showing his back to Grisholt's guards and letting them know what he thought.

Outside, the Orator cried out the introductions. Gunjar's name could be heard, but Grisholt did not bother standing up to watch.

He no longer felt lucky.

21

Demasta followed his employer outside and slammed the door behind him. He turned, not bothering to nod at the four extra warriors standing in the corridor, and all of them fell into step behind Curge as he stalked away. *Little shite*, flashed in Curge's mind. Some of these lesser houses and stables had to be watched, and Grisholt in particular. It was as his father said: never turn your back on a hungry dog. He'd get Bezange to keep an eye on him. He walked through the whitewashed walls a short distance before climbing the stairs leading back to *his* viewing box. His house had maintained their ranking for so long that it was difficult to think otherwise and that the other two owners were merely temporary, unwanted guests. Curge consoled himself with that very thought. *Hungry dogs*, he thought as he directed Demasta to stand just outside with his men. *And now, wolves*.

Curge opened the door and snatched a silver goblet from a serving tray, startling the wench holding it. He downed the wine in gulps, smacked his lips while staring at the wall, and waited for her to refill it. Once done, he made his way to his seat and plopped down on the green satin cushions.

"Decided to join us, eh?" Nexus asked him. Curge didn't

bother looking at the old wine merchant who, in his opinion, was a noisy nuisance. The gold-faced Gastillo he could bear as he'd been brought up near the fights, but not this silver-haired, black-eyed weasel trying to learn everything at once and believing himself to be the best. The arrogance of the man cut at Curge's patience. It was only a week ago he'd lost a fighter to a Free Trained, something that put the merchant in his place. Curge didn't know how much control Nexus was wresting from his taskmasters during this season, but while in the city and assuming in his role of manager, Curge believed the merchant was probably close to driving them insane.

"Don't answer me, then," Nexus said in an unbothered voice.

Curge glared past the fitted brick of the box and into the arena. The fight had finished. One gladiator strutted off the sands while another had to be walked off by a pair of men.

"You missed it." Gastillo sounded bored, his words carrying the barest note of metal as they passed the lips of his golden mask. "The Stable of Grisholt almost lost a man this day. To another Free Trained lout. The upset of the day, I imagine."

That softened Curge's mood somewhat. When his agents saw both Grisholt and Caro place their wagers, he gave the nod to Bezange to find out who Caro was wagering on and placed his own wager. He couldn't remember the last time any of Grisholt's lads had actually won a match, but he had to shake his head at the simplicity of the ploy. Instructing his fighter to lose, making a show of placing coin on him while having another man place a much larger wager on the opponent wasn't unheard of amongst the owners. One had to have gold to keep it all running, but pompous Grisholt was just so *obvious* about it. It made Curge ill. The gold he'd won would relieve some of that discomfort, some of which he'd pass off to Bezange for detecting the scheme in the first place, but he told himself once again to keep an eye on the man and his stable of fighters.

"You wouldn't know anything about that, would you?" Gastillo asked.

"What's this?" Curge tore his attention from the arena and focused on his companion to the far right, sunlight flashing off Gastillo's metal face. "Are you stabbing at me, good Gastillo? A man of *your* honour? Let me remind you, since your brain is obviously cooking under that sheet of cheap tin you're wearing, that I *lost* a warrior just recently. A particularly expensive investment, I might add. We'll see how well you take such a loss when the day comes about. And it will. And I'll be right here when it does, remembering this exact moment."

"It was saucy of you," Nexus agreed in smug fashion.

"Don't come to my defense, Nexus," Curge said out of the corner of his mouth, waving his goblet underneath his nose and inhaling its scent. "I haven't the stomach for it right now."

Nexus and Gastillo exchanged looks, sly ones at that, and returned to watching the sands. Curge took in the sheer stony scope of the arena, noting the seats were half-empty. He knew in his blackest of hearts the pair would not stay quiet for long.

"Sour mood you're in," Nexus said eventually.

Curge rolled his eyes. "Who wouldn't be sour when he has to put up with the likes of you beside him?"

"Seddon's heaven," Nexus bit back. "If I'd known the entertainment was going to be as good up here as on the arena floor, I'd have come here much, much sooner. Usually, the men about me *listen* to what I have to say. These little lashes you throw out are amusing."

"I hope my boot amuses you when you find it up your hole."

Nexus's smug expression sagged almost immediately.

"That's better." Curge pressed on. "I like it when you're quiet. Just like a woman. Eh, Gastillo?"

But Gastillo did not answer.

"Ahhh that's right, you're still kissing his ass behind my back. Let me guess the conversation when I'm not about. 'That lad looks about done—yes, you're quite right, Nexus.' 'I believe these Free Trained punces are thicker these days than any other. Yes, once again you're quite right. It surprises me how observant you are in your first season of the games!'"

Nexus's lips puckered as though his wine had soured, but Gastillo's golden face was unreadable.

"You go too far, you loud bastard."

"That's the first real thing you've said to me since I arrived here, Nexus," Curge said. "Just remember whose tongue is in your ass when I sit down. Or perhaps, if my words are too salty, you might seek company that's more agreeable?"

"I'll be looking forward to our matches together, Curge. If your hellpups are as good with a blade as you are with barbs, perhaps I'll manage to stay awake. Oh hold on, that's *right*—one of your dogs was killed by a Free Trained. You'll be busy with blood matches, I expect."

"You can be sure I'll have time for your lads, once that's done," Curge rumbled.

"I look forward to it."

Curge regarded Nexus for a moment and saw the hard stare directed back at him. Say what one would about the man, Curge told himself, the wine merchant was more than willing to sling barbs. Unlike the gold-plated tit on the far side.

"What does Gastillo have to say about that, hm?" Curge asked in a loud voice. "You look like you might be shivering over there underneath that shiny face of yours. When does one of your lads grace the arena sands? When will we see Gastillo's hellpups fight?"

The golden visage didn't move. "Soon," brushed past the metal lips.

Curge let him be, hoping that Nexus might learn something about keeping a quiet tongue.

22

A boot nudged Halm, waking him from his sleep. The early morning smells of the surrounding forest made him crack his eyes wider and sit up amongst some sparsely growing grass.

"You're taking to sleeping outside very well," Muluk informed him.

"After the Pit, anywhere's a good place to sleep."

"You're right there."

"Anything to eat?"

"Only if you brought it yourself." Muluk walked deeper into the forest.

"Where are you going?" Halm asked.

Muluk turned and grabbed his crotch before disappearing behind some thick trunks. Halm ignored the gesture and spied the other Kree already on his feet and crutches.

"Fine morning, good Goll."

"You Zhiberians call everyone good?"

"It's a fashion I've taken after the Sunjans. Are you buying us breakfast this morning?"

"Why not," Goll grumped. "Buying everything else for

us. No reason to stop now."

"My friend, good Goll." Halm beamed, getting to his feet. He placed his hands behind his back and stretched it with a crack.

"That didn't sound good," one of the nearby coach guards commented.

"Sounds terrible but feels good. Now for that breakfast."

"You're welcome to eat with us." The driver walked towards the vehicle. "Not much, but I can spare you a bit."

Both pit fighters nodded their approval before moving closer.

A little later, the rays of sunshine piercing the overhead canopy of green, they sat in a circle around an uncovered basket full of breads and hard-boiled eggs. Sweet red jam was applied with knives and eaten with gusto. They drank water from a barrel at the rear of the koch, measured out with a deep ladle.

"How was the alehouse last night?" Muluk asked from where he sat, the corner of his mouth flecked with the remains of his single egg.

Halm grunted.

"What was that?"

"Yes," Goll asked drily, "what was that?"

"I said"—Halm swallowed his last bite of bread—"I almost had a fight." The Zhiberian then recounted his experience in the alehouse and the words exchanged with the old man and his two dangerous-looking companions.

"A damn good thing you didn't fight them," Goll scolded. "You're to fight later this week, and I'm counting on you to win. Anything between now and then… well, you walk away. Run if you have to."

Halm shrugged at this as if it were no matter.

"I'm serious about this," Goll continued. "You risk yourself in such a manner, and you're no use to any of this. What can you contribute?"

"My stories of distant lands?" Halm beamed. "The women I've bedded. The company I've kept."

"That might be something to hear." Muluk chuckled.

Goll shot a dark look at his fellow countryman and pointed a warning finger at Halm.

"All right," the Zhiberian conceded before Goll could say anything more. "I'll do as you say."

That placated the Kree as he settled back with only a hard look at his portly companion.

"Right, so where's this Thaimondus?" Muluk asked of the driver. The man, a middle-aged sort with a face darkened by the sun, jabbed a hand in the direction of the lake.

"Down there. You'll see a palisade. And a wharf with some small fishing boats. All his property. He's like a small lord here."

"You know about him?" Goll asked.

"Only that he used to train fighters for the games… and now lives here."

"What's he look like?" Muluk wanted to know.

"Small man. Old now. Haven't seen him for a while, but I've heard he's become sickly. His mind addled."

From where he sat, Halm's face drooped.

"He's usually walked around by a pair of his lads." The driver focused on Goll. "Two big men. You'll see them soon enough."

Halm drew a hand across his forehead. Even in the shade, he was finding it uncomfortable.

Goll noticed immediately. "Those men you almost fought…"

"Might be them." Halm's words caused the Kree to close his eyes, seemingly wishing it wasn't so.

"We could be finished then," Muluk said for them both.

"Shut up," Goll snapped, flustered. Then to Halm, "We could be finished, you realize."

"It might not be them," Halm offered.

"Might not," Muluk added.

"Are you some damn echo here," Goll slung at his fellow Kree, who became sullen and set his jaw.

"These two men, one of them walk around bare-chested like myself? Tall man?" Halm asked the driver.

"Aye that. I've seen him such."

Goll squeezed his eyes shut in quiet agony while Muluk rubbed the side of his face.

"I didn't know," Halm muttered at them both. "There was no way of knowing. They were right on me from the moment I was in the place."

"What should we do?" Muluk asked.

"Find out if it's really them," Goll answered, setting his shoulders. "Then go from there. My thanks for the meal. We'll be back before noon if we can—or send word otherwise. If we're able."

"We'll be here then." The driver stood up to tend to the horses.

The three gladiators got to their feet and followed the dirt road. They passed houses built on either side without any forethought other than simply claiming the spot as their own. Small gardens with wild garlic divided up the space between the rough dwellings while stone chimneys smoked idyllic plumes into the quiet morning air. The sun hid itself behind some low-hanging clouds, giving the land and the lake a pleasant, dull quality.

"Nice little place." Muluk eyed the free chickens strutting about. Goats could be heard somewhere to the left.

"Nothing here to do," Halm said.

"Daresay this is just the start of a little town." Goll swung along on his crutches. "The lake ahead is quite large. Plenty of land about. Quiet. I'd like to see this place again in twenty years."

Halm scowled, struggling with both his like and his loathing for the quiet life. And the idea that he might have made an enemy of Thaimondus without even knowing made all other thoughts trivial. It was a wonder he managed to get down breakfast.

They approached the lake, a great, dark-blue thing laid out before them like a poorly framed mirror with a small rocky beach. A small wharf jutted out into the water, long and set low to the surface, with three small boats tied to its length. The town had been built alongside the small waterside clearing, but to the left and right, a fence of elms almost completely ringed the rest of the water's edges.

"Like one big pisspot," Muluk commented.

"Doubt the people around here would call it that," Goll said without humour.

"Why? It's true."

"It does look like a big pisspot. Even with the wharf and boats," Halm added.

"Or shitepot," said Muluk.

"They wouldn't shite or piss in their drinking water," Halm retorted. "What fool does that?"

"Look." Goll grated. "Let me do the talking when we're inside. Don't say anything unless spoken to. Make no comments about anything. Just silence."

"Sounds to me he doesn't feel we're up on our social skills," Muluk said.

Halm didn't bother answering as he was vigorously scratching at his crotch.

To the left of the lake, narrow logs almost the height of two men rose up from the bare earth where they'd been rooted. The tops were sharpened to raw points while dull metal spikes protruded from the wall. They walked towards the large wooden gate set into the barrier and could see a tile roof rising up a ways beyond, smoke slinking from a chimney.

"Someone's home, anyway," Muluk said.

"Rap on the wood," Goll instructed.

The Kree looked about a moment before pounding three times on the gate, not moving the timbers in the slightest.

"Good morning!" Muluk called out, causing Goll to squint.

No answer from beyond.

"What now?" Muluk asked.

"We wait."

Halm's unease grew as his guts squirmed, seemingly rearranging his insides.

A man could be heard humming to himself then, drawing closer to the gate. Two others could be heard talking and chuckling. Then came the sound of boots climbing steps, and a head peered over the wall.

"What is it?" the head asked.

"Is this the residence of Thaimondus?" Goll asked, craning his neck backwards.

The head's jaw rolled as it chewed on something. "It is."

"We've come to speak with him."

"What about?"

Goll frowned. "That's between us and him."

"No, that's between you and me. You tell me what about,

and I'll mention it to him when I get around to it. And the longer you wait, the less important it is, I figger."

The head spoke rough Sunjan, and Halm had to concentrate to make sense of the thick accent.

"We wish to hire him as our taskmaster. We're pit fighters. From Sunja."

"Course you're from Sunja. Free Trained are you? No trouble to tell."

Muluk shared a *who is this punce?* frown with Halm, who wasn't feeling well at all about this. The encounter with the locals the night before, coupled with this bastard on the wall, were cutting a very clear picture of people living in this area.

"Please pass on that message," Goll politely asked.

"When I get the chance," the head answered, still chewing.

"Then we'll wait here."

"Move on back a bit. Over there in the grass. Don't piss on anything."

With an exasperated sigh, Goll turned to move.

"Course," the head continued, "I might pass on that request a little faster if you toss me a coin."

"What?" Goll snarled.

"A coin. What's the matter? You deaf? Or just stupid?"

Even Halm scowled at this topper above them. It was a young man, unshaven, with a shock of curly brown hair. He gripped the points of two logs with fingers that looked like fat sausages.

"I'm not paying you anything."

"Well, then, that'll be two coins now."

Goll balked. "You must think I'm an idiot."

"I *do*. I truly do. And be careful now. Any unpleasantness and the price goes up once more."

"We'll wait," Goll told him.

"You'll wait a long time, then."

"You have to come out some time."

"No, you stupid topper." The head sighed. "You don't understand. I'll make it simple for you. You listening? Hey, cripple? You listening?"

Goll's jaw clenched. "Go on."

"No, I asked you if you were listening. You answer me first, and then we'll go to the next bit."

The crippled Kree smiled then, as harsh as a gleam of steel, and Halm saw the restrained fury in his eyes. "I'm listening."

"Good. Try not to be so thick, eh?" At this, chuckles could be heard behind the closed gate. "Always heard you lot were stupid, eh. Stupid. But never believed it. I'm the sort where I have to *see* it, right? Have to *see* it. Lads," he said to the men laughing behind the gate, "you should see this crippled ball licker. He looks like he's ready to burn something. Hey, cripple," he directed back at Goll. "Get happy there. It's four coins now."

Goll glanced at Halm, and the Zhiberian wanted nothing more than to strike that pile of shit on the wall.

One of the head's hands stuck out from the wall, fingers flexing. "Toss them up here. The only way you'll see anyone here. Old Thaimondus hisself wants the coin. Told me to get it from you. Coin first, then we'll let you in."

Rubbing his face, Goll struggled with his purse and fished out four gold coins. He tossed the first one up at the head. It bounced off the wood, and the man made no attempt to catch it.

"In my hand, you angry tit, in my hand. Toss it here."

Muluk walked over and picked up the gold piece.

He was about to throw it up when the head spoke. "Ah no, no, no, that's not fair. The cripple tosses it. Come on, little man. Toss it here. Pretend one of those sticks is up your ass."

Holding his temper, Goll tossed up all four coins, one after the other while balancing himself on the crutches. Some attempts failed, but after a while, the head grew bored with his sport and eventually made the effort to catch the gold.

"That's good, cripple." The head smiled in nasty fashion. He nodded to the men behind the gate. Sounds of a plank being removed and falling to the ground could be heard.

The gate slowly opened inwards.

Halm's gut sank.

The brute standing right in the widening opening was none other than the shirtless giant from the night before.

And the big man smiled at him.

23

"Breed," the giant hissed with evil delight. Half a dozen other men stood about, dressed in leather vests and capped off with ill-made cloth hats. All carried swords and spears, and none appeared particularly friendly. Some still chuckled in wicked amusement from the head's taunting of Goll.

"Welcome, breed," the giant greeted and stepped aside, gesturing for them to enter.

Goll lumbered in, heedless of the monster's recognition of Halm, and for that alone, the Zhiberian wanted to throttle the Kree. Muluk followed him in, and Halm reluctantly brought up the rear, wary of the big man exuding hateful mirth.

Two men behind the gates pushed them closed, bringing the count of armed men to ten. Halm didn't like the odds in the least, and the presence of the great, evil, smiling brute before him made him feel terrible. Four of the spearmen with brazen smirks on their faces blocked Goll from proceeding any further. Beyond their crossed spears stood a fine-looking house built on a knoll.

"Ah," the head called out, stepping down from the wall's rampart. He was dressed in fine pants and a grey shirt open from the neck down to his upper belly. "I'm afraid I misled you a bit. The price to get in here was four gold pieces. To see Thaimondus will cost a bit more."

Goll scowled at him, the colour creeping up his neck like a furious rash. "Thaimondus!" he roared.

The smiles on the gathered men bled away. Two of them even looked back to the well- made house facing the wharf and water. Other smaller houses were behind the wall, along with a barn and a smithy, all squatting well away from the prized house lording over them all. At the startling yell, people milling about with chores looked up.

"Thaimondus!" Goll repeated.

The head's amusement disappeared, and he took two steps towards the Kree, but Muluk stopped him by blocking his path and staring into his face with a questioning glare. The spearmen about them tensed, and Halm placed his back to his two companions, his hand on his sword's pommel. Before him, the giant's smile didn't dim in the slightest. The man had even taken to punching meaty fists into alternating hands.

"He's heard you already, you stupid punce," the head said. "Dog balls, you'll wake up the whole town."

"What do you care?" Goll asked.

"I don't, truth be known. Ah…"

From the house on the hill, two men emerged from a door and stood on a deck facing the wall. Halm inwardly groaned. The henchman with the grim look helped the bowed-over frame of a much older man, Thaimondus himself—the same saucy bastard who had ridiculed him the night before. The old taskmaster came into view dressed in a red robe of considerable worth.

"This will not end well," Halm spoke under his breath, catching Muluk's ear.

"Is it him?"

"Aye that," Halm said wearily. "In the wasted flesh."

"I'll do the talking," Goll insisted.

Halm gestured *be my guest*.

"Father," the giant called out, "the *breed* from last night is amongst these dogs."

The dark one's face split into a murderous smile while Thaimondus steadied himself by grabbing onto the deck's railing. His unpleasant features screwed up and glowered down at them all. He swished his hand, unsteady for the moment it took, and the spearmen blocking the three moved aside.

Goll called out. "Master Thaimondus, I wish—"

"Shut up," Thaimondus snarled with all the fury from the previous night, squashing Halm's hope that he might have been drunk after all. To his regret, he could see that Thaimondus, in his charming years, was a right vengeful old prick.

One of the old taskmaster's hands stabbed in Halm's direction. "You." He seethed, his lips puckering up in hate. "You piece of *horseshite*. Miserable sack of maggot juice. I spit. I spit on you and any who claim you as family."

And he did, graphically summoning up curds of phlegm but generating only a weak bauble of a dribble that stretched for a moment from his lower lip before finally breaking away and falling to the ground. The sight and sound of it made Halm cringe. Even Goll looked back at the Zhiberian with a concerned expression, silently demanding a greater explanation when there was no time to tell.

"You there," Thaimondus screamed out, "cripple! What are you doing with this topper?"

Goll closed his eyes as if in mortal agony and faced the

taskmaster. "He travels with me and my other companion. We're gladiators—"

"*Pah.*" Thaimondus jerked his hand in the air. "You're not *gladiators*. Gladiators wouldn't be here talking to me while the games are on. Who are you? Unless, Saimon paddle my ass, unless you're Free Trained shite. That's it. That's it, isn't it? You're *Free* Trained rabble. Dog *balls*. Should've seen it earlier. Boys thinking since they have a blade they're men. I'll tell you what, cripple, you and your daisy friend there can leave now and don't look back. This fat breed and I have some unattended matters to finish. I said I'd find you, breed—but Saimon take me, I never figured you be knocking on my front door so early in the morning!" A rusty laugh left him, sounding like a woodsman taking a saw across a frayed tree trunk. "Saimon's black hanging fruit, we'll string you up nice and proper," Thaimondus cackled with wicked glee, clasping his claws together in anticipation.

"You can't have him," Goll announced.

This drew the taskmaster's attention, and he took a moment to address the upstart. "Watch me, cripple. There're no Skarrs about. This is *my* land, and you stand upon it. You and anyone on it are my property in my eyes, as sickly as they are. Any thinking man here knows that."

"Then we'll fight you," Goll stated.

From where he stood, Halm felt a rush of admiration for the Kree. Even Muluk was adamant in his pose. The Zhiberian's fondness for the pair grew.

"Fight you?" Thaimondus exclaimed. His frame shook and he leaned to one side. In alarm, the man near him reached out and steadied him. The rotten sounds erupting from Thaimondus's one-toothed maw were foul to hear, forcing Halm to glance elsewhere. He saw the workers beyond the spearmen—men, women, and children, all poorly dressed—and knew in an instant that Thaimondus probably was a self-proclaimed lord here in this wooded land.

Worse, he might very well be a tyrant.

"I'll fight," Halm shouted and drew his blade, "him."

He pointed his weapon at the giant. The big man eyed Halm's sword with interest and cocked his head in a question towards the taskmaster.

"Neven?" Thaimondus laughed so hard his breath came in short dangerous gasps. Halm wished the man dead right there, but the ancient taskmaster recovered. "What do you say, Neven?"

Towering Neven growled and bared surprisingly fine teeth as he tensed his powerful-looking upper body, causing everything to bulge.

Muluk cast an incredulous eye at the Zhiberian, his meaning clear: *You're dead*.

"I wish to wager!" Goll shouted, catching everyone's attention.

"Wager?" Thaimondus asked. "Wager what?" He put the question to the head. "Didn't you get all their coin already?"

The head frowned and cast his eyes downard.

"Youuu dolt," Thaimondus fumed. "What is it you wish to wager then, cripple? Entertain us."

"If we win, you will…" Goll paused.

Halm wanted to tell him then there was no way in Saimon's hell he was going to be trained by that shrivelled ass.

Goll continued, "You will release us. And pay us a hundred gold coin."

Thaimondus leaned over the railing. "Do you have a hundred coin on you?"

"No."

"Then lick my ass, you brazen pup. A hundred gold. You'll get your lives, and that's that. The fight's to the death as well, if you have the balls for it. There'll be no love tapping on my land."

Goll didn't back down. "To the death, then."

"I'll have that Mademian blade of yours soon enough, breed," Thaimondus said to Halm in a cracking voice.

Halm bristled at the mention of his prized weapon while Neven brightened with desire.

"Neven!"

The giant glanced about at the sound of the taskmaster's voice.

"Fetch something to pound the breed's ass into the dirt."

With that, Neven lumbered off. Halm saw the muscles flex in his powerful back.

"Make a ring right there," Thaimondus croaked at his guards standing around. "Keep it in the dirt. Easier to cover up when things get messy. Move back, cripple, you're blocking my view. My lads won't hurt you. Not yet."

Swinging along on his crutches, Goll got out of the way and stood to one side with Muluk. Halm wandered over to them with a sorry half-smile on his face.

"Now, this is good," Halm said. "My thanks for making the fight to the death. Clears up matters."

"Can you take him?" Goll asked, causing the Zhiberian to frown at the question.

"You're not judging his chances by his size, are you?"

"I am," Goll said.

"You didn't do that for me."

"Well, you're… you."

Those words took a moment to sink in, and when they finally did, Halm frowned at the Kree. He then slapped his belly. "Get ready," the Zhiberian said as he backed into to the center of the ring formed of guardsmen.

"For what?" Goll asked but got no reply.

The people living behind Thaimondus's wall gathered behind the spearmen, watching with anxious faces.

Soon Neven returned, flourishing a long-shafted mace. He swung the weapon back and forth, from left hand to right, loosening up thick muscles as he entered the ring. Neven's dusky features were lit up with wicked mirth. Halm's answering smile was tight-lipped and sly.

"Introductions all round," Thaimondus shouted over their heads. "Welcome all to the games of Thaimondus."

The spearmen yelled out their appreciation while Halm noted none of the people beyond shared it.

"Neven of Sunja!" Neven roared and flung his arms wide. He turned around on the road, immersing himself in the guards' applause.

Then it was Halm's turn.

He held his sword overhead. "Halm of Zhiberia."

Thaimondus's face twisted up in thought. "Zhi—"

Halm rushed the giant. Taken aback, Neven retreated a step and lashed out with the mace, making the wind whistle from the force of the blow. Halm ducked under the swing, slashed at the man's bare washboard of a gut and opened it up with a heavy spurt of red. Neven's face blanched, and he buckled over, pressing a hand against his wound.

An instant after Neven bent over, Halm spun around and hacked the larger man's head clean off with one fell chop.

The body and head crashed into the dirt. Neven's corpse

moved at the waist as if considering rising once more to fight, but then it wilted and became still. Halm inspected his work before gazing up at the old man watching from the deck.

Thaimondus clutched at his fine robe as if stabbed through the heart.

Goll's jaw hung open, and when Halm locked gazes with him, the Kree's face broke out into a smile. Halm slapped his fat belly once more in an unspoken *"See?"*

The wail from Thaimondus made everyone hearing that ghastly sound shudder in fright. Halm then remembered Neven had once addressed the old man as father. He'd just killed the old man's son. He realized he felt more than fine about it.

The old taskmaster held onto the railing as if to yank it up and heave it across the road. He swore, hot and loud enough to scorch the very air about him. He clawed at the air, cross-cutting it with enough feeling to draw blood. After long seconds, he settled down and caught his breath. He eyed Halm with a glare black with hateful rage.

"Tarcul." Thaimondus breathed loud enough for all to hear. "Bring me that breed's head."

With that, the man at his side made his way to the ring.

Goll cleared his throat and called out to the old man, "Another wager?"

"To Saimon's *hell* with your wager!"

Halm held his sword out at arm's length, watching the gathered spearmen for any with balls enough to come forth and test him. They did not, preferring rather to wait for the next champion of the village. Tarcul came forth, pulling his broadsword out and swishing it before him much like Neven. The man wasn't smiling as the giant had been, but as he drew closer, Halm could see the family resemblance.

"To the death?" Halm asked.

"I'm going to stab this up your hole, Zhiberian."

"Come on, then. Time's wasting."

"Kill him, Tarcul! Avenge your brother!"

Halm's brow knotted together just as Tarcul attacked, heaving his broadsword about him like a living hellion held by the tail. They exchanged a brief clashing of blades before spinning away from each other. Halm's expression was measured yet wary, but Tarcul's was sparkling hatred. He slashed, slashed, and lunged, his sword snapping out like arrowshot. Halm parried, parried, and whirled away as his foe shot by him. Overextended, Halm spun around, almost impossibly fast for a man of his size, and half-lopped off the wrist of Tarcul's sword arm. With a grunt both agonized and surprised, Tarcul dropped to his knees, his sword falling from a hand hanging by a thin, gushing sliver of flesh.

Tarcul looked up, perhaps about to plead for mercy.

Halm's Mademian blade flashed in an uppercut, splitting the man's jaw and face up the middle and flinging his entire body backwards. It landed with a thud. His legs shivered once and became still.

The Zhiberian put his back to the corpse and regarded the deck of Thaimondus. "Any more sons you want me to kill?"

The taskmaster sputtered with venomous fury, his face purpling at the energy coursing through his frail frame. It took a few heartbeats, but the hateful blast of "Kill him!" finally pierced the air. "Kill the breed! Someone *kill* that fat breed!"

The spearmen looked at each other first before the gladiator, for this *was* a gladiator before them, and that was all Halm needed.

He killed two of them with short, well-placed slashes, opening up a throat to a surprised gurgle and splitting a chest with a single, violent note of a shriek. The Mademian's fine edge sliced through their leather shirts as if they were soft butter. Then a spear stabbed for his gut, but he parried it, went forward, and stabbed the wielder through the back when the man dropped his weapon and tried to flee. Seeing no danger from that quarter, Halm turned around and faced another spearman, who held his weapon before him while his eyes bulged with fright.

Across the way, Muluk had brained two men with Neven's mace and was facing down a third.

Goll had tripped the head—the same man that had taunted them from the wall and taken their coin—and speared him with a crutch. The wretch lay on the ground, grasping at his trousers' crotch, which bloomed darkly. Goll took only a moment to line up his fallen opponent's throat before smashing once more with a measured length of wood. The man at his feet went into violent spasms slow in stopping.

"Bad day all 'round." Halm smiled at the remaining spearman.

"Kill them!" Thaimondus screamed still, falling to his knees and baying the words like a wounded hound. "Saimon take me now if you don't kill them! Kill, Killllllll!"

The spearman chose to fight.

He jabbed his weapon at the Zhiberian's chest.

Halm caught the spear behind the steel's head, stepped forward and thrust. The spearman shrieked, released the weapon, and sought to run. The Mademian blade sank into his ribs, splitting them apart and driving the man to the earth.

With barely any effort, Halm rooted the blade free of the corpse and gazed around. There was no one else. The men who had surrounded them, the guards of the old taskmaster, were chopped down where they stood or tried to leave. His eyes met the drawn face of Muluk, who was holding Neven's mace across his pelvis with two hands, and then the pensive features of Goll.

From the deck above, a red-faced and nearly insane Thaimondus squealed and thrashed and cried out for hellions to rise up from Saimon's hell. He pleaded for the dark to take his soul—which he would give up willingly—in exchange for killing the three he-bitches that had robbed him of his sons and men. Spittle flew. His fingers slashed the air, seeking soft flesh while his screeching continued, long and harsh. His strength finally left him as he sank to his knees, his words lost in a dying wheeze of frustration.

It only truly ended when Halm climbed up onto the deck and drove his sword through the old man's throat.

24

They weren't really sure what to make of the villagers.

Like beaten animals, the men, women, and children crowded around, staring at the dead bodies until one of the women spoke up and told some others to get the little ones back until the mess was cleaned up and the bodies buried. Goll watched them with a stoic face, wondering if he would have to use his crutch as a weapon once again. He and Muluk retreated to the house of the now dead Thaimondus and divided their attention between a resting Halm and the gathering crowd. The men stopped just under the deck and gazed up at the Zhiberian. The sun stayed behind its tattered blanket of clouds, keeping its glare to itself.

"Well," Goll announced, "that was interesting."

"Not as interesting as the next few moments." Muluk glanced at the gathering villagers with a worried expression.

"Aye that." Halm leaned over the railing and faced his companions. "I'll sleep soundly this night. This lot had bad to their core. The old man in particular. Something wasn't right there. What's next?"

Goll balanced on his crutches and rubbed at an eye. "I really don't know. Give me a bit to think."

"This place looks good," Muluk said. "Grounds well kept. Nothing in ruins."

Goll frowned. "I'm wondering how well these men were liked. Those people over there aren't exactly cheering our names."

"Not yet." Halm's arm creaked out from where he rested on the railing and pointed a finger.

A woman approached them, dressed in a brown-and-white dress that flowed all the way to her ankles. Her hair, long and dark, was tied back into a single ponytail exposing her sun-browned features, which were plain but not unattractive. Halm recognized her as the barkeep from the tiny alehouse.

"Who killed these men?" She stopped with her hands at her sides. Behind her, the men of the village dragged the corpses into a pile while another brought around a long wagon with two horses.

"You didn't see what happened?" Goll asked her.

"I didn't. Just rose to this, and a bloody morning it is. So who's responsible?"

Goll looked at Halm while Muluk pointed.

Halm sighed wearily at being singled out. "Lads," he muttered.

"You?" The woman scowled. "I know you. You're the one from last night. Drank a pitcher. I remember."

"I suppose it isn't hard to remember a new face in this place?"

"No, it isn't. Well then, you've had a busy morning. See you got some revenge."

"I did, and… I did." Halm nodded slowly, weighing his words. "We're just wondering how the people will take to us now, seeing that we killed the lot of the guards around here."

"Well, I can tell you, they're happy with them being dead."

"They are?"

"Yes. This lot held us captive for the last two years. Threatened whole families. Didn't allow anyone to leave unless it was in the back of that wagon there, the same one being used to carry them off now."

Goll regarded her curiously. "What this?"

"Yes, they were pigs. Old Thaimondus was never a kind sort. He came here only five years ago perhaps, but even then, he cheated the men working on his properties, the same men who built this house. That wall. Their payment was to be allowed to build their own homes inside the wall, under the protection of Lord Thaimondus."

"He was a lord?" Goll asked.

"In his own mind, he called himself a lord. Demanded taxes. Brought in men who were thieves and rapists. Those spearmen. The last two years, the village had shrunk from perhaps a hundred and fifty people to a mere hundred."

"Why didn't you contact the constables in Sunja? The street watch?"

She shrugged. "We did. Nothing ever came of it, and no one returned. After the first attempt, everyone was rounded up right there where you killed the big one, Neven. Thaimondus cursed us all and said if any tried to leave, he'd execute twice the number. But his mind was addled as well. We all knew that. Everyone knew it was rotting. He'd lash out at anyone, anytime, and forget about it seconds later. So we've been living under the whim of a mad man."

"He remembered you," Muluk said to Halm, to which the Zhiberian faintly shrugged.

"The people aren't exactly rejoicing," Goll pointed out.

She raised her chin and considered them all. "Well, that's the meat of it now, isn't it? These people aren't warriors. We're all wondering who the new masters are."

This mortified both Goll and Muluk while Halm gawked at her. "What's your name?" he asked.

"Miji."

"Miji, you tell these people, we want nothing from them."

"Ah, we might want the house," Goll jumped in, flashing a cautious look at Halm. "And the coin these bastards took from us. And half of anything we find inside the house."

"But nothing else," Halm cut off the Kree.

Miji considered the three. "I don't think anyone wants the house. Except for the few possessions that Thaimondus stole."

"Why not?" Halm asked, sizing it up behind him. "Solid build."

"People from this village were killed in that house. And raped."

That took the pleasant look off Halm's face.

"Then, we'll leave it as well," Goll said. "What's done with it is up to you and all the rest. We won't lay any claim. Give us a few moments to search it, though."

Miji nodded and went back to her people.

"Saimon's blue pisspot," Muluk breathed, watching the woman walk away. "This man was a hellion bastard."

"Bad all round," Halm agreed.

"Well, get on in there and take a look around," Goll ordered. "I won't lie to you. I thought for a moment there we might've had our training grounds, but I won't train in this place. Bad all round. Maybe even cursed now."

"Killed and raped," Muluk said. "That's…" He couldn't finish.

Halm studied the white corpse of the taskmaster, the face pointed towards the lake. With a grunt, he hooked his foot under the dead man's belly and heaved him off the deck. The body crumpled in a heap below, facedown in the dirt and grass.

Then the Zhiberian hoarked and spat upon the carcass.

"That's what I think about that," he said.

In the ensuing silence, the three pit fighters regarded the people whom they had just unintentionally liberated.

After a few moments, Goll somberly suggested they go through the house, and the others agreed. They searched the premises, finding several items of worth, but left it all, remembering and believing the valuables might have been stolen in the first place. A small oak chest opened with a key found on Thaimondus's carcass, and they found close to five hundred gold coins, tarnished and dark in the shadows of the house. Another small chest contained well over a hundred silver.

This, they decided, wasn't all theirs. Perhaps none of it. Nevertheless, Goll found two small cloth sacks and filled them with half the gold but left the silver.

"I'm not certain about this," Halm said, getting an agreeing rumble from Muluk.

"I am." Goll tied off the sack. "This coin is ours. Don't worry, they'll be happy enough with what's left, especially with the old prick gone. The rest of the coin they can divide amongst themselves."

Halm and Muluk still appeared uncomfortable.

"Look." Goll turned to Miji, another woman, and three men who waited just outside the door. "Miji, we found a large sum of money here. Most of it is probably yours. We've claimed a little less than half, and the rest, along with anything else of worth which probably was taken from you, is here. But if you truly feel it's *all* yours…" Goll held out the heavy sack with one arm.

The villagers shook their heads.

"You keep that," Miji said, causing Goll to glance at his companions with a knowing look. "Coin well spent to be free of the bastards. As for the things in the house, we'll go through it and take back what's ours." She studied the house for a moment. "We'll burn the rest."

"We'll take our leave then," Goll said quietly.

"Where're you going?" Miji asked.

"Sunja."

"You can't walk that distance."

"We have a koch waiting."

"Your pardon," one of the men spoke up, "but that koch is gone."

Goll blinked, handed the sack to Muluk, and swung himself out into the sun. He arched his head up and winced.

Past noon.

"But we have horses you can have," the villager told him.

"Thaimondus owned the horses," Miji added. "Down the lane, there's a stable."

"I'm the stable hand," said another man, dressed in a worn shirt and trousers and with a black bandanna around his grey head. "If you want them, I'll have them for you."

Halm unconsciously met the gaze of Miji, who didn't avert her eyes. The Zhiberian smiled at her, suddenly careful not to bare his ill-kept teeth.

"Do you have a wagon?" Goll asked.

"We do, we do," the stable hand said.

"Not leaving you in a bad spot, are we?" Muluk asked.

The man scratched at his bandanna before he hiked it up

over his forehead. The word *punce* was spelled out in scar tissue. It started from his right temple, below the hair line, before stretching across in horrific fashion to touch the other side. "Tarcul and four of his lads did this to me. Never did find out exactly why. And I'm fortunate as there're others who got worse. Eyes gouged out. Fingers chopped off. You sons aren't leaving us…" The stable hand's eyes watered up suddenly, his mouth clamped shut, and all became very still, the air charged with emotion. His companions placed hands on his slumped shoulders, comforting him. Goll averted his eyes.

"Not leaving us in a bad spot," the stable hand finally got out. "Not in the least." He wiped at his face. "You've delivered us from one, in fact."

The stable hand sniffed hard then, clearing his flooded sinuses, and smiled gratefully.

25

The house of Thaimondus burned as if a star itself had dropped out of the heavens and crashed upon its roof. Halm raised a mug of beer and took a deep pull of it. Putting the taskmaster down had been just the stroke of good fortune he needed out of the arena. The death of Thaimondus and his sons, including the pack of dogs they had collected to keep Karashipa in line, seemed to transform the villagers. No longer did they wear long, emotionless faces but were actually smiling. Upon recognizing Halm, several made it a point to come up to the Zhiberian and thank him for killing their demented overlord. They even thanked Goll and Muluk, and that night, after the bodies of the dead had been placed inside Thaimondus's looted house and the valuables and remaining money returned to their rightful owners, the town had a public feast near the water's shore, butchering and roasting four pigs and countless chickens.

It was perhaps the best meal in a very, very long time for Halm.

Ale, dark beer, and wine were served then, and Miji's alehouse became a place to visit after the food near the lake's edge. Most people piled inside the palisade to watch the torching of the house, but Halm remained behind. He could see the glow of the highest flames perfectly from the deck of the alehouse. The wild spiraling of glowing embers rode currents of smoke to the heavens.

When he heard the door squeak behind him, his hopes spiked.

Miji appeared alongside him with mug in hand. Halm glanced at her and nodded, holding out his own mug. She tapped it, and they both drank, later watching the distant blaze.

"All this wine and such," Halm asked, "won't it break you? It's a lot to give up freely."

"It's just enough." Miji looked into his eyes. "And nothing breaks me."

"Oh. I like the sound of that."

Miji became quiet then. "I was almost raped by that old bastard."

Halm winced and took in her profile. She wasn't a beauty, but she wasn't hard to look upon either. In fact, the more he saw of her, the more he liked.

"I'm sorry."

Miji shrugged. "Happened two years ago. I'm glad he's dead. And I'm very happy to celebrate the death of them all."

"I'm right happy to celebrate with you."

"Do you always go around shirtless?" Miji asked.

"Ah, yes. Almost always."

"I see. You have something wrong with your lip?"

Halm blinked at her. She had picked up on that. He chuckled then, baring his terrible mess of a mouth.

"Your teeth are bad," she said with a frown. "But otherwise, you're not too hard to look upon. Any wife to speak of?"

Halm glanced to the glow of fire. "No, no wife. No children. Too old for all that."

"Horse shite."

"Well, all right. No *interest* in any of that."

"You're not a daisy, are you?"

That made him sputter in his beer. "No! Lords, no. Not that I have anything against…" He shrugged.

"Only asking."

"You seem quite interested."

"Maybe I am."

"Looking to get married?"

"To the right one. Like us all. Maybe even raise a family."

That made the Zhiberian wince yet again. "I have no desire for children."

"None?"

Halm shook his head. "Much rather bash heads in the Pit."

"Where are you from again?"

"Zhiberia."

"Are all Zhiberians like you?"

"No. Just me." And he smiled. Miji smiled back. Halm saw that her teeth were fair and clean, but she was missing her right incisor. She raised a hand to her ponytail and gave it a long sensual stroke before directing her attention back to the fire.

"Can you do anything else besides fight in the pit?" she asked.

"Like rutting?"

Miji chuckled then, the sound quite pleasant to Halm's battered ears and relieving. He was glad he'd made her laugh yet scolded himself for being so bold. Only a moment ago, she had told him she'd almost been raped, and here he was making jokes. He wouldn't blame her in the least if she'd slapped, scolded, or outright left him for such a slight. Such brazen comments were usually reserved for the serving maids or prostitutes he bought for a night's pleasure. Looking at this dark-haired woman beside him, he had to remind him she was neither, and he didn't want to chance offending her, not after catching her eye.

"Not rutting," she said.

"My apologies for that. Very bad of me."

Miji looked at the fire. "Can you hammer a nail? Or farm?"

Halm sighed. "No and… no. No interest."

"Nothing at all."

"Nothing like that. My apologies."

"You apologize a bit."

Halm caught himself on the verge of doing it once more.

"So what can you do besides apologize? And fight?"

"*That* I can do. And enjoy. Not much else, however."

She took another mouthful of beer. "I'd been to Sunja three times before that topper stopped any of us from leaving the area. Every time, I longed to get back here. It might not seem like much, but I grew up here. I enjoy these walls of trees much better than those of the city."

Halm decided not to ask her about her parents.

"Now, it's getting on time for me to think about getting married." She regarded him again, her hazel eyes holding his attention.

"Isn't it the man that asks the woman?" Halm frowned. Sunjan culture wasn't all that different from Zhiberia.

"I'll ask if I feel like it." She was softly defiant. "Does that worry you?"

"Oh no. Daresay I should thank you for the warning."

"Daresay you should."

They shared a light chuckle then and turned their attention back to the fire.

*

Someone kicked Pig Knot where he lay sleeping, jarring him awake to the irregular wheeze and rumble of surrounding snores. He sat up against the wall and wiped his face with a dirty palm, glimpsing the moving shadows of three men becoming indistinct and merging with the gloom. They offered no apologies and trundled along as if on an open street, talking in loud voices and uncaring about the many sleepers covering the floor. One even carried a large cloth sack.

Pig Knot frowned and rubbed his face in recognition.

The sack looked like Halm's.

The sight of it got him to his feet. He felt his stomach grumble at him and even a pang of nausea from a distinct lack of food. The Sunjan had spent the day staying low and conserving his energy, hoping that his companions would return. He had no coin for food, and the few bites Bindon had given him were consumed quickly, but the fountain did sate his thirst. Twice during the day, he'd asked the Madea if there were any fighters unable to battle their opponents, seeking to fill the position. There weren't, however, and Pig Knot had remained in the Pit, listening to men just a few feet away eat bread and fruit, smacking their lips in unnecessary fashion.

Sleep was a welcomed escape.

But this morning was different. Or was it still night? It was difficult to determine below the arena. Noting the lack of activity, he decided it was sometime before dawn. Pig

Knot recalled the sack bouncing just a little, slung over a shoulder. He was certain it belonged to Halm. He knew it. And a topper had taken it.

And before he knew what he was doing, he got to his feet and followed.

The air was warm and ripe with bad breath and seeping gas, and Pig Knot stepped over legs and arms as if they were pitfalls. Snores ripped the stillness. Eventually, Pig Knot spotted his quarry walking up the stairs to the outside. He hurried towards the stairs, the torchlight in nearby sconces burning low and deepening the foul shadows. When he reached the base, the men were lost in the dark above.

A scowl twisting his face, Pig Knot climbed.

When he emerged outside, it was under a thousand stars twinkling behind cottony wisps of smoke, lighting up the dark ceiling of the world. Pig Knot stood and took a deep breath, savouring the city's breath over the stale stink of the air below.

The three men trudged away from Gate of the Moon and melted into the semi-dark of a street.

Pig Knot followed, not knowing in the least what he might do, only that his friend's possessions were being stolen. How long had Halm left them there? He allowed he'd probably do the same if the thing was just lying about and unclaimed for a few days, but the Zhiberian was alive. And he'd need that sack of shite for his next match. He wasn't about to let some pit fighter claim it as his own. The thought of a fellow Sunjan stealing something from a visitor to the country galled him as well.

The streets were near empty, the few people either heading home or visiting the alehouses and taverns with their warm, glowing windows. Laughter rolled across the way. Pig Knot knew this area, knew it rarely slept but rather exhausted itself. Many a night he'd frequented this particular strip as it was crammed on both sides with places to spend coin on drink and women. A group of drinkers spilled into the street, raucous and stumbling, blocking his view. He sped up, stealing quick checks over the drunkards' heads as he navigated his way through them.

The three men turned and headed down an alley.

Pig Knot cut through the crowd and sped up until he reached the mouth of the backstreet. He took a cautious peek before slipping around the corner. His boots shuffled along fitted stones, their surfaces draped in shadows and pressing in on the few hollows of dying lantern light. The three men were halfway through, silhouettes against the night.

"You three," Pig Knot called out, making himself heard over the din of the nearby drinking establishments. "That's my friend's property you have there."

The three stopped in their tracks. Heads turned around.

"There's a leather sleeve for the arm, greaves, and a pointy brass helm."

"What if there is?" one of the heads asked.

"It's not yours."

"Curious," a different voice said. "I have exactly what you say right here. But your friend left it in the dark. Never came back. I don't think he wants it anymore."

The three shades split apart.

"He wants it," Pig Knot declared, moving closer. A corner of light illuminated him for a brief moment as he passed through it.

Thoughtful silence at that, brimmed by the muted merriment of the night's drinkers.

"Perhaps you want to try and take it?" came the challenge, sounding as if it were sheathed in a smile.

"Try?" Pig Knot growled, getting closer to the three. "You don't know me."

No sooner did that final syllable leave his lips than all four men lunged for each other, to the clatter of a dropped sack and drunken laughter in the night.

Leathery hands gripped and sought to take down Pig Knot. A fist flashed off his brow, snapping his face to the left. He returned the punch with one of his own, connecting and making a man gag. Two shadows clung to him. One snaked a leg around his own, and all three men dropped into a pool of darkness. Hands groped on Pig Knot's thighs while another set clamped down on his throat. Grunts and hisses stabbed the air. Pig Knot kicked out, hitting something solid and driving it back from his legs. He wrapped his forearm over the paws on his throat and jerked them to the right, twisting underneath his attacker's weight. The man fell forward, releasing his hold before his face crashed into the fitted stones of the alley floor. Pig Knot untangled himself and rose, kicking the scrambling figures at his feet. A man charged into him from the side like a swung maul, driving him into a hard wall. Pig Knot looked down as his attacker's head swept up, cracking off his jaw and bouncing his head off hard timbers. He saw stars and wondered for a split second if they belonged to the night. Two fists thundered into his gut, tenderizing the muscle there and making him breathless.

The Sunjan punched an elbow into his attacker's back, forcing him to his knees with a grunt of pain. Fingers flashed out of the gloom and mashed Pig Knot's face. He half-blocked a punch with a flick of his arm. The hand on his face clawed, ripping open the stitches there with sinewy snaps. Pig Knot roared. The shadow snarled back. A fist flew out of the dark and Pig Knot ducked, hearing the crinkle of knuckles breaking against solid wood. He cut loose with three quick blows that buckled the man over with pained huffs.

Pig Knot reached down and felt hair, gripped scalp, and cocked back a knee, intending to drive a nose out the back of a head. A fist cracked across his face, breaking his own beak with a startling pop of pain and sound, causing him to yank free a small mat of hair. Another fist hammered his face before two more axed into his stomach.

Instinct taking over, a grimacing Pig Knot rammed an open palm into a face, feeling a nose shatter, giving back what he received. The man staggered back, cupping his features and hissing in pain and rage.

Pig Knot charged but was nearly taken off his feet by a solid shadow and punched twice before being whirled about and slammed against the opposite wall of the alley. A hand gripped the Sunjan's shoulder, but he twisted under it and smashed a crotch. The owner collapsed with the barest *urf*. Pig Knot straightened and something *else* came at him. The night erupted with the brazen smack of flesh on flesh as he blocked three quick punches before stepping outside the man's swing and driving his fist over a thick shoulder. Hard knuckles cracked off a chin, toppling the shadow.

Fighting to draw air into his lungs, Pig Knot backed up until lantern light found him. Something rasped against the cut stones of the alley, and a pair of arms lashed around Pig Knot's legs, bringing him down. A man crawled over him, hammering fists into the Sunjan's body and drawing grunts of pain. The attacker pinned Pig's Knot's arm under a knee and mashed an elbow down across the Sunjan's skull. Then again. Then a furious pummelling of elbows erupted from the man on top, every blow as hard as the stone beneath Pig Knot's back. Skin swelled and split. Blood spurted. His head bounced off the stone.

Wheezing, Pig Knot's open palm flashed up and crunched into his foe's jaw, lifting him up with enough force to make his spine bend. Pig Knot freed his trapped arm and grabbed his attacker's chin. He held him at arm's length a second before unleashing punishing strikes into a purpling face, releasing the unconscious man on the final blow. Pig Knot rolled the boneless figure off and used a wall to force himself to his feet. Something barrelled through the darkness, and he twisted out of the way, allowing the wall to flatten a face. Pig Knot kicked the stunned man in the gut twice, whipping his boot up from the road and into a buckled midsection. The smashed lout collapsed outside the circle of lantern light.

Panting, Pig Knot whirled to the left then the right, misstepped, and caught himself against a wall. In between gasps, he listened. Laughter, distant and taunting. Moans at his feet. Something hissing as if a throat had been cut.

Pig Knot put a hand to his face and felt the ugly blooms of swelling. Blood slathered his hand.

Then a light shone his way.

An old man stood in a doorway, holding a lantern aloft and blinking at the fright Pig Knot knew he'd become. The old stranger shivered, beard twitching in horror, his evening robes dark and kept closed with a rope belt at his waist. Heads poked around his hips. Pale, fat faces.

Children.

"Close the door," Pig Knot rasped.

Finding his courage, the grandfather hurriedly backed in, pressing a hand into the faces of his young ones so that they wouldn't see the things in the alley. A moment later, the door shut, and Pig Knot was once again swallowed by the dark.

He staggered across the men on the road. A hand clutched at his ankle. Pig Knot twisted around and stomped on the joint before punishing the owner with several kicks to the body. He stepped away from the now-rubbery grip. Someone moaned, and Pig Knot was only half sure it wasn't him. He found Halm's sack and straightened up, frame heaving, and painfully hung the thing over a shoulder. Standing amongst bodies writhing as if they'd been gutted, Pig Knot glared.

He turned this way and that, waiting for one of them to rise and stop him.

They did not.

He tongue-checked all of his teeth as he staggered from the alley, tasting blood. He spat. With the sack over his shoulder, Pig Knot walked away very slowly, unsteadily at times...

Back towards the Pit.

Somewhere during that walk, shadows surrounded him, called to him as if they were standing on some faraway shore. He heard them but didn't answer.

And when his knees buckled and he collapsed to the road, they rushed in.

26

Light blazed through his personal darkness so strongly that when Pig Knot opened his eyes, he first thought he was dead. As it turned out, he wasn't. He was on his back with his face pointed towards an open window. He turned away from the light, grimacing at the tightness in his neck, and gazed up at the familiar sight of bare timbers comprising the ceiling.

With a groan, he touched his head. Stitches. *More* stitches. His fingers felt more harsh seams amongst the knobs of his face. By the hair of Saimon's black crack, he was thankful he was unconscious when *those* went in. He pulled himself into a sitting position and blinked at the cot he lay upon. Three other cots filled the room. Three open windows.

"Bindon?" he whispered. There was no doubt he was back at the healer's house, but he was puzzled as to how he'd gotten there. Just at the foot of the cot was the cloth sack holding Halm's possessions, but he had no recollection of what had happened.

"Bindon?" he asked, louder this time and directing it at the open stairway.

A metallic *clunk* came from below, heavy and ominous-sounding and frightful enough to startle Pig Knot. It hit the bottom step, paused as if gathering strength, and then proceeded upwards, becoming louder, closer. Wood squealed under a tremendous weight. The approaching noise drew Pig Knot's gaze to the stairs, and he grew increasingly anxious. He noted the surgical tools on the table next to the window. Several sharp-looking knives and even a hand axe lay there.

The footsteps became louder. The wood yelped.

Pig Knot again considered the table and the assembled cutting instruments.

Then a helm rose in the stairwell—the back of one—and even as Pig Knot watched, the figure paused upon hitting the landing before slowly turning around to address the next flight of stairs. A full visor covered the helmet, which was Sunjan in design. Pig Knot scowled. It was military. Worse, it was the helm of a Sujin. The Skarrs were the lighter infantry, tasked with defending the city and, to some extent, policing the streets along with the constables, but the Sujins were not. They were the frontline assault troops of Sunja, the heavy foot, comprised of men from every walk of life, even killers and criminals who, if one believed the stories, were once imprisoned and given the choice to join or perish within their cells. Most Sujins served along the front, deployed in strength and warring with invading Nordun, whose own forces seemed to have no end.

And here was one, walking up the stairs towards him.

Like a nightmare of metal, flesh, and bone, the soldier grew with each step he took. The lowered visor hid the man's features, allowing only the black pits of his eyes to glint in the light. A heavy chainmail shirt with iron plates lashed to his frame gleamed, and the pommel of the Sujin shortsword seeped into view. Daggers in scabbards lined the soldier's waist like a short fence.

Pig Knot looked at the knives on the table and knew nothing there could penetrate this *thing* coming up the steps.

And the hellion *still* grew with each step, matching the rising unease in Pig Knot's breast.

Another figure came up the steps behind this slow-moving mountain, but the Sujin didn't allow him to dwell on whoever it was. When the solider reached the top step, the crest of his helm bumped into a beam Pig Knot had believed out of reach. Perhaps it still was, to him. Not to the monster now occupying the upstairs room with him. Pig Knot took a breath and didn't take his eyes off the warrior. If he really needed it, the window would be a last attempt at escape. That thought made him uncomfortable, for all manner of bad things might happen on the day a pig flies.

The Sujin stepped away from the steps, stooping over slightly to allow the second man to come into the room. Pig Knot recognized him but couldn't recall the name. He was perhaps in his early forties or late thirties, dark of complexion, as if he'd fallen asleep in a forge when he was a child. Flecks of harsh grey colored his temples, and lines were scratched out beneath his eyes—evil-looking eyes as sharp as the edge of a blade and every bit as cold. He wore grey trousers, rough-spun cloth, and a blue shirt that hung off a muscular frame. Like the Sujin, he wore a sword at his waist.

"We meet again." The man smiled thinly.

"Seems so," Pig Knot agreed, wary of this stranger and still not certain about the massive Sujin in the room. "He a friend?"

"Yes. You can say that."

"What's your name again?"

"Toffer. And you're Pig Knot. Interesting name."

"Oh, I'm interesting, all right."

Toffer moved to one of the beds, deemed it to be worthy, and sat down. He folded his hands and stared hard at the Sunjan.

"You got into another fight last night, the second one in almost as many nights."

Pig Knot frowned. "What do you know about it?"

"I saw the first one where you took on a handful of gladiators. Not Free Trained either. Those were groomed war pigs if I ever came across any. And you put them down. While *pissed*, no less."

"All I wanted then was a place to drink."

"And they didn't want you there; I understand both sides. But when they sought to punish you for it, by Seddon's ball sack, you gave back."

They were probably just as drunk, Pig Knot thought, but he didn't voice his opinion.

"You are indeed a *scrappy* one." Toffer chuckled in admiration. "I like that. You've run up a bill with my friend Bindon this day. We both wondered how you'll be able to pay. You managed the first instance, but I suspect this time will be different."

"I'll pay him."

"I already did."

Pig Knot straightened on his cot. He didn't like that in the least. Owing debts to friends, merchants, and even healers was one thing. The feeling he had about owing coin to Toffer wasn't something he was sure he could sleep easy over.

"Yes," Toffer explained. "You owe me now. And I do require payment. My friend here"—he tilted his head to the brooding Sujin—"needs coin as well. In case you don't already know, you were a mess last night. You're a sewn-up mess this morning. We carried you here, me and a few others. I thought that one of your nature would appreciate the gesture, especially when you left those three men in the alley last night."

Pig Knot started, but Toffer kept on. "I also know those three lads aren't particularly happy with you. Probably searching for you right now, in fact. You were half-right in fighting them in a dark alleyway, but you probably should have stayed away from the light."

Toffer traced a finger around his jaw. "My guess is they saw your face. In any case, anyone who looks upon you now, well… you're memorable. Let's leave it at that."

"What do you want?"

"My coin, of course."

"I don't have any."

"You have that sack at your feet," Toffer pointed out.

Pig Knot fumed. "That's a friend's. Not mine to give."

"I understand. Well, that means you must pay me. Pay us." Another dip of the head to the menacing hell pup standing to one side. "And I wish to be paid soon and in full."

Pig Knot glanced to the window once more. Truthfully, he felt terrible, but it might indeed be the time to bolt. "Said I don't have any."

"Well, what do you have of worth?" Toffer peered at him down the length of his nose.

"Nothing."

"Ah, but you're wrong," Toffer hissed. "A man who can

hold his own against a handful of house pit fighters isn't *nothing* in my eyes. I'm interested in your skills, young man. *Those* are invaluable. I want those."

What was this topper speaking about? Pig Knot's expression shifted into dark confusion.

"You fight in the games this season," Toffer said as though suppressing bad air. "Your first fight was a terrible mess. I won coin off you, but you were shite, honestly."

"My thanks," Pig Knot said sardonically.

"What I saw in the streets, however, changed my mind about you. You're a killer. An animal. One of Saimon's hellions unleashed when riled. And I smell opportunity."

"Like what?"

Toffer's eyes bore into Pig Knot. "Not the most intelligent, it seems."

Pig Knot didn't like that. "I can tell you're the smart one around here."

"Really? How's that?"

"If you were alone right now, I'd toss your ass-licking carcass right out that window."

Toffer's expression soured. "You think I need him?"

"I do. You had a few other lads with you in the pool, I remember. Strength in numbers, right?"

"That's right."

The Sujin's baleful gaze seemed to intensify, or perhaps it was Pig Knot's growing nervousness.

Toffer spoke. "Well, you know I have the numbers. You also know I have at least one Sujin with me. But honestly, when you have one such as Klytus here, well, you don't really need many more."

"Hmm," Pig Knot conceded.

"Well, here's my offer. I'll get you a fight in the Pit. I can do that. Even if your match isn't until later, I can move it up. You win that fight. You fight like you did on the streets there, win, and you'll repay me."

That sounded easy enough, but Pig Knot had to ask, "And if I don't fight and perhaps pay you later?"

"There is no later," Toffer said curtly. "There's no refusal. If you breathe the words, Klytus will convince you otherwise. And if he's convincing you, the longer he takes, the less interested I'll be in having you fight, because you'll have all of your fingers broken. Probably some ribs. Your jaw. And anything else he can snap. Of course, I just might heave you into the Pit with your wounds anyway and let the dogs devour you. The choice is yours."

"Give me a moment."

Toffer smiled. "You have. One. Moment. Klytus."

Upon hearing his name, the armoured Sujin animated with a rustling of mail links and took a heavy step forward, arms dangling at his sides and fists clenching.

Pig Knot inwardly winced.

The Sujin grabbed the end of the cot and lifted it with a creak. One of the warrior's huge hands reached for Pig Knot's head.

"I'll do it!" Pig Knot blurted, and the hand stopped. The helm turned in the direction of Toffer.

"Excellent," the other man said. "That wasn't so bad, after all."

Klytus released the cot, allowing it to crash to the floor and making Pig Knot shudder with the impact. The Sujin backed up to the steps once more, moving as if his limbs were controlled by unseen strings. Pig Knot felt something snap beneath him and believed he sank a little lower in the straw.

"Now then," Toffer said. "Business. You rest here for the day. Relax. Heal. I'll make the arrangements. We'll try to get you into a fight tomorrow perhaps. Or the day after. I've left another coin with Bindon, so you'll have food to eat."

"My thanks," Pig Knot said without meaning it, watching Klytus distrustfully. "Except I can barely see out of my eyes. They're swoll—"

"Then stop prodding them with your fingers. You'll see well enough when it's time to fight. Besides, I've seen you fight, remember? These taps will only spice up the stew."

Pig Knot's shoulders sagged in defeat.

"Ah, don't worry. I have nothing but confidence in your skillset. You'll pay me back from the coin you win." Toffer stared him in the eyes. "And Pig Knot, don't think about leaving the games or the city. That would be… unwise. You only see two men here this day. I can tell you there are many, many more of us."

Pig Knot paused. "I won't. Leave, I mean. What's one fight?"

"Excellent. That's my sentiment exactly. What *is* one fight?" Toffer smiled, but then it frosted over. "Just don't lose it."

Pig Knot blinked with uncertainty.

"Well, that's all I have to say." Toffer exhaled and slapped his knees as he rose. "I'll meet you here again once everything's been arranged. Don't go anywhere except the shite trough."

"I have the chamber pot underneath. I've been here before."

Toffer nodded, studied Pig Knot for a moment longer, and finally departed, plodding down the steps until he disappeared from sight. Klytus followed him like some monstrous dog nipping at his master's heels. Pig Knot once again marvelled at the size of the man. He figured he'd avoided a close thing.

Sounds from the street drifted into the room, eventually swallowing the heavy footfalls of his visitors. Pig Knot lay back on the cot, no longer concerned with how his backside seemed to sink in the middle of the bed, and wondered if he had just made a very bad decision.

27

Early that morning, as a red sky simmered below the horizon, Clavellus climbed aboard a wagon his men had prepared the night before. The vehicle soon left his estate in a plume of dust, travelling upon wheels that would soon need replacing. The morning heat beat down on the driver, but the two other passengers rode under a cloth canopy covering the rear like a tent. Clavellus held a rough hand towel to his face and neck, soaking up the moisture already gathering there, and gnawed on his inner lip for a moment. He was taking a great risk in travelling to the city, one he lied about to his Nala, but he could no longer wait. His patience just wasn't there anymore. He doubted the three Free Trained men would come back to him, not after the verbal lashing he delivered while half drunk, so he decided to search for them. He took Koba along, who sat across from him wearing only a pair of brown trousers that looked much too warm. His upper body, broad and muscular, was bare and sweaty, and several times during their trip, Koba wiped the moisture from his body and palmed it off on his leg.

Early morning and the sun had only just begun grilling the land.

"I don't like this," Koba said once more as the wagon rattled along.

Clavellus ran his trembling left hand over his beard and regarded the man. "Too late to go back now."

"I don't want to go back."

"Well, now you're just being difficult." The taskmaster smiled crookedly.

"Machlann didn't want to come."

"No, Machlann didn't."

"I would have thought he'd want to."

"Machlann isn't... as fond of the place as I am." However, he knew it wasn't true. Machlann was one of three trainers who'd been cast out along with Clavellus years ago. Pinnak had fallen from his horse while crossing a stream one morning and had his ribcage crushed by a single hoof. Basen had simply up and died shivering while eating a meal of fish. Both had met their ends within three years of being exiled from the games. Machlann was the only one to have lived as long as Clavellus, and the trainer had admitted the night before to his taskmaster that to even gaze upon the city would tear his heart in two. And he didn't want to break down before the Bear—the nickname they'd given Koba.

Clavellus had stayed away from the city himself since his exile. There were other smaller cities in the country, farther away, but if he had to go or needed something, more often than not he'd travel to them or to one of the smaller towns. Not even Nala asked to enter Sunja's capitol anymore, and as time went on, fewer of her friends remaining in the main city came to visit her. For that, Clavellus was eternally sorry and, as a result, he'd attempted to make his wife's life as comfortable as possible with what they had.

"Do you miss it?" Koba asked him.

Clavellus met his trainer's eyes and, with a ghost of a smile, looked away.

Once they passed the grassy flatlands of Plagur's Reach, the city rose up on its immense plateau like a tarnished crown saddling a dusty wave of rock and dirt. The wagon shook as its four horses pulled its weight up the terraced road towards the main gates and towering walls. Both Koba and Clavellus subtly braced themselves as their driver urged the horses up the incline. The huge fitted blocks of granite composing the walls of Sunja grew larger as they got closer while banners of colour hung from crenellated heights and fluttered in an easterly breeze. Traffic into the city increased, and at times, the travellers leaving the city had to carefully squeeze past those arriving. Shouts of warning and anger in languages other than Sunjan pierced the dusty air, and Clavellus looked out the rear of the wagon to see men and women hauling wagons bearing livestock and other dry goods down the terraced road.

Koba had turned to watch the river of people, wagons, expensive koches, and animals, showing Clavellus his profile and his hideous scar.

"Is it always this way?" the trainer asked with wonder.

"It is. Sometimes worse."

Koba's incredulous smile made Clavellus momentarily feel better about returning.

They entered the city after being approved by a knot of Skarrs wielding spears or bows guarding the south gate. Rows of impassive warriors stood at attention outside on stone ledges, with their backs to the wall, their mail armour already dimmed by dust. More Skarrs threaded their ways through the deluge of wagons and people, hailing and searching vehicles and goods before allowing them to pass.

A face covered by a metal visor threw back the tarp covering the rear of the wagon and peered inside at Clavellus and Koba at the same instant another Skarr demanded the driver reveal the purpose of his visit. Clavellus's man answered more questions before the Skarr gave the signal to pass on. The warrior at the rear let the tarp drop without a word.

"They're careful," Koba stated.

"It's a time of war," Clavellus reminded him.

Soon the road became a little smoother, the crowds thicker. The driver steered them onto a wider venue specifically for wagons, and they made good time towards the Pit. Clavellus peered out through a slit in the cloth, beheld the droves of people dressed in both drab greys and explosions of vibrant colours, and reminisced about another time with a sigh and an ache. He half-expected to see men who were ghosts now, standing along the street, perhaps even with a wave for him. But there were none.

Just more people.

Sunja had grown fat with them.

Before noon, they arrived at the Pit, and Clavellus instructed his driver to stay with the wagon. Anything that needed to be done, Koba and he would manage. The older man and his big trainer eased out of the wagon, and for a moment, they stood and basked in the menacing yet majestic size of Sunja's Pit. Red brick and massive oak timbers, Vathian black-veined marble columns, and Sunjan might completed the four-level structure capable of holding thousands. Brick archways ringed the very top, decorated with plunging waterfalls and warrior figures of scintillating blue and gleaming copper. Painted murals depicting battle scenes from the arena's bloody past covered the lower walls, depicting men and beasts alike in heroic or ferocious poses.

The smell of sweat permeated the scene, but it was barely noticed due to the extraordinary sight.

"It's…" Koba whispered in awe and faltered, not possessing the vocabulary to place his thoughts into sound, and Clavellus barely heard. Elation filled him, as he secretly had feared to never be able to return to the one place where all of his skill and knowledge meant something. It was still dangerous, even with the death of old Curge, but it felt as if a thick noose about his throat had been removed. Any fear of the risks evaporated in the presence of the Pit, Seddon save him and Nala forgive him. He didn't care. The arena was truly his first love, and he'd missed her dearly.

He gazed upon on the open square about the arena, the people already heading into the Gate of the Sea. He heard the rising excitement in their voices and sensed the rumble of energy in the air. They had gotten here right on time.

"This way." Clavellus led his trainer into the Pit's stony breast.

*

Later that day, when the sun scorched the people in the stands, men raked the sands below, covering up the blood before the next fight began. The games were in full ferocious bloom, and the sand soaked up sweat and blood enough to become a thick broth that took effort to cover. In the viewing boxes at ground level, heat shimmered off the areas untouched by the last fight. Through that dancing veil, the people glistened. *Hellish heat*, Clavellus thought, straining to see who sat in the stands. It was one thing he hadn't missed about the place. The temperature reached him even here, below the surface where it usually was cooler. Not this day, however. This day transformed the arena into a brick oven.

The old taskmaster stood at the arched window and gazed out, running his fingers over his chin, bearing the stickiness of it all while simply enjoying the spectacle of armed might, flesh, and blood.

Koba's mouth hung open as though about to catch grapes while the trainer's eyes never left the sands. He stood beside Clavellus, bowed over to see better, his attention birdlike. Clavellus had to thank the Madea for allowing him to enter the Pit. Though he was not the Madea of his day or an old friend, the official remembered his name and was indifferent enough to the unwritten decrees of dead men. He saw nothing wrong with allowing a former taskmaster of champions to enter and watch the glory of the games. And in the Madea's eyes, Clavellus was still a taskmaster, regardless of no longer being active. He permitted him his own private viewing chamber.

Free Trained men fought this day although Clavellus had missed perhaps the first two matches. He quickly pulled his shaky hand down over his face and peered outside, memories flooding his person. The stone and brick of the Pit had aged much better than he, and he fondly patted one side of the arched window.

"More wagering?" Koba asked.

"In between the fights, yes. There's a schedule posted at the end of each entryway. People can see who fights whom there and place their wagers when they wish, really."

"The Free Trained are shite."

"They are," Clavellus agreed. "Well, usually are. There are some that might hold promise, and those who do are quickly snapped up by the established houses. Future fodder, you see. And it's best for them. The house fighters despise the children playing in games meant for men. Hate them. Feel as if the Chamber sullies the sport by allowing them onto the same field."

"Then why do it?" Koba asked.

"Coin. Fodder. One has to feed the masses something before the main events, and there aren't really enough pit fighters—trained and prepared gladiators—to fight in every match. Allowing these men in lengthens the season and earns the Chamber more coin. Earns the owners more coin. It's best this way."

"Business," Koba hissed.

"Yes," Clavellus agreed once again. "Business. Exactly."

Just then, the Orator bellowed the introductions for the next pair of fighters, much to the crowd's thunderous delight. Clavellus didn't recognize the name of Gastillo, nor Prajus, who belonged to his house. The gladiator wore armour that shone in the sun; a lovely vest of scale that shimmered in the heat covered his upper body while a black iron helm with a face cage protected his features. Clavellus had always liked that style of helm. It made a man look intimidating. Prajus's arms were bare and muscular and covered in metal bracers. A set of bronze greaves protected his lower legs up to his knees, where thick spikes protruded. Clavellus inwardly winced at the spikes. There was only one reason why the gladiator had such, and that was to gut his foe at close quarters. A knee strike tipped with one of those would kill a man—slowly. Prajus stood with his legs spread apart and held a broadsword and shield, both well maintained. The shield had the iron head of a dragon on its surface.

Fine equipment, weapons. Clavellus knew money when he saw it. Gastillo outfitted his boys well.

The other man wasn't allied to anyone. He wore an old

leather vest and pot helm, with a narrow slit and perforated mouth area. Clavellus wondered if the topper could see from the thing, let alone properly breathe. Leather bracers covered the fighter's arms, and strips of leather protected the upper thighs. His lower legs remained as bare as a babe's ass and practically begged to be cut out from under him. A wooden shield banded with iron and a broadsword filled the Free Trained man's hands. The arms of the man were beefy but with more fat than muscle, and certainly not toned like his opponent's.

Clavellus sighed heavily. This wasn't going to be pretty.

Upon the scream from the Orator, the fighters moved. The Free Trained was called Valobra, from Balgotha. Some champions had trickled down from that country just beyond Marrn, but this one appeared to be on his own. Clavellus observed the man was nervous in his movements while Prajus, the House of Gastillo gladiator, seemed as relaxed as if he'd downed half a cask of Sunjan firewater.

The old taskmaster shook his head. The Free Trained had been tossed to a hellpup.

Valobra rushed Prajus, swinging for a head, then a shoulder, and finally thrusting for the gut. Prajus ducked, leaned away, and parried before backing away. The crowd, *oooohing* at the sudden flurry from the Balgothan, became silent, stunned by the quickness of Prajus. Then their voices rose in eager anticipation of the house fighter's response. Prajus did nothing, however, and simply stayed light on his feet, knees bent and guard up, waiting and poised with confidence.

Counterstriker, Clavellus gauged. The man was a counterstriker, looking to punish his foe after he'd committed to his own attack and with his guard lowered.

They weren't the most exciting to watch, but when they did lash out, it was with extraordinary speed and deadly consequences.

Clavellus then realized with a chilling detachment that the pit fighter from the House of Gastillo wasn't wasting time. He was *prolonging* it.

Valobra turned and sized up his foe while Prajus stepped to his left, shield protecting his forward leg, sword ready, never taking his eyes from his opponent. Solid form.

The Balgothan lunged at his opponent to a ragged cheer from the audience—and missed. Prajus got out of the way and seemingly swatted at the Free Trained warrior as he rushed by. With their positions changed, Valobra showed his back to Clavellus and Koba.

Clavellus frowned.

Koba hissed.

The crowd erupted in a harsh rumble, aware one man had been hit.

That seemingly innocuous strike had slashed the Balgothan's back to the spine, the leather cut open like an ugly, toothless mouth. A sheet of blood seeped across and under the material, running over the man's ass and onto his legs. Valobra moved as if quilled with arrows. Clavellus knew the battle rush was the only thing keeping the Free Trained on his feet.

Even as he thought it, Valobra painfully lashed out with thrusts and slashes, targeting everything yet connecting with nothing. Prajus nimbly ducked and dodged, deflecting a sword and passing up an opportunity to drive the tip of his blade through the man's gut.

Clavellus shook his head ever so slightly. Valobra had truly gotten the poor draw, as Prajus was in no hurry.

He was playing to the crowd.

Valobra stabbed for Prajus's arm, which the fighter took on the shield. The Free Trained made a wide looping cut that Prajus ducked under, which made Clavellus palm-wipe his face in embarrassment. Then a final desperate flurry from the Balgothan, heralded by a dramatic roar the spectators drowned out. Swords clashed in that unnerving clang of edges.

This time, Prajus didn't get out of the way. This time, Prajus stood right before the man and allowed each attack to roll off him in a dizzying display of defense. Then he flicked his wrist at his opponent in apparent boredom, halting the man in his tracks. The house gladiator stepped away as Valobra dropped to his knees, clutching at the red line across his chest. Blood dripped from the cut like snow thaw. Valobra pressed his forearm against it to stem the flow, but it spilled over his flesh. Prajus stood strides away, keeping an eye on his opponent and not relaxing his impressive guard in the least. Although the man was making an example of the Free Trained, he wasn't entirely taking him lightly.

Confident, but not overly.

Clavellus concluded the House of Gastillo was a force attending the season's games.

A grimacing Valobra got to his feet amongst a cruel shower of insults and wailing. The audience hadn't changed in the least, the old taskmaster observed. They were still bastards and bitches as fickle as weather and just as quick to change.

Hearing them and deciding to put on one last show, the Balgothan slashed mightily, his blood fanning the sands and actually backing Prajus up a step. The air crinkled as

Valobra's slower blade probed and tested Prajus's defenses, each thrust turned aside. He finally stabbed, unbalancing himself, and Prajus stepped into his man. Unstoppable, he smashed the edge of his shield across the man's pot helm twice, the sharp sounds startling.

Prajus cracked him twice with the shield and stabbed him once through the throat.

The Free Trained did a little breathless jig on the spot. Then the blood burst forth, and he collapsed to the sand.

Prajus stood over the fallen man, blade dripping.

The arena exploded in adoration.

Even Clavellus nodded at the impressive display of arms.

"He's one I'll have to be careful of," a voice rumbled when the cheering died down.

Clavellus and Koba turned to see Dark Curge standing in their chamber, watching them with icy eyes. Dressed in shiny green satin with black trousers, the bald, one-armed owner did not visit alone. A shorter, solid-looking boulder of a man stood behind him, wearing a thick X of studded leather crossed his otherwise bare muscular chest.

"You came back," Curge whispered in awe. "I never thought you would. My father did, but…" He faltered and shook his head in disbelief.

"Curge," Clavellus greeted cautiously, as if one twitch might provoke an attack. Koba straightened up at his side, waiting for a gesture from his taskmaster, but Clavellus gave no such signal.

"You aren't supposed to be here," Dark Curge rumbled, ignoring Koba entirely.

"I decided to chance it."

"I could kill you right here."

"You could murder me right here," Clavellus corrected.

"There's no law backing you or forbidding what I did in the past."

The word *murder* made Koba shift uneasily. The taskmaster hoped his trainer would not do anything rash... *yet*.

"Only my father's."

"Only your father's reputation. I see you took that as your own?"

Curge nodded sagely. "One thing he left to me. Amongst others."

"I doubt there's anyone left of the old guard to remember Curge casting me out."

To this, Dark Curge smirked. "More than you would like. They haven't all died of old age."

"Who's left?"

"I'm sure you'll find out on your own if you've the balls to come this far."

"Hmm. What about this Gastillo?"

"Once a pit fighter. On his own for a few seasons now. Well financed but... manageable. Truth be known, the House of Curge still dominates these games."

Clavellus could not suppress his own smirk. "I'll ask around on that."

"Have you found the Free Trained men that visited you?" Curge asked, his eyes sly.

The question caught Clavellus off guard, and in the moment he took to think of an answer, Curge had him.

"Yes, I know about them," the one-armed man rumbled. "There's... little that happens in the Pit that I don't know about. I've known perhaps even longer than you." His smile opened like a long, gleaming stitch pulled apart. "I know they're searching for a taskmaster of their own. Seeing you here makes me believe you are thinking about coming back to the games, so I'll be brief, old master. Any man taken under your wing will be punished on the sands. Gutted. One by one, so that you'll *know* you made a mistake in coming back. I'll place a bounty large enough on any of them to make the Domis shite themselves and the Madea break a sweat. And once started, it won't end. I'll let slip that your head is also up for payment, just to make things more interesting. Saimon's hell, I just might hunt you myself. Surprise you, like this time, eh? The streets won't be friendly to you in the least, not amongst those who kill for a living. Do you truly wish to be constantly looking over your shoulder? Checking every shadow? Not I. And when you're gone and your estate is in ruins, I'll ravage that as well."

When he finished, deadly tension thrummed between the four men.

"There's no need for any of this." Clavellus locked gazes with Curge. "What happened was long ago."

"My father said you'd say such things," Curge droned on, sounding bored, "just as he said you would crawl back. He knew you better than I. Obviously, he knew you better than *you* knew him. You went against him. Challenged his word under his own roof. In front of his fighters. You questioned the word of *Curge. Now* you know how deep a mistake that was. Only now… after all these years."

For a time, neither man spoke. Clavellus felt as if he'd just been punched hard in the guts, and he struggled with his composure. To show weakness here would mean spilled blood.

"It's a surprise that you didn't lose more than just your arm," Clavellus finally retorted in a controlled voice.

"This?" Curge lifted his stump and regarded it with

pursed lips. "What was it you once said? 'Pain is just a friendly tap to get your arse moving.' *This* got me moving—quite fast in fact. The man that did this—well, I aimed higher with my cut, and my life with one arm is considerably easier than his with no head."

Curge lowered his arm. "Stay away, Clavellus," he growled, all cordiality having bled from his voice. "Be good to yourself and die peacefully in bed. Perhaps with that old bitch you call a wife if she still draws breath. You've stayed away for so long. Why trouble yourself now with returning? With knowing I'll make you and yours *bleed* for transgressions against my father? The House of Curge remembers. Always has. Always will. When you leave here this day, do not come back. Know that I'll be watching. And listening. A maggot could squeal within these walls, and I'd hear of it. You won't get this warning again." The big man shook his head and suddenly appeared almost apologetic. "This day, I'll be merciful and allow you to take in the spectacle of the games. Just to see what you've missed all this time. My gift to you for the old days. Think of it as a cup of water... offered to a man dying of thirst. But don't linger here."

Curge's eyes became as hard as the glare off polished Vathian marble. "In fact, get out the moment the day's fights are finished. Do you understand?"

"I do." Clavellus swallowed.

Satrisfied, Curge's face softened. He glanced at Koba, and the corners of his eyes crinkled in amusement.

Then he turned dismissively and left, his burly henchman following, showing his back. They left the door open.

Koba strode across the room and peered out, turning left and right and watching for a few moments while Clavellus took a deep steadying breath and longed for a tankard of firewater. His heart and lungs seemed to have stopped sometime during Curge's visit, and he struggled to hide the pent-up anxiety pounded into him by the warning of his once student. He'd wanted to return, and he'd done so.

Now he wondered if he had the balls to go further.

The banishment had not lessened. As long as one remained of old Curge's line, he would make it known that Clavellus was still a pariah to the games. Thinking back to the instance when he crossed the brooding bastard, in front of his fighters no less, filled him with a quivering stinger of regret lodged deep in his bones. He should've just let old Curge have his way back then. He should have just given the order and walked away.

But he didn't.

Seddon above, he thought. To be lectured by old Curge's only son left him wishing for a taste of venom. The very man whom Clavellus had taught perhaps everything he'd ever known about combat, and to have his once student *warn* him… the underlying, insolent *dare* in his words. That was a nail that Clavellus knew he couldn't swallow.

Then he smiled feebly. Young Curge—Dark Curge— had done well. He'd gotten inside his old instructor's head. Clavellus saw the trap clearly then, and the realization spread over him like the sun's heat. Curge didn't want him to stay away. Just the opposite. Curge wanted him to *partake* in the games with whomever he was training. Whether he knew Clavellus didn't have any gladiators at the moment was unsaid and uncertain. And how he'd known about the Free Trained was beyond him. Regardless, Curge wanted his old taskmaster back in the Pit.

With whoever had the balls to stand with him.

To take up steel against Curge's own students.

The old teacher versus the pupil.

"He's gone," Koba returned, appearing every bit as tense as Clavellus felt.

"No, he's not. Not really," the taskmaster said distantly, appearing calm on the outside while hiding the conflict within. He'd run from Dark Curge's father, but running from the son did not sit well on Clavellus's heart. The sheer audacity to confront and lecture him did not sit well on his mind. And embarking upon what Clavellus had *known* all along he'd finally do, what he'd done for half his life, even in the shadows of Sunja's games... did *not* sit well on his nerves.

Outside, the crowds had quieted down.

"We have to get moving," Clavellus said finally.

"Are we leaving?" Koba wanted to know.

"Far from it."

28

The day following the burning of Thaimondus's house, Halm and Muluk felt as if spikes were being hammered into their temples while their stomachs upheaved with a storm's strength. They were far too hung over to travel, so an irritated Goll reluctantly gave in to staying another day in Karashipa. The next day, however, the Kree rallied his dried-out companions at dawn and left the little village when the sun had just pulled itself above the distant treetops, turning the sky gold-white. They rode away on horses as Goll decided there was no need to take a wagon. The horses would be handful enough.

Feeling eyes on his back, Halm turned around once on his mare, and saw the small gathering watching them leave. Miji stood there, just a shape set against the picturesque scene of sleepy, roughshod houses and the black mirror of the lake beyond. Goll purposely steered his horse directly behind the Zhiberian, blocking his view and regarding him with an annoyed question on his features. Halm cleared his throat and righted himself in the saddle, a wistful expression on his face. His mare's ears flickered to the quirky chortles of morning birds as he got used to the sway of the animal underneath him. The villagers had provided them all with saddles and saddlebags in addition to the horses, and Goll in particular had struggled getting onto his gelding, which was a sturdy sixteen hands high and the tallest of the three animals.

"Think I'll miss this place." Muluk glanced about as he rode beside the Zhiberian. "Good place to live. Not in the city."

"Aye that." Halm caught himself the moment he said it.

The stocky Kree smiled at him. "So, you ah…" He flexed his brow with sly meaning and tossed a nod towards the village.

"No," Halm answered. "Just talked."

"Talked? What is it with you and talking? All Zhiberians like you?"

"No. Just me."

"Lords above." Muluk turned in his saddle and looked back at an uncomfortable Goll. "You hear that? He *talked* to her."

"You expect him to club her across the head or something, you tit?"

Muluk scowled uncertainly at his countryman before directing his attention back to Halm. "Well, did you kiss her even?"

"No, none of that. Nothing. Only talk."

"And here I thought that look on your face was from being spent." Muluk scratched at his dark hair. "Next alehouse we get to, I'll show you how to do things right. Guaranteed."

Behind them both, Goll groaned and gazed at something interesting in the underbrush.

Muluk ignored him. "I know just the one for you."

A bemused Halm eyed the Kree. "It's all right, good Muluk. I think I'll be seeing that barkeep again in the future. I'll wait on that."

"Pah. Your choice. I'll ask again later when you're drunk."

"No more drinking," Goll declared firmly.

"What?" asked a surprised Muluk.

"No more drinking. You, I don't care, but for him," he dipped his head at Halm's back, "nothing. Not even a sip. He'll be fighting soon, and it's all poison to a man fighting."

"Bit strict, isn't it?" Muluk asked.

"You'll find my boot strict in your ass if I catch you buying him a drink."

Muluk frowned and shot a disapproving glance back at his countryman. "Uncalled for."

"I'm telling you both, but especially *you*, Zhiberian. If you're serious about this, you will now observe what I had to observe while preparing for my matches here. On my own. No spirits of any kind. Only practice and rest. With a day of rest before the match."

"I like that part," Halm confided to Muluk.

"What's the good of it?" Muluk demanded. "You can't drink. And you aren't interested in a woman. Damn boring if you ask me."

"I'm not asking you, you black-bearded punce; I'm telling you," Goll warned. "And you better not encourage him, Zhiberian. You'll be a laughing stock if the whole of Sunja sees you with the print of my broken toes stamped into your ass."

"Where exactly is he going to be training anyway?" Muluk asked.

"I don't know. I'll find a place."

"Like Thaimondus and Clavellus?"

"I did what I could with the information I had." Goll defended himself in a cool voice. "What happened wasn't my fault. And just in case you haven't noticed, your fat ass is in a saddle provided by that information, however indirectly."

Muluk scratched at his unruly black curls as he glanced at Halm. "Seems to be thinking hard about asses this morning."

"I was too, last night," the Zhiberian said. "But nothing came of it."

That left Muluk smirking.

"I'll take care of it," Goll promised. "With the coin we have and the coin we'll get from selling the horses, we'll—"

Muluk turned around in his saddle. "Sell the horses? We just got them."

"We can't care for them in the city. It's an expense we can't afford."

"I'm getting used to it!"

"You haven't had to *care* for the beast yet," Goll countered. "One day of feeding and brushing it out and shoveling its shite, and you'll be talking differently."

"Hadn't thought of that."

"Well, think on it. Think on this as well—I'll be able to rent another room if you wish, in our favourite alehouse. You'll be able to sleep in peace."

That brightened Muluk, and he bared his yellowed teeth. "There'll be no peace if I have my own room."

"I really don't care," Goll retorted. "Rut whoever you please if you're drunk enough to. Rut the horse goodbye if you like. Halm is the one I'm concerned with."

"You hear that?" Muluk asked his burly companion. "You're *his* now."

Halm kept silent.

"This is serious business, Zhiberian," Goll insisted. "From here on in, we do things my way. Follow my instructions, and we'll all come out better for it. I guarantee it. *I'll* be the taskmaster. We'll build something from the ground up. Draw fighters to our name and banner. We'll have our *own* house. Something that will make the other houses take note of us."

"I've taken note of you," Muluk quipped out of the corner of his mouth.

"What was that?"

"One drink and you're through," Muluk said a little louder, making Halm smile. "Just talking to the Zhiberian, dear."

Goll lapsed into silence. The only sounds heard for the next little while were the plodding of the horses, the low conversation of Halm and Muluk, and the gentle creaking of full saddlebags. The land crept past them as the air stayed a comfortable temperature. Cloud cover seeped in from the east and stretched across overheard like fine cotton, and for once, all was fine with the world.

They took their time for fear of risking saddle soreness and entered the city at suppertime. Goll sold the horses to a willing merchant closing up his stall and almost heading home for the evening. Sixty gold was added to their fortunes, even though Goll believed the merchant didn't pay full value for the three horses. He leeched another fifteen gold off the man from the sale of the saddles.

"Carry this," Goll handed a sack to Halm and Muluk, "and guard it with your lives."

"How much do we have now?" Muluk asked.

"Wait until we get to our room," Goll answered. "Then we'll see exactly. But I think we're a third of the way there."

"A third," Muluk said.

"We'll need more," Halm added.

"Yes, we will," Goll said guardedly. "We'll need more. But I think we can all agree that this time three days ago, we were in a much harder place. Things are moving for us. I can feel it."

Muluk eyed a shapely woman moving through the milling crowds. "I could feel that."

Both Goll and Halm stopped and took a moment to appreciate the curves, barely hidden by a wisp of a dress. Goll got them moving once again through the streets towards their favourite alehouse. A thick blue-grey cloud like the underbelly of a thunder god dragged itself across the purpling sky, and the sun had almost dropped from sight when they reached the building. Sounds of laughter and conversation perked their ears before they lay eyes on the place. They crossed the threshold with weary feet. Goll immediately left his companions and swung himself though the drinkers and eaters and to the barkeep. The portly man leaned towards him when beckoned, and Goll spoke into his ear.

"He's a determined bastard, isn't he?" Muluk said.

"He is. He is," Halm had to agree.

"Think anything will come of all this?"

"You have anything else better to do?"

Muluk met Halm's steady gaze. "I do not, good Halm."

"Neither do I, good Muluk. Neither do I."

"Then... let's see where it all goes."

Halm nodded in resignation. "What's to lose? I can't think of anything."

"Except your life, I suppose."

There was that. Halm shrugged it off.

Then Goll waved them over.

"I have us the only three rooms just above the bar here." He held out three keys. "Take one, and that's yours for the night. We'll meet in mine. I've ordered food to be sent up as well as a couple ale pitchers. Water for you," Goll directed at Halm; then at Muluk, "I figure it's best to keep this one in good cheer else I hear the groans all night and tomorrow."

"You won't hear a word from me." Muluk beamed as he took a key, clearly happy with Goll's gifts.

"Nothing for me?" Halm asked, taking his own.

"Just the food and water. No beer or ale, and certainly no firewater."

"A bit of wine?"

Goll scowled as if he hadn't heard that last bit before turning and making his way towards the stairs through the people. Muttering, Halm followed with Muluk. They climbed above the crowds, hauling themselves up the stairs to the second floor, which was open to the main floor below. A wide, scuffed walkway was bordered by a rounded wooden railing, which was all that kept one from falling into the masses below. Halm looked up at the ceiling, inspecting the slanting planks nailed to the ribs of thick timbers holding everything up.

Halm fitted the key and opened the door to his room just as some pipe music started below. He peered through the railing and saw a group of men start playing while rosy, long-haired sirens twirled and pranced before them, attracting onlookers. Feeling tempted himself, as he enjoyed such revelries, Halm turned back to his door and felt the heat from Goll's stare. Without meeting his companion's eyes, he entered the darkness and closed the door behind him. Fading light from a far, shuttered window barely illuminated the interior, and he fumbled his way. He dropped the cloth sack with the coins on a bed that looked to have had its middle squished, as if it had endured far too much action over the years. But he was thankful for a cloth blanket draped over the straw for cushion, with another, thinner blanket pulled neatly on top, suggesting a woman's touch. The heavy wooden frame appeared surprisingly strong for an upstairs room of an alehouse, double sized and otherwise enticing. A single, square table lay beside it, along with a washbasin, a pitcher of water, and a chamber pot poked halfway underneath the bed. Three long fresh candles, stuck in individual clay cups, also presided on the table.

With the music from outside surprisingly muted, Halm gazed upon the room and sighed contentedly. He sent a silent thanks to Goll. It was hard to fault the man when he provided accommodations such as these. Another tired groan escaped him, and he plopped down on the bed, discovering it quite soft. He swung his legs up and lay back, boots still on, while folding his hands behind his head just and savouring the luxury. The ceiling above was a murky lattice of wooden slabs and bare timbers, and for a moment, he studied them while listening to the pipe players below. Each eye blink became heavier than the last.

Someone knocked at his door and opened it, allowing a wide gash of light to fall across the bed and floor.

"What? You sleeping already?" Muluk asked in shock as he stuck his head in.

"No." Halm sat up.

"Come on then. The food's here."

"Already?"

"You *have* been sleeping."

Halm rubbed at his face. "Perhaps a little there."

"Come on. Eat now and sleep afterwards."

With a grunt, he followed Muluk to the room at the end of the walkway, where the door stood half opened. Inside, Goll's table was filled with a platter of lamb and beef, bread, and two pitchers with cups.

"You sleeping?" Goll asked with the corner of his mouth hitched up. He placed a slab of lamb on a slice of bread and folded it up.

"I did for a bit." Halm sat down.

"That's good. You eat what you can and sleep. Tomorrow, we work."

"What about me?" Muluk got comfortable in his own chair.

"You," Goll said, "will have the most important task of all. You'll stay here and guard the gold."

"What?"

"You heard me. Someone has to do it."

"Why not just leave it in a bank?" Muluk helped himself to the meat and bread.

Goll paused before biting into his food. "I thought about it, but I'd be forever going back and forth to the place. No, we'll keep one man here. Perhaps even two eventually. With the barkeep down below and you above, no one will bother you. Plus, no one knows it's here. And in case you were wondering, we have a little over three hundred gold pieces to our names. A small fortune."

Both Halm and Muluk stopped in midchew. Neither man had ever been so close to so much money. It was bewildering. Halm slowly looked at the bed.

"I've hidden it," Goll said, "but don't worry. If anyone

really searched for it, they'd find it. Reminds me—here."

Goll leaned back and winced, still tender from the beating Baylus the Butcher gave him on the very first day. He pulled up his leather purse, undid the drawstrings, and counted out five coins to Halm and then to Muluk. The men watched in wonder.

"This is yours. Your first coin other than what the house will provide for you, being food and rooms. Spend it on whatever you wish. But Halm, no drinking. And you, well, understand that I don't know when you'll get another handful of coins from me, if ever again. So make this last. You lads understand?"

They nodded and made their gold portions disappear.

"We'll head to the arena tomorrow and see when and who you'll be fighting," Goll told Halm. "With luck, perhaps we can get a little more information on the dog. And you must win. I'll be wagering a lot of coin on you."

Halm didn't say anything. Two thoughts were on his mind: the whereabouts of Pig Knot and what Miji might be serving in her little alehouse down by the lake.

Below, the pipe players carried on. Caro had heard better playing in far better establishments with far prettier women. With a contemptuous snarl, he nursed his mug of ale and wandered to a window, minding himself as he moved through the gathering crowds. He placed a shoulder against the frame and alternated between peering out into the street and up at the second floor. The fat man and his companions had returned as he thought they might when they first disappeared from the city. They appeared to be in fair spirits, which coin would do for a pack of motherless dogs. Not many could afford private rooms in the alehouse, especially Free Trained shite surviving match to match *if* they were lucky. No, something else had happened. They came into money somewhere.

He sipped from his mug once more and caught the eye of a blond serving maid, wearing a dress exposing a dark gash of cleavage. There was no temptation there, however, as Caro focused on what he had to do. His attention lay on the rooms above and the men keeping them.

He would send word to Grisholt in the morning.

29

Voices in the street woke Pig Knot from his sleep. He cracked open his eyes and took a deep breath, paused a moment, and then stretched his limbs, clawing at air. Relaxing, he gazed up at the ceiling and smelled the pungent saywort Bindon had rubbed on his wounds the night before. Pig Knot screwed up his face at the odour. He smelled as if he'd been dragged through a forest planted in a shite trough.

He then sensed a presence in the room and turned his head. The shuttered window lay open, and dull daylight cut across the room, revealing the tall form of a giant standing quietly at attention.

Klytus. In armor.

The huge Sujin shifted his weight, causing a floorboard to squeal.

Groaning, Pig Knot looked at the window. Clouds blotted out the usual sunshine. He snorted, clearing his sinuses and again abhorring the smell smeared onto his person, then rubbed at his eyes and regarded the mountain of metal standing before the stairs. The man didn't come any closer, and Pig Knot believed it was because the ceiling was too low for him and he didn't like to stoop.

"What is it?"

Klytus was brief. "This day, you fight."

Pig Knot sighed and wearily swung his legs over the edge of the bed. He felt the stitches and swollen bruises over his face. Bindon had actually brought up a mirror to him at one point, and that was a fright he didn't need to repeat. The Sunjan's face looked like a sliced and battered peach. He'd wear a visor if he could. Perhaps Halm's.

"All right." He got to his feet.

*

Descending the steps to the Pit's general quarters felt like wading into a rank sewer. After days of being aboveground and in relatively fresh air, Halm's nose wrinkled at the smell wafting up from the darkness before him. The foulness crept over his tongue and throat with every breath. He turned around to Goll, coming down behind him and favouring his foot with the broken toes.

"What?" the Kree asked him.

"This place stinks."

"Are you only just discovering that?" Goll jerked his chin at the steps, orange in torchlight. "This place smelled like shite when I first came here, and that was at the beginning of the games. Now, I'd sleep in the morass of a pigsty if I had a choice. Move on."

They reached the bottom, and the Zhiberian inwardly cringed once more at the number of men present. It felt like a market day, with the merchants and buyers all crammed into a public latrine. Men moved through the torchlit shadows like white eels in deep water. Something was squishing between his sandaled toes, and he didn't have the courage to find out what it was. It all made him greater appreciate having his own room. Goll maneuvered around him and made his way to the Madea and his prickly fence of Skarrs. Already the arena official was pondering over his matchboard and consulting his papers.

And there stood Pig Knot.

Standing at the mouth of the white tunnel, Pig Knot wore a vest of leather armor and held a sword and shield.

Another man, dressed in brown trousers and a white shirt, talked with him. Pig Knot listened as his companion leaned in and spoke aggressively, his teeth flashing at times.

"That's Pig Knot." Halm pointed.

"What?" Goll turned.

"There."

Goll peered in that direction. "Are you certain?"

"Aye that. And he just slapped on my helm."

As they watched, Pig Knot fumbled with the straps under his chin as the other man continued to talk. Then the Sunjan disappeared from sight as men passed through their line of sight.

"You there," someone said nearby, distracting them both. A short man emerged from the figures milling about. Long sideburns scythed down his sallow cheeks, and his dark though greying hair was cut close to the skull. He wore a brown vest over a white tunic, exposing a set of powerful-looking arms.

Halm glanced in the direction of Pig Knot. He was striding up the white tunnel while his companion had seemingly vanished.

"My master wishes to speak with you once more. At his residence," the man said.

"Who's that?" Goll asked. "And who are you?"

The shorter man moved in closer, conscious of the press

of bodies. "I'm Borchus. I speak for Clavellus."

The name of the taskmaster froze both men.

"Clavellus wants to see us?" Goll asked, unconvinced. "The same man that called us... what was it?"

"Punces," Halm supplied dutifully.

Goll nodded. "I remember 'masterless pit dogs' myself."

"Asslickers."

Goll lifted a finger at that one, approving of Halm's memory. "And there were a few other cutting words as well. So why does he want to see us?"

"You'll have to see him about that." Borchus hung his thumbs on a leather belt. "I was only instructed to locate you and deliver the message. Especially you." He nodded at Halm. "Hard not to pick you out of a crowd. How much do you eat to keep that striking figure?"

"Depends. How tall are you?"

Borchus's brow cocked as if hooked from above. "Ah, that was wit," he deadpanned. "You surprised me. Give me a moment to compose myself. I'm breathless. My ribs."

Halm opened his mouth to say more, but Goll cut him off. "You tell him we'll see him tomorrow."

"This day would be best, I think."

"My friend said tomorrow," Halm said.

"Since all of your fat clings about your waist, how is it you still cannot hear?" Borchus retorted, his face expressionless.

"Not sure, why don't you climb down off your chair and try shouting again?"

"You don't wear a helm when you fight, do you?"

"All right." Goll eyed both men. "We'll be there. And we'll leave shortly. After we get the third member of our group."

"Ah yes, I've heard of him. I hope he's not the size of this one. Doubt if there's enough cattle about to feed two." Borchus straightened, unimpressed. "I'll wait for you outside the city's southern gate."

With that, he turned and walked away.

"Little shite." Halm gnawed on his lower lip in reflection.

"You weren't helping, trading jabs like that."

Halm held out a hand. "Like what? *He* started. I would've finished it if you hadn't cut in."

Goll ignored him. "We'll have to go. Clavellus wishes to speak with us."

"Pig Knot's fighting. We have to wait for him."

"I'm not waiting for him."

"We wait for him." Halm's gaze hardened. "He'll want this chance."

"I don't think he will."

"What do you mean you don't think he will? I know the man. You're wrong."

Goll paused for a moment, mulling. Halm didn't know what was going on in that skull of his, but he shored up his stance and made it clear he wasn't moving.

"Fine," Goll said through tight lips.

"Over there then." Halm pointed at the white tunnel. "Won't have time to place a wager. Sounds as though they're about to start…"

*

Let him cut you a bit. I mean cut *you. The people who watch these things want to see blood, and you're going to give it to them. I want you to perform a bit. Can you do that? Let him cut you, think that you're on the out, and then gut him. Slice him like a fish, up through the belly and across the throat. Take his miserable life. Do that. But let him cut you first.*

The instructions Toffer had given, leaning in close, breath reeking like a pocket of gas escaping a dead man's swelling gut, did nothing to inspire Pig Knot to win. All he heard was the poison in the man's words; all he smelled, the foulness from his mouth. All he felt was the uncertainty of doing *any* of this, and he believed he'd feel much better once the nasty business was concluded.

Let him cut you, echoed through the Sunjan's mind like words spoken to a sleepy child. He lost track of where he was going until the gatekeeper roused him with a cry of warning. Pig Knot realized then that he had walked by the man and was climbing the steps to the portcullis. Standing inside the gate, another man stood and angrily shooed him away, having not received the signal from the Orator.

The gatekeeper actually slapped him on the chest when he drew back.

"Anxious or just stunned?" the gatekeeper asked.

"Bit of both, perhaps."

"Well, hold on. Wait until I get the signal and pull the lever."

Pig Knot nodded.

Let him cut you.

And then gut him. He didn't quite understand why the need for the theatrics, but an order was an order. Debt was debt.

He barely heard the gatekeeper's words, but he understood the slap across the back. He got moving, climbing the steps towards the rising gate. He entered the arena to a foul barrage of jeers and insults, stalling him just past the threshold. The crowd, at least those that remembered him, had spread the word about his last match. Across from him, shifting from foot to foot, was a man armoured in leather and armed with a sword and shield. A pot helm covered his features, and for that, Pig Knot was grateful. He caught the name, Sadar, but he didn't hear where the man was from. Didn't matter.

Let him cut you.

Pig Knot sighed. Across the way, Sadar focused on him, unmoving and seemingly waiting for the Orator's signal.

"Begin!" The single word punctured Pig Knot's thoughts like a spike.

Sadar wasted no time. He was smaller than Pig Knot, but his arms and legs were bare and wiry, giving him the look of a well-greased animal. Pig Knot took a huge breath of apprehension. Sadar quickly crossed the sand, closing the distance.

Pig Knot groaned inwardly. The man had push.

Sadar swung both sword and shield at Pig Knot in an alternating flash of steel, causing the Sunjan to hide behind his shield and retreat from the storm. A sword crashed off the borrowed helm of Halm, suddenly skewing his vision. Pig Knot backed up furiously, trying to right his helmet. His foe pressed him, stabbing for legs and arms and barely missing, making Pig Knot dance. The Sunjan couldn't properly see. He gave up and ran from the man, wanting distance so he could correct his helm.

The arena burst into scalding laughter.

Pig Knot reached the other side of the arena, chagrined, but he got his sight back with a quick adjustment. Above, dark clouds had rolled in, cloaking the arena in that gloomy twilight of thunderstorms, their billowing mass veined with lightning.

Closing in on the Sunjan, Sadar rolled his shoulders.

Let him cut you.

Those words were going to hurt. Sadar appeared ready to *maim* him.

The man stabbed for his head, and Pig Knot deflected it with his shield. A sword went for his arm, and Pig Knot parried that one as well. Then it was shield edge, sword tip, and a slash seeking to spill his guts. Pig Knot ducked, parried, and parried again before thrusting back and having his sword turned away. Sadar saw an opening and lunged, which was greeted with an appreciative *ooooooh* from the onlookers. Pig Knot sprawled out of the way, souring the thousands of voices into an arena-wide groan.

Seddon's rosy ass, Pig Knot cursed. *One bad fight and they—*
Remembered.

Sadar's sword swept low, hunting for legs and causing Pig Knot to jump. He backpedaled, keeping his sword before him. Sadar closed in quickly once more, his limbs gleaming with sweat. His shield came up and over, his whole body behind the swing, and Pig Knot reacted in anticipation of the follow-up stab underneath, seeking his stomach.

He glimpsed the steel just as he moved away. Sadar sped by, sending up sand as he dug his feet in to stop his momentum.

Sadar turned around and bellowed. That suited Pig Knot fine. He felt like screaming himself. Then, for the first time, he noticed his sword arm. A cut the width of his shoulder lay open and bled thickly. Somewhere in the past few seconds, a sword had bitten him.

Sadar cocked his head like a bird about to pluck an eyeball from a skull. The crowd chanted his name, louder and louder as more people joined in, the words pulsing like a storm surf.

Pig Knot blinked at the wound, flexed his arm, and grimaced at the burn.

He'd been *cut*.

Sadar flew at him.

Pig Knot dropped to the sand and chopped the left leg out from under the man, sending him crashing into the sand like a dropped sack of heavy grain. In that lightning bolt of spent time, the fight was over. The crowd gasped at the sight, and when the Sunjan got back to his feet, he could see why.

Bare legs. There was a reason why greaves were a good thing.

Sadar had made the mistake, however, of not wearing them. Perhaps he felt they were too heavy. Now he lay on the sand, bawling like a lamb beholding the butcher. The left leg was cut almost entirely off just below the knee, hanging on by a shred of thick meat and spurting blood into the sand. Sadar had dropped his sword, and if it wasn't for the inner band of metal on his shield, he probably would've lost that as well.

Pig Knot could see red bone in that wound. It made him wince.

"Mercy!" Sadar cried out.

The crowds screamed, outraged at the sudden twist of events.

Sadar threw up both his arms, his shield leaning away from his left. He moved his sliced leg, causing the bloody mouth to stretch wider. Pig Knot's shoulders slumped.

"Mercy!" Sadar pleaded again and tore off his helm. Lad could not have been more than twenty, if that. His lips trembled, but Pig Knot could no longer hear him. The incensed screams from the onlookers suddenly drowned out all other sound.

Damn.

He gripped his sword, the steel red from Sadar's blood. *Gut him. Slice him like a fish…*

Grimacing, Pig Knot shook his head… and turned away.

He walked back to the portcullis, catching bits and pieces of curses heaped upon his name. Some truly inventive ones rose above the angry clamour of the audience. Any moment, he expected a spear to nail him through the back, but it didn't happen. He waited until the gate came up and ducked under it, not bothering to look back at the man whose life he'd spared.

He wondered if Toffer would be upset. The fight hadn't gone the way he wanted.

Thinking further, he realized he truly didn't care.

Walking back through the white tunnel, he didn't pay attention to the man inside the portcullis, the gatekeeper, or the Skarrs standing guard.

He wandered back to general quarters, appreciating the pearly gleam of the tunnel, taking the helmet from his head and breathing the hideous-tasting air. Toffer would be waiting for him. Pig Knot wasn't looking forward to the meeting, but a win was a win, and any time one came back from the sands with only a gash to the arm was a good thing. The tunnel ended in the crowded torchlit general quarters, and he steered towards the mighty matchboard. He faced the Madea, who eyed him without emotion for a moment.

Pig Knot waited.

"You win your fight?" the Madea asked over the din of the massive underground chamber.

He nodded.

The Madea still waited until a runner brought the official word. Without a word, he handed a leather purse full of coin to Pig Knot, who hefted it in a fist. He remembered to thank the ring organizer and turned to leave.

There, standing in his way, was a man.

It wasn't Toffer.

"Get scratched, did you?" Halm grinned at him.

All at once, Pig Knot's mood brightened. It was good to see a friend's face coming back from the Pit. "Maybe if I had those rolls of yours, it wouldn't have bothered me."

"Maybe, maybe," Halm agreed. "I see you're a few coins richer."

Pig Knot shrugged and noticed the Kree standing next to him. "Goll. How goes the limping?"

That didn't win him any smiles. Goll frowned. "We're leaving. You can come with us or not."

"Leaving? Leaving what?"

"The city," Goll said.

"We have a meeting with a taskmaster." Halm eyes shone in the sparse lamplight.

"What?" Pig Knot asked. "What about?"

"Tell you on the way."

"Well, wait—I have your sack over there," Pig Knot said ruefully. "That shite still stinks, by the way. And I have to see the healer."

"For that scratch?" Halm scoffed. "Old woman. A rag will plug that. Let's get going."

"Wait." Goll went to the Madea, talked with the man, and then returned. "You fight in three days," he reported to Halm.

"Three days, eh? Did he say who?"

"House of Curge. No surprise there."

Halm agreed. "None at all."

Pig Knot glanced about for Toffer.

"Looking for your friend from earlier?" Goll asked.

"Aye that. See him?"

"He left. Probably at the Domis right now if he wagered on you."

"I'm sure he did."

"Who was he?"

"Just a man I owed. All settled now."

Halm clapped a hand to Pig Knot's shoulder. "Good to see you, Pig Knot. We have some interesting news for you."

*

Rubbing the sleep from his eyes, Caro leaned against the stone wall of a tailor and weaver store and studied the front of the alehouse containing the remaining Free Trained man. He employed several other spies, all funded by Grisholt's recent winnings in the arena. The henchman he'd replaced in the alley reported that two of them had left much earlier, so Caro assigned a man to follow the Zhiberian and his companion.

After sending his night man off to get some sleep, Caro resumed watch with his breakfast, a couple of hard-boiled eggs and a chunk of bread. He'd taken up sleeping in an alleyway two buildings away on a pair of blankets he'd stolen from a weaver's open stall. The alley had become the designated area for him or any of the other men working for him. Hanging farther back between the structures to avoid attention but remaining close enough to keep an eye on the entrance to the alehouse, he sipped on a wooden cup of water and quietly finished eating his food. It would be all he'd get until the evening.

He'd almost gotten over the fright Curge had given him, wishing he could somehow exact revenge on the bald ogre. Caro's career as a fighter had been a short one, for he realized early that he couldn't endure the constant training. Gathering information, placing wagers, and any other work of an agent agreed with him much more than retching his guts out while a trainer screamed insults at him. He believed that if he performed well enough, Grisholt would take care of him. These days, loyalty was valued in a man, and Caro just didn't see himself slaving in a field somewhere or under a merchant's roof.

The shady dealings were infinitely more agreeable.

The morning stretched into early afternoon, with no sign of any of their marks appearing. People filed in and out of his field of vision, but they were all the wrong ones. He pissed in the alley when the need took him, grateful for the break in the monotony. Soon his thoughts were on other things he could be doing, but he squashed those and forced himself to enjoy the hunt. For this was a hunt of the best kind.

Just then he glimpsed the pensive face of one of his hired hands passing by the mouth of the alley.

Caro's expression became curious.

This man, Ballan, subtly directed his attention down the street before passing from view. Caro came forward, cautiously glancing one way and then the other. There, amongst the people going about their business, walked the Zhiberian, his fat belly bared to the sun and bouncing about in a manner Caro found distasteful.

The agent retreated a step back into the alley. The fat man was returning to the alehouse. He walked alone. Caro eventually saw the Zhiberian wore an expression of urgency. Reaching the alehouse, he jumped the steps to the front door and disappeared inside.

Caro waited.

The Zhiberian emerged once again—with another man at his side.

Worse, they were carrying cloth sacks with them—sacks that, if Caro didn't miss his guess, were full of coin. He detached himself from the alley and tracked the pair heading back the way the fat man had come. Ballan stretched across the way, catching Caro's attention and seeking guidance. Caro wasn't sure of what to do. Even though he carried a sword at his waist—he'd carried the weapon since the encounter with Dark Curge—his agents didn't carry much more. They were eyes and ears, not fighters, and certainly not capable of attacking two dangerous men in broad daylight.

Caro gave Ballan the briefest of hand signals, *follow them*, and got moving himself. He kept back to avoid being noticed. The pit fighters walked quickly, straight through the middle of the crowds, who instinctively parted for them. Some people meandered into Caro's path, threatening to slow him, so he shouldered past or shoved them out of his way, hearing their curses in his wake. Ballan kept up just at the edge of his vision, keeping closer to the store- and stallfronts. Caro had no one else to draw upon this hour of morning as they were all sleeping somewhere. It was just the two of them in pursuit of the pit fighters.

They trailed twenty paces behind their quarry, following them to the southern gate of the city, where a knot of watchful Skarrs made Caro hesitate. The Zhiberian and his companion entered the tunnel, where murder holes allowed scant grey light to filter down and checker the traffic entering and exiting Sunja.

Caro followed, immersing himself in the crowds and flowing past the Skarrs. Despite his forced expression of boredom, he sensed the city guards watching him right up until he entered the tunnel. Once inside, he searched for his targets amongst the moving bottleneck of people. The passageway ended, and he emerged on the other side and located his prey boarding one of two wagons driven by men he didn't know. Once they were aboard, the vehicles rolled from the city, following the terraced road, all to the rumble from gathering thunderheads.

About ten strides on his right, Ballan stopped and stared, seeing the same thing.

Caro held his chin and looked about. With a quick flick of his chin, he set Ballan to follow. The agent watched him go, smelling rain on the air and watching the clouds move over the city. Then he felt the first few pelts on his forehead. Wherever the wagons were heading, Ballan was in for some exercise and wet weather, not that Caro cared. He didn't have to do it.

The rain flickered from drops to a drizzle as the wagons rattled down over the cliff, following the winding road to the softly undulating farmland of Plagur's Reach far below. There wasn't anything Caro could do now except to go back, rouse one of his remaining thugs, and send him off to Grisholt.

His employer would want to know the Free Trained had left the city yet again and, this time, perhaps even taken their coin with them.

Then another idea struck Caro, which made him head towards Sunja's Pit.

The matchboard.

Halm of Zhiberia would be displayed on the Madea's matchboard for all to see if he was to fight in the coming days.

Increasing his stride, Caro's hopes grew that the day would not be a total loss and a more lucrative one would be just on the horizon.

30

The warning from Curge four days ago had stayed with Grisholt for a long time after he'd returned to the security of his walled estate. Not just anyone would come into his viewing chamber and start threatening him, and if his father had been present, blood would have smeared the floor. Though the House of Grisholt had fallen from its days of glory, it was still a name and a force to be wary of. The more Grisholt dwelt on what had happened, the more rotten with indignation and insult he became. The *gall* of the one-armed bastard. Grisholt replayed the entire episode, trading barbs with Dark Curge and backing him up with his cutting words. Grisholt paced his grounds, stopping and staring out over his estate walls and muttering with heat, "I should have told him to…" before mentally re-enacting the scene—but with Curge withering and retreating in the end. In some cases, the confrontation took on the feel of a dramatic Perician play where both hero and antagonist fall in a merciless hand-to-hand fight in the final act. Brakuss and his lads die, heroically taking down Curge's brute, while Grisholt stabs the old topper through the throat and emerges from the battle sporting a gallant cut above an eye, a gash that, once healed, becomes a sophisticated scar that endears him to any woman he meets.

If only he had the opportunity to face Curge again. It would be a different meeting. He would tell that ogre where he truly stood in Sunja and that his threats were as worrying as a fragrant cow kiss in a road.

The entire episode soured the gold he'd won from Gunjar losing his match. The fighter had even survived with minimal damage, and while both feats should have made the owner delighted, Grisholt fumed instead. Caro had delivered his lord and master his sizeable winnings in a leather sack after the gladiator's fight, and Grisholt remembered the heft and the gravelly jingle of the coins as they landed on the floor of his koch. He didn't even bother to count it while he rode back home. The owner merely sat and stared out the window at the people passing by, glaring at any that met his stare.

He hadn't been to the city since.

The urge to take out his frustrations on his servants, as his father would've done when he was alive, was fought down and controlled. Instead, Grisholt became stricken with long bouts of brooding, making him miserable even as he portioned his winnings and channeled coin into the areas of the house and business needing it. The incident smouldered in his head as bright as freshly forged steel.

Grisholt would make Curge regret threatening him. He'd remember the outrageous breach of etiquette and make him pay… at a later time, perhaps when he was close to his deathbed. And why wait for a natural death? His father had spoken of removing the heads of houses before. Certainly the House of Curge could be dethroned from its current position in the Pit. They had enjoyed their dominant status for too long, it seemed to Grisholt. Years, in fact. Perhaps it was time to seek alternative means, beyond the combat of the arena, to bring down the house. It would most assuredly benefit Grisholt to do so, and he knew the other houses and stables would welcome the change, however it came about. Only a sizeable amount of coin prevented him from pursuing this course of action. Gold would be needed to hire killers bold enough to strike down Curge, gold that Grisholt did not have.

So he mulled in black fashion until word reached him that the Free Trained men had settled into three rooms of an alehouse. That was very interesting news indeed and perked the owner up considerably. And then came another report of the pit fighters leaving the city, perhaps even carrying their coin with them.

Always something, Grisholt thought. Caro had sent a man after the Free Trained to see where they'd gone. Caro himself had gone to the Pit and discovered that the Zhiberian was scheduled to battle on the sands in a few days, fighting one of Curge's lot, no less. Not that the match was of any importance to Grisholt. The master of the stable couldn't help but think the Free Trained's gold could have already been in *his* hands if he'd been more organized and had the proper men in place.

But he hadn't been prepared. Grisholt wasn't about to make that mistake again.

Rain fell as he entered the regular common room of the gladiators, now devoid of most of his warriors except for the summoned few. Torchlight revealed five great tables, of which only a pair were occupied. Six men gathered around them, men whom Brakuss had chosen from the Stable of Grisholt ranks. Men who weren't particularly fussy about getting their hands dirty beyond the arena.

Cutthroats.

Killers.

The pungent smell of unwashed bodies made Grisholt screw up his nose for a moment. He wasn't surprised about the men Brakuss had recruited. The chosen men had trained hard for the arena; in fact, the brutes had to be watched closely for fear of fighting *too* hard in their sparring matches. Grisholt recognized the one already responsible for removing another gladiator from the active roster. Inflicting wounds and crippling potential money earners was something the owner couldn't afford. Part of his role was to recognize the strengths of an individual and to determine where that person would best serve the interests of the house.

In this case, regarding the gathered men, their eyes glittering like rats', Grisholt approved of Brakuss's selection and gave his one-eyed henchman an appreciative nod. The house master stood before the men divided up and sitting at two tables, sizing up their bare arms and chests. Scarred and muscular, they looked rough, ready, and even eager.

Golki sat like a skinned bear, with round eyes that hadn't blinked since Grisholt came into the room. Perhaps the most powerful of the gathered fighters, Golki preferred using two long-shafted, diamond-shaped maces in combat and actually had to be physically restrained at times from continuing well past the finish of sparring matches.

The menacing Kurlin sat at the end of the same table as Golki, his hands flat on the wooden surface as if divining spirits. Grisholt had heard from his taskmaster Turst that

Kurlin was the sort who also enjoyed punishing his fellow fighters a bit too much. Turst even asked Grisholt to reconsider entering him in the games, as he was a blood match waiting to happen. Kurlin was perfect for such shady work as Grisholt was offering.

Morg and Sulo were usually grinning butchers, quick to anger and even quicker to use any and all dishonourable tricks known to put a man down. Morg in particular had blinded a man by jamming a thumb into his head up to the first knuckle. Grisholt still remembered the morning it happened and the victim's shrieks. He wasn't overly fond of the pair as he knew they scorned and taunted most around them.

Then there was Lantus. Grisholt inwardly chided himself for not anticipating *his* volunteering in the first place. Good enough with a blade to enter the arena, Turst held the opinion that he would never improve his fighting ability. Lantus seemingly knew this as well, so he cheated at every opportunity. Lantus was one of those types who couldn't be trusted at all and had to be motivated with brazen threats of physical punishment or even death. He wasn't someone Grisholt felt confident in or comfortable around. He didn't linger on the man and was more than a little wary of his presence in the group. The old house manager wondered if it might be better just to kill the snake outright. Lantus would have to be watched by the others, and he would make it a point to convey those thoughts to Brakuss. Perhaps Golki or Kurlin should kill him after the task was completed.

The final man was cut and drawn looking, as if starved for some exotic dish. He kept his muscular arms folded. Inked pictures of knives ringed Plakus's biceps, and he ran his tongue over his lips in anticipation of what Grisholt had to say. Plakus had a dirty fashion of flapping that lengthy muscle about his jowls whenever he was training or thinking hard. It was unnerving.

Six killers.

Overall, Grisholt couldn't have been more satisfied with the choices Brakuss had made.

"Boys," he greeted and waited for a moment. "I have a task for you. Something that you'll be well paid for and that will earn my gratitude. It might even open up other opportunities. One never knows. In any case, word has come to me that a small group of Free Trained fighters have come into a large sum of coin. I *want* that coin. There are at least three of them, possibly four, and they have no idea of you or your intentions. Presently, they have left Sunja with coin in hand, but they'll return in a few days. When they do, my eyes and ears in the city will inform you of where they are sleeping and how many you'll be facing. I want you to take whatever they have. If they have hidden their gold, torture them until they reveal where it is—then kill them. Do whatever is necessary to loosen their tongues. Bear two things in mind: Get the gold, and be quiet about it. Is that clear?"

The lot of them had become increasingly more attentive, leaning towards their manager. When he finished, they nodded eagerly.

"Excellent." Grisholt folded his arms and tugged on his beard. "Bring whatever they have back to me, and I'll be quite generous with your shares. Do well, and we just might begin a new business. With my spies out and about and listening to the very heart of the city, I've a feeling more opportunities such as this one will arise. In any case, I believe we are on the threshold of becoming exceptionally wealthy."

Grisholt didn't bother giving these lads a speech about doing it for the greater glory of the stable. It would only be a waste of breath and time. They'd work for him because of the coin but also for the potential to butcher. He almost felt remorse for bringing these men together for such fell purpose. A terrible force was about to be released into the world.

"From here on, keep this a secret. Do not speak with the other fighters. I don't want anyone else beyond this room to know our plans. Also, keep your identity a secret. Cover your faces when you have to. Be stealthy. Kill whoever crosses you, but do it quietly. Be as ghosts with long knives. Understand?"

They did.

"Excellent. Brakuss will give you the particulars and anything else you need to know. Your contact in the city is Caro, and you'll follow his orders. Understood?"

Another series of nods.

Grisholt let out his breath in a hiss. He looked at each of the men in turn, meeting their dangerous gazes.

"Well then…" He was suddenly chipper. "Enjoy the hunt."

31

Not wanting to leave Muluk behind with the gold for an extended amount of time, Goll had Halm rush back to the alehouse to get both him and the coin. A pair of white, cloth-covered wagons waited for the two men when they reached the south gate, and blocky Borchus got down from the first wagon and directed them to jump into the second. The storm clouds overhead cleared their throats and bulged with veined lightning, and no sooner did Muluk's boot leave the ground than Halm felt the first few pecks of rain. The canopy of the wagon kept them dry, however, and the driver instructed them to untie a canvas if the rain began blowing in. They left the city by mid-afternoon, rumbling down the incline and heading towards the estate of Clavellus.

With the wagon bumping and shaking them gently and the rain pecking against the shell of the wagon, Halm looked at Pig Knot and Goll.

"What have you two been talking about, hm?"

Pig Knot smirked. "About this idea of a house. Not bad, I must say. The Kree has big ideas. So you're all in on this?"

"I am," Halm said brightly.

"As am I," reported Muluk, but uncertainty made his face a touch long.

"Well, I'm in as well then."

Goll's face became pensive.

"What?" Pig Knot asked.

"I'm not sure I want you to be a part of this."

"Goll," Halm began, "we've already talked—"

"*We* talked about this. You and I. He wasn't here. And I've been waiting for your return so I won't have to repeat myself." Goll regarded Pig Knot as rain pelted off the canopy overhead and thunder rolled off the plains. "I've seen you fight. I'm not impressed. You won this time, but I'm sure if I'd watched it, I still wouldn't be impressed. I want men who are committed to making a legitimate house successful."

"I see," Pig Knot said. "But you don't even know what this Clavellus wants. Do you?"

"I expect he'll want to talk about the games," Goll said.

"Oh, you expect? Well, before you cast me out or call me unworthy, why don't we see what he wants to talk about. I just might not want to be a part of your house, anyway. Seem to have hit a roll on the sands on my own." Pig Knot patted his leather purse for emphasis. "Like yourselves."

Goll regarded the two small sacks of coin on the wagon floor. "Yes, we've had our share of good luck, and I'm inclined to think it'll continue."

"Let's just keep it at that then. You really are looking to join a house?" Pig Knot asked Halm.

"Aye that."

"Why?"

"Partly because of him." Halm indicated Goll. "And my own sense of time. I'm starting to think there might be more beyond living from season to season, getting drunk, and cracking heads in the months leading up to the next round of games. I..." Halm fluttered then, realizing he had a small audience. "I want a bit more than that. If I can."

"You've had offers before with established houses. Why with him?"

The Zhiberian felt the wood of the wagon's frame pressing into his back and the canopy billowing against his shoulders. "This one is just starting. Or at least I feel it's about to start. With another house, I'd be just a fighter. Here, I would be... well..."

He grinned then, exposing his terrible yellow and black teeth overlapping each other and making his mouth look like a steel trap for wild animals. "It's stupid."

"Not until I laugh at it." Pig Knot's eyes twinkled.

"That's just my point."

"Out with it. You want to tell it, so go on."

Halm sighed and shrugged. "I think this could be a piece of history. The more I think about that, about being a part of it, the more I like it. I think Goll is the person to take whoever joins him there. He has push."

"Oh, he has something, I daresay." Pig Knot smirked.

"You should listen as well, Sunjan," Goll countered. "You might be inspired to do something with your life. Other than swinging a blade while drunk and becoming a punce in the eyes of thousands of people, like your first fight."

"You saw that?" Pig Knot asked.

"I did."

"Well, I wasn't drunk then. The other man was drunk. I was only hung over."

"Like anyone could tell the difference on the sands. You were suffering, and the world saw it. I think you only do things halfway. I'm telling you this because I'm saving you the trouble of quitting later on. I've seen your type. The first bit of hard work that comes up, the first hard day of formal training, and you'll break."

Pig Knot looked away.

"Well?" Goll asked.

"We'll see," Pig Knot muttered, but Halm smiled inwardly. Goll had made the Sunjan angry, and when Pig Knot was angry, he was at his best.

"We'll see," Halm agreed and met Goll's hard eyes.

The rain continued, increasing the men's fear that they might have to be called into service to push the wagons through the muddier sections of the road. The problem never materialized, and as rain seeped through the cloth canopy above, the conversation lulled, and the rocking of the wagon put all four to sleep.

An abrupt stop and a cry from the driver woke them all at once.

"We're here." Goll screwed a palm into his eye and wiped it.

"Dying Seddon. Next time I'll walk," Muluk complained, arching his back.

Outside, men called out greetings while wet footsteps approached from all sides.

"Sounds like enough of them out there." Halm looked up into the darkness of the wagon just as a drop of water spattered onto his right shoulder.

Then the canvas was pulled back, revealing a group of men staring at them all. Lanterns glowed in a mist of rain, swinging from their handles with little squeals. The dark halved their faces until one man raised his arm, urging them to get out.

"Well? Get out of there, you damned gurry, get out afore I yank you out screaming." His voice thundered, startling the four. "Damnation, *out*! Out, I said. You think I'm holding this thing open for your benefit? P'rhaps you'd move faster with my boot up your ass? Move, you cripple. Slip, slide, or just damn drop, *but get your pitiful ass-licking hide out of there!*"

The pit fighters hauled themselves out, feeling the ache in their joints from the long ride. Muluk grimaced when he landed and straightened up slowly.

"What's the trouble, my missus?" the same man thundered, bawling out the question as if he stood upon a hill. "What's the trouble? Eh?"

"Dammit, man, you don't need to scream at us," Muluk shot back.

"Scream?" the face rumbled in mock puzzlement and held up a lantern. The speaker's expression curdled at the question, hitching up one side of perhaps the most majestic grey moustache any of them had ever seen. *"I haven't begun to scream, you ripe prick!"*

Muluk flinched from the barrage as did Halm and Pig Knot. Goll wavered on his crutches but weathered the blast.

"We're—" was all the Kree got out.

"Eeeeee," the older man drowned him out in the deepest bass, "I know what y'are—you're a pile of maggot shite that's got me out in this warm pisspot of a night. Y'followed one order right, albeit slower 'n a winter's shite, so see if you can follow the next afore I get *sour*. Come this way, and make sure you're right on my tail as for the love of Seddon's rosy ass, y'don't want me *behind* you."

With that, the speaker strutted through the wedge of men behind him, all of whom split apart like a flimsy curtain. In the glow of lantern light, rain fell in a slant.

"I'd get moving," one of the guards said solemnly.

Not bothering to look at his companion, Halm did just that, feeling the squish of wet sand beneath his foot. The others fell in behind him with Goll bringing up the rear. They were in the open, but most of the lanterns squeaking in the breeze fluttered and gave only a glimpse of where they stood. White walls of wood and brick gleamed in the wet dark, and the screamer who had greeted them marched towards a single, open door.

Into this, he disappeared.

The four men followed him in and stamped their feet on a fitted stone floor. Light from lanterns perched on shelves revealed a spacious room filled with worn wooden tables and benches. A shadowy archway appeared at the back, stretching almost to the ceiling and wide enough for two people to step through shoulder to shoulder.

"Sit 'n' shush." The mustached man's words came out with heat.

Three of them complied while Goll stopped before their guide. "Don't you—"

"Sit your ass down, y'right talkative bastard. The man you want to see will talk to you soon enough, but not I. Seddon above. I should be drinking at home in front of a fire."

Simmering, Goll hesitated for a brief moment before finding a bench and lowering himself on it.

A manservant came into the room from a side chamber, carrying four wooden cups and a pitcher. Silently, he poured each of the fighters a drink of mead. Outside, the night sky cleared its throat in a grumble that made them look at the thick timbers of the ceiling as the rain hissed with increased force.

"Looks like we got here just in time." Muluk sipped on his mead in approval.

"We'll have to go back out in it," Pig Knot muttered.

Halm wondered if they would have to walk back. He thought about asking, but one look at the moustached bawler who spoke twice as loudly as necessary convinced him to wait.

The main door opened, and three men entered. The first was the big brute with the missing left ear and the ugly scar that reminded Halm of lips. Rain coated his bare, muscular shoulders and chest in a wet sheen. Then Clavellus and Borchus came in, their clothing soaked from the angry burst of rain. Clavellus moved to the head of one table and sat down with a huff, his right hand holding a silver mug. He smoothed his bushy white beard, flicking the water at the floor.

"Damnation," the taskmaster growled. "We need the rain but not a flood."

He scratched his bald head and regarded the men sitting before him. "I'll get to it right away as it's late and I know Machlann has drinking to do. *I've* got drinking to do, for that matter. You men came to me about a week ago, looking for a taskmaster. I've called you back here to tell you I'm interested. I've reconsidered."

His words faded into the sound of a downpour outside. Halm glanced at Goll, but the Kree stared hard at the taskmaster.

"You've reconsidered," Goll stated.

"I have." Clavellus said, his white beard flexing.

"Just like that?"

The taskmaster took a moment before answering. "No. Not just like that. I have my reasons, mind you, which are of no concern of yours. I'm offering you my staff's services here, use of my property. Even rooms if you wish. All for a reasonable price."

Behind him, the one who had greeted them, Machlann, half turned and glanced out towards a shuttered window, scratching at his ear.

"You seemed against the idea before," Goll stated quietly. "'Motherless dogs,' I believe you called us."

"Punces," Halm added.

"That was then." Clavellus took a pull of his silver mug. He savoured its contents, swallowing slowly. "This is now."

"You came into very good reasons," Goll said thoughtfully.

"And they'll stay mine. You wanted a taskmaster and trainers. You have access to one. I'll even reduce my fee, just to erase the bad memory of our first meeting. But I doubt you'll find anyone else to take you on. If you are still searching, that is."

Goll didn't look at his companions. "We accept."

Clavellus nodded and regarded his drink. "Then before we talk any further, refresh my mind on what it is you wish to accomplish. You *are* about to start formal training while the games are in progress. The other houses train for months leading up to the season. I mean, we can't very well prepare you to face a gladiator who's been training for months. Or years even."

"We want to win."

"To win. Bit simple, isn't it? They all want to win."

"One match at a time. As many victories as we can manage. As I said before, I wish to start a new house. That begins now. With you, we'll do what we can in the current season. We'll ready ourselves for our matches as best we can and let Seddon figure the rest out."

"My experience, Seddon doesn't figure much when it comes to the games."

"Well, we'll do what we can, fight until we can't, and look towards next year. The next season."

"You speak for these men?" Clavellus asked pointedly.

"I do."

"You're the head of this new house?"

Goll hesitated. He turned and met Halm's gaze. The Zhiberian nodded. Then Muluk, but he folded his arms and shrugged more in resignation. Pig Knot shook his head, grinned, and waved a hand as if it mattered little.

"They don't seem as set on this course as you are," Clavellus observed.

Goll didn't comment on that. "I'm the head of the house. The master. I'll deal with any who are judged lacking. You just have to weed them out."

Clavellus thought about it and gestured towards Halm. "My agent Borchus says that one has a blood match with the House of Curge. Of all the houses, Curge is the… *last* one you want hunting you."

The taskmaster became reflective then and took a drink. "This all of you?"

"No, I don't expect."

"What's your final number then?"

"Not decided yet. You say we can stay here?"

"That would be the wisest thing to do," Clavellus said. "No one to bother us out here. The city can be distracting at times."

"How many can you hold?"

"Here?" Clavellus grunted. "Machlann?"

Machlann stopped twiddling with the ends of his huge

moustache and straightened. "Thirty. Thirty-five if we really squeeze them. Or cut off the fat."

Halm didn't like the sound of that.

"I'll let you know," Goll said, thinking to himself. "I expect we'll have at least that."

"All Free Trained?"

"All. But they won't be Free Trained any longer. It'll be the start of a house."

"Have you registered this with the Gladiatorial Chamber? That's a large lump of coin if I remember correctly."

"It is. A thousand gold. We have some of it."

"Some of it." Clavellus rocked on his bench. "How were you intending to get the rest of it?"

Goll cleared his throat. "Wagering."

"Wagering." Behind the taskmaster, his trainers stiffened at the revelation. The agent Borchus studied his feet with a scowl. Clavellus took another sip before continuing. "You mean to wager the coin you have. On who? Your fighters? The very ones you're asking me to train?"

"Yes."

"Do you realize how that sounds?"

The Kree kept his tongue, and Clavellus took another drink of his mug, emptying it. "This one has balls, Machlann. What do you think?"

"Has shite in his head," Machlann replied without rancor.

Clavellus smirked. "Koba?"

The one-eared fellow gave a dismayed shake of his head. "Unfit."

The taskmaster regarded Goll with gleaming eyes. "Shite in his head. Unfit. You hear this, Goll? That's what my trainers think of your money predicament, and I'm inclined to agree with them. This might never begin at all, not without coin. The Chamber doesn't deal in credit. Not even with an established house. Certainly not with a group of Free Trained with high ambitions. And the banks will laugh at you."

"We'll get it," Goll said. "The next fight is Halm's. In three days. We have that time to prepare him."

"Against one of Curge's brutes?"

"Yes."

"You're Halm, yes?" Clavellus asked the Zhiberian.

"I am."

"What do you think your chances are?"

Halm smiled. "Oh, I'll win it all. Guaranteed."

In the flickering of the lantern light, the lengthy silence that greeted Halm's lofty reply was almost as frightening as the storm clouds overhead. Not one of the trainers reacted, not even Borchus.

"You will, eh?" Clavellus eventually responded, not amused. "So why do you need us?"

Halm's smile dimmed, and he answered in a much more humble tone. "It all helps."

Clavellus pondered that for a moment. "Then we'll see, won't we? Machlann here is my oldest trainer. Koba is my second. Both men are hellions who have trained a few pit fighters out here for the smaller games of Vathia. You think you can follow their instructions?"

"I do." Halm spoke earnestly, humour gone from his face.

"What about you, then?" Clavellus asked Muluk.

"Can't fight. Been put out of the games."

"Really? By who?"

Frowning, Muluk flicked his head towards Halm.

"So why are you here?"

Muluk fidgeted. "I can fix armour. Do a few blades. That sort of thing."

Clavellus studied him before switching to the last man at the table. "And you?" he asked Pig Knot.

"I'm still in it."

"Can you follow instructions?"

"Aye that. At least until it suits me not to." Pig Knot smirked. "I've done some training in the past. I'll not be jumping through rings of fire; I'll tell you that right now. Saimon piss on that."

Clavellus arched his head back as if smelling something and shared a look with Machlann.

"Well." The taskmaster leaned forward. He placed his left hand on the table, and Halm noticed it quivered incessantly. "We'll see, won't we? As for you, Goll, you have to come up with that coin. Doesn't look like you'll be fighting anytime soon this season, not in your condition. I'll place myself and my trainers at your disposal for the next few days, just to see what we're working with and to prepare your fat man as best as possible. Put him through a few paces. If he's capable—and fortunate—maybe he won't get killed out there on the sands. Against Curge's lot, it's slay or be slain—and get dragged away with meat hooks. Furthermore, it's a blood match, so I think you'll be motivated right and proper."

"Aye that," Halm said quietly.

"Well then," Clavellus announced, "I think that's all for the night. I've had my servants prepare rooms for you in the back, so you may sleep here. In the morning, we'll start training you. Where are you all from?"

"Sunja," Pig Knot said.

"Zhiberia."

"Kree."

"Kree."

Clavellus nodded to both Kree. "I've known some of your countrymen. It remains to be seen if you measure up to them. Tomorrow, we'll get an idea. And, you, Goll, you're rolling dice in a few days. Seems to me it all comes down to what the Zhiberian can do. I don't share your... confidence in your man. But let's see."

"Thank you," Goll said, "for doing this."

Clavellus waved it away. "I'm not doing anything for free. If anything, you'll give us one or two days' amusement. Perhaps a little longer..."

With that, the old man slowly got to his feet and dusted himself off. "In the morning," he told them all and left. His men followed him out the door.

Outside, Clavellus motioned his men to walk him back to his house. They crossed his threshold seconds later, wet with rain. There, the taskmaster turned on his staff, picking at the soaked shirt stuck to his chest.

"Well?"

Machlann spoke first. "Unfit, like Koba said."

"They'll break in half a day," Koba added.

Borchus remained silent.

"Nothing to say?" Clavellus asked.

"No," the short man replied in a tired voice.

The taskmaster almost chuckled at that. He should have expected such an answer from the agent.

Then he was all business.

"All right, then. Listen. Don't *kill* them," Clavellus warned his trainers. "Punish them. Push them past their limits. Break their spirits even, but don't kill them. See if there's even anything there to work with. That Zhiberian in particular will need a day to recover. If you can show him a few tricks to keep him alive, then do it. If he wins, we'll go from there. But if he loses, well, we don't have anything to worry about. It's done, finished before it even begins."

"Why are we even doing this at all?" Machlann wanted to know.

Clavellus didn't hesitate. The trainer had been with him since Sunja and was his oldest friend. "Partly because... I miss it. These lads are in Sunja's Pit. The games are the best in the land. Better than anything Vathia can field. I want to see if we can do it once more. This Goll youngster has push. We just might be seeing the start of another house."

"We might. That all?"

Koba stared at Clavellus, the only one who was in the room with him when Curge had confronted him.

The taskmaster's face puckered. "You know I went to the games the other day."

"Aye that," Machlann said. "And?"

"I met Curge."

Machlann's moustache drooped.

"He warned me to stay away."

"And that was it, eh?"

"That was it."

The four of them stood in the entryway of Clavellus's house, the rain crashing down outside.

"Will you train them?" Clavellus asked.

Koba nodded at once.

"Aye, I'll train them," Machlann said a few thoughtful

seconds later. "Hope for the best. But they're Free Trained. It'll take something to unlearn their bad habits and teach them anything. And like you said, we don't have months. The season's *now*."

"No," Clavellus said. "Right now, we only have tomorrow and the next. Then, we'll see if the Zhiberian can win. If he doesn't, it'll be all over. They won't have the coin. But see what you can do with him and that other one in the short time you have."

Both trainers nodded at their taskmaster, and that was all Clavellus could ask.

"Just don't kill them tomorrow…"

32

The rain had stopped during the night, leaving the morning air smelling clean and sweet. Grey clouds spotted the sky, hanging without direction while the sun rose below them. While Nala still slept, Clavellus rose from the fine sheets of his bed and gathered up a breakfast of cold cheese and bread in the kitchen area, where he ate at the main table. He heard Koba and Machlann somewhere outside, his old friend's voice breaking the stillness of the morning like a maul bouncing off beach rock. Nala would probably complain about him and eventually move to another spare bedroom farther away from the training grounds. Clavellus didn't mind. He looked forward to the commotion. Even if it was for just a morning, the prospect of working again, of crafting men into pit fighters, made his blood pump through old passageways with renewed vigor.

Upon finishing his meal, he stood and left his dishes for Ananda to take away and then strode to the balcony area overlooking the training grounds. The sun was only just peeking over the horizon, causing the deep blue overhead to fade into blinding orange and fragmenting the clouds. The sight of mornings after summer storms always made him feel rejuvenated and filled him with thoughts of the land scrubbed clean. He felt his left hand tremble against his thigh, and then he felt the want of something to drink stronger than tea. Wine would be the very thing. He went back inside to a cellar no longer well stocked. There he found a bottle and cracked it open, filling his silver mug from the night before. On his lands, he had a small vineyard and employed people to work it, which only just kept him in grapes.

Mug in one hand and bottle in the other, he returned to the balcony.

Machlann's voice once more pierced the morning quiet like a rooster with a pair of shorn balls.

"Get out of there. Get out and stand. *Stand,* I said, don't *slouch.* Koba, if that one slouches, you have my permission to brain the bastard. Seddon above, you're a fat one. Aye that. You heard me. I said fat. You've already fought in the games? No doubt they were right mesmerized by the rolls on you. Did you suffocate your opponents? Unholy Saimon below, you're a fat one. And you! Any more hair on you? Your father must have rutted with a dog to birth the likes of you. Oh, you find that amusing? Well then, Koba, why don't we amuse ourselves further, eh?"

As he approached the balcony, Clavellus saw the men through the stumpy columns. He put his bottle on a table outside and kept his mug to his chest as he pressed his pelvis against the railing. Below, three fighters stood at attention on the wide berth of sands. Koba stood behind them, shirtless but covered in his training leathers, while Machlann stood in front of the men from the previous night. They were clothed in white loincloths without even as much as boots or sandals. All appeared very much awake, and Pig Knot was even smiling.

Clavellus smirked at the sight.

The topper had no idea how Machlann disliked lads doing exactly that.

A battered Goll stood outside of the common room, standing on his crutches and watching intently, waiting. The Kree appeared to be the only one who might have had some merit about him, but he wasn't healthy enough to go through the paces the trainers were about to have the new meat do. Not many were, Clavellus reflected.

"*Eeeeee,* you he-bitches are mine now," Machlann informed them with a growl, "and here's what you need to know. What I say, you do whether you can or cannot. If you don't, the pain is yours. What Koba says, you do. If not, the pain is yours. In my eyes, you are not worthy to be here. Stains of horse shite have more right to be here than you do. I've voiced my opinion on this matter to Master Clavellus and Master Goll, and this morning… I'll prove it to them."

"Master Goll?" Pig Knot sounded as if he'd tasted something poisonous.

"Speak only when spoken to." Machlann didn't look at the Sunjan. "Else, pain will be yours. Now then, morning exercise. Do as I do, else the pain is yours."

Pig Knot, Muluk, and Halm stared at the older man with looks of disbelief.

"You *do* know what exercises are?" Machlann bellowed.

The men didn't answer, which was good. Machlann took a breath, extended both of his arms, and lowered himself until his upper legs were parallel with the ground. And there he stayed.

"Sweet Seddon," Pig Knot said loudly enough for all to hear, "if he lets slip a cow kiss, we're all dead men."

Muluk and Pig Knot broke into grins and chuckles.

Then Koba came into view, scowling and all business. Near his thigh, he carried a club the length of his forearm.

Machlann straightened and studied the three men. "P'rhaps you didn't hear me."

With that, Koba cracked his club across the meat of Pig Knot's bare thigh, hard enough to make the man yell out in pain—a bit too loudly, Clavellus thought. He didn't like the dramatic ones in the least.

"What was that for?" Pig Knot demanded, half turning.

Koba lashed his lower back with the club, bringing forth yet another cry of pain. Pig Knot backed away, breaking ranks and almost bumping into Muluk.

"Hit me once more with that—" Pig Knot warned, rubbing his tender flesh and pointing a warning finger.

Koba moved to do just that.

"Hold off," Machlann yelled. The older trainer glanced up at Clavellus with a knowing look before turning about. "You didn't hear my rules? You're either stupid or deaf. And I hate to think Free Trained shite such as you might be that stupid."

"You're a right noisy little bastard." Pig Knot still favoured his thigh.

Machlann scrutinized the man for a moment before holding out a hand to Koba. "Sticks, my son, if you please."

Koba turned and walked off to a rack of wooden and metal weapons. He collected a pair of light clubs like those he usually carried, and returned to the open sands. Machlann took one of the weapons and slapped one end into a leathery hand. Koba gave the other to Pig Knot, who took it with a question on his face.

"Come at me, lad," Machlann ordered.

"What?"

Machlann waved him in.

"I'm not fighting you, you old tit."

"Boys," the trainer addressed Muluk and Halm, "some room is needed. Move away from him."

No longer smiling, both the Kree and the Zhiberian stepped back until Pig Knot and Machlann remained. Above the training grounds, spearmen who patrolled the walls of the villa stopped to watch, sensing the tension rise in the air. Clavellus leaned forward, much interested in what was about to transpire.

"Defend yourself," Machlann ordered the much bigger man.

"You're unfit," Pig Knot said in dismay.

The trainer walked towards him.

"I'll crack you open," Pig Knot warned.

The trainer's eyes became slits. He sprang at the bigger man, swarming him with a series of strikes at various points. Pig Knot deflected the first blow, barely turned aside the second, and ducked the third before the fourth one rang off his forearm, generating another loud yelp.

He placed some distance from the smaller, wiry frame of the trainer, shaking his arm and red faced with chagrin. "You old topper! I'll brain you for that if you don't stop now. Stop *now*."

Machlann moved in on him, bent over ever so slightly, stalking his foe.

"Stop, I said, or I'll take your unfit head off!"

Machlann didn't appear to hear.

For a moment, an uncertain Pig Knot seemed to realize the old man wasn't about to stop either, so he bellowed his frustration and charged, swinging for the head.

Except the head was no longer there.

Defying his age, Machlann ducked and let loose with a startlingly swift barrage to Pig Knot's bare ribs, shoulders, head, and legs, a heavy-handed percussion that sounded like a giant's footsteps. The club turned Pig Knot's head to one side and buckled his midsection while the lower strike bounced off a knee. Machlann attempted to spin into another strike, but Pig Knot surprisingly shoved him away. The trainer stumbled forward a few steps, kicking up sand as he went, before stopping and regaining his stance. He spun around, amazingly steady for one his age, and held his club before him.

Machlann's dislike for the man reached his face, and Clavellus knew the trainer wasn't impressed with the black-haired brute. Nor was he, truth be known. The lad was in a fight, and he didn't realize it. Machlann would punish him. Watching the fight from where they stood on the wall, the guardsmen dappled the sands with scalding chuckles. They knew Machlann's reputation.

Not enjoying the attention from the guards, Pig Knot closed with the trainer, swinging his club back and forth. Once within range, he lunged.

Machlann bounced his club off the big man's wrist, disarming him almost magically and making Pig Knot cry out. The trainer cut loose with another blistering combination of strikes, one flowing after the other, the sound of each fleshy impact breaking the quiet like the unbroken thrumming of a drum, staggering his foe. An eyebrow burst apart, a shoulder crumpled, a throat choked. Pig Knot froze on the last strike as if run through the gullet. Machlann hooked a leg, dropping his foe to a knee and forcing him to plant an outstretched palm hard in the sand. When Pig Knot looked up, dazed and bloodied, Machlann clubbed him three more times—short, powerful strikes that seemingly had no power. However, each time he struck, Pig Knot's frame rocked as if battered by catapult shot.

One last blow across the forehead burst open the stitches there and knocked the man flat on his back.

Pig Knot did not move again.

The guardsmen burst into rumbles of delight. Machlann glanced up but did nothing to silence them. Both Halm and Muluk appeared uncomfortable, squinting in the sunlight, and kept quiet.

Machlann's chest heaved as he stood back from the fallen man. Clavellus reflected that the old trainer was indeed showing his age. Pig Knot was tough, the taskmaster would give him that, but his hesitation in attacking an old man, who he perceived as a weaker opponent, had been his downfall.

"Errrrg," Pig Knot moaned, spat out blood, and rolled onto his stomach. "I'll kill you. I'll kill you. Seddon above. I'll *kill*…"

Machlann looked down at his fallen adversary for a moment and regarded Clavellus.

The taskmaster nodded curtly.

Getting the approval, Machlann walked over and soundly trounced the back of Pig Knot's skull with one blow, flattening him and ending his threats. The trainer stayed in the pose for a moment, waiting for a reaction, and when none came, he relaxed and straightened. Taking deep breaths, the trainer turned to his students.

"This maggot made a mistake," Machlann said to Muluk and Halm, who were suddenly much more attentive. "He thought I wasn't going to hit him. He made another mistake of not seeing the threat I posed. Anyone—no matter the size, age, or sex—can be a threat. That's your first lesson.

Remember it else I take this," he waved his club, "to your face."

Pig Knot groaned and got an arm under his face, lifting it out of the blood-soaked sand.

"Besides not understanding I meant him harm, he had no defense to speak of, and when he did swing at me, it was all power. No technique. And not one combination to be seen."

Machlann eyed Pig Knot testing his nose and dabbing fingers to his bleeding brow. He allowed him a moment, then, "To your feet, youngster."

Pig Knot didn't comply right away. Instead, he glanced over his shoulder at the trainer. Sand clung to Pig Knot's bloody features. Insolence glared there.

"*Eeeeeee!* Saimon's black hanging fruit," Machlann growled and bared a rack of teeth where only half still remained. "You get to your feet this instant afore I shove my boot up your dog blossom."

Shaking his head to clear it, Pig Knot struggled to his knees, heaved out a breath, and stood, swaying ever so slightly. He continued wiping away the sand caked to his person.

"Form the line once more." Machlann seethed, displaying his half set of teeth.

Muluk and Halm got into place, and Pig Knot took up his spot to the Kree's right.

"Now then," the trainer huffed. "I've made my point. Disobey me, and I'll smash you right and proper. Now then, do as I do. Arms out."

Once more, Machlann squatted, gripping his club by the ends as he held it out before him for balance.

This time, even though he was the last of the three, Pig Knot did as he was told.

Machlann held the pose for a moment before straightening. "One," he counted.

The three did the same, and once completed, the trainer squatted once more. At first, the men did the exercises without any difficulty, but by the twentieth dip, grimaces appeared while grunts perforated the morning. Koba walked between them, tapping them with his club on the bare thigh or shoulder if they weren't low enough. By the count of thirty, the three were growling in agony. Pig Knot collapsed two counts later, slowly rolling over onto his front as if expecting a club upside his head or back. Machlann shook his head at Koba, waving the other trainer off.

By the count of forty, Halm bent over with his hands on knees, signalling he was done.

By forty-four, Muluk gasped and ceased. The old trainer went on to fifty before he stopped with sweat on his brow. Without a word, he walked over to a huge rack of wooden swords and gestured for the three men to take one.

"Find something and fast."

Halm and Muluk exchanged looks.

"Why not real ones?" Halm asked.

But Machlann didn't answer him. Koba stepped in from behind and cracked Halm across the small of the back, hard enough that it echoed briefly. The Zhiberian straightened, more in shock than pain, and glared at the trainer. Koba stood ready, his club swinging loosely as if expecting a charge.

"What was that for?" Halm grated.

Koba thrummed his club into the meat of the Zhiberian's gut, doubling him over and leaving a respectable red welt. In the stillness that followed, Halm composed himself, nodded, and kept his tongue.

Pig Knot scowled in pained fashion. "Now why did you—"

Machlann turned on him and smashed his club into the Sunjan's midsection, robbing him of his words. To his credit, Pig Knot barely flinched this time and only partially buckled over in pain.

Clavellus watched, stroking his beard and wondering if they got the lesson being taught. There were no further questions from the warriors, and the taskmaster smiled. The Free Trained weren't so dense after all.

Holding their tender spots, they then picked wooden swords. Clavellus knew the practice sticks were about the weight of a regular blade. Their silence pleased the taskmaster, and he took a pull of his mug, relishing the dry bite of the wine.

"Pick a wooden man and stand afore him," Machlann commanded then, gesturing to the high crosses on the eastern side of the grounds. As ordered, they chose their wooden crosses.

"Now then, Master Koba."

The scarred trainer stood by the line of the three novices, facing his own wooden man, and gestured with his club. "Basic cut. Chop down with one hand on the left arm."

And he demonstrated, his club clacking off the wood.

"Follow through. Bring the sword up and cut across the gut," Koba instructed and demonstrated. "Twist your hips for power. Watch me."

The three did so, the connections ringing out. Koba repeated the combination, battering an arm before slashing across the lower torso, again and again. He finished and gestured for the three men to commence attacking. The training area came alive with the rhythm of multiple hits. Clavellus smiled. To him, the sound was that of a once-still heart finally beating.

Machlann watched the warriors with a hawk's eye, keeping his thoughts to himself. The men were only practicing two basic cuts merged into a simple combination. The idea was to make not only their brains understand and remember the movement, but their muscles as well.

"Keep it up until I say stop," Koba yelled over the racket of wood on wood. "Don't pause between strikes. Flow from one into the other. Flow, I said."

Clavellus knew his trainer would keep them at it for about two hundred strokes if possible. Then they would switch to the awkward left. The trainees' sweat coated them after only thirty strikes, their shoulders gleaming under the sun. Machlann glanced up and scowled at him, delivering a silent message that he was none too impressed with the raw meat.

"Training has started?" Nala asked in voice laced with bad humor, diverting his attention from the trainer below.

"It has." He turned around to face her, admiring her uncombed silver hair tumbling about her shoulders and remembering how black it had once been.

She stood there in sea-blue silk robes and regarded him with a frown. "So I'll be hearing this for months on end?"

"Yes." He heard Koba instruct one of the men to twist his hips with greater power. "I'm afraid so."

"And you're drinking this early in the morning?"

He swished the contents of his silver mug, only half full now, and realized he had no memory of drinking it. "The morning heat drove me to it."

"I don't believe that at all."

"Sorry again. The lads are bare chested down there," he offered, hoping to change the subject.

"And I'm not interested in that in the least. I heard Machlann bellowing this morning. I'm going to move to the guest room on the far end. You're welcome to visit, but if you're going to be getting up at the break of dawn, perhaps it's best you didn't."

"Perhaps." Clavellus drew his trembling left hand across his brow. He'd known Nala wouldn't be happy this morning. "It might be only for a short time."

"Why is that?"

"They don't have the money to pay us yet."

"I see. So you're training them out of charity?" she asked without dismay, and he loved her for it. She was never about gold.

"For the time. Just to see what they're about."

"And are any of them worthy?"

To that, he didn't quite have an answer. He mulled it over for a second before simply saying, "It's too early to tell."

"It's your time, then. I'll be far and away from it."

"Not too far, I hope."

"Far enough," she said, but he saw the barest smile covered up. With that, Nala turned about and seemingly glided away, the blue silk trailing after her. All this time, and he still thought her to be the most beautiful creature he'd ever laid eyes on. He watched her fade in the shadows of the inner rooms before the clattering below drew him back to the task at hand. The bottle of wine was on a nearby table, and he took a moment to refill his mug.

They were working on their left hands when he turned back.

Clavellus watched them practice the drill over and over, observing their technique and making mental notes for improvement if Koba or Machlann missed anything. The notion that Free Trained lads were practicing on his grounds made him sigh. Had he lost his mind? In any case, they were there, and one in particular had a fight soon. He'd make certain that Halm knew a trick or two before his time.

33

The practice drills continued until midday with only a few scattered periods of rest, and when Machlann ordered them to file into the common room for a meal of porridge and fruits, exhaustion crippled their once-proud walks into shuffles. The shuttered windows had been thrown open to allow fresh air to flow through, as well as daylight. The three men nearly collapsed at a single table and commenced spooning warm porridge into their gullets. With no handy rags and the temperature of the room still warm, sweat ran freely off their forms and stung their eyes.

"This is unfit," Pig Knot grunted, his brow sporting a fresh red crust. "They'll kill us before we get back into the arena."

"My legs and arms feel like they're about to fall off," Muluk whined, his eyes downcast, taking his time with his meal and gulping down water from a cup.

"Certainly are working us," Halm agreed. "I thought that old topper was going to kill you."

"Pah," Pig Knot spat. "Wore himself out trying. He only had a stick. This," he said while tapping his skull, "is thicker than rock."

"You'll have to hit him with it next time," Halm said. "I'm not about to be brazen around either of them."

"Why?" Muluk asked, his eyes appearing glassy.

"They *know* things," Halm said. "It's that simple. That one-two chop we've been practicing is only the start of it. I see the method to it. They'll add on more; you'll see."

"More?" Muluk almost dropped his spoon. He looked mortified. "I can't do any more. I'm not in the games. I shouldn't be swinging wood with the likes of either of you. I was supposed to be an armourer. Sharpen a few blades and pound out armour plating."

"What about that?" Halm asked. "Why did you line up with us?"

Muluk shrugged morosely. "It was exercise. Couldn't see anything wrong with a little exercise in the morning. But then after Pig Knot was beaten, I *feared* leaving. Figured those hellions would both lay their clubs into me."

"I wouldn't stand for it," Pig Knot said.

Muluk fixed him with a look. "Oh yes, you probably wouldn't stand for it. What would you do? Grab an ankle from where you were lying on the ground? That might slow one of them down. After the beating you took out there? Seddon above, man, that old bastard made you look like you were well on in age."

"You both keep that to yourselves," Pig Knot warned.

"Noticed that Koba fellow?" Halm asked them.

"What about him?" Muluk asked back, wary.

"He was swinging just as much as we were. Even when he was going about and shoring up this or that. That lad might not be for the arena, but he's far from done."

"We're being pushed to the edge of our deaths, and you're admiring them," Pig Knot said with disgust.

"Hard not to." Halm looked towards the window and saw no one outside. "My shoulders feel like chains have been wrapped about them. I haven't felt this way… well… *never*. I'm thinking what might happen if we had a year to train."

"I could never do it," Muluk confessed immediately. "I'm done *now*."

"Why are you here again?" Pig Knot asked him.

"Feels like to lengthen my arms."

"Perhaps you should stay with working metal," Halm suggested.

"Just might, if this house business ever comes about. Where is Goll anyway?"

"Probably with them."

"Hmm."

"They called him Master Goll," Pig Knot said, his lips curling with the taste of the title. "Not sure I like that. Not sure I like *this*." He indicated the whole interior of the room.

Neither Halm nor Muluk voiced their thoughts on those words, losing themselves in their meal.

When they finished eating, they left the empty bowls and cups and climbed onto the nearby tables. The great thick planks didn't even creak when they lay down.

"Just a few moments," Pig Knot muttered.

But the others were already falling asleep.

*

"So how is it you came to look like this?" Clavellus asked, sitting at one end of a table and eating a slice of dried beef from a large plate. Koba and Machlann flanked him, eating from their own plates of meat and fruit, while Goll sat across from the taskmaster. They ate in the shade of the balcony on the edge of the training grounds, where servants had prepared a table. Over Machlann's shoulder, Goll saw the heat shimmering off the white sand, and knew that the afternoon would be a particularly brutal one for his men. *His men*, he thought, and figured they were now. He would be the master of a new house. Almost by default, it seemed, since the others did not question it.

"You mean this?" Goll pointed at the fading bruises about his jaw. "I fought in the Pit about two weeks ago."

"Did you win?"

"I did."

"Who was he?" Clavellus asked.

Goll clenched his jaw. "Baylus the Butcher."

Both trainers regarded the Kree in a new light.

Clavellus leaned back in his chair. "You fought Baylus? I heard he died about two weeks ago."

Goll nodded.

"You killed him?"

Another nod.

"Seddon above, you're fortunate to be with us at all. Baylus was... *unique* from what I understand. I never saw him fight, but I've heard enough stories about the man. They rightly called him a butcher."

"He was."

"And you killed him. Boys, we have something of a celebrity at our table this day. Sweet Seddon. How was the fight? Evenly matched?"

Goll had to take a sip of water before swallowing his food. "Not at all. He was killing me. I... I'd never faced anyone like him before."

"Why is that?"

"He was... playing with me. And the more he played, the angrier I became. Lost my concentration. Stopped fighting my fight. I was trained by the Weapon Masters of Kree. Was supposed to defeat the best on the field. And here was this once champion toying with me and making me bleed with almost every step."

"How did you kill him?" Clavellus asked.

The water in Goll's cup rippled, and he stared into its clear depths. "He was about to kill me, I believe. The crowds certainly wanted me dead. But then he didn't. Instead, he allowed me to get to my feet. I remember him feinting. He'd been feinting for much of our fight, and I finally recognized what he was doing, so when he feinted again, I stabbed him through the knee. Then the other leg. That brought him down. After that, I got on top of him, pinned his weapon arm with my knee, and stabbed him through the brain."

Both trainers stopped eating and stared at the Kree.

"He'd cut me up badly, my left arm in particular. I can barely manage the crutch on that side. But I killed him." Goll drained his cup.

"A once-champion spared your life, and you repaid him by putting your blade through his head?" Machlann asked in his rough voice.

"I did." Goll sniffed. He met each face in turn, shrugged, and went back to eating beef. "I admit… it was a mistake."

"Man's got push," Clavellus said to his trainers, but Machlann didn't smile at the comment, nor did he go back to his food right away. Instead, he sat and mentally weighed Goll's story. Koba chewed on a strip of dried meat but didn't appear to taste it. Clavellus knew what they were thinking. Perhaps it was a mistake. It certainly wasn't the first time they'd heard a story like Goll's, of mercies shown in the arena that were never repaid. Some would feel badly about the death of Baylus, and there would be more who'd be wary of killers like the Kree.

"Perhaps you are best suited as a house master then," Clavellus said, and when Goll didn't answer him, he let the subject drop. Perhaps Goll wished he could have that moment back. Perhaps he would have spared the Butcher in turn, repaying the gesture.

Or perhaps he would've killed him again.

"Well," the taskmaster said, changing topics. "What about your boys here? They're not in the best physical shape. This morning showed us that. Those two cuts they were practicing shouldn't have drained them like it did."

Goll agreed. "Not at all. My thanks for taking the time. Do with them what you will. But please keep in mind, Halm fights the day after tomorrow."

"Understood. When does that other one go in? The one with the tied-back hair."

"Pig Knot. I don't know. Don't really care, to tell the truth."

Once more the trainers paused, and this time, exchanged looks.

"Why is that?" Clavellus inquired, his eyes narrowing.

"I've seen him fight. He's not house material. Too sloppy. I've had doubts about him from the beginning. His will is questionable. I don't think there's much there to work with." With that, Goll addressed the trainers directly. "If you wish, break him this day. Single him out and make him realize that taking up the steel is hard work. I expect you to do the same to anyone else I bring to you."

Machlann cocked an eyebrow while Koba went right on eating.

"Who else are you going to bring us?" Clavellus asked,

clenching his hand to slow its shaking.

"We'll need more men," Goll stated. "Correct me if I'm wrong, but a school or stable or house has between twenty to thirty fighters. Sometimes as many as thirty-five."

The taskmaster nodded that he was indeed correct.

"When the house is reality, I'm going to go to the ranks of Free Trained and announce it. I expect there will be more than a handful who will take up the offer. Not all will be ready, but over time they will. With your help."

"Free Trained." Clavellus exhaled.

Goll regarded him questioningly.

"I want to let you know something," the taskmaster began. "I have a past with some of the houses in the games. They don't like me, you see. Why doesn't really matter now, but I've been told… to stay away from the Pit. That anyone trained by my hand will be hunted on the arena sands and killed. Anyone we prepare for the arena will have that on their necks. What are your thoughts on the matter?"

For a moment, Goll didn't reply. "No matter. We're Free Trained in all eyes anyway, even if we have the name of a house to say differently. The first year will be difficult, and the second even more so. But if I can get the men I want and win a few matches, with you carving them into professional fighters, the respect will follow eventually."

"The House of Curge, in particular, will make our lives difficult." Clavellus waited for the outburst of disbelief, but none came.

"We already have a blood match with them. Halm of Zhiberia killed one of their fighters. It doesn't worry me. The houses will leave us alone in the end, barring any blood matches, present or in the future."

Clavellus's conscience felt lighter. Unloading that burden

was easier than he thought, although he wasn't certain this Kree knew the extent of Curge's wrath. "It may be dangerous outside of the arena as well," he said quietly.

"I'm not concerned," Goll said. "It's dangerous for us now. And we'll be training here once we have the coin."

"Once you have the coin, you may."

"Then I hope for good things."

Good things. Clavellus reflected on the words. "I hope you have luck finding the men you want," he finally said.

Perhaps, the taskmaster thought, he should hope for "good things" as well.

34

They walked through the city streets in a wedge with no one man following another but rather moving along with the shared aura of danger. Armed men walked about Sunja all the time, and no one blinked at their presence. These six, however, exuded violence barely kept in check. They wore leather cuirasses, their bare muscular arms swinging, and carried an assortment of weapons and blades strapped on or hanging off their persons. Heavyset and towering over most of the people about them, they sauntered with an exaggerated air through the masses, parting them with dangerous looks. One of the more powerful-looking men shoulder-bumped a farmer and drove him to the road. Other people saw or heard the incident and just got out of the way with a greater sense of urgency.

Skarrs covered in gleaming mail shirts and polished shields stood at guard posts and eyed the warriors but allowed them to pass unbothered. The ever-patrolling Street Watch took no interest in them either, for no one came forth to report any wrongdoing. Once the authorities were out of sight, the acts of intimidation increased. They shoved ordinary men out of the way, eyed women with lolling tongues and groped their bottoms, and kicked at livestock cluttering up the street.

With the wind blowing towards him, Caro stood at the mouth of an alleyway and watched the six strut down the street like big children aware they had no equal here and the master was nowhere in sight. He didn't like the look of them in the least and knew, just *knew*, these were the men sent to him by Grisholt. Caro wondered about the old man at times, and if they truly *were* from Grisholt, he'd sent elephants where cats were needed.

A whiff of roasting pork cut across Caro's nose and hooked his attention for a moment before he turned back to the approaching men. As he looked on, he saw Ballan leading the way only strides ahead of the brutes. That finished it. They were from Grisholt, walking abreast of each other as though on parade, heedless of the attention they were attracting. That made Caro sigh in exasperation; it was just his luck to have to deal with these swaggering choppers.

Right then, one brute on the far end stopped in his tracks. An old man harangued him about something. The bald warrior made to strike the feeble codger, who fell backwards with dramatic flair. Fortunately, the Street Watch was nowhere to be seen. Caro fumed. He hadn't even met these toppers, and already he was wishing them dead.

As he came closer, Ballan spotted Caro and glanced over his shoulder to one of the lead warriors, who flicked his chin at the spy to *keep going*. Caro wished they would do just that. He could hire better men than these for the task at hand. It was just Grisholt's thinking to save a few coins by letting loose his pit fighters.

"Caro," Ballan greeted him with an expression of futility.

"Ballan," he replied. Behind Ballan, the six gathered at

the head of the alley like a logjam of bad intentions.

"This is Kurlin, Lantus—"

"You lads certainly made an entrance." Caro cut Ballan off, inspecting the newcomers with a steely countenance. He held no fear of this lot, having come across enough of their types back in the day when he fought in the Pit. Like dogs, they had to be shown who was in charge, and if they didn't acknowledge him, he was prepared to strike one down as an example to the remainder.

In this case, the six men stared back, judging the intimidating agent.

"I know of you," Kurlin said. "You fought in the Pit years ago."

Caro neither confirmed nor denied it but chose to ignore Kurlin. "You lads follow me now while you're away from the stable. Understood? No more scaring the locals. This isn't the arena, and if you catch the attention of the Skarrs or the Street Watch or even asslickers like yourselves and cause trouble, I'll not help you in the least."

"No one here will start anything," the one called Lantus said. "Not until you give the word. Don't worry."

"I'm already worried." Caro gnashed his teeth. "This way."

He led them down the alley and onto the next street. There was a three-story inn there, built of huge timbers with green streamers hanging from its heights. Into this he brought them, and he sat them down in a secluded alcove, away from the scant patrons visiting the place. Once they settled in, he warned them all to be silent and sat at the head of the table.

"Ballan, buy us something to eat and drink," Caro commanded and sent him off. With his elbows on the table's rough surface, he regarded the sitting men over his tangled knot of hands. They studied the interior of the inn like a pack of dogs that had been penned for far too long.

"We'll eat something. Then I'll show you to your room," Caro informed them.

"Our room?" Lantus screwed up half his face in disdain. "We only just got here."

"Aye that," Kurlin said for the other fearsome men. "We've been at Grisholt's villa for damned too long to pass on the tastes of Sunja. Give us a night at least."

Already begins, Caro fumed. "You'll follow my orders while here, and I speak on behalf of *Master* Grisholt. You'll be housed in a cellar nearby, and when the time comes, and I expect it to happen soon, you'll move out and finish your business. I can't be rounding you lot up if you're scattered about the city. Any revelry you intended to do while here will wait until you've finished the task. Understood?"

A rusty sickle of a smile spread across Lantus's face. "Seems like we've left the thumb of one master for another."

In the shade of the inn, the gladiators glowered.

"Yes," Caro stated coldly, "you have. I'm certain Master Grisholt has made you an offer, so know this: My men are all over the city, watching and listening for these Free Trained dogs. When they come, you do what you have to do, and get out. Then strike hard for the villa. I'm sure you'll be granted a reward for your services."

Lantus and Kurlin exchanged quiet looks while the other fighters eyed Caro like sleepy dogs on chains.

"We'll be ready," Kurlin finally answered. "Don't you worry."

"We're... *professionals*," Lantus hissed, and the entire table of them seemed to relax as though in on a private joke.

None of it made Caro feel any better.

The gladiators forced the conversation after that, which was something Caro didn't relish partaking in. His feelings about the six men seemed truth enough: they were gruff, barely civilized men who probably took what they wanted whenever the urge struck them. How Grisholt even brought them under his wing with the intention to train them was something Caro would have to ask him about personally. The thought that they might even betray the whole house…

Ballan didn't return, and Caro knew he'd gone back into the street to carry on with his own work even though they had others watching the alehouse, the Pit, and the southern gate to the city. The food came a short time later, two large platters of roast pork and beef with sliced onions and potatoes heaped on the sides and covered in a brown sauce. A serving maid made two trips with the meal, and Caro saw her face pale at the unwanted attention from the assembled brutes.

"Well, the first good thing I've seen all day," said one.

"You're a fine-looking thing."

"What's under that dress of yours? Shame to hide yourself," sneered another.

Those that didn't speak ogled the young woman with lust. When she came back with a platter of fresh fruit, one of the men, an unshaven lout with huge arms, grabbed her wrist and pulled her into his lap with a roar. At once, the hounds around the table let loose with howls of glee. The man, whose biceps were inked with daggers, buried his face into the nape of the woman's brown, shoulder-length hair while a hand snaked towards a breast.

"Squirmy one," he hissed.

"I'll have a squeeze," said another.

"Open that up," called a third, pointing at the front of her clothes. The woman screamed.

Caro thumped the table with his shortsword, drawing all attention.

"Let her go," the agent said to the one with the blades painted on his arms. "Now."

"Whining, are you? Give a moment." He resumed his rough search for the buttons on the maid's shirt.

"Let her go *now*," Caro said, rising and bringing his sword to guard in a movement the gathered men recognized.

"You've trained with a sword?" Lantus asked.

"He'll find out," Caro promised. "What did I say?"

The table became quiet then, but the insolent smiles remained.

"Let her go, Plakus," Kurlin finally said, sounding bored.

Plakus did so, throwing the fleshy bear trap of his arms wide and releasing her. He sneered at the standing Caro, not entirely convinced he was truly ready to do anything with his weapon. Sobbing, the serving maid ran from the alcove, leaving only the men to sort things out.

"Either you boys aren't very smart," Caro began, "or you're testing me. Don't test me again."

"He was only playing," soothed Kurlin. "Weren't you, Plakus?"

"Aye that," Plakus rumbled. "I'll play again once you're out of sight."

"Who says you'll be out of my sight?" Caro demanded.

"Then I'll have to blind you, won't I?" Plakus countered.

Caro cocked his head, his ire at the brazen words rising. Lantus held out a hand and waved it at the tensed-up Plakus.

"Calm down there, hellpup. Calm down." Then to Caro, "Boys are in the city for the first time in a while. Won't happen again. At least, not until the work is done."

"See to it then," Caro warned him. "I won't have another instance like this."

With that, Caro stabbed the shortsword into a slab of pork and jerked it off the platter. He shook it at them all. "I was one of you once. Don't think I've forgotten how to use a sword. Mind yourselves."

With that, Caro shucked the pork off his blade and left the fighters to their meal. He showed them his back as he crossed the floor, and when he was halfway across, the alcove behind him erupted in unchecked laughter. His face and ears burned at whatever had been said at his expense. Caro met the barkeep behind his counter while the serving maid was nowhere to be seen. *Probably halfway to Marrn now*, he thought.

He gave the barkeep five silver coins. "For you, and for the girl." He handed over a gold piece. "Make sure she gets it."

With that, Caro turned about and placed his back to the counter, eyeing the feeding frenzy back in the alcove. He kept his sword out, the flat of the blade tapping his leg with each beat of thought. No fouler pack of he-bitches could Grisholt have sent him. The idea struck him that Grisholt might very well be doing a little cleaning himself, ridding the excess flesh from his ranks. It was unfortunate Caro had to be in contact with them. Another exasperated sigh left him, first the episode with Dark Curge and now this.

Trouble clung to his ass these days.

Across the way, the one called Kurlin ate with gusto, pausing once to salute him with a fistful of pork and a greasy smirk.

*

Koba found all three men splayed out on the tables, resembling dead men waiting to be butchered, so he rapped his club off the nearest set of shins to get him howling. Muluk yelled out and clutched his lower legs in pain, waking in an instant. Koba administered the same to Pig Knot next, catching him just as Muluk's cry roused him from sleep. The trainer didn't reach Halm in time as the Zhiberian jumped off his table, grinning at the obvious disappointment on the big man's face.

"Not this time, you don't," Halm said and winked, placing the table between them. The great scar on the side of Koba's face wrinkled as he frowned.

"You've crippled me!" Pig Knot wailed as he hobbled along. "I'm crippled!"

"I'm crippled!" Muluk took up the cry. "Sweet, dying Seddon!"

"On the sands," the trainer ordered, herding them into daylight. The sun had gone behind some clouds, but the sand grilled their bare feet. Machlann stood waiting for them, dour and squinting in displeasure.

"Where were they?" the trainer asked.

"Sleeping on the tables." Koba's voice was tainted with disbelief.

"Sleeping?" Machlann bellowed. "*Sleeping?* Well, that nap will just be taken from your sleep this night since you started on it already without permission. You stupid dog blossoms. I hope you're well and rested this afternoon as I've all manner of torture in mind for you. Seddon might take pity on you and strike you dead, but I doubt that. No, right now you're with me, and I'm about to show you why you don't sleep in the middle of the day. With your approval, Master Clavellus."

Machlann turned his head in the direction of the balcony. Clavellus stood there with his mug in hand, gazing down imperiously with Goll next to him.

The taskmaster nodded to continue.

"Master Goll?"

"Break them if you must," Goll yelled out.

Pig Knot stopped wincing upon hearing the words. "Right serious, aren't you?"

Koba lurked behind him.

Machlann faced the three men with an expression of barely suppressed smugness. "Right serious is all Koba and I are about, you steaming piece of shite. Dog balls. After this afternoon, meat hooks will seem a blessing to you."

None of the three had anything to say to that.

Truth be told, they were frightened.

More practice on the wooden men, the same chop-and-slash technique they'd done all morning. Machlann watched them from the side, his voice blaring unpleasantly through the summer air.

"Terrible shape, all of you. Eeeeeee, what are you lads doing? What are you doing? And two of you are still in the games? Not for bloody long. You've no stamina to speak of. None that I can see. Can you see any, Koba?"

"None."

"Hear that? You there. Pig Shite!"

"Pig *Knot*," Pig Knot grated, sweating as if he suffered from innumerable puncture wounds.

"You're swinging that stick as if you're fanning someone. *Eeeeeee*, put your hips into it. More power. Stop *tickling* and carve your name out on that timber, boy! *Eeeeeee*! Swing! Don't worry if you break the sword. We have lots to spare. Swing! Smash it over that wood because your foe is training to do the very same to you and gladly."

Machlann stopped and studied Pig Knot, who doubled his efforts, clacking his wooden sword repeatedly off the cross. After a barrage of heavy strikes, his strength began to wilt.

"Harder!" Machlann roared. "This isn't some tavern wench you've hauled off to a dark corner. Hit it! *Eeeeeee,* Saimon's black hanging fruit. I'm not so sure I've seen such weak limbs or shortness of breath. A child would put more push into it. Dying Seddon."

Machlann marched over to Pig Knot and grabbed the sword. "Watch!"

In a flurry that stunned and amazed the three fighters, the trainer laced off a steady one-two combination that made the wood tremble with each impact.

"See my hips? See how I'm twisting them as I throw the cross strike? That's *power!* And I'm not even rutting! *Eeeeeee.* I should be five years dead in a grave, and I'm making that timber rattle more than you ever did."

Machlann tossed the sword back to the Sunjan, who got back to work with a weary expulsion of breath.

"Koba, these lads might have warmed up as much as possible considering."

A stern Koba nodded his agreement.

"Then let's get them working."

Halm straightened and rubbed his shoulder, his face a snarl of exertion and disbelief. It did not go unnoticed by Machlann.

"That's correct, my fat little slab of pork. Now the work begins, and I pity you all. Stand aside with Koba there, Zhiberian. He'll take care of you. Try not to bore him." Machlann smirked and glanced towards the balcony.

"Here." Koba gestured, wanting Halm to follow. They moved away from Pig Knot and Muluk, who were both listening to Machlann's guttural shrieks and shouts. The big trainer pulled on a worn hauberk and hood over his sun-bronzed torso and head. Once that was on, he put on a stout iron helmet that swallowed up his face. Righting the helm, he picked a round shield from a rack and fitted it onto his left arm. A second shield went onto his right. Then he turned to the gladiator, his eyes gleaming behind the visor.

"You fight soon. I want you to come at me and take my head off if you can. Everything you have, everything you know, use now. I can only improve you by knowing what you can do."

"Might kill you." Halm stared at the man.

"*Pah!* You can try. I'm wearing this." He spread his arms to show off the metal mesh of the hauberk, which covered all of his torso and his upper legs. "At best you might knock me out."

The trainer loosened up his arms and rolled his head on his shoulders. "Now, come at me. Everything you have left."

Halm looked at the balcony. Both Clavellus and Goll were no longer watching the others but focused on him. They stood motionless at the railing and leaned forward.

"Now!" Koba urged.

And Halm came on.

The Zhiberian tore into the metal man, but his arms were tired from bashing wood for the better part of the morning. Still, he swung for his trainer's head and arms and even tried to feint but then realized Koba wasn't attacking and gave up. Koba blocked everything with his shields, backing up when necessary, his arms deflecting each strike away from his body.

When Halm paused for breath, Koba bashed his arm with a shield, sending him staggering for balance. "You wait too long. Don't be lulled by the shields. I can put one of these edges into your face and break it."

Halm didn't doubt that he could and suddenly wasn't certain he *wouldn't*. Unlike the trainer, he wore nothing except his loincloth and felt very exposed.

Koba urged him to come forward.

Halm thrust, and Koba turned it aside, spun, and bashed a shield across the back of the fat Zhiberian's head, sending him forward kicking up sand.

"Mindful of the spin. If that was a sword, you'd be wondering why your body was lying on the sand in full view, if you get my meaning."

Halm did. He regained his balance and dug his bare feet into the sand, feeling the grit between his toes.

Then he rushed his trainer.

*

Clavellus and Goll watched from the balcony, observing the paces put to the three men and keeping to the shade when possible. Clavellus sipped on his mug. He switched from wine to mead, savouring the dull edge of the drink before swallowing it, reflecting on what he was seeing below. A pensive Goll had his own mug filled, but it rested on the nearby table.

"Your man's powerful," Clavellus observed. "But he's not using that two-strike combination he's been practicing all morning. And he tires quickly. The first gladiator to realize that and draw the fight out will kill him. Or maim. And you say he has a blood match with one of Curge's lads? Let's hope they don't figure it out."

"Perhaps they won't." Goll kept his eyes on Halm, struggling to strike his trainer.

"Perhaps." Clavellus smiled and sipped. "But truth be known, I only said that to make you feel better."

Goll looked at the man, but the old taskmaster merely grunted and kept his eyes on the sand below.

*

Machlann wailed like a dying bear. "*Eeeeeee*! What was that? What *was* that? Seddon's kog and bells, boy, you swing that stick like you have one jammed up your dog blossom! Widen your stance the width of your shoulders. A narrow stance takes away from your base, your power. Slows you down, and Seddon knows you move like a sick cow as it is."

"I've won two matches this season," Pig Knot countered, panting as he straightened and stepped away from his wooden practice man. He lifted a hand to his brow and mopped away the moisture there while his bare, hairy chest gleamed with sweat. Muluk paused as well, bending over at the knees.

"You did?" Machlann exclaimed, clearly appalled. "That's… disturbing. Either they didn't know what they were doing, they were worse than you, or they were drunk when they stepped onto the sands. Tell me if I'm wrong?"

Muluk held up a hand, distracting both men and sparing Pig Knot's from answering. "I'm done."

"You're *what?*" Machlann's blue eyes widened. "You're what? Saimon's blue pisspot. What do you mean, *I'm done?* You think you have the authority here to just *stop* when you feel like it, my missus? Say it again. I dare you. You best get back into a stance before I take to paddling your balls. That's after I squeeze the juice out of them with my fist."

"I'm no longer in the tournament," Muluk explained with heavy breaths. "I'm just the armourer."

"The *what?*"

"The... the armourer!"

"Then why did you line up this morning?" Machlann demanded.

"Figured I'd have some exercise."

"*Exercise?*"

Muluk blinked fearfully at the reddening features of the trainer.

"And now you've had enough?" Machlann snorted.

Muluk looked at a panting Pig Knot for support and found none. "Ah, yes," the Kree answered hesitantly.

"On your guard and come at me."

"I'd rather not."

"On. Your. Guard."

Grimacing, Muluk straightened his back and regarded the angry trainer with growing apprehension.

"By Saimon's black balls, you come at me this instant, or I'll make it *hurt*, so help me sunny Seddon," Machlann growled.

Shaking his head, Muluk walked to the trainer with his wooden sword held at length, resigned about the beating he was about to receive. Machlann wasn't impressed in the least with his approach. When the Kree swung at him, the old man cracked his club across the other's wrist, making him drop the sword before stepping in and battering him about the skull. He hit the Kree three times in rapid succession before Muluk fell to his knees, holding his head and dripping blood from his nose.

"You're a right proper bastard," Pig Knot hissed. "He said he was done."

"He'll think twice about wasting my time. I'm no nursemaid. Nor am I here for a bit of unfit *exercise*."

"He's *done*."

"Aye that, he's done. I hope that he's a better armourer than swordsman. You hear that, you sun-baked cow kiss?"

Muluk rolled over on the hot sands, grimacing in pain, still holding his head.

"You're right to stay down there. Wasting my time when I could be forging others. You think I do this for *fun*? Seddon's rosy ass. I'll chew you up and shite you out in the morning if you ever waste my time like this again. You hear me, topper? Armourer. *Pah*! I swear if I ever see or hear of you talk about fighting in the games, I'll thumbscrew your eyes out. Get out of my sight!"

Getting to his knees, covered in sand and dust, a dejected and exhausted Muluk made to rise.

Machlann stepped up behind and kicked him to the ground.

"*Crawl* off the sands, you miserable piece of maggot shite!" Machlann shouted. "Maggots *crawl*, not walk."

His head slouched between his shoulders, an exhausted Muluk did just that. Machlann simmered behind him, hefting his club as if debating whether to let the man go or to lay into him once more as a lesson to the others. In the end, he allowed Muluk to slink away, untouched, onto the stone ringing the training sands. There, the Kree sat and drew his legs up to rest his chin on his knees.

The trainer whirled upon Pig Knot with angry eyes. "You still here?"

"I'm still here, you old bastard."

Machlann didn't flinch at the insult. "This means I have only you to watch over now. You best be on your game from here on, my missus. I only smashed him. You, I don't care for at all."

Pig Knot glared at the trainer.

"Keep that anger close by," Machlann warned. "You'll need it for the rest of the day."

*

Pig Knot tried to feed off the energy of his anger, but it didn't last. The trainer pushed him through seemingly meaningless drills that were embarrassing for him more than improving his current set of skills. They worked on principals of leverage, angles, and taking advantage of unprotected joints when close to an opponent, which Pig Knot knew nothing about. Machlann delighted in displaying the Sunjan's lack of knowledge to Clavellus and Goll, who remained silent onlookers. Several times, Machlann had Pig Knot overreaching or off-balance before slapping him violently into the sand. They also practiced over-the-shoulder cuts and back slashes, attempted to connect the attacks into a seamless flow, and followed the technique with counterstrikes. Machlann would demonstrate twice at most and then have Pig Knot try, and if he failed, the trainer would flounce him with his club across a shoulder or a thigh and scorch the air with a cutting remark at his lack of skill. The old trainer worked him hard and cursed him harder, and by early evening, both were sweating, but Pig Knot was almost exhausted.

"All right, you shite-caked topper," Machlann announced after returning from a water barrel near the smithy, "have a rest. In a moment, Koba will show you a few things."

Pig Knot had no wind to reply as he sank to his hands

and knees. He pressed his forehead to the hot sand. A moment later, Halm collapsed beside him.

"Seddon above, I'm done," Halm wheezed through his ruined teeth.

Pig Knot only panted.

"That hellion," Halm gasped, "had me swinging at him for damn near half the afternoon, and only at the end did I seem to please him, but my arms feel like rocks."

"You still think this is a good idea?"

"What's that?"

"Becoming part of a house?"

"There's no house yet." Halm worked his parched throat. "But yes, I do. Attempting this, this day, only tells me… more that, while I think… I might've had potential, I'm past my prime. And if I'm past it, you certainly are."

Pig Knot lifted his head from the sand. "Yet here we are."

"And to what end? I'm too old to farm or anything else. I was only ever good at cracking heads together. This might even be my last season. And to think they have lads who train for *years* to go into the arena before they even set foot in one. That's something I find unthinkable. No wonder we were always defeated in the second month of the fights. We were fighting ones like ourselves, louts with some skill but who would be outclassed by these hellpups who trained for it. Now I see what they mean when they say house gladiators hate us. Most of the Free Trained strut around thinking they're dangerous when they're not. They're unpolished animals trying to win what they can before the real fighters step onto the sands."

"Not always. You killed one this season."

"My first and probably my last." Halm shook his head.

"Here, this day, I'm thinking there's so much more to learn and no time for any of it."

"You don't sound so happy."

"I'm not."

They became quiet then for a moment, resting on the hot sand, gathering themselves before having to go back at it.

"This is gurry," Pig Knot said with venom. "All of it."

"Stay with it," Halm stressed. "That could be us up there one day, gazing down on our fighters. All we need to do is win a little. Just a little coin to get ourselves established."

"I've been swinging my arms, been watching a friend get pummelled, and been beaten and yelled at practically all day. You really think it's going to get better?"

"I do."

Pig Knot shook his head and was about to retort when Muluk appeared with a water bucket and two cups. The smell of the drink took away anything Pig Knot had to say, and both he and Halm grabbed the cups and guzzled.

"Easy, you toppers." With distrust, Muluk eyed the trainers standing on the other side of the practice area and talking in front of the weapons rack. "You fill up too much, and they'll take it out of you."

"You still here?" Pig Knot gasped. "After that beating you got?"

"No worse than what I might've gotten from my father," Muluk replied with a rueful smile. "But I'm still here. There's work to be done over there." He finished with a nod to the open smithy and the bare anvils.

Pig Knot scowled and shook his head once more.

"*Eee*, you. Pig Shite!" Machlann suddenly shouted, taking their attention. The two trainers, shining under the waning sun, wandered to the side of the smithy.

"Surprised he knew your name," a bemused Halm said under his breath.

"Just my luck," Pig Knot said.

"You'll be with Koba for the rest of the day. You, fat man, are with me," Machlann finished with a throaty wheeze and coughed.

It was Halm's turn to scowl.

"Still happy you're here?" Pig Knot asked.

"Shut up." Halm climbed to his feet.

Feeling somewhat vindicated, Pig Knot got up as well, with Muluk scurrying off to some shade. The Sunjan walked towards the waiting bulk of Koba, who motioned for him to move into the open part of the sands, where Halm had been for most of the afternoon. Deep scuffs and gouges marred the white surface, evidence of the violent dance Halm and Koba had performed earlier.

"You going to crack me with that stick as well?" Pig Knot grumped.

The trainer stared at him for a moment before pulling on his helm. "No. Once I'm ready, you come at me. Try and hit me."

"Not worried that I will?"

Koba paused. "No."

"No," Pig Knot agreed with a weary huff. "I wouldn't be either. Not this late in the day anyway."

Across from him, Koba adjusted his helm and scratched at the hauberk under an arm. He then gathered up his shields and clumsily fitted them onto his arms. Once ready, he stood back from the gladiator and waved him on.

"I'm ready," Koba informed him.

I'm not, Pig Knot wanted to say but held it in.

"Everything you have left, now. Try and take my head off."

"What're you going to do?" Pig Knot asked.

"I'll stop you. Tell you what you're doing wrong."

"Bit dangerous for you, isn't it?"

"I survived your friend there," Koba said grimly. "I think I'll survive you."

Pig Knot shrugged and charged. He took two quick steps and delivered a slash ripping upwards from the earth like a striking snake. Koba deflected it and stepped to his right. Pig Knot matched him, going into the one-two stroke he'd learned that morning and wishing he had real steel. Koba deflected with both shields, one after the other, and the solid sounds of each block rang out. The Sunjan dug down deep and threw himself at the trainer, baring teeth and swinging for a head, an arm, and finally a leg before feinting and slashing for a leg again.

Koba ducked, dodged, and smashed the final cut away.

"Don't feint," Koba said.

Pig Knot didn't hear him.

For the next few moments, he drew on reserves of energy he did not know he possessed. He whirled his club at the trainer, attacking the man as if he embodied all that was wrong with his life, and each time Koba stopped him, his frustration deepened.

"I'm spent," Pig Knot panted after one last flurry and dropped to the sand. "Seddon above… I'm… I'm done."

Koba loomed overhead.

"You could've… could've struck back," Pig Knot said.

"I could've."

"Why didn't you?"

The trainer didn't answer as something caught his attention enough for Pig Knot to follow his gaze. There, in the dying shine of the evening and walking around the far edge of the sands, was a servant dressed in light robes. Blond hair, a heart-shaped face, and skin browned just enough by the sun, she headed towards the main house.

"Seddon above." Pig Knot smiled. "That one's enough to make a man pause and think right thoughts."

Koba's face, hidden by an iron visor, turned back to the gladiator.

"Right tender, too, from what I can see," Pig Knot said in a greedy tone. "Wearing too damn much though."

Only then did he see the narrowing of Koba's eyes and the stiffening of his posture. An angry heat, which made the sun feel like ice, emanated from the man.

"Get to your feet," the trainer ordered in a controlled voice. Pig Knot didn't like the sound of it or the fury barely contained.

"No harm meant," Pig Knot said. "Only appreciating the—"

For the first time that day, Koba attacked in anger, slinging the edge of a shield towards Pig Knot's head. The Sunjan got out of the way, but the other shield magically took him upside his face, hard enough to make his teeth rattle, and twirled him about like a broken top. He landed facedown in the sand and took a long moment to flex his jaw.

"Get up," Koba told him.

Pig Knot considered the trainer for a moment. His words came out as whimper. "I didn't mean anything."

"Get up," the trainer repeated, the edge still in his voice.

Suddenly fearful, Pig Knot hauled himself to his feet.

35

When the sun finally fell from the sky and the trainers released them from their drills, both Halm and Pig Knot collapsed, their limbs wailing. Both men groaned and wished for death, feeling as though they had been dragged behind a koch a considerable distance. Muluk attempted to rouse them from where they lay, but they waved him off.

"Up and for the baths, you sacks of shite," Machlann roared, pointing. "Seddon's rosy ass, you've stained and stunk up my sands enough for one day. Up! Up, or by Seddon I'll stab your eyes out with my prick! *Eeee.*"

That got them moving.

They staggered to their feet and stumbled towards a door held open by a manservant. Steam clung to them and filled their senses upon entering the chamber, a wide area with flagstones set into the ground. Ahead, just barely seen through the oppressive clouds, lay a wide bath ringed with round beach rocks fitted closely together. The entire area lay before them, fashioned after the famous bathhouses of Sunja, and its waters appeared calm and shimmered in ghostly lamp light.

"This is for us?" Halm rasped.

"It is." The servant gestured with an arm.

Slowly, disbelieving, they dusted off their feet and bodies, painfully aware of how filthy they'd become, and stripped off their loincloths. The walls were made of black wood with long benches wide enough to lie upon. Low tables stretched out before the bath waters, set in a depression marked with iron drains and placed before the low wall holding back the waters.

"Lie on the tables," the servant instructed, "or sit."

Neither Halm, Pig Knot, nor Muluk spoke. Naked, they splayed out while more men entered the room carrying buckets of warm water. Soon, the three were set upon and scrubbed down with coarse cloths and soap. Sore, knotted muscles were massaged.

"Dying Seddon!" Muluk exclaimed into the crook of his arm as he lay on his back. "This is wonderful."

"What are you doing here, anyway?" Pig Knot asked nearby.

"Don't say anything, else that hellion Machlann might hear you," Muluk shot back, genuine concern in his voice.

At the end, the servants emptied the buckets over the men's heads with a splash.

"You may relax here for a while," one servant informed them. "Just know that supper will be waiting for you. The longer you linger here, the colder it will become."

With that, the three servants retreated outside, closing the door behind them.

"Not as nice as the baths in Sunja." Halm sized the place up as the pooled water at his feet leaked away into drains. "But after this day…"

"Don't complain," Muluk warned a second time. "These walls might have ears."

The three of them hobbled to the clear waters and sank into the depths up to their chins. Groans of relief cut the smoky air as they settled in.

"Dog balls, this is better than rutting," Halm hissed, water lapping at his chin.

"Fool," Pig Knot said.

"I'd almost consider coming back tomorrow if this is what's at the end of the day," Muluk said.

"After what Machlann said?" Pig Knot asked.

"Hmm. Well, perhaps not then."

"You're still sore?" Halm asked of Pig Knot.

"Aye that. That one named Koba nearly took my head off. All because of…"

"Of what?" Muluk asked.

"Aye, of what?" Halm added.

Pig Knot's brow scrunched in confusion. "There was a serving wench crossing over to the house there."

"The little berry with the blond hair?" Halm asked.

"Aye that. That's the biscuit."

"She is," Muluk agreed.

"Well, I was eyeing her. Might have said something as well—I can't remember. Next I knew, the brute was pounding me with a shield. And doing the work too. I think I lost two teeth at one point."

"She must be something to him," Halm said.

"I know that *now*," Pig Knot reflected. "Just didn't know it *then*. That bastard damn near killed me. If it was a real fight and I was rested…" He trailed off with vengeful eyes.

Muluk *tsked*. "First Machlann and then Koba. You aren't that good at making friends."

"That Koba knows what he's about," Halm stated quietly. "Both of them."

Muluk glanced over his shoulder to check if they were indeed alone. "Why does he make that sound? That *eeeee* sound, it's strange."

"Perhaps you'll make that sound when you get his age," an amused Halm said.

"I don't expect to live that long."

"*I* don't expect to live that long," Pig Knot grated. "I'm getting the feeling they're not wanting me around here."

The men became quiet for a moment, and then Halm said, "We're on the cusp of something here. If you think they're working you hard now, just wait until later. I think they do this to weed out the lesser souls."

"You think I'm a lesser soul?"

"I think if you truly want to stay here, you'll have to do much more." Halm stared him in the eye. "And I think it'll be worth it."

Pig Knot mulled. "I don't know…"

"What else do you have to do? Or be?" Muluk asked.

"Nothing and nowhere," Pig Knot admitted, "but there'll come a time when that argument won't work anymore. And it's coming soon, I figure."

They finished their bath, dressed in clean loincloths the servants had left for them, and ate their meal of porridge and dried meat while half-asleep. Goll was nowhere to be seen, nor were any of the trainers or the taskmaster. Once they were done eating, a manservant directed them to their small rooms, which were really nothing more than deep alcoves. Heavy curtains hung over each entrance for privacy, while inside were a bedpan, a cot, and little else. The men sank into their beds exhausted and left the evening behind.

They had little doubt the next day would be just as difficult.

When the following day began, Pig Knot was all for doing what he could with it, though embers of loathing for the trainers burned in his head and chest. The three men ate in relative silence, feeling as though another day's sleep was needed. Their muscles and joints ached in ways never before realized, and Muluk wondered loudly if the baths were open. The servants feeding them informed him they were not but would be in the evening. That brightened the Kree's spirits.

When they finished eating, they filed out onto the sands and stood abreast of each other. Waiting for them were Goll, the two trainers, and Clavellus.

"Feeling stiff this morning?" Machlann roared, breaking the morning stillness and causing a flock of black birds to take flight.

None of the men dared reply.

"No matter, Master Clavellus." Machlann stepped to one side. The taskmaster stood with his silver mug in hand and studied the three of them.

"You, Halm of Zhiberia, will be with Machlann this morning. He wishes to speak with you before you leave this morning."

Halm blanched at the words.

"To the arena," Clavellus explained with a smile. "Easy, lad. We aren't kicking you out yet. But you do have some work ahead of you tomorrow, in the form of the House of Curge. Listen well to what Machlann has to say, and then rest up. You'll be taking up steel tomorrow."

The taskmaster singled out Muluk. "I'm told you're to be the new armourer."

"I am, Master Clavellus."

"Then you see that smithy?"

"Aye that."

"That's yours to work if you lot become an actual house."

Muluk blinked and took in the smithy, his eyes suddenly attentive. It was perhaps the first time someone had offered him anything substantial in a long time.

"But your fighting days are finished," Clavellus told him.

Muluk didn't say anything upon hearing the news, and the taskmaster went on to the next man.

"Pig Knot?"

"Aye, Master Clavellus?"

"You're to stay here with us while the others head into the city." The taskmaster shook his head. "You have a hard day ahead of you. A hard day indeed. And I for one look forward to seeing what you're capable of."

"Oh." Pig Knot became downcast. He wasn't looking forward to a day where he was the centre of attention with both trainers. Goll regarded him with a stoic air, and that didn't surprise him in the least. He vowed to make it through. Before him, the gazes of the two trainers stayed rock steady, but Pig Knot thought there was a flick of eagerness there.

"It's going to be a long, hot day, lads," Clavellus declared, and Pig Knot knew he was right.

"Best of luck," Halm said before leaving his side.

"As you," Pig Knot muttered back, inwardly steeling himself for the trials he'd have to endure alone. A part of him became venomous. Why did he have to prove himself to these men? He didn't really want to be here anyway. But he was here, and so were they, trying to break him so they might toss him out. Break *him*. That thought almost made him smirk. Being part of a house was something he still wasn't sure of, but he'd show them this day that he was worthy regardless. He would not allow them to choose.

He would be the one doing the choosing if he stayed or left.

Koba stepped away from the gathered men and motioned to Pig Knot that he should follow.

Setting his jaw, Pig Knot started after him.

As the pair of men walked off to the open sands, Clavellus motioned Halm and Muluk over to where he, Goll, and Machlann stood waiting. Machlann pinched one end of his huge moustache while Goll appeared pensive. Halm wasn't certain of what to expect.

"You're heading into Sunja this day," Machlann stated. "One can't teach everything in a day and expect a man to remember it all. Not possible. Not with this trade. So do what you have to do for victory. Finish the fight as you would if you weren't fighting for the sake of a house. But fight intelligently, remember the few little things you learned here, and perhaps we'll see you here again in two days."

Halm nodded and waited for more, but none came.

"That's all?" Halm asked, appearing surprised.

"That's all."

"Have a safe journey," Clavellus said to them both. "Borchus will ride with you into the city."

"My thanks," Halm said to Machlann, but the old trainer swished his hand and considered him with hard, piercing eyes.

"I haven't done anything. Not yet."

"You're coming as well, Muluk," Goll said, visibly surprising him with the decision.

With that, Goll swung about on his crutches and led

them to the waiting wagon. Borchus was up front with the driver and barely noticed them get aboard. Moments later, they were all rattling out the front gate of the villa and headed towards the city of Sunja.

Clavellus stood with Machlann and watched the wagon roll away, until the gates closed.

36

They reached Sunja at mid-afternoon, when the sun was at its strongest, passing through the outer gates and inspection points without incident. The three men had dozed off during much of the trip but woke upon reaching the final road up towards the south gate. They heard Borchus answer questions being asked of him, and then the wagon moved again. The journey had been a weary one, and arriving in the city roused them much. Outside, Borchus directed the driver to bring the wagon to a livery stable, where it and the horses would remain until it was time to leave.

"We're back," Halm said pleasantly when the transport finally came to a halt.

A moment later, Borchus pulled back the sheet of canvas covering the rear.

"All out," he announced in a tired voice. "The wagon'll stay here until it's time to leave. As well as Bagrun."

"Bag who?" Halm asked.

"The driver."

"Ah."

The three climbed down as Goll patted Muluk on the shoulder. "Grab that as well." He indicated a sack on the wagon floor.

Muluk pulled it up and made a face as he slung it over a shoulder. "Heavy."

"But you're so strong," Halm said soberly before breaking into a grin.

"You're better off placing that in a bank." Borchus's grey eyes conveyed a deep weariness.

"No, it stays with us," Goll said. "Easier to place wagers rather than making trips to a banker all the time."

"It's your coin," Borchus said indifferently. "Where will you be staying?"

Goll gave the agent directions to the alehouse they usually frequented and asked where he would be sleeping that night.

"Sleep?" Borchus asked. "I'll decide on that later. I've work to do before the night is done. Some of it best finished when ale and beer and firewater have been drunk in very large quantities."

"How will we find you?" Goll wanted to know.

"I'll find you if it's necessary. Win or lose tomorrow, I'll be at the Pit." The short man looked at Halm then. "Don't disappoint me, fat man."

"I won't." Halm frowned good-naturedly. "Dwarf."

"Dwarf?" Borchus scoffed. "Best you can do, Zhiberian? I'm truly disappointed now."

With that, the short, blocky agent turned and left the livery yard. The men followed him out, allowing Bagrun to work.

Back into the crowded streets of Sunja they walked, periodically eyeing the wooden shop fronts, merchants' stalls, and houses built side by side. They didn't talk as they moved through the throngs of people although Halm and Muluk paused at times to allow Goll to catch up when he fell behind. The sun was just falling from the sky when the alehouse tavern came into view, and a small crew of lamplighters moved down the street, fueling the hanging baubles and illuminating the road with their torches as they passed.

The barkeep gave them keys for two rooms, and Goll paid the man for two nights.

"No need to return right away. Pig Knot is in good hands." Goll handed Halm his key. "Muluk and I will share while you get one all to yourself. And sleep. No drinking."

"Of course," Halm said. "Do you think he'll make it?"

"Who?"

"Pig Knot."

"You mean the training?"

"Yes."

"No," Goll said, "I don't."

"He'll surprise you."

The frown on the Kree's face voiced his thoughts on the matter, and he directed them all to an alcove beside the one they usually drank in, which was occupied. Roast beef was ordered, along with water pitchers, and the three ate in relative silence, occasionally watching patrons interact with each other. Once supper was done, they retired upstairs.

Halm paused at the railing before his door and leaned over, watching the people below with a wistful expression.

"What's wrong?" Muluk asked him.

"Just watching the crowd is all."

Muluk stopped at his shoulder and gazed down. "It'll be noisy here this night."

"I'll sleep all the same."

"You better." Goll left his door open as he went inside. "Bring that in here," he called out to Muluk.

"Aye, bring that in there." Halm pointed at the sack of coin. "What sort of guard are you, anyway?"

"The cheap kind." Muluk scratched at his unruly head of hair.

"If I win tomorrow, I'll shave that headpiece off your scalp."

"If you win, I'll let you." Muluk disappeared into his room. A moment later, the door closed.

The sounds and smells from below wafted up and held Halm in rapt attention. He listened to the peals of laughter and bawdy conversation and even watched one couple climb the stairs to the second level and enter the remaining room at the end. Their door banged shut, and for a moment, he heard the muted giggle of the woman. The sound took the Zhiberian back to thoughts of another woman, not so pretty—but then again, he was no prize either, he knew—and what she might be doing this night. He hoped she was alone, perhaps even thinking of him in kind.

Miji with the dark hair tied back, the narrow face, and the hazel eyes reminding him of a cat's.

He thought of her until weariness tugged him away from the rail and the dark doorway of his room beckoned.

Below, with his back against the wall and near the entrance, Ballan watched the big man turn away and close the door behind him. He'd watched the three men from the very instant he spied them outside marching down the street, and what truly piqued his interest were the sacks they carried. Ballan wasn't a gambler—he didn't have the luck for it—but he would wager that one of those cloth sacks held quite a bit of coin.

He lingered for a few moments, heedless of the growing

revelry around his person. When he was certain they weren't coming back out for the night, he moved outside and walked back to where Caro would be waiting. He cut across the street and walked for a short time before darting down an alley. There, draped in darkness, Caro sat upright and dozed with his chin down and his back against the stone wall of a tailor and weaver store.

"Caro."

The agent's head snapped up. Caro blinked at Ballan, and the henchman was close enough to see the shortsword laid by the waking man's thigh.

"They're back."

Caro wiped his face and inhaled deeply. "When?"

"Just now. They're at the alehouse."

The agent's eyes glittered in the shadow. "Go to the cellar. Tell Lantus and the rest what's happening then come back here. Wait…"

Ballan paused.

"Wait… they'll be fighting tomorrow. That's why they're here. Halm is fighting in the arena against one of Curge's lot. This is a chance for us… to take what they have. In the morning."

"Why the morning?"

"We can't rob them at night. Too many people. But in the morning, whoever is in there will be sluggish. They won't see Lantus and his louts go in, and if they do, they certainly won't pay heed to them," Caro whispered. "We'll strike in the morning."

"If we wait until after the fight, they might have more," Ballan pointed out.

"And they might have lost everything. No, tomorrow morning is the time."

Caro looked at Ballan.

"Go to the cellar and rouse the lads. Tell them they work at dawn."

*

Since they had come into the city, Lantus and the other once-gladiators had been confined by Caro to the cellar of a nearby torchmaker, a man who wasn't too concerned with whom he took gold from or for what purposes. Lantus didn't like Caro. There was too much weasel in the man and too much loyalty to Grisholt, who was the mother of all weasels in his eyes. When Brakuss approached him and asked about doing some work outside the arena, Lantus took it. It wasn't that he didn't like fighting in the pit—he could fight, make no mistake, and damn Turst for thinking otherwise—but Lantus felt that all he'd learned at the Stable of Grisholt was simply going to waste. Outside the arena, he could do much more. *So* much more. It wasn't until Brakuss that he'd realized the direction he had to take. And a robbery at that. He couldn't believe his fortune. That idiot Grisholt didn't trust in him at all, yet he had tasked him with something of *this* magnitude. But then he got thinking… perhaps Grisholt was counting on the presence and the loyalty of the other five men in the pack to keep him in line.

When Caro had packed them away in the cellar and told them to stay there until needed— whenever that was— Lantus saw his chance. There in the narrow confines with walls made of stone and timbers, with the lingering smell of shite and piss, the men sat, lived, and talked. He talked with Kurlin who also wasn't entirely pleased with his lot in life. He was a schemer yet hadn't thought of betraying Grisholt after the coin was stolen. *Get the gold and be quiet about it,*

Grisholt had told them. Why not simply get the gold and leave? Divide it amongst the six? The light that sparkled in Kurlin's cruel eyes informed Lantus he'd fishhooked the man. He was perhaps the one he most worried about going forward with his plan. Kurlin wasn't stupid, and secretly Lantus was very wary of him. Kurlin possessed a craziness that unnerved most, something unfit that only surfaced in sparring sessions and in Sunja's Pit. Once he started swinging, it was never a sure thing that Lantus would stop.

Then there was Plakus, who occupied himself by taking a knife tip and tracing the daggers inked into his flesh. Plakus agreed in even shorter time than Kurlin, a crooked smile growing on his face as Lantus informed him of his intentions. In less than half a day, Lantus had split the group and went after the remainder. The others agreed to the new plan almost immediately. Lantus wasn't at all nervous about convincing jackals like Morg and Sulo. They lived only to hurt people. Golki didn't care who he got to smash as long as he was being paid while doing it. Once all of them were with him, Lantus held a general meeting during which they all sat down and talked in quiet tones spiked at times with outbursts of impatience. They listened to the world above them as they waited in the cellar with a new awareness and a newer, much more exciting purpose.

Ballan arrived that night, just as the lamplight was almost consumed. The man threw open the doors to the outside world and stepped noisily into the cellar depths, screwing up his nose at the smell, which Lantus had grown accustomed to. The spy's face was a murky orange in the meagre light, but his distaste could still be made out.

"You're to muster before dawn," he informed them all. "They are at the alehouse now."

"Why dawn?" Lantus asked from where he squatted in a corner, fingers playing impatiently along the edge of his shortsword.

"They'll be asleep. As well the rest of the city. Little trouble taking them unawares."

That was met with silence.

"I'll rouse you when it's time. Be ready."

"Ballan, is it?" Lantus called out.

He paused on the steps, looking puzzled. "You have something to say?"

Lantus's smile erupted like stitches being pulled apart one by one, and he stared at the man. "Nothing at all. We'll be ready."

Ballan hesitated, apparently divided on something, and gazed at the shadowy outlines of the men in the cellar.

"Do that," he said finally and climbed out of the cellar. A moment later, the solid slap of a closing door rang through the sour air.

Kurlin looked at Lantus. "What was that about?"

"Once we have the money, they'll no doubt try to find and stop us. Grisholt will contact his eyes and ears in the city to find out what happened… but they'll be dead. Ballan, I think, will be the first man I kill."

Kurlin snorted in amusement. "Why is that then?"

Lantus shrugged. "No reason."

37

Even though Muluk snored throughout the night, Goll slept well despite waking twice at throaty notes that roused him with a jolt. When dawn's light seeped around the shuttered windows like gold poured from the sky, Goll awoke and felt the magnitude of the day. He lay in his bed, staring at the dim wooden beams above, and just thought. Whatever gold he possessed would be placed on Halm though he wasn't positive of the outcome. Everything balanced on the Zhiberian and whether or not he could defeat Curge's gladiator. If he failed, Goll's plans would be set back to a point of starting over completely, and it was doubtful Clavellus would allow them any grace for using his facilities and trainers. He could ask, but that would only happen if Halm lost.

Halm must not lose. Goll rose and laboured in getting dressed, feeling the pull and yell of his wounds. He splashed water on his face from a nearby washbasin. As uneasy as he felt, he still felt the need to eat something.

"Get up," he said to Muluk as he washed.

"Uhhh." His countryman moaned and punctuated it with a half-dead snort. Goll stood back from the basin and took in the form of the man, sprawled in his bed as though he had leaped into it from a great height, with a single blanket somehow knotted about his limbs in a tangle rivalling anything a sailor might tie off.

"Get up, I said."

A pause. "Why?"

"It's dawn."

"My point. It's *dawn*," Muluk moaned. "Why are you up so early? Damnation, man, don't you sleep?"

"Up. We'll buy some breakfast."

"Where? It's *dawn*, Goll." He whined. "The tavern's kitchen won't be open."

"Always someone awake and willing to sell something from the street stalls."

"Where?"

"We'll find something."

"You go on," Muluk moaned. "I'll stay here."

Goll frowned and went to the sack of gold tucked under the bed. He sat on the bed's edge and bent over, counting out five coins.

"I'm not buying you anything if you stay here." He pocketed the coins.

Muluk snored.

"Protect the coin," Goll ordered him.

Muluk snored louder.

"I mean it."

"Go eat or… something," Muluk trailed off sleepily, uprooting his pillow and jamming his head underneath it.

Not pleased in the least, Goll gathered up his crutches, went to the door, and threw back the bolts. He closed it behind himself none too quietly and walked to the next room. He pounded on it twice before Halm's sleepy voice inside stopped him.

"What?" the Zhiberian grated.

"Get up."

"Why? It's *dawn*, you punce."

Goll took a breath. "Get up this instant."

Beyond the door, groans and the sound of stumbling perked the Kree's ears. Moments passed, and Goll was just about to yell when the door burst open, exposing him to the unpleasant gust of the Zhiberian's morning breath. Halm had his trousers and boots on, with everything above the waist on display.

"Did you wash?" Goll asked him.

"Real men don't wash," Halm growled, half-asleep and making the Kree grimace at the revelation.

"Come along then, *real* man. Let's find something to eat."

"This early? The kitchen won't be open."

"You sound like old man Muluk."

Halm squinted and looked about. "Where *is* old man Muluk?"

"Sleeping."

"Why isn't he coming along for breakfast?"

"Because we're both real men, and he isn't."

"Real men aren't very smart," Halm grumped.

"Nor do they smell as if someone used their mouths as shite troughs during the night."

Halm closed his jaws. "Uncalled for," he muttered, appearing offended.

"Come on, and let's see what's what. I'm hungry, and you need to be up. Some boiled eggs would be good."

That got an agreeing grunt from the Zhiberian, and both of them made their way along the walkway, past the first room, and down the stairs. Below, the barkeep slept behind the counter, his head in his arms and his back rising and falling with each breath. Scattered throughout the interior were other patrons sleeping in alcoves or passed out on the wooden floor. Bright sunbeams crossed the legs and torsos of some but weren't yet strong enough to wake them. Goll and Halm made their way down the steps, which groaned, but that wasn't enough to stir them.

"They're all dead asleep," Halm said, "like we should be."

On one step, the wood squealed loud enough for Goll to wince. He half turned on the Zhiberian. "Go back and sleep if you wish. I won't be listening to you complain about getting up so early all while I'm eating."

"Doubt you'll find anything out there anyway."

"I'll find something."

Halm glowered. "All right, I'll come along. Right after the latrine."

Goll didn't say anything to that, for he suddenly felt the urge as well. Sighing, he followed the bigger man.

*

Just before dawn, as promised, Ballan returned to the cellar and woke up the six.

He waited for the men on the cellar stairs, watching them emerge from the shadows of the place like dismal wraiths unleashed from their holes, caked in leather and metal and brandishing all manner of frightening weapons. The place smelled terrible, rank as rotting offal, and Ballan kept his hand close to his mouth.

"What's wrong?" Lantus adjusted scratched leather bracers on his forearms. "Not flowery enough for you?"

Ballan didn't answer. Lantus sneered and checked his weapons. The others mirrored him, slapping shortswords into sheaths and daggers into belts and boots. One hefted a huge battle axe, shocking Ballan. He wondered how he'd missed such a weapon when they first came into the city. None wore helmets.

"Now then." Lantus smiled. "Where's the meat you want us to carve?"

The one called Golki came up to stand on Ballan's right, pig eyed, nostrils flaring. Ballan flinched, getting a round of dark chuckles, and backed away from the brute.

"Scares easy, doesn't he?" the one called Kurlin observed.

"The sweeter the blood, they say," said the lout with the daggers tattooed on his arms.

His unease growing, Ballan led them out of the cellar and into growing daylight. "This way," he whispered and hunched over as he passed through an alley. The men behind him made no such attempt at being secretive, swaggering along with their leather and weapons creaking, breaking the morning stillness. Some of them muttered amongst themselves, and when Ballan turned to order them to be quiet, Lantus scowled hard enough that, for a moment, he thought he would be knifed right there.

When Caro came into view, standing just back from the mouth of the alley and keeping watch on the sleepy-looking alehouse, Ballan's relief was enormous. Caro turned about at the sound of their approach and glared at the warriors.

"Why don't you scream as well?" he asked acidly. "Rake your blades off the sides of the buildings? Let everyone know you've arrived."

"Perhaps we will," Lantus replied, and Ballan could see the pit fighter didn't like Caro's tone. "Or maybe we'll just make someone scream."

Caro ignored that. "Are you dogs ready?"

"Watch your mouth," Kurlin seethed, sliding his shortsword free of its scabbard. Behind him, the others bared their own weapons.

Caro studied them all with greater attention, and Ballan had to admire his leader for having balls of sheer stone and doing so without so much as a flinch.

"Mind who you're speaking to, *dog*," Caro countered, unblinking. "Else you do your morning's work without paws."

Kurlin bristled, not liking the quip in the least.

"This one's a scrapper," Plakus threw in, nodding appreciatively.

"He once fought in the pit or something like that," Lantus said over his shoulder.

"And moved on to better things," Caro stated in a dangerous tone. "Now shut—"

Ballan abruptly slunk back into the alley, seeing something across the street and attracting the attention of all with him.

There, two of the men had emerged from the alehouse's entrance.

The killers in the alleyway quieted, their audacity simmering.

"There they are…" Caro hissed from where he pressed himself against the wall.

"Only the two of them?" Lantus asked from just behind him.

"Only two."

"There're three," Ballan supplied.

Caro raised a hand.

The pair of men stopped on the step, as if waiting.

*

"*Now* what?" Goll asked, turning on his crutch.

Halm blinked at him. "Forgot my blade."

"Go on and get it then."

Halm considered the open door but then waved a hand. "It's all right. Lead on."

"Are you certain? Don't want you to get there and change your mind."

"Bit harsh this morning, aren't you?" Halm said.

"It's a big day. An important day."

"I know it."

"Then act like it."

"Like you?" Halm grinned, flashing his horrible teeth. "No. I'm happy the way I am. I'll fight this day, and I'll win. Or I'll probably be dead. Dark Curge's lad, remember?"

Goll sighed. He did.

"Ah…" Halm flourished his hand once more. "Let's find something to eat, friend Goll. You've got me up this early, I mean to test that purse of yours. See how deep it is. Perhaps even bring back old man Muluk something."

"Perhaps." Goll broke into a stride.

They walked on.

*

Caro watched the two men walking down the street away from both the tavern and where they lurked.

"Well?" Lantus asked, his shoulder against the wall. "They're the ones, right?"

"They don't have anything with them," Caro noted. "No cloth sacks. It's all in there." He nodded at the tavern.

"Then we're off." Lantus motioned his men forward.

Caro turned on them. "You stupid punce. Wait at least until these bastards are well and away. The third one—the one they called Muluk—might come out anyway. The whole of Sunja doesn't want to wake to a street fight."

Lantus's answering scowl hinted at his waning patience at being called names.

Caro stuck his head around the corner and saw the pair walk away, down the narrow street, past crates, closed stalls, and assorted other debris. Rays of light lit up their upper torsos as they meandered along. Then they were gone from sight. The smell of sewage wafted across his nose, pungent and offending. Somewhere a rooster crowed, twice. Nothing moved on the street.

Caro looked back at the waiting killers. "All right. Look for a cloth sack in one of the upstairs rooms. We don't know which, but there are only three. Search them all. Be careful of Muluk and kill him. Get the coin and get out. Think you can do all that?"

Lantus screwed up his face at the orders. He purposely bumped his shoulder into Caro's as he passed, knocking the man against the wall. Kurlin followed, his shortsword gleaming and ready for a fight. Caro kept his mouth shut this time. Morg shoved Ballan up against the nearby building, grinning maliciously at him.

In seconds, the six fighters left the secretive shade of the alley and looked around. Sunlight made their dusty colours seem all the more vibrant. They crossed the street and plodded up the front steps of the tavern, their boots clopping off the wood and causing Caro to shake his head.

"Ballan."

"Yes?"

"Those are six right bastards I'd just as soon gut as trust." Caro became pensive for a moment and then continued,

"Go rouse whoever is nearby. Have them strap on steel and meet me back here."

"You expect trouble?"

Caro's features hardened. "I expect something…"

*

The night had been a rough one, and heaps of sleeping bodies filled both the floor and the alcoves. The smell wasn't as bad as the cellar, a mixture of mostly spilled beer or ale. Beams of light speared through shuttered windows, tethering their ends to the wooden floor. Snores rumbled, undisturbed by the wooden footsteps of the six entering the alehouse. Even the old barkeep slept, his head in his arms behind the counter.

Lantus glanced about and noted every sleeping patron in the cavernous interior. They were sleeping, but he had been trained not to take chances. It wasn't his fault they were here, and he had to ensure no one saw their faces.

Kurlin looked at him, not easy to look upon at any time and right now appearing quite evil.

Lantus's fingers flexed on his sword's hilt. "Kill them all. Quietly."

The men broke away from their leader, eager to please.

*

In his bed, Muluk smacked his lips and cracked an eye. Like a bird taken to wing, sleep wouldn't return to him, and for that, he cursed Goll in his native tongue. He lay there, staring up at the ceiling, and just listened, eyes closed, feeling the air flow in and out of his body. Breakfast. Too damn early for breakfast.

Urk.

Whuck.

Clack.

The sounds made him frown as they drifted from downstairs. They reminded him of a throat being cut or a head being smashed. He thought it strange to hear any noise this time of the morning. Then a silence fell, deep and unsettling, in which he waited expectantly for the next soft note but heard nothing. Muluk scoffed and figured it was probably a few drunks stumbling off tables in their haste to get to a latrine.

With that, he sniffed deeply, wrinkled his nose up, and rolled onto his side. He wondered absently if the lads might bring him back something to eat. Another sniff then and a rub at his nose.

Once again, he tried summoning sleep.

*

The street meandered quite a distance away from the alehouse, and Halm and Goll followed it until they came to a stall occupied by an old woman in a thin yellow dress. She sat behind a bare stone grill situated against the wall of a store with its shutters closed. Her sun-ravaged features questioned the two men.

"You have food here?" Goll asked.

"I do," she crackled back. "You lads speak funny. Where're you from?"

They stopped before the stall. "I'm from Kree, and this one's a Zhiberian."

She watched Halm warily, careful not to meet his eyes.

It caused him to chuckle. "I'll not do anything wrong, good woman," he said pleasantly. "My companion and I just want to eat."

Still on guard, she puttered about her stone grill and produced a large iron frying pan.

"Can you pay?" she asked.

Goll held up a single gold coin. The sun caught the metal just so and made it twinkle.

No longer shy, the old woman got cooking.

*

The smell of blood soured the air and covered the floor in thick, ever-widening gobs. Some of it drained to the earth below through knots and seams in the wooden planks while the rest simply flowed with all the grace of slow-moving ice. Lantus dropped the head of the barkeep, angling it so the gush from his cut throat would not spatter his boots. It wasn't that he worried about getting blood on himself, but he realized he'd have to step out into daylight once again and probably have to leave the city with haste. Even fresh blood was difficult to clean off, but he hated when it became sticky.

They'd made quick work of the people sleeping in the alehouse. The barkeep himself was a simple haul and gash. Barely a hitch, except for the unsettling hissing a person makes when their gullet's been sliced open. Even with the grunts and breaking of bones, most of the patrons barely stirred in their drunken slumbers. Lantus decided he didn't mind the lack of a challenge.

"Come on," he whispered, motioning the others to follow him towards the stairs. They pulled themselves away from their individual acts of butchery, leaving the tavern floor and nearby alcoves with still-bleeding corpses. Blood coated the hands and leather of some and covered all of their blades. Golki held his diamond-shaped maces before him, bringing up the rear and shaking one iron head at the wall.

A tattered piece of red scalp splashed against the wood and slunk in spurts to the floor.

Lantus went up the stairs, eyes set on the three doors at the top, taking two at a time.

He froze at a wooden squeal behind and turned about to see Kurlin, snarling as if he'd just stepped into a steaming cow kiss.

*

That one piercing squeal of wood, as sharp-sounding as one of Goll's sleep farts, spiked the silence and made Muluk open his eyes again. Like it or not, he was quickly waking to the shrill murmurs of what almost sounded like birdcalls. It took him a moment more to realize the sound was the stairs. People were coming up, their boots softly clomping off wood.

Muluk squinted in the room full of shadows, leaned over the edge of the bed and spied the dark lump of the coin sack peeking out from underneath.

Goll, he thought, *didn't bring enough coin.*

He sighed in weary wonder.

*

Dying Seddon, Lantus thought. He hoped he had killed the carpenter of those stairs below. If he spied one of the dead bodies with a hammer or any other tool on the way back down, he'd make it a point to stab the topper again. He reached the walkway and waved his men up and past him. Morg and Sulo grinned with anticipation as they passed. Golki lifted his twin maces. Plakus hefted his battle-axe.

Six men lined the walkway, two at each door. They readied themselves to kick in the doors and charge. All eyes latched onto Lantus, who crouched behind Plakus.

Lantus raised his hand.

And dropped it.

38

The soft rattling outside his door continued until Muluk sat up, a hand to his forehead. Goll had apparently paused outside the door, and squinting at the line of light at the base seam, Muluk could see that Halm was there as well. The pair was trying hard to be quiet.

Then the door flew open.

Two men barged into the room, gleaming shortswords out, and took a second to spot where the Kree was sleeping. Muluk jerked himself over the side of the bed, suddenly very much awake. The killers charged him, shouting, and Muluk did the only thing he could.

He threw his blanket.

The blanket covered one man's upper torso, and he thrashed to be free of it. Muluk faced the second man, who rushed around the expanse of the bed. He swung his sword at the naked Kree, who slept without a stitch on, and missed the top of his head by a hair. Muluk sprang at him, grabbed him up in a bear hug, and with whatever strength he possessed, squeezed about his midsection. A gasp of surprise and pain burst from his victim's lungs.

"To Morg and Sulo!" Muluk heard from outside, and

panic rose in his gullet. He threw his attacker into the other, already freed of the blanket, and slammed both of them into the wall where they stumbled to the floor. Naked and unarmed, Muluk ran at the door.

Just as a man appeared there with a pair of heavy maces.

Golki's face twisted up in anger and swung a mace an instant before Muluk crashed into him. The mace swept a killer arc over his head, splintering a chunk of doorframe as Muluk forced him backwards onto the walkway. A man with a fearsome battle-axe flashed by, but Muluk could pay him little mind. He and Golki crashed through the wooden railing and fell roaring onto the bar below.

Golki landed on his back with a solid slap of flesh on wood, still holding his weapons and with Muluk on top of him.

The impact was enough to jar the Kree for a moment, but then he regained his wits. He looked up in time to see the brute with the battle-axe about to leap. With a huff, he scrambled off the motionless body and the bar and onto his feet, landing barefoot in blood and nearly losing his balance. Muluk glanced down, too energized to feel horror at the mess coating the tavern floor, and fleetingly took in the dead bodies. He grabbed one of the maces from the slow-moving Golki, who did nothing to stop him.

"Kill him, Plakus!" another yelled out—two more men were racing down the stairs.

Above him, Plakus jumped.

He landed *through* the section of the countertop, up to his knees, his face a shocked rictus of pain. The battle-axe slipped from his fingers as he doubled over as if bowing to royalty.

Mace in hand, Muluk raced to the stairs to head off the two descending men. They met at the bottom, and a ferocious monster of a man swung a sword at his head. The mace wasn't the choice weapon of the Kree, but he wielded it like a heavy blade. He blocked the sword and knocked the lead man off balance with a countering two-handed swipe, flinging him out of the way and into the gore-covered floor. The second man slashed at Muluk's stomach, drawing a line that spat blood. Muluk sprang back, noting the two men he'd thrown into the wall of his room now charging down the steps two at a time.

The Kree lashed out with the mace. His foe ducked to one side, escaping the scything arc of the heavy weapon. Muluk crashed into him and heaved him into the descending men. All three attackers dropped to their knees, hands grasping at wood to halt their falls, giving Muluk a few more seconds.

The first swordsman pulled himself up from the blood on the tavern floor, snarled, and attacked. He slashed right and then left and finally stabbed. Muluk evaded both attacks and smashed the sword to the floor before stepping in close and uppercutting with his mace. The weapon crushed his foe's jaw, cracking his head back in a spurt of broken teeth and dropping him to the floor.

"I'll gut you!" someone shouted from behind.

Muluk whirled about to face the first man to untangle himself from the clutter of limbs on the stairs. He drew back his sword for an over-the-shoulder chop. The Kree deflected the swipe with his mace and parried another, and for a moment, the pair stood toe to toe exchanging heavy blows. The sword finally punched through Muluk's guard and flashed across his lower ribs, parting flesh. Muluk retreated, backing towards the bar and eyeing the remaining killers, who were rising from the stairs, recovered and angry.

"You think that stings," Kurlin hissed with a grin behind his guard, nodding at Muluk's bleeding wound. "I'll make you sing."

He lunged at the Kree.

*

Halm smelled the toasting bread and smiled. Perhaps an early rise wasn't a bad idea at all. He sipped on a cup of water while Goll eyed a pot full of boiling eggs, next to the bread.

"This," the old lady said, her bottom lip hanging as she pointed at a jar, "is honey butter. Very good. Made just this week."

"Honey butter?" Goll asked.

"Yes, and this…" She brought up another jar and attempted to open it. Halm reached out, but she drew back with a shake of her head. With a little grunt, she opened the jar. "This is redberry jam. Very sweet."

The jam intrigued the Zhiberian. He had a taste for sugary things.

"How much longer for the eggs?" Goll asked.

"I just put them to boil. Are you in a hurry?" the woman asked him.

The Kree shrugged. "Not really."

*

Lantus held his wrecked jaw and crawled along the floor. Golki moved weakly on the countertop like a shell-less turtle on its back writhing pitifully, attempting to turn over, while Plakus, in obvious pain, bent over at the waist where he had crashed through the wood, his battle-axe on the floor.

Muluk and Kurlin savagely exchanged blows, sword and mace clanging. Muluk then twisted away from the counter, weaving between the heavy tables and benches to throw off his opponent.

"Morg, Sulo, go around!" Kurlin cried as he navigated the obstructions.

Muluk changed course and retreated back around the corner of the bar, leaving bloody footprints in his wake.

"He's a slippery one, Kurlin," Morg shouted, grinning and seemingly enjoying the hunt.

The naked Kree got behind a table and shoved it towards Sulo, slowing him. Muluk then faced the two men rushing towards him. He circled Morg's flank, placing the killer between Kurlin and himself. Kurlin cursed and opted to climb onto a table to go around his companion.

Morg stabbed for Muluk's gut. The Kree parried it and burst his opponent's nose with a counterpunch. He changed targets and crashed his mace into a stunned Morg's chest, driving him backwards and causing him to stumble over a bench.

Kurlin jumped from table to table, moved in, and slashed downwards, missing the naked man's head narrowly but cutting a sliver of flesh from the outer curve of his right shoulder. The Kree cried out, the force of the blow causing him to slip. He fell to his knees, and as he went, he grabbed Kurlin's ankle and yanked him off his feet, landing him flat on his back.

Then Muluk scuttled on hands and knees under a table.

Sulo maneuvered around the bodies just as Muluk sprang out from underneath a thick slab of polished wood. He slashed downwards at the naked man, cutting a shallow line down his bare back. Muluk bolted for the far wall where he righted himself just in time to see Sulo pursuing.

Muluk dropped to a knee and threw the mace with both arms.

The weapon bounced off Sulo's unprotected shins and sent him crashing down between tables just as a nearby Golki, still on the bar, flipped himself onto his belly.

Muluk drove a fist into the piggish face, snapping the man's head to the left and dropping him once more. Wasting no further time on him, Muluk bent over and grabbed the other mace.

A wounded Sulo struggled to his knees just as Muluk crushed his skull with a *clack* and a fleshy splash, the impact toppling the killer against a table.

Grunting, Muluk backed up and looked at his shoulder. Meat, red and raw, oozed distressing streams of blood down his flesh. He could still work the arm, but it stung to Saimon's hell.

Across from him, both Morg and Kurlin got to their feet.

"That's one," Muluk breathed, glaring at them both. He hefted the mace with two hands and shifted his weight from foot to foot.

"No one's coming to save you," Kurlin growled, raising his shortsword. Morg extracted a dagger for his off hand and circled to his right.

Muluk bared teeth. "Or you."

"Kill him," screeched a red-faced Plakus, still transfixed by the shards of the countertop, the cords in his neck protruding. Near him, Golki struggled to rise again.

On some unheard signal, Kurlin, Morg, and Muluk flung themselves at each other.

For a moment, blades seemingly stitched together as the three traded blows. Muluk stopped one sword and then another, purely on the defensive and maneuvering to place one man between himself and the other. He parried Kurlin's sword to the floor and uppercut with his mace, letting it fly to crunch into Morg's jaw and halting him in mid-attack. The man flopped to the floor as Kurlin righted himself. Muluk swarmed him, throwing his arms about the other's torso, and both fell heavily over a table, suddenly wrestling for Kurlin's sword.

They landed on bloody floorboards with Kurlin on top. Muluk punched upwards, missed, and grabbed for a wrist, frantic not to give his adversary a chance to stab downwards. Kurlin roared, his face blazing red, and forced the sword down, using his body weight to push the tip of the blade towards the other's contorted face.

Muluk abruptly gave up resisting and whipped his head to the right. The blade sliced down and grazed his hairy head, embedding itself in the wooden floor. Kurlin's eyes widened as Muluk heaved with his hips, throwing the other off balance and into a table.

Muluk struggled to his feet and noted the blood spattering his left arm. A moment later, he heard ringing in his ear.

That hesitation was all Kurlin needed. His face contorted in hatred as he extracted a dagger from a boot and charged. He stabbed for Muluk's gut, and the Kree caught the arm as it thrust forward. The tip of the blade pierced Muluk's gut, and Kurlin dragged it to one side, drawing a dollop of blood across the floor. Muluk rammed his shoulder into the man's nose, bursting it like a water bag and making him cringe in pain.

The killer still had enough strength to shove Muluk back. The Kree stumbled three steps and collided with a table. He threw his arms out to right himself, his left hand slapping the wooden surface when an unsteady Lantus rose up behind him, wrecked jaw hanging hideously, and hacked downwards with the battle-axe he had picked up from the floor—lopping off three fingers of Muluk's left hand and burying the blade in the table, the underside splintering.

Muluk screamed in pain.

A livid Lantus screamed back.

Muluk twisted about and grabbed him by his wrecked mouth, dug his feet in, and pulled the man forward. Howling in pain, Lantus could not resist and collided with the table's edge a split-second before a raving Muluk crashed an elbow into the back of his head, driving him down onto the wood facefirst with a crunch. Knotting up a fistful of hair, Muluk yanked the man's neck to the battle-axe edge not fully buried into wood and sawed with every ounce of energy remaining. The steel licked bare flesh in rapid jerks. Blood spurted. Lantus sagged.

That left only three.

Kurlin razored a new line down Muluk's back with his sword, taking him from his left shoulder down into the meat of his left buttock.

Muluk roared and released the head in his grasp. He whirled about in pain, backed up, and crashed into the bar where Plakus, still impaled in the wood, grabbed him about the neck and squeezed.

Kurlin's eyes lit up as he charged, intent on plunging his shortsword through Muluk's chest.

Muluk kicked, his bare foot snapping into the face of the man and crumpling him with a whimper. Plakus growled in agony and rage in Muluk's ear, struggling to get a better grip on his neck. Muluk drove an elbow into his captor's gut and twisted around, his own blood slicking his neck and preventing Plakus from establishing a firm hold. He pushed away from the wounded man, breaking the hold.

Plakus roared.

Muluk gathered up a fallen shortsword, his chest heaving, his back scalding, and his limbs aching. He eyed Golki flopping off the bar and staggering towards the alehouse entrance, the first man to attempt escape.

Plakus roared again, writhing savagely as he righted himself, attracting attention.

Muluk slashed open the trapped man's throat and left him gurgling. Plakus's face paled almost immediately. The dying killer clawed at the gruesome cut with red fingers before finally collapsing, slumping over the front of the bar.

Chest heaving, Muluk turned around and saw Kurlin struggle to his knees, an arm on a nearby table. A dagger in his right hand.

"You," the killer breathed.

With an overhand chop, Muluk split Kurlin's head open to a cheek, where he left the weapon. He didn't have the energy to pry it out, his own blood loss weakening him almost to the point of collapse.

A door clattered open as Golki stumbled through, allowing a wide beam of sunlight into the alehouse.

The man disappeared outside, and Muluk groaned. Filling his lungs, he hurried through the bodies and blood, pushing himself well past his limits. He snatched up a dagger dark with gore and staggered out the door in pursuit.

A fist smashed him across the face, breaking his cheek and driving him to the flagstones. Muluk hit hard and rolled, still possessing enough sense to instinctively keep moving. Golki growled something beastlike from above, and then

Muluk felt the man's weight crash down on him. He squirmed, disoriented, and got a hold of an arm. Golki stabbed with his dagger, cutting Muluk under his arm, across his ribs. The Kree grimaced, twisted, rolled the bigger man to the road, and got on top. Golki squealed and cut the outside of Muluk's thigh, the burn of the steel bright enough to make him dizzy. Golki kept on cutting, *sawing*, each frenzied slash going a little deeper into the muscle.

With a final, furious scream, the Kree rammed a knee into the weapon arm of his foe, pinning it to the road, just before jamming his near fingerless slab of a hand into the killer's face. Muluk fended off desperate fingers clawing for his eyes and heard the garbled screech beneath him before angling the dagger in his right fist towards the man's face...

And stabbed.

There was a sick crunch and a sudden spasm where Muluk was almost bucked from his would-be-killer. Then the body slumped beneath him.

Muluk gazed down and was too tired to do anything but gape.

He eventually rolled off the dead man, who had been stabbed through the centre of his face hard enough that the cross guard of the dagger pinched into an eye and the corner of his mouth.

Muluk tried to rise, but his legs wouldn't work. He looked down at his naked, bleeding self, and saw the mess of his frame. Cuts laced his body and were only just beginning to send out one mighty crescendo of pain. He tried scratching at his nose only to flutter the bloody stumps of his fingers before his eyes.

Then his world tilted.

Along the street, the world awakened with hard claps of

wood banging off wood. Blurry figures, ghosts shimmering in the daylight, streamed into the road to the left and right of him. They surrounded him, seeping inwards at the edges of his darkening vision. He sat and waited, legs splayed out before him, the pain rushing in with tidal force. A little wheeze left him then, signaling the last of his strength.

Someone grabbed his shoulder, turning him to the right. The sun flashed off metal skin and two eyes that blazed.

"Who are you?" a voice demanded.

Muluk blinked, took the barest of breaths.

"I'm the…" he paused, "arm… *errrr.*"

Blackness foamed over him then, full of black motes sparkling like evil suns, and he tumbled below its surface.

39

The crowds choked the street in front of the alehouse, making it nearly impossible for Goll and Halm to get any closer to the place. The pair exchanged puzzled looks before Halm took the lead in parting the people, sliding towards the drinking establishment. Halm stopped before a line of Skarrs in full battle dress, cordoning off an area where their Koor officers stood studying a dead man lying in the street. Blood stained the street stones, and the pit fighters' confusion turned to concern.

"What happened here?" Goll asked of a man nearby.

"Big fight this morning."

"What? Who?"

"Don't know. There was one barely alive. They carried him off to a healer."

Goll looked at Halm. "Get inside. Look for Muluk."

The Zhiberian nodded, his own concern spiking, and made for the alehouse entrance.

Four Skarrs stood watch outside of the doorway, and one of them focused on the huge man appearing before them.

"I need to enter," Halm said.

"Who are you?"

"Just a man who stayed here last night. Some valuables were inside."

The iron helm's visor hid the Skarr's face. "It's unfit in there."

"I've seen worse."

The Skarr considered him for a moment. "Wait here." He went inside. Halm glanced back at the dead man in the street. The Street Watch was a full complement of about two dozen Skarrs, and it seemed to take all of them to hold back the masses of people. A moment later, the Skarr returned and waved Halm across the threshold.

What the Zhiberian saw made his jaw hang open in shock.

Blood covered the floor of the interior, and the smell smacked him full in the face. More Skarrs filled the room, hauling pallid bodies to the center and lining them up. Halm recognized the faces of two serving maids and the barkeep but not any others. There were five warrior types, each displaying the frightening wounds that killed them. Three Skarrs chopped away at the ruined bar where a brute of a man lay impaled and bent over. A section of the wood was peeled away, revealing how narrow braces beneath the thin wood had speared the dead man through his knees and thighs.

"Who're you?" a Skarr Koor asked him pointedly, standing in the middle of the floor sticky with drying gore.

"I…" Halm blinked. "My friend and I stayed here last night. We have our things in the upstairs rooms."

"You know any of these people?" the officer asked.

Halm pointed at the dead serving maids and the barkeep, identifying them by profession only. "I don't know the others."

"Where were you this morning?"

"All of these people were sleeping when my friend and I left the tavern. We went for something to eat."

The Koor dismissed Halm and waved him on up the stairs. The Zhiberian walked over the bloody floor, feeling and hearing every gummy step he took. He ascended the stairs to the walkway and saw that a section of the railway had been smashed as well. Shaking his head, he peered below once more, and the scene looked even more horrific from above. He hurried to his room and saw that the door was open but that nothing appeared disturbed. His sack of armour remained on the floor.

Then he proceeded to Goll and Muluk's room, eyeing the broken railing directly across from the open doorway.

The bed was a disheveled tangle, and the room's meagre furnishings had been brushed aside as if in a skirmish. There, under the edge of the bed, rested the cloth sack containing whatever wealth Goll had managed to gather.

Scratching at his nose in relief, Halm crossed the floor and picked up the sack, feeling the weight. He checked the contents, frowned grimly at the coin, and tossed the bag over his shoulder. He returned to his own room, gathered his equipment, and with both sacks slung over his shoulders, made his way back down the stairs.

The Skarrs allowed him to pass, and Halm stepped out into sunshine that was already uncomfortably hot.

Goll waited, looking anxiously at him.

"I have it."

The tension left Goll's face in a gush but then tightened once more. "Where's Muluk?"

"Not inside. Not one of the dead."

"No?"

"No. Whoever it was murdered *everyone* in there. There were five armoured men in there by the looks of it, plus the one in the street."

Mulling over the information, Goll abruptly swung his way to the nearest Skarr.

"Where's the survivor?"

The soldier pointed as he gave directions, and Halm and Goll cut a path through the crowd eagerly straining to see the dead. The traffic beyond thinned out for a short period before the waking city, with its raucous dealings, overwhelmed them. Neither companion had time to be accosted by braying merchants or slow-moving people, and their worry had risen considerably by the time they located the healer's house.

Halm rapped his knuckles on the wooden door of a two-story house with open windows. He couldn't wait and entered, startling a middle-aged man working over a patient on a table. The Zhiberian's throat constricted. White bandages bright with blood covered the body while another ringed his head in thick loops, leaving the face with one purpled cheek, exposed.

Muluk's eyes flickered in his direction, and the Kree tried to smile.

"Who are you?" the healer demanded, rising from his work with a roll of cloth bandages in his hands, challenging the pair.

"We're…" Halm checked behind him to ensure Goll was there. "We're his friends."

"*Late*… friends," Muluk rasped with a weak smirk.

The healer considered the newcomers for a short time before backing away. Halm and Goll crowded Muluk's bedside, mortified at the damage done to him.

"He's not going to die," the healer informed them.

"He thinks…" Muluk corrected.

Goll leaned in. "Who did this?"

Muluk met his stare, the eye above his bruised cheek bloodshot and sickly yellow. "Don't know."

"They didn't take anything," Goll told him. "Thanks to you."

"He killed six men with nary a stitch of clothing on him, the Skarrs tell me," the healer stated in quiet awe. "Nary a stitch. That's a Kree for you, as bare-assed and brazen as they come. They brought him to me about mid-morning."

"You did all of this?" Goll asked.

"Most—as I don't have an assistant these days. The Skarrs helped for a short while before going off. By that time, I had most of the deepest cuts stitched. Need to bandage them now, which was what I was doing when you two came in. He's not so chipper. The blood loss almost did him in."

"Killed… them all." Muluk's voice was strained, his eyes eerily dull.

"You did that." Halm placed a warm hand on top of the Kree's head. "Aye that. Right and proper. Where was that ferocity when we fought in the pit?"

"Not… to the death, then."

"Lucky me, eh?"

"Do what you have to do," Goll instructed the healer. "You'll be paid for your efforts. Halm here will aid you for a short time, but later we'll be off for the Pit."

"Fighters, are you?" the healer asked.

"We are. This man as well."

"Plain to see. A proper beast, he is," the healer said.

Goll's concerned face broke into a smile. "He is. He is,

indeed. And he's one of ours."

The effort it had taken to speak drained whatever strength Muluk had remaining, and he closed his eyes. Halm crowded in to assist the healer as Goll collapsed on a nearby seat and sighed in relief. He was glad Muluk had survived the attack, but he was even happier that the gold had been untouched. He wiped his brow with a palm and mulled as the men worked on his countryman. One thought came to the forefront.

Who were the six men?

Worse still, could there be others?

*

The final fight in the streets with the one called Golki was shocking, and one that Caro knew would be with him for a while. When the man on top finally killed the once-gladiator, Caro hesitated, wishing Ballan back with a few lads with steel. He thought of going into the building himself, but then people arrived, seeping from their dwellings like rats to crumbs. Then the Street Watch hurried into the area, establishing order. Caro couldn't risk entering the tavern with them around and stayed in the alleyway until his henchman arrived behind him with five others, all carrying blades. Caro motioned for them to stand behind him and hold their tongues. He stood and watched as a group of Skarrs carried the sole survivor away while a small number of them entered the alehouse. Caro could only guess at the grisly mess lurking inside, for none of Grisholt's other dogs emerged freely or captured by the Skarrs.

That meant only one thing.

Caro instructed Ballan and his lads to stay in the alley before he slunk into the crowd. He overheard that everyone inside had been butchered, even the barkeep and his family. That set the agent's jaw. The dead patrons and owners rendered him speechless with guilt for not fully appreciating the killers' appetite for malice. As gruff as they were, he had never expected them to kill everyone in the tavern. He'd certainly never called for it. The memory of their stupid grinning faces scalded his memory, and it gladdened his conscience to know they were dead.

Except the one who had fought back. The one called Muluk.

One man had torn apart Grisholt's pack of killers. He wasn't certain he wanted to return to the man's estate and report the news of their failure, so he deemed it best to send someone else.

The idea of entering the tavern took him, but by then, Halm of Zhiberia and the cripple had returned. The Zhiberian went inside and emerged later with two cloth sacks, the appearance of which made Caro's heart flutter in exasperation. Reluctantly, he returned to where his men waited and gave instructions to Ballan to keep an eye on things here. Caro took two men, and together, they followed Halm and the cripple to the nearby healer's house. An alley across from the building offered some refuge from the hot morning sun, and there, Caro stood with his two spies, attempting diligently to appear at ease while maintaining watch on the open windows of the house.

As the commoners of Sunja meandered through the street, blocking his sight at times, he couldn't help but feel a touch of wonder.

One man had killed *six* trained gladiators singlehandedly.

Caro didn't have any idea who he was.

But he knew a rock when he saw one.

40

Blood frothed from lipless slits as the healer pulled back cloth bandages and dabbed saywort on the worst wounds. In the beginning, Halm held down the breathing mess that was Muluk, but then the Kree slipped into unconsciousness.

"For the best, really," the healer answered the unspoken questions from both Halm and Goll.

"Seddon's ass, what is that shite you're smearing on him?" Halm asked, screwing up his face.

"What?" the healer asked, clearly unaffected by the odour. "This?"

"Yes, that. Smells like overripe onions. Or an unwashed dog."

"I don't smell a thing. Regardless, it's saywort. It'll speed up the healing."

Halm looked upon the jar the healer held with a face filled with disgust.

"What's your name?" Goll asked, diverting his attention from the Zhiberian.

"Shan," the man answered, continuing to apply the ointment.

"We have to go," Goll explained. "This brute fights in

the afternoon, and we've spent most of the morning working with you. Here…" Fumbling for his purse, he counted out five gold pieces and handed them over. "I hope this is enough?"

"More than enough." Shan took the gold, Muluk's blood staining his hands.

"Keep him here until we come get him. If it's longer than two or three days and that gold runs out, we'll pay you again. Fair enough?"

"More than fair," the healer said, taken aback.

"Do you have any extra bandages? Can we have them for him?" Goll pointed at Halm's belly.

"Certainly." The healer gestured toward a wall filled with rolls of cloth. "Take what you want."

Halm took three, thanked the healer, and jabbed the bandages into his sack of gear.

"We're leaving," Goll announced. He placed a hand on Muluk's arm, held it briefly, and released him.

A pensive Halm rested his hand on the Kree's forehead before nodding sternly at Shan. He then gathered up his sacks of equipment and coin and followed Goll out the door.

Outside, Halm fell into step with the Kree. "What do you think happened?"

"I don't know," Goll answered. "And I'm not happy about it. We weren't careful enough. Should've had more men with us to guard the gold."

"Or placed it in a bank."

"Or placed it in a bank," Goll gave up. "Didn't think thieves would be so cutthroat in Sunja."

"More than cutthroat. They were butchers. You didn't see the people inside. They cut up everyone. No one survived except our lad back there."

"Were they after the coin?"

Halm thought about it. "All three rooms upstairs had their doors booted in. I figure they knew."

"How did they know about it?"

"Perhaps they saw us?"

"Perhaps. Perhaps they didn't even know about the coin at all, but I'm going to assume they did. And they attacked in the morning. That tells me they had been watching us since last night. Perhaps even longer. And they made plans to strike early in the morning. There were six men. We were probably expected to be in the alehouse as well if we didn't rise for breakfast."

"Would've been a different fight," Halm scowled.

Goll agreed with a nod. "But you can't dwell on that right now. You have your own fight. Try and keep up."

With that, the Kree moved faster towards Sunja's Pit.

Halm kept up as best he could with the man on crutches.

It was past noon when they arrived at the arena, and the Domis were just opening their shutters, accepting wagers on the fights of the day. People meandered about the square though there weren't many placing wagers. Halm wondered if the morning's action had anything to do it, or perhaps it was still too early. Goll swung his way up to the first window and placed his wager, and Halm saw the look of interest on the Domis's face when he heard the amount of coin. Goll took his marker and placed it inside his purse.

"Now, we get below," the Kree informed him.

"Was that all of it?" Halm asked as they walked towards the Gate of the Sun.

"Most of it. We've been spending a little more than I wanted, but yes, most of it's just been placed on your hide.

Lightens the load, I must say."

Realizing what rested on his shoulders took the wind out of Halm, and he lagged behind.

"Hurry!" Goll shouted at him, prompting the Zhiberian to move faster.

Within moments, they were below the Pit and descending towards general quarters. The air reeked of fetid latrines, a cloying stench that made Halm wonder if he'd had really fought and lived underneath the arena for so many years. When the stairway opened up, torchlight revealed an enormous underground chamber filled with writhing bodies seeming to be stumbling over one another.

Goll stopped at the sight. "Seddon above. Must be a big day."

"Never imagined…" Halm trailed off, unable to describe what he was seeing and feeling.

"You see this?" Goll half-turned to him. "And I know if we are successful here this day, we'll rescue several of them from this hell."

"Only to place them in another."

"For some, perhaps." Goll became thoughtful as torchlight flicked over his bruised features. "Perhaps."

Then he continued his descent.

They made their way to the matchboard and the intimidating wall of Skarrs standing at attention, facing outwards. The Madea sat behind his heavy wooden desk, perusing documents and charts of information, making the matches days before they would happen. Goll studied the mighty board behind the arena official, perhaps the best-lit area of the entire chamber, while Halm stood nearby, searching the shadows, on guard for would-be thieves. He was certain nothing would happen in general quarters, but a part of him wouldn't allow relaxation.

"You're two fights away from your match," Goll informed him.

"Hmm." Halm looked up at the chart, seeing the matched-up names and not understanding a word.

Then Goll's mouth hung open.

"What is it?"

"Can't you see it?"

Halm didn't want to reveal his illiteracy. "No, what?"

"Pig Knot fights the day after tomorrow."

"Pig Knot? That's soon, isn't it?"

"Very soon," a familiar voice commented to one side. Both men turned to see Borchus staring up at the matchboard. "But don't worry. I've sent word back. He'll be here in time. His opponent isn't a house fighter; that much I can tell."

"How do you know?" Goll asked.

"There's no black circle next to the fellow's name. If it was a house gladiator, there'd be a black circle next to or around the name. Pig Knot's opponent isn't marked, so chances are he's a Free Trained. Who it is isn't really important. If I wanted to find out, I would."

"Where were you this morning?" Goll asked the shorter but much thicker man.

"About," Borchus replied, unconcerned. "Why?"

"Muluk was attacked and almost killed."

The agent's face became drawn. "*Almost* killed? He's alive?"

"Alive at a healer's house but sliced to pieces."

The news made Borchus's face crunch up in thought. "Do you have any enemies?" he asked, not bothering with offering condolences.

"Besides Curge?" Halm asked.

"Yes."

"No, no one."

"How many attackers?"

"Six," Goll informed him. "They killed everyone in the alehouse. Muluk was the only one who survived."

"Six men?" Borchus's eyes narrowed. "Why would they do such a thing? You still have your coin?"

"We do."

"Perhaps they knew about it, then?"

Goll didn't reply, studying the agent's face.

"I'll look into it," Borchus said, mulling. "Concentrate on your fight. You'll have your hands full with him."

"Who?" Goll asked before Halm could.

The agent frowned. "You just looked at the matchboard. You can read, can't you?"

"Of course I can read," Goll snapped back. "I just saw Pig Knot's name."

"His name's Bhor," Borchus informed them, leaning in close yet not meeting their gazes, wary of the other men walking about in the underground chamber. "One of Curge's many favourites."

"Why are you whispering?" Halm asked, aware that he was whispering himself.

"Just a plump child with his belly hanging out, aren't you?" Borchus smirked as if adoring a newborn producing words for the first time. "No idea of who you walk amongst down here. Of who takes note of the matchboard? Why the Madea has the number of Skarrs about him? There are games within games here, fat man, manipulated by forces concealed by shadows. Far and above what you know or think you know and well beyond the myopic urges of the

Free Trained. Look about. You think all the men down here are fighters? Hmm? Did you pick *me* for one?"

"You do look it," Goll muttered.

Halm didn't comment, not liking Brochus's *fat* jabs in the least.

"And that's why I'm here. I blend in. Much easier to do what I do."

"And what's that?" Halm blurted, heat in his cheeks.

"Calm down, large one. Not the thinking type, are you?"

"I think fine. Having a right proper thought about you now, in fact."

"Wondering how I get the best of you in our verbal exchanges, no doubt."

Halm's face scrunched up in dislike. "Wondering if you'll ever grow any taller, you shortened piece of maggot shite."

Borchus stared at the Zhiberian for a moment as if he hadn't heard anything at all. "Well, I'll be on my way then. I've things to do. Try not to perish out there. Coin has been wagered on your head."

"Wait. Where are you going?" Goll demanded.

The agent became sly. "Who are you to ask about my business? Hmm? Concentrate on your bulbous lad there. That's all you have to do this day. Try not to think too much, however. This place smells bad enough as it is."

With that, Borchus moved away from them and quickly disappeared within the tide of bodies and shadows.

"I'm truly beginning to hate that little stump," Halm grumbled.

"I can see why."

"What does *myopic* mean?"

Goll regarded his companion, his brow knotted up in doubt. "Weren't you educated?"

"All Zhiberians are educated."

Somehow, Goll doubted that. "Come on. We've got to get you suited up. I'll help."

"You think you can?"

Goll scowled. "Was that a jab? After you just asked about *myopic*? I just said I'd help. Might not be as quick as before, but I'll do what I can for you."

Halm glowered for a moment.

"And it means shortsighted."

"Oh." Halm's expression lightened. "That's not so bad."

Goll could've taken the time to explain that it was an insult, but he was becoming much too occupied with preparing Halm for battle. They made their way to the entrance of the white tunnel, found an open spot nearby, and dumped the contents of Halm's sack onto the floor.

*

In another part of the Pit, in the area designated for gladiators from established schools and houses, Dark Curge paced in his waiting chamber exclusive to the House of Curge. Ten fighters filled the confines of the room, and Curge stared out at the ground level through a brick arch at shoulder height. This day, he opted to watch the fights from here, not wanting the company of half-faced Gastillo or the excitable Nexus. From this window he'd watch, looking upon the sands with his boys. He reached out, pressing the pit of his good arm against the stone, and cupped a fistful of sand. Feeling the grains, he made a fist and withdrew it, kneading the particles out the bottom of his hand where they fell to the floor.

Curge didn't look at the armored frame of Bhor, who dominated the center of the chamber. The old owner and once gladiator glared at the falling sand, his face as hard as the stone surrounding them all. None of the others spoke, and in short time, their attention focused on their master.

His hand emptied, and Curge made a show of opening his fist, finger by finger, revealing his bare palm.

Dark Curge's eyes settled on Bhor's frame, his leather curiass dull in the light.

"The man you face this day slew Samarhead." Curge spoke calmly, but his eyes blazed with checked fury. "Kill him. I don't care how you do it or how long it takes. Kill him. Samarhead was a brother, and to have your brother taken down by shite-feasting vermin is an insult that must be… not only paid back in blood… but made an *example* of. Men fear to whisper our names. Show them that they are well and right to have that fear. This day, out there, no mercy. No pity. Kill this… Zhiberian."

Bhor lifted his heavy war hammer, the curling motion making the muscles of his thick arms flex. Spikes the length of fingers decorated his powerful shoulders like monstrous sea urchins. A full caged helm concealed his features, making him appear even more intimidating.

Curge took a breath through his nose, the tension in the room close to bursting. He stepped in close to his pit fighter so there would be no misunderstanding.

"And bring me his crushed head."

*

The outfitting done, Goll stood back and studied Halm: conical helm, leather sleeve on his sword arm, metal bracers and greaves, square shield on the left arm. It all appeared so very worn, and both Goll and Halm wondered if it would fall off him on the first step or during the fight. The only things new on the Zhiberian were the bandages on the wounds sustained in his fight with mad Vadrian.

"Remember what they taught you," Goll said.

"Who?"

"The trainers."

"Taught me?" Halm exclaimed softly. "My arms and legs are still stiff from the gurry they had us doing." He chuckled at how concerned the Kree became. "Fear not, good Goll. I don't. Neither should you. I'll either win or lose, and if I lose, I don't think I'll be alive. I'll do what I can for the house."

"You must."

"I will."

The Madea called for Halm, making the Zhiberian look up. "It's time."

"Luck to you, Zhiberian," Goll said in a sombre voice.

Halm chortled, baring rotten teeth. "I told you once already—"

Goll joined in, saying the words with him, "The only luck I have is bad."

They shared a smile at that.

Almost shyly, Goll stuck out his fist. Halm regarded it for a moment before tapping it with his own, holding his Mademian sword. The contact seemed to lift the Kree's spirits.

Then Halm got walking. His huge belly, brazenly on display, quivered with each heavy step.

The white tunnel.

He marched past the Skarrs standing at attention and made his way to the gatekeeper. The old man, bent over and mining at his nose, paused as Halm came into sight. The same gatekeeper as before, Halm saw.

Above, the crowds cried out anxiously.

"I remember you," the gatekeeper hissed. "That fat gut of yours. Right saucy, aren't you?"

Halm shook his head. Compared to Borchus, it almost seemed a shame to trade barbs with the gatekeeper, like smashing a child. He kept quiet, gazing up the stairs, which ended in a thick iron portcullis. Black bars stamped blue sky.

"Not so talkative this day, eh?" the gatekeeper leered with evil mirth. "Frightened, I s'pose."

"Frightened you might die on me right here, and I'll have to pull that lever," Halm replied calmly, knowing the keeper wouldn't keep his mouth shut, and silence, at least in his feeble mind, was weakness.

"I still have plenty of life left in me, youngster."

"You must whisper that in the goat's ear just as you shag it."

The fury on the gatekeeper's face amused Halm, but he supposed it wasn't wise to get the old man's blood going in such a way.

"I hope you die out there this day." The gatekeeper shook.

"As do I, especially if it keeps me away from the likes of you." Halm shrugged.

With that, the gatekeeper yanked down on the lever, and the man above, just inside the portcullis, stepped back at the clanking of chains and the rusty rattle of the rising gate.

"So quick to get rid of me, my *myopic* prick?" Halm asked the old man.

"Get on, you brazen pisser."

The Zhiberian did just that, privately delighted that he had learned and made use of a new word.

The crowds erupted in an applause that momentarily stunned him when he stepped out into the light. Fists shook and pumped the air. Women screamed at him. He turned around, still numb from the reception, taking in the seats of the arena and noting how full they were. The place positively teemed with people this day. He scuffed at the sands, lowering his helm for a moment and grinding his jaw. Even though he wore sandals, he could feel the hot sands underfoot and around his toes.

Across from him, his opponent stepped out of the mouth of the raised portcullis.

"This day," the Orator blared, "we have the second blood match between this pit fighter and the house hunting for his head. Already he has two victories to his name, and he seeks to defy the fates and add yet another. To do this, he must first survive the wrath of the House of Curge. He is… Halm… of *Zhiberia*."

More startling applause came, the sound crackling in his ears like violent rains. Halm wasn't sure if he should wave to them all or not. He chose not to, knowing full well how fickle the crowds could be once blood began to fall.

"Across from him is a killer of men. He is Sunjan born and no stranger to the games of the Pit. There is nothing he enjoys better than punishing his opponents with his heavy hammer, destroying whatever it touches. A stout follower and a master from the House of Curge, he has taken a vow to avenge the life of his fallen brethren, whose life was taken by the man he now faces. From past matches, I know he will not rest until his hammer has cracked open the Zhiberian's skull. He is *Bhor…* of Sunja!"

Hearing his name, Bhor lifted his weapon in salute to the masses and in the direction of the vacant chair of King Juhn. The cheers the Sunjan received were as loud as Halm's reception. The warrior's warhammer possessed a thick spike for puncturing heavier armor.

Halm figured his bandaged stomach would be a tempting target for his opponent, just like all the ones before him. Bhor's armour appeared to be only leather, despite the array of spikes pricking his shoulders. Light. The man would be fast.

And he looked unsettlingly powerful.

"Begin!" the Orator shouted to the rousing approval of the onlookers.

Bhor immediately marched towards Halm, and the Zhiberian tightened his grip on his Mademian blade. The Sunjan wore a full-cage helmet, covering his features entirely and making him exceptionally menacing.

"You're a right pretty one!" Halm shouted.

Bhor did not reply.

Right serious, too, Halm thought.

Twenty strides away.

He felt his bandages, tight across the wounds, and shifted into a crouch. Bhor brought the warhammer up to his chest. The people's cheering quieted a touch as the distance closed. Halm shook his head once more. Bhor was a large man bearing down on him. The Zhiberian gauged where he might put his first strike—the gut, which Bhor only seemed to be partially guarding. Or a limb or hand. The arms had bracers and the legs greaves. He also wore spiked gloves as Vadrian had.

Ten strides.

"I'll kill you," Bhor growled, loud enough for only Halm to hear.

It wasn't as though he hadn't heard such things before. "Come on then," Halm said.

Five strides. Bhor whipped the warhammer up over his

head. That he could lift such a murderous hunk of metal was something amazing. Halm cocked his arm.

They leaped at each other to the rising delight of the crowd.

And a moment later, the Pit exploded with sound.

41

Below the arena, the awesome blast of cheers partially muted by the stone made Goll look up. He wasn't the only one, as several others stopped what they were doing to gaze upwards at the murky heights. Only for a moment did they look, however, before turning their attention back to their own preparations. Any moment, Goll expected chunks of stone to fall around him. Then the harsh thunder subsided into nothing. And the Madea was calling out the names of the next fighters to walk the tunnel.

That sudden roar rattled Goll's nerves. He'd been taken in by the Weapon Masters of Kree at the age of twelve, and one of the very first lessons he'd learned from them was that of self-reliance. Yet, here he was, relying on another to forward his goals. The fear in his guts taunted him. He couldn't even make the journey to the stands this time around, couldn't bear to watch, choosing to wait for Halm either to return through the tunnel on his feet or to be carried out in the meat cart. The thought of having placed almost *all* of their coin on the head of one Zhiberian made his stomach sink. He should have been smarter. He should have placed a smaller wager. If Halm had lost, Goll's plans would be swept away.

The moments stretched on as he leaned against the stone lip of the white tunnel's entrance, feeling something like a worried wife wondering if her champion would come home.

Then, from around the far corner, a man appeared, walking tall.

Goll stopped breathing. He couldn't believe his eyes.

As each step brought Halm clearer into view and closer, Goll couldn't see any indication of a wound on his fleshy frame. As far as he could see, there were none. Halfway down the tunnel, Halm reached up with one hand and pulled off his helm, lighting up the white stone with his infectious grin. Goll exhaled and smiled back, feeling both disbelief and a surge of joy.

"Didn't take long at all," Halm informed him.

"Not at all," Goll agreed. "I didn't have any time to go to the stands."

"Surprised?"

The Kree couldn't help but grin. "I am. I'd be lying otherwise."

"Well, come on," Halm told him as he bent over with a groan and began stripping off his greaves. "Let's get this off me and get topside. We have a marker to cash in."

He won, Goll's mind flashed, almost as stunning as the rainburst of sound he'd heard earlier.

"Some bad news, however."

Goll's face momentarily darkened. "What's that?"

"Bastard Curge will probably have another man on me in a week's time."

"You killed Bhor?"

"Aye that. Didn't you hear?"

"I heard the people, but—"

"The very place shook on its foundation when I killed him." Halm flipped off one of his greaves and slapped it on the stone floor. He got to work on the other one.

Goll thought of the wager and the coin wanting for him. He couldn't stop smiling. "Zhiberians," he whispered.

*

In the viewing chamber at ground level, Curge stiffened as if a spike had been driven through both feet, and he gripped the brickwork of the archway. His men behind him remained deathly quiet, not daring to even breathe in the wake of the stunning loss. The Zhiberian had already left the sands, and men dragged Bhor from the Pit to the open gate, where a cart waited. That cart would transport the fighter's dead body from the sands to the waiting firepit, where all the day's dead would go.

Curge couldn't believe his eyes. The bastard Zhiberian had finished Bhor *faster* than Samarhead if that was possible. The fight replayed itself in his mind: two pit fighters, closing, closing, Bhor with his warhammer overhead and Halm with his sword and square shield at the ready, the crowds barely heard, and then…

Bhor swinging, warhammer screaming downwards on a slant, but the Zhiberian… the Zhiberian *lunging*, arm punching out and stabbing the taller Bhor through the torso, leaving the sword in him as the fat man ducked inside the arc of the descending weapon.

Dodging it entirely.

Bhor dropped to his knees a heartbeat later, warhammer already released, head slumping as though he was about to vomit, and then he simply rolled over.

Halm righted himself, walked over to his opponent, and

worked his blade free, the steel's tip bright with blood. More of it bubbled up in the puncture hole of Bhor's leather vest. The people screamed approval while Bhor feebly sought to cover the wound with his hands.

The Zhiberian towered above him, ignoring the crowd, and merely waited for the man to die.

It hadn't taken long.

Curge clenched his jaw and fumed, only faintly aware of servants raking the sands to cover up the blood, of his own men standing behind him. Streams of images raced through his mind, and he made the effort to slow them down, studying the battle in black and white. The Zhiberian was fast, deadly fast. That was clear to him now. And he was a counterstriker, waiting until his foe had committed to an attack before launching his own. That fat belly of his was only a ruse, a ruse that had taken two of his most promising men from Curge, and even the insane Vadrian if he wanted to include him.

Dark Curge inwardly cursed himself for not paying greater heed to this pit fighter.

It was a mistake he wasn't about to make again.

*

Later that evening, in the house of Healer Shan, Goll and Halm sat about Muluk's sleeping form, still confined to the same table they had left him on. Goll sent an untouched Halm out to fetch some food and drink, and he brought back a small feast of fresh bread, a pair of roast garlic ducks, and water, with a bottle of mead as a before-bed drink. He spread the food out on another table, the smell of the meat filling the room, and asked Shan to leave them to their privacy. The healer closed the outer shop, asking the men only to close the door and shutter the windows if they decided to leave. From where he sat, Goll asked if he had any beds and if they could stay there for the night.

"I do." Shan scratched at his head of sandy hair. "But wouldn't you be more comfortable in an alehouse or inn?"

"After this morning? No," Goll replied. "I'll pay you for anything you have upstairs. You do have some, correct?"

"I do, but they're for patients."

"If you have anyone come in the night, we'll sleep on the floor."

"Well, no need for that..."

"If it's needed, we'll do it."

A smile appeared on Shan's lined face. "Then the upstairs is yours. I live through that door there. Knock if you need me."

"We will," Goll assured him. The Kree grunted and thought for a moment. "Do you know of any men who might be hired on as watchmen?"

"Watchmen?"

"Guards."

"How many?"

Goll took a breath and considered the question. "Perhaps two or three. If you know of any."

"I'll put the word out. I might know of a man."

"Good."

Shan regarded the sleeping form of Muluk then the bulky Halm. "I'll leave you all til the morning. Oil lamps are on the shelf when you need them. Cots are upstairs."

Goll nodded his thanks and returned to his meal, Halm on the other side of the table. The Zhiberian was already well into his portion of the duck and smacked his lips loudly as he ate.

"Go at it quietly, man," Goll told him. "You'll wake up Muluk."

"I'll save him some."

"We both will."

"You think we need a guard?" Halm asked.

"I'll feel better about it."

Halm leaned in and lowered his voice. "How much did we win?"

Goll sighed. "Not quite enough."

"No?"

"No."

"What if I throw in what's left of my coin?"

"Not enough even then. We need several hundred more. We'll have to… have to wager on Pig Knot."

"Ah." Halm smiled, digging into his food again. "The coin is as good as ours then. He'll not let you down."

Goll didn't share the same confidence.

*

At about the same time Halm and Goll were holding Muluk down so Shan could work on his wrecked body, Pig Knot felt as if his arms and legs were about to drop off. Under the hellish glare of both the morning sun and the pair of trainers, he marched about the open sands with a timber beam that must have weighed as much as a grown man across his shoulders. His path, as laid out by Koba, took him the width of the sands, where he would squat once before rising and struggling to the other side, where he would sink into another squat to complete the circuit.

Even when Koba did a complete two rounds seemingly without breaking a sweat, Pig Knot knew he was going to die. Perhaps somewhere during the second completion.

He surprised himself by doing six.

There was no way he could rise when he dipped that final time, and dropping the timber from his shoulders was no easy task either. They allowed him a brief moment of rest before once more having him take up a wooden sword and lay into the practice man, drumming out the exact same two stroke he'd done the day before. Pig Knot paced himself, but when Machlann shouted it was time to eat, the Sunjan's limbs felt rubbery with exhaustion.

In the common room, he could barely use his arms to feed himself the soup they gave him.

There was more training in the afternoon, weapon practice and even some sparring with Koba, all while both Machlann and Clavellus watched with judging eyes. Pig Knot knew the old trainer waited for him to surrender, to quit and walk away, every time he gave an order. The moustached bastard wasn't interested in leaden arms and legs or the exhausted pain. Even Koba, who sparred with him, swung his wooden sword and shield with heavy strength while Pig Knot could only defend himself and counterstrike with whatever weak reserves he possessed. Ever since yesterday, when Pig Knot had eyed that young tart, he sensed Koba projecting an air of suppressed hostility towards him, one that the Sunjan wanted to dispel.

By midafternoon, hopes of that disappeared and were replaced by wondering if he *should* simply quit. He didn't seem to be learning anything, and the bruises on his arms and legs from Koba's strikes were only getting bigger. Any moment, he expected a shout from Clavellus, commanding the trainers to ease off him, but the taskmaster seemed more interested in his damned silver mug that had to be nailed to his hand, often flashing in the sunlight.

Pig Knot continued sparring with heavy-handed Koba.

The Sunjan withdrew into himself, listening to that voice telling him he didn't need such abuse and that he could do quite well on his own. Every time he heard it, a part of him believed it, but then the stubborn part of him saw Machlann's wretched face *waiting* for him to surrender and walk away. The clacking of the wooden blades distracted him only a little from that voice while his muscles increased their pleading for him to stop. Just… *stop.*

Machlann stood in the shade of an overhanging roof extending from the ramparts, watching and waiting. The guards patrolling the walls were only half interested in the same man having his guts torn out. Pig Knot grimaced when Koba slapped his right bicep with the flat of his sword once more.

"*Eeee* stop looking at *me* and *them* and focus on *him,*" Machlann bawled. Then to Koba, "Seems we might have a right proper daisy in our midst, eh? A right proper daisy."

Koba withdrew back into his fighting stance, waited until Pig Knot was ready, and attacked again.

This time, Pig Knot parried the blow and became locked up with the trainer, hissing with exertion. Koba frowned at the situation and seemed to wait. Pig Knot took the moment to push forward, pistoning his legs into the sand.

The frown became a snarl, and Koba twisted his upper body, ramming his forearm into Pig Knot's wrist and slapping him to the ground in a spray of sand.

"*Eeeee* what was that?" Machlann bawled. "What was *that?* You right stupid punce! What did I tell you about leverage? What did I tell you? Don't you ever do that again, or I'll cut your bells off and string them up for wind chimes! On your feet! On your feet!"

Pig Knot exhaled, practically spent, yet he somehow stood. Machlann walked over, glaring hot enough to melt stone, and gestured with his club.

"Lock it up again," the trainer ordered. "Lock it up. Go on. You were eager enough to get into a shoving match just now. Now I'll show you why you never *ever* do such a thing."

Koba assumed his stance and waited for Pig Knot to cross swords with him as they had done before. Not seeing the point, Pig Knot nevertheless complied. He didn't want to be clubbed across the head once more and have to endure more stitching.

"Now," Machlann growled, "lean in, half strength, so you'll understand."

Koba glared at him from behind the crossed blades. Pig Knot still wondered what he'd done. What was the woman to the burly trainer?

"This is a situation a trained gladiator won't commit to, unless it's a Free Trained flick of maggot shite. Now look here. You're pushing ahead, using all muscle, when this is problem of leverage. You don't push forward when steel is locked as all of your power is committed into going forward, and it's too easy to put your sorry head into the dirt. And if someone is doing it to you, by Seddon's ball sack, you punish him. You use your free arm, as Koba did. Twist your upper body and strike the wrist here."

Machlann tapped Pig Knot's wrist and forearm and glared at the man.

"Do that with enough force while the other is trying to push through you, and you send your daisy into the sand, bare assed and ready to be packed. Understood?"

Pig Knot blinked.

"Go ahead, then. Push forward as you did before," Machlann said.

Without thinking, Pig Knot did just that.

Koba twisted and rammed a fist into Pig Knot's weapon hand, sending him sprawling to the sand once more. He rolled over only to have Koba drop and make to stab him through the middle. If it were a real fight, Pig Knot would've been skewered.

"See?" Machlann asked loudly.

"Aye that."

"Machlann," a voice called, pulling both trainers back from the Sunjan sprawled out on the sand. "Go through that a bit until he understands what you're talking about."

Like a dutiful dog, the trainer promptly nodded and switched his attention back to Pig Knot.

"You heard the taskmaster. On your feet."

Groaning, Pig Knot did just that.

"Once more, Pig Shite," Machlann growled at him. "Once more. And then again. And again until I say stop or you drop. I have a fistful of gold that you'll quit before the day's done."

Pig Knot huffed, red-faced, as he stared at the man. He liked that wager himself.

However, by evening, after a torturous day of drills and half-learned fighting techniques, Machlann yelled at him to get out of his sight. The day was done, and the Sunjan had done it. Pig Knot could scarcely believe it. He'd survived the day and lived to breathe. On legs that ached with each step, he limped from the training area and headed for the baths. His arms felt like pliable lead and sported dark welts that glowed. Sweat caked his person, and he felt well and truly filthy from the day's exertions. With each step, he wanted to quit.

Wanted to just leave it all behind, yet he knew, standing in his wake and most certainly waiting for him to do just that, were the two trainers, along with the drunken taskmaster on his balcony. Pig Knot wished for one sip of whatever the bastard was drinking from his silver mug.

Then another notion formed in his skull.

The trainers had tried hard to break him this day. Damn hard. Placed coin on it even.

Pig Knot stopped in his tracks, not five strides away from the common room door, and looked back.

There, discussing matters between them, stood the two trainers, their features dusky with the failing daylight. They eventually felt his stare and matched it.

Pig Knot smiled and nodded. *You did what you could… and I'm still here.*

Neither trainer said a word.

With that message sent, the Sunjan turned about and went inside. He fell asleep in the hot waters, shrouded in luxurious steam. He dreamed of the drills and a laughing Machlann whipping him relentlessly, screaming at him that he wasn't worth the time or effort. Koba lurked in the background, grinning malevolently while sharpening a steel blade. Horns sprouted from his head.

"Only getting started!" Machlann shrieked, barbs bursting from the whip's length. *"Eeee only getting started!"*

Only words, but Pig Knot knew they were true. They *were* only getting started. That was why no words were spoken at the end. He'd lived through the day, but there would be more to pull himself through, more exhausting exercises, more bloody drills, and more wagers on when he'd quit. All while the trainers whipped him.

Fine then. The words shored up his resolve. *We'll see if they can break me… for I'm not about to quit. Not now. For spite's sake, if anything.*

Something pulled Pig Knot back from the dream.

He opened his eyes to a concerned face. A servant had roused him. For that, Pig Knot quietly thanked him.

And somehow, the exhausted man made it back to his room, not even bothering to eat, and collapsed on his cot.

*

"Well?" Clavellus asked his trainers, swishing around the black beer in his mug until it came dangerously close to spilling. He'd walked downstairs and met the two men in front of the main doors to his home.

Machlann went first. "Physically, he's lacking in wind, but he's still a brute. Given time, we could strengthen his endurance. Given time. Mentally, nothing there. He's only half at it. Only half push. He'll be gone in a day. Guaranteed."

Clavellus peered into the depths of his drink and took a sip. Savoured it. "Koba?"

"Machlann's right."

The taskmaster grunted and thought some more on it.

"He's stubborn though," Machlann commented in an uncharacteristically quiet tone. "I'll say that for him. A few times this day, he was pushed to the brink. Each time, he looked over at me and got back up. Something to be said for that."

"You just said you'd break him in a day," Clavellus said.

"Oh, I will, I expect. This stubbornness to stay at it isn't because of a desire to fight as a gladiator but more like taking a piss in my face. Spite, pure and hot, is what's keeping him in there."

"Spite isn't enough." Clavellus looked at the sands. "Not here. And not in the Pit."

"Spite he's got plenty of," Machlann grumped. "But as I said, another day and he'll be gone. Some might think it, but spite isn't the same as willpower, and of that, he's got very little left."

"You won't get that day."

A touch of a frown crumpled up the old trainer's forehead.

"That last one the men allowed through the gates there. One of Borchus's boys. He must have almost killed his horse getting here. Brought word from Sunja. Apparently, Pig Knot's to fight the day after tomorrow. Another Free Trained match. He'll leave tomorrow morning, so as of now, what scant training there has been is now finished. At least until he gets back."

Machlann shook his head. "He won't be back. Seen it before. Once he gets away, the notion of coming back here won't be on his mind. He'll slip away into the crowds. Probably become a guard somewhere if he can stay away from the drink. He won't be back."

"Well, either way, appears you'll be free of him," Clavellus remarked and caught a hint of satisfaction in Koba's hard features. Just a lapse, and then it was gone, but the taskmaster had seen it. He didn't comment, however.

"Koba," the taskmaster addressed his younger trainer. "Give him a little longer to rest in the morning. That'll be our gift to him. Give him that and see to it that there's a wagon ready to haul him off to Sunja."

"You're giving him a wagon?" Machlann asked, not hiding his surprise.

"I'll put the cost on Master Goll's bill," Clavellus said

with a considering pout. "It's business, after all."

The words got smiles from his trainers, but inwardly, Clavellus didn't convince himself. He wanted to see the man in action. He wanted to see a fighter prepared by his staff battle on the sands. The beer in his mug beckoned, and he took another swallow. Seddon above, he should never have gone back to the Pit the other day, as it had only served to make him want *more*. He might tell Machlann and Koba otherwise, but even with the short time the Free Trained had spent on his grounds, he already thought of them as *his*. Not the final warriors he would have produced if he'd had even a year to work with, but still… his.

"'S'all business." Clavellus felt the burn of the lie even as he muttered it.

*

The next morning, Pig Knot woke with a loud snark of a snore and stared at the ceiling untouched by morning light. He struggled to a sitting position and swung his legs out, sensing the lateness of the day and wondering why no one had called him. He dressed in a clean loincloth and stiffly walked out to the common room, hoping for something to eat before the day's torture started once more.

There, Koba filled the doorway, waiting.

"No training this day."

The words sank into Pig Knot, jolting him as if they were spikes. Were they casting him out? It was possible. Perhaps they'd decided he was finished, impatient for him to make up his own stubborn mind. Fine then, he felt his resolve firming up. Let them cast him out. It wouldn't be *him* quitting. In that, there was a small victory.

"Why?" he demanded defiantly, ready to argue even

though part of him wanted to be gone.

"You fight tomorrow."

Pig Knot's brow knotted up in a question.

"Get something to eat," the big trainer told him, turning around. "You leave for Sunja this morning."

Koba left Pig Knot standing and blinking amongst the tables.

After only a moment, however, the pit fighter got moving.

42

The wagon arrived in Sunja in late afternoon, letting Pig Knot off at Sunja's Pit, right before the Gate of the Sun. Pig Knot had slept most of the day, only roused when the wagon stopped at points along the way.

"Stay there," said the driver, whose name Pig Knot didn't even know.

"What?"

"Stay there. Easiest place to be found. Borchus will be about."

"Who?"

"Short man, looks like a wall."

"Ah." Pig Knot remembered. "He's around?"

"I'm always around," Borchus said drily as he emerged from the shadows of the tunnel. He waved the wagon driver off as he walked up to the taller Pig Knot. "Did you wear these clothes before?"

Pig Knot frowned at himself. "It's all I have."

"You don't spend your coin on fashion, do you?"

"Oh, and you do? With that black vest of yours? What's that from? Pig?"

"Imagine you've slept with enough to know." Borchus

chewed on the inside of his cheek. "Look, I really would enjoy a bit of jab and parry with you, but I don't have the time. I've business to attend to. If you wish, I'm heading in the direction of a healer house where some of your friends have gathered."

"Oh. Well then, lead the way."

The agent took him to the healer's house with two lamps burning brightly inside open windows. Two familiar men sat about a table, and Pig Knot smiled at the bare belly of the Zhiberian, leaning back on a chair while conversing with Goll.

Borchus rapped on the door. Halm got up and allowed him to enter, not looking incredibly pleased to see the smaller man. But his face lit up once he laid eyes upon Pig Knot.

"Well, look who it is!" Halm exclaimed and offered his fist. Pig Knot returned the grin and tapped the fist with his own.

"Just in the city for a night, boys." Pig Knot noted Goll wasn't overly excited to see him. "Greetings, good Goll. Don't get up."

"I wasn't about to," Goll replied drily.

Halm dismissed the Kree with a hand and urged Pig Knot to enter.

"Where's Muluk?" Pig Knot glanced around. "You sell him off?"

The smiles dimmed.

"Only joking, lads," Pig Knot said sombrely.

"Muluk's upstairs," Halm told him. "There was an attack at the tavern. Six men came in the morning and killed just about everyone in there. All except Muluk. He gave a damn good showing. Killed all six bandits with nary a stitch on him."

"Muluk killed six men?" Pig Knot gasped, the idea bewildering.

"Killed them and protected our coin in the process," Goll said. "We're richer this day because of that man. And this one." He nodded to Halm.

"To Muluk," Halm said, not taking any of the credit. "I would've fought anyway, coin or no coin. He kept the idea of becoming a house on the table."

"Can I see him?" Pig Knot asked.

"Sleeping now," Goll said. "The healer gives him something to sleep. A wise thing to do."

"It's not pretty," Halm added. "Muluk wasn't easy to look at, even at the best of times. Now he's…" The Zhiberian made a face.

Pig Knot felt the wind leave him. He found a chair, hauled it to the table, and sat down.

"Thank you for bringing this one to us, Borchus," Halm said begrudgingly.

"I was heading in this direction," the agent said, studying the interior of the house. "Had to speak with this one as well."

"Me?" Pig Knot asked. "You could've talked while we walked over here."

"Didn't feel like it then. Regardless, this fellow you fight tomorrow, they call him Skulljigger. Not a particularly pleasant name, in my opinion. No doubt unpopular with the ladies as well. In any case, I did a bit of questioning on your behalf. The man's already won two fights. Crippled one opponent. It would seem he favours attacking the legs and then torturing his foe until he collapses. Or surrenders."

"Well, thank you for that," Pig Knot said appreciatively.

"It would seem, though, that your reputation is known

amongst the people. The Domis expect the odds to be slightly in your favour."

"Any advice?" Pig Knot asked.

"Don't get killed."

Halm frowned. "Give the lad some real advice if you know any."

Borchus considered it for a moment. "There's nothing to tell. Skulljigger has won all of his fights by attacking the legs. From what I gather, no one has yet found a weakness."

"He's a house gladiator?"

Borchus shook his head slowly. "No. Just an animal."

Pig Knot rubbed his chin. "Well, thank you all the same."

Borchus went to the entrance. "I'll be off then." He averted his eyes to the floor and closed the door as he went out.

Halm strode over to the open windows and watched for a moment before pulling the shutters to. "Nice of him. For a change."

"That was helpful," Pig Knot said as Halm returned to the table and sat down.

"How went your training?" Halm asked him.

The Sunjan shrugged. "What training? I scant remember what we did. My arms and legs still ache. All they did was grind me down to the bone while whipping me with their sticks. Training. Pah."

"But you're still here." Halm looked pleased.

"You seem taken with this whole notion that being part of a new house is a good idea, and while I've only known you for a few seasons, I *think* you're a smart man. Not as smart as I, of course…"

Halm shrugged, not offended in the least.

"But I think I'll stay and see what happens. Just to see

where it all goes. With your permission of course, Master Goll," he said with a mocking smile.

But Goll did not smile back.

"This is why you're not fit to be in a house," the Kree said quietly. "This is why I don't want anyone like you near what we're attempting to accomplish."

"Goll—" Halm started, but the Kree silenced him with a glare.

"You heard him. The man has no respect for me or for the paces the trainers are putting him through. Don't you think, just for a *moment*, that the reason they're working you so hard is to make certain that you want to be a part of a house? Those men know what they're doing, and if you had a brain, you'd be spending the better part of the day learning all that you can from them. I've seen you fight, Pig Knot. I've seen you dance and flounce around the Pit in a drunken mess as if you were keeping flies off a sick cow's ass. You haven't shown anyone *anything*. You aren't good enough for a house, and I don't think you belong with us. I *know* you don't. My opinion, you're too headstrong to know what you are doing."

Pig Knot scoffed, no longer smiling, and straightened. "You can't tell me they know what they're doing."

"You forget the beating an old man put into you?" Goll challenged. "You were spitting out sand, put there by *an old man*. And you *still* joke about them? I tell you, there is a joke at this table, but it isn't those trainers. *My* house will be for men who are serious about competition and who are willing to work for it. Not someone who believes he has skill but when he has the opportunity to improve his abilities, chooses to close his mind to learning and discipline. And *that's* what belonging to a house means. Work. Discipline. Doing what you are told and following through until it's *done*."

"I'll show you tomorrow." Pig Knot tensed his jaw, mortified to be talked to in such a manner. "I'll show you."

"You'll show me something." Goll got to his feet, not sounding convinced. "I'm heading upstairs. Try to sleep some before the day. Why not head out for a mug of beer or mead while you're here?"

The Kree hobbled up the stairs then, leaving a heavy air of resentment about the room. Pig Knot scowled at his back and met the indifferent gaze of Halm. Neither man said anything until Goll was out of sight.

"You want to prove him wrong?" Halm asked quietly.

Pig Knot smiled and exhaled, making the attempt to relax. "Certainly. What do I have to do?"

"Prove him wrong."

That struck Pig Knot hard. "Are you agreeing with him?"

"I *said*… prove him wrong. In every way. He's already got an opinion of you. I have one myself actually because I know something about you from seasons past. But truthfully, I don't know what goes on in your head. I do think Goll is mistaken, however. For I know there is no quit in you." The Zhiberian chuckled darkly. "Never did I see it in those seasons past. Not even when you lost. I think this Skulljigger can hack off both your knees, and I *know* you won't quit. But that might not be enough."

"What *is*?" Pig Knot leaned forward and struggled to keep his voice down, but anger was flowing through him now, thick and hot and ready to scald. What would be enough to convince them that he was good enough?

Halm allowed the question to hang in the air for a moment and studied the workmanship of the table.

"Just… prove him wrong," he finally said.

43

"What's this?" Pig Knot asked, gesturing at the morning food on the table. The night had been a long one for him, full of self-reflection and frustration. The rebuke from Goll and the advice from Halm still stung, and waking up to eat something good was perhaps the only thing keeping him in a positive frame of mind. He'd slept upstairs with the other men, wincing at the sight of Muluk yet wishing he could afford a tavern room. And a woman to go with it.

"It's breakfast," Halm mumbled through a mouthful of cheese.

"Just cheese, a loaf of bread, and some sliced apples?"

Goll and Halm exchanged looks.

"You're not at an inn now," the Kree quipped. "And you fight this day. A heavy stomach isn't a good thing."

"And you have that problem at times." Halm grinned and winked. Some bread crumbs clung to the corners of his mouth.

Pig Knot wasn't pleased and sat down heavily at the table's head. He threw a slice of apple into his mouth and chewed loudly. "How's Muluk?"

"Still asleep," Halm said. "The healer gives him

something to keep him sleeping most of the time. He'll be awake later."

The Zhiberian swallowed. "You ready for this day?"

Pig Knot nodded.

Goll looked at Halm and sighed heavily.

Once the men finished breakfast, Goll told Halm to take Pig Knot to the Pit and spend the morning warming up. They would meet there later in the afternoon. The two friends left the healer's house and took their time getting to the arena. The downtown area of Sunja could be garish at times, with its old wooden store fronts, wandering and stationary merchants, livestock, and stalls of foods and goods, all seemingly connected by the bawdy streamers of color crying out "festival" when there wasn't one. Navigating the people was another matter, but Pig Knot found he far preferred this to the isolated training grounds of Clavellus and his pair of hellions.

The pair of them wandered around the open area surrounding the arena, lounged under a sun that had yet to reach its blazing height, and talked about past seasons. Neither wanted to descend into the hellish belly of the Pit until it was time, as they knew it would be hellish in both sight and smell. They watched the people come and go from the Gate of the Sea, and Halm eventually handed him his Mademian sword to loosen up with. Pig Knot stood before him, hefting the weapon while Halm sat on the edge of a public fountain.

"Not much of a trainer, are you?" Pig Knot smiled, swinging the bare blade left and right.

"Not yet," Halm replied. "So enjoy it now. Might be different in a year."

"You see yourself as a trainer?" Pig Knot asked.

"I see myself as... an *owner*."

"Goll won't let you be an owner."

"Goll won't let me be a master of the house, but I can still own part of it. If I help build it." He paused and after a moment said, "You could, as well."

Pig Knot stopped swinging the blade at that point and stared questioningly at him. He didn't want to push the subject because he didn't care to be lectured once more. There were more pressing matters on his mind. Then he noticed the men sauntering into the square, taking up points about the area where Pig Knot was swishing his sword. He recognized Toffer approaching with a swagger and a gleam in his eye. One of the three men accompanying him was the tall monster of a man whose name he couldn't recall, but Pig Knot knew him to be a Sujin.

"Found you. Excellent." Toffer beamed, showing teeth in what he probably thought was a smile.

"You found me." Pig Knot glanced back at a curious Halm and indicated all was fine. "Coming to the games this day? I'm fighting."

"I know, I know." Toffer came closer. He wore ordinary clothing, but Pig Knot was wary of the sword at his waist. "Who do you think got you this fight?"

"What?" Pig Knot asked, startled.

"Yessss," Toffer hissed and nodded at Halm before returning his attention to Pig Knot. "That was me. I have some influence around these parts, you see. And don't worry about your last fight. I must confess that I was a little disappointed with you not killing the man, even though I was more than clear on how I wanted the match to end. You remember that conversation, don't you?"

Pig Knot's attention flicked from Toffer to Klytus—that was the monster's name—as he eyed the other two men.

"I remember it."

"Then you know what you did wrong."

"Things change when you're in the arena." Pig Knot suddenly huffed, growing impatient. "If you have something to say, then out with it."

"I do have something to say, in fact. I'm willing to forget what happened last time *if*... you kill the man this time."

"You want me to slay a pit fighter?"

"I want you to gut this pit fighter."

"You have something against these men?" Pig Knot asked, genuinely puzzled.

"I have my reasons. You just win this day and win in spectacular fashion." Toffer stepped in close, no longer smiling. "*Kill* the topper. Take his head off his shoulders and do it this time. Hear me? *Do* it. Or I won't be in as pleasant a mood next time we meet."

"Yes, you've certainly charmed me this morning."

"Do you see me laughing? I've made funnier lads disappear, *Pig*. Don't disappoint me this time, or I'll find you... and that conversation won't be as civil."

Pig Knot kept his rebuttals to himself. Toffer's expression had shifted from old friend to murderous bastard in a short time. He suspected swords were only one, perhaps two verbal jabs away.

"I understand." Pig Knot nodded.

Toffer pursed his lips and glared. Then he abruptly turned and stalked away. Like a bad tide rumbling out, the three men backed away from Pig Knot and Halm, Klytus being the last to turn and walk away. The Sujin towered over the thickening crowds of people walking towards the arena.

"Who was that?" Halm eventually asked. The fat man sat on the fountain edge, his great belly bare and tanning in the sun. "An old friend?"

"Not at all. More like a boil on my ass."

Halm's brow flexed in disdain, and he squinted in the bright daylight. "Doesn't sound pleasant."

"No." Pig Knot swished the blade about him and stabbed at an imaginary Toffer. "Not pleasant at all, truth be known."

*

The day flowed into afternoon as people walked into Sunja's great arena in anticipation of bloody entertainment. When they were ready, Pig Knot and Halm proceeded to general quarters and picked up the weapons and armor needed. Pig Knot selected a leather cuirass that might have been scrubbed in sand at one point in time, with equally worn metal greaves and bracers to protect his legs and arms. The helm didn't have a face cage—all of those had been taken— but it did possess a thin nose guard. The sword and shield he decided on were also old, but the armoury only took from the Pit's dead, and at times, the selection wasn't the best. Above, the first two matches had been fought, and Pig Knot waited until he got the signal to enter the tunnel after the conclusion of the third fight. Fighters draped in torchlight and shadows moved about the Pit's underworld—hard, dangerous men best avoided at any time.

"Some of these lads will join us, you know." Halm stood with Pig Knot, off to the side of the white tunnel and to the left of a flickering torch.

"Goll's going to choose from these?"

"Mmhmm." Halm nodded.

"Frightening."

"It is. It is."

As if hearing his name, Goll parted a group of warriors and swung into sight, stopping before the two men. An indifferent Borchus accompanied him.

"There he is," Halm exclaimed. "Although you seem to have picked up a dog."

Borchus didn't reply, nor did he seem to hear.

"You look ready," Goll addressed Pig Knot.

"I am."

"Just to let you know, I placed everything we could afford on this fight." Goll glared at the gladiator. "Everything."

"Don't worry about a thing," Pig Knot said. He and Halm both decided not to bring up the visit by Toffer. Neither could tell how the Kree's sensibilities would react to such information.

The Madea rose up and bawled the fighters' names.

"It's time," Pig Knot said.

Halm fist-tapped him.

"I want a few last words with you in private," Goll told Pig Knot. "You two head on to the box."

"We have a viewing box?" Halm asked.

"I arranged it." Borchus held onto his belt. "Imagine that."

Halm locked gazes with the smaller agent. "Good fortune to you, Pig Knot."

Pig Knot lifted his sword to show he'd heard. Goll shuffled ahead of him towards the tunnel.

Pig Knot saw his opponent and slowed in his tracks, a little startled. The man called Skulljigger was moving towards the same tunnel, just putting an open helm over his head. He wore a vest of leather as well, with the same accompanying trappings, but carried a sword and off-handed hand axe instead of a shield.

But it was his face that caught Pig Knot's attention.

It had been dark that night, but he remembered the face. The bruises, faded now, but still there, only made Pig Knot more confident of his identity.

Skulljigger was one of the men who had tried to steal Halm's equipment and whom, along with his companions, Pig Knot had left bloodied to a pulp in an alley.

Feeling eyes on him, Skulljigger turned and met the gaze of Pig Knot. His expression knotted up in puzzlement, then more puzzlement, before the slow, knowing slink of a moist smile etched from one corner of his mouth. Skulljigger nodded and then smiled at the Sunjan, with what few teeth he had remaining.

Pig Knot nodded back, feeling his own smirk rising.

"Well," he purred as Skulljigger plodded on down the tunnel. Toffer's order suddenly didn't seem so bad.

"Are you ready for this?" Goll asked, facing him on the threshold of the tunnel.

"I am," Pig Knot replied.

"You truly wish to be a part of the house?" Goll asked, his eyes boring into Pig Knot's face, searching.

Prove him wrong, Halm's voice echoed in his head.

"I do."

"Then you know what you must do this day."

Pig Knot nodded.

Goll leaned forward and hissed. "*Lose.*"

The word made Pig Knot's jaw drop. He blinked in astonishment at the Kree, feeling his gut fall and splash somewhere upon the fitted stones beneath his feet. Pig Knot searched the face of the man before him, trying to summon breath to give sound to his question.

"There's no time." Goll's words stopped him. "If you truly wish to be a part, the only sure way to do so, to convince *me*, is showing you can follow a master's orders. *Lose*. Our coin, *all* of it, I placed on the head of this Skulljigger. You lose, hear me, and we will have the funds to register our house and plenty left over for most everything else."

Pig Knot's head gave the barest disbelieving shake. "But—"

"*Lose*," Goll hissed, on the brink of being furious. "If you've never listened to anyone before in your miserable life, *listen now*, Saimon damn you."

With that, Goll looped around him and made his way towards the viewing boxes.

Leaving a stunned Pig Knot behind.

*

Goll followed the passageway to the viewing chamber underneath the arena stands, those reserved for the house gladiators. There, Halm and Borchus waited for him. Halm turned from the archway looking out onto the sands at ground level as Goll entered.

"All ready?"

"I hope so." Goll gave both him and Borchus an anxious look. Borchus was the only one who knew of Goll's wager, as he had informed the agent himself. Seddon himself placed the man at the Domis's window at the same time Goll meant to make his wager, and the Kree decided then to let him know whom *not* to wager on. For peace's sake. Goll would be hard pressed to explain the coin after Pig Knot's loss to

Borchus, so this way was safer. He'd also be hard pressed to explain the coin to Halm, but the Zhiberian was already on his side. It was the only way to ensure the house could be established, and Pig Knot was too much of a risk any other way.

No, in his mind, Goll had done what needed to be done. And if Pig Knot truly wanted to be a part of what one day would be known as history, he would lose. A part of Goll was still uncertain about which way the Sunjan would flow, and for that, he cursed the man.

Borchus nodded, his face revealing nothing of what he knew, and turned to the archway. Goll moved to stand between the men and stared out at the sands. Everything depended on a man he had no faith in, and he hated the very situation. Pig Knot was only half-inspired to succeed on the sands and a drunkard the other half, and everything in the balance hung on *him*.

Goll had never been more nervous his entire life, not even when he was fighting.

Outside, the fighters walked into view.

The Orator bellowed out introductions and called for the fight to begin.

44

Across the sands, Skulljigger shifted from foot to foot, holding his sword and axe at guard. Pig Knot blinked at him over the edge of his shield, a block of ice weighing down his gut. *Lose*, Goll's face demanded of him. *Lose!* The word made Pig Knot moan inwardly. If only the Kree knew what he was asking and whom Pig Knot was fighting. *Seddon above*, Pig Knot thought as he remembered Toffer in a flash.

The day had become utter shite.

Skulljigger motioned with his weapons, goading Pig Knot to come closer amidst the growing jeers of the onlookers. Pig Knot wanted no such thing. All he wanted was to be in a tavern somewhere with a woman on his knee and a drink in his hand.

Lose.

The cold certainty hit him that he was going to perish this day, and his stomach fluttered.

Skulljigger grew impatient and came across the sands, seeking a fight to the death.

"Seddon smiles on me this day," Skulljigger cried above the rumble of the audience. He grinned evilly as he closed the distance. "I'll make you sing!"

The sword and hand axe swung at Pig Knot, one after the other in a gnashing of flashing steel. True to Brochus's report, the attacking pit fighter focused on his legs. Pig Knot stepped back and got behind his shield, grimacing as the weapons laid into the barrier. He stepped to one side, trying to throw Skulljigger off balance, but the man followed him without error and attacked relentlessly. He slashed and hacked, cutting for a knee and swinging for a head. Pig Knot deflected what he could and ducked under the arc of the axe. The steel clipped the top of his head, ringing his skull and flinging him to the right. Skulljigger pounced, grazing his sword off Pig Knot's right bracer and convincing him for an instant that his arm was gone. The Kree's shield and sword got tangled together, forcing him to back up in a splash of sand.

Skulljigger stopped and watched Pig Knot scurry out of reach. He spread his weapons and looked towards the crowd, imploring them for patience. *He* was doing *his* part. Having done that, he started hunting once more.

Pig Knot watched him over the edge of his shield once more and didn't know what to do. Win or lose, he was well and truly—

Skulljigger slashed for legs, driving him back. He slashed again, spinning around and whipping his axe across Pig Knot's eyes, missing by a finger. The man's momentum put him momentarily off balance, and Pig Knot stepped into a cut and parted the leather of his foe from shoulder to buttock.

The onlookers held their breath for a moment, and Skulljigger staggered back, his hand reaching behind to check for blood. Finding nothing amiss, he took the time to pull the ruined vest from his muscular torso with a growl.

The people's cheering grew. They saw he wasn't done in the least.

"You should've pressed on," Skulljigger hissed.

I should be somewhere else! Pig Knot bit back.

The pair jumped at each other then, exchanging brutal thrusts and slashes and avoiding over-the-shoulder downward cuts looking to split flesh from head to crotch. Sand scattered with each step as the men clashed, rang steel off steel, and grunted, throwing their strength into every swing. Several times, Pig Knot found himself performing the familiar-feeling one-two cut and slash he'd practiced with the trainers, and he wished then that he'd learned what followed.

Then with a scream that rooted him in place, Skulljigger brought his blade down and split Pig Knot's shield straight down the middle, cutting his forearm to the bone. The sword jerked away with a squeal of metal and wood. Pig Knot shook his arm free of the shield. Skulljigger lunged low, seeking the legs yet again, and missed. His momentum carried him beyond Pig Knot's reach and allowed some distance to form between the two.

Pig Knot inspected his arm and the messy redness dribbling from the mouth his foe's blade had opened. It dappled the sands in a trail leading back to Skulljigger. The Sunjan grimaced, focused beyond the pain of his arm, and turned his body sideways, getting behind his sword and making as small a target as possible.

"Hurt?" Skulljigger asked. "Not finished yet."

He plunged forward, his weapons whirling in a pattern Pig Knot had no answer for. The Kree stopped the sword twice before a flat axe crunched into his left shoulder, lodging in bone and seemingly slicing a knob of flesh off.

Skulljigger stepped in close and kicked, laying his boot flat against Pig Knot's armoured gut and sending him flying across the sand and onto his back with a jarring thud. Blood spurted, and somewhere he felt the axe sink a little deeper before being pulled out.

A dazed Pig Knot scrambled instinctively to his knees, looked up, and had his chin shattered by a sword pommel. The world became lopsided and stopped with a jolt when he tasted sand. A voice screamed at him to roll, *roll over*, and he wailed as he tried to move his sluggish legs from underneath his weight.

"Topper!" Skulljigger shouted, distressingly close.

Pig Knot turned onto his side, into shadow.

Skulljigger stabbed him through the knee, the tip cutting through tendon and bone and spiking downwards to the sand.

Pig Knot wailed hideously, shivering on the sands as if he lay on a sheet of ice. The cut transfixed him in place though he trembled as if in convulsions. Shouts reached him through his pain-gripped mind. A mash of garbled voices and curses and screams to do something, just *do anything* before it was too late. The pain in his leg shot up into his body as if the very sands had grown teeth and ripped him back and forth like a rabid animal. A hand stripped him of his helm, grabbed his braid, and wrenched him around, straightening his body.

Pig Knot lashed out with his good leg, a kick energized by pain, and knocked a leg away. Skulljigger collapsed to the sands. Pig Knot rolled over, feeling his stomach turn cold then sick, feeling nothing in his fingers. He crawled and reached his sword where he had dropped it. He gripped the blade itself, cutting his fingers in a sizzle that didn't hurt in the least. He held the weapon with his crippled hand, willing it to work and trying to correct his hold.

Prove him wrong!

A burp of agony left Pig Knot then, and his buzzing hand relinquished the steel. The weight fell, but he didn't care as he saw his ruined knee, a gush of fluid erupting from the sliced flesh and bone, and nearly swooned.

Nearby, Skulljigger stood. The fighter favoured his knee, but the rest of him was just fine.

And he was smiling.

Around the arena, the crowds called for Pig Knot's death, and the rising chant drowned out the voices Pig Knot thought might have belonged to friends. Steel gleamed in the sun, almost mystically, and there was no one between him and the killer creeping towards him.

"Watch," Skulljigger demanded of the audience. *"Watch me!"*

Pig Knot opened eyes that had become caked with tears and dust. Skulljigger stepped in close, a savage face with red teeth, and drew the blade back for the killing thrust.

Prove him wrong!

The sword flashed.

*

He heard voices.

They clambered over him like a warm surf.

He felt pain twinkling like stars in a distant, black canopy where figures moved.

Lightning bolts sank into his flesh and yet were not felt, but he was somehow aware that things—bad things—had been done to him. Probably *very* bad things.

The sounds of people, a crashing of voices, neared and

then pulled away and slowly, slowly, receded. Warmth enveloped his whole being.

More hands, pulling, pushing, rolling him onto his side.

On his back.

He was on his back. That felt very important to him for some reason he was in no capacity to contemplate. For something was... was gnawing on his legs. *Both* legs. Little stinging bites made holes in his flesh as if delivered by white maggots.

Maggots?

Was he... dead?

Was this death?

Then...

Nothing.

45

Halm lost control and struggled out though the archway, screaming as if Seddon above had touched him directly between the eyes. Heat shimmered on the arena floor, adding to the sensation that it was all a humid dream. The last thing Goll saw, besides the writhing of the Zhiberian's legs and arms as he scrabbled through the window, and the flurry of sand in his feverish wake, was the sun shining down on the figure in the center of the arena, with sword held high. Thousands upon thousands of voices christened that shining blade with their united power, a frightening force that made the very walls tremble and made the steel almost blinding to gaze upon.

And the man in the center, the one the Zhiberian struggled to reach in nightmarish slow motion, plunged that fiery streak of light down as if stabbing the very earth itself. Again and again… and again, in arcs of the darkest crimson.

Before the bulk of the Zhiberian took him down.

"This way," Borchus directed Goll, pulling him back from the arch. "There's nothing we can do."

They limped away from the tempest of sound and fury exploding in the area. Horns sounded, deep oceanic monsters that split the wall of human voices as neatly as an axe to wood, commanding the end of all things. But Goll limped away on his crutches, shocked by the level of violence he'd seen on this day, violence that he was surely as guilty of as the blazing warrior with the falling sword.

"The Zhiberian is on his own this time," Borchus said in a voice that might have been a shout. Goll wasn't certain. "We have coin to collect."

"Not yet," Goll heard himself saying.

"What?"

"Not yet."

With that, Goll regained his self-control and shuffled in the direction of the general quarters. Men got out of his way, and he saw Skarrs, more Skarrs than he'd ever seen in one place before, swarming into the white tunnel. Gladiators watched them with faces full of confusion and excitement. The Madea and his own cadre of guardians stood up and peered in the direction of the tunnel.

It was there Goll stopped, to the right of the Madea's raised stage and desk.

"You men!" He roared with the blood in his ears and madness in his eyes. "Listen to me now! Listen! Those of you who wish it, who want it, come forth and be known to me. I am Goll, the killer of the one called The Butcher of Balgotha, and I call on any... *any* who wish to join my house of pit fighters this day."

Faces obscured by sooty half-light stared at him, roused by the sound of his voice, puzzled by his meaning.

"If you see yourselves as better than the man next to you, if you are clamouring for the attention of the established houses, then consider the stable I am starting. You will have a taskmaster, trainers, food, and a place to sleep. You'll no longer be alone in the games, and you'll be considered an equal to the house gladiators. It's a hard path you've chosen, but if you wish, you don't have to walk it alone. Join now, train with us, and we'll fashion you into a pure pit fighter."

"How much will it cost?" someone yelled out.

Goll turned in the direction of the voice. "Nothing."

"You'll take a portion of our winnings though?" asked another.

"Yes. But no more than any other house," Goll answered.

"Weapons and armour provided for?"

That was a good question. "In the beginning, it might be difficult…"

"What do you mean *might* be difficult?" the voice demanded from the back. Goll struggled to see who it was, but there were simply too many. "The regular stables or houses or whatever they call themselves all give the best to their lads. Not something pulled or patched up from the dead. We can't be expected to use shite all the time."

"And you'd still be Free Trained in the eyes of the other houses," another voice added with dreary candor. "You wait and see. You think them punces pound on us now for being here, wait until they hear of a house made of you lot. They'll hunt you down like dogs on rats. Snap you up and grind—"

"What about drink?" shouted another.

"Drink?" Goll asked, feeling his brow knotting together in annoyed puzzlement.

"Well aye, drink. Beer, wine, that sort of thing. Would it be allowed?"

"No." Goll shook his head, thinking it to be the stupidest question of them all. "You can't expect to perform at—"

"Not for me then," the speaker called out. Then the dam broke.

"What do you want? A lake of Sunjan gold?"

"Be all right now, wouldn't it?"

"No spirits of any kind?" a different voice demanded.

"Fishhook that," grumped another.

"That's all thirsty work, you crippled shagger. Can't expect *men* to do it all and not have a sip of *something* at the end!" protested someone near the front. Goll saw him, a filthy-looking brute dressed in only a soiled loincloth.

"Not for me!" someone called out, Goll recognized the voice as someone repeating himself, but louder.

"Aye that, the drink kills it."

"The thought of them righteous bastards will be up our dog blossoms keeps me out."

"Will I be able to work on my farm?"

The question stunned Goll, and he sputtered his reply. "No, you… you couldn't manage both—"

The packed crowd shook at the edges as fighters drifted away or turned their backs and struggled from the center. More heads turned, and the unstable whole rippled and began breaking up.

"Too much, lad," someone muttered close by.

"You're asking a lot," said another.

"Not for meeeee!" the tormenting voice screeched and crumpled into an unhealthy-sounding gale of giggling before drifting away.

Goll stood dumbfounded. How could this be happening? It was the opportunity of a lifetime! He was throwing open his house's gates from the very beginning, and they were laughing at it. *Free Trained.* He shook his head in dumbfounded disgust.

The mob gradually dispersed amongst bursts of laughter, sly looks of contempt, and mutters of discontent. The day was young still, and there were matches to prepare for.

Goll couldn't imagine what was going through these bastards' minds.

But not all of them wandered away. Five remained.

Goll looked from face to face, puzzlement growing into subdued excitement.

"What then?" he asked.

"I'm for joining up," said a big man dressed in a leather curiass, his muscular arms bared. His head was shaved clean and possessed a few dents as if it had been kicked about.

"As I," said another, one of the shorter men staying behind. Slim, dressed in plain clothes and wearing a blade off his hip. "Seems you impressed a few, at least. I'm Junger of Pericia."

Goll stared at him, working his mind around the accented Sunjan.

"I'm Sapo," said a beast of a man. A paw of a hand rested on the shaft of a mighty axe. Even though he only spoke two words, Goll knew him to be a native Sunjan.

"What of you then?" the Kree asked of the others.

"I'm Tumber, from Vathia," announced the man with the shaved and battered skull.

"Torello. Sunjan," said another.

"Kolo. Sunjan born."

Goll nodded at them, but then his attention was taken by a tower of a man emerging from the shadows with a great flowing mustache and beard, perhaps the tallest figure Goll had ever seen on two legs not made of stone. While tall, he wasn't as meaty as the others and actually appeared on the edge of starvation, which caused Goll a twinge of dismay. An aura of menace emanated from his person, and the Kree wasn't the only one watching this near-emaciated hellion approach.

Then Goll realized this lanky monster wore a necklace of crow heads.

"Brozz," the man said in a low voice. His Sunjan hissed with a barely noticeable accent. "From Sarland."

The Kree peered up at the Sarlander watchtower, took a breath, and studied each of them in turn. "You understand what you're about to do?"

"You've made yourself clear." Tumber nodded once. "I speak for myself, however."

The others gave their answers in similar fashion, and Goll made a quick count. "Six," he stated and felt pangs of both disappointment and eagerness. Big things sometimes came from such small numbers.

"Follow me then." Goll shuffled towards the white tunnel.

"Where are you going?" Borchus asked him at his side.

"To gather our fallen," he responded.

*

"Away from him!" Halm roared as he pulled himself from the archway, kicking up sand. The arena was a storm of sound with the weight of thousands of voices, heavy as a battering of mauls. He wasn't certain the pit fighter had heard him or not.

Then Skulljigger turned about.

He held his bright and bloody sword at guard, stepping back as Halm came forward, but the Zhiberian leaped at him and caught him around the midsection. They crashed into the sand as if fallen from the heavens, sending up sand and dust. Skulljigger snarled and pushed a set of savage teeth away from him with one hand, discovering a hand clamping about his sword arm's wrist.

They twisted and wrestled until Skulljigger got his legs under him and shoved off, rolling out from under the heavier Halm.

They separated, stood up, and glared at each other.

Halm stood over the mess that was his friend, panting and dividing his attention between him and the pit fighter.

"You bastard!" Halm shouted and felt his words devoured by the deafening roar. Skulljigger's lips moved, but he couldn't hear. He gestured with his wet blade before flicking it, sending scarlet into the sand.

The Zhiberian looked at the crumpled form. There, blinking as if he'd just woken and wincing in a bloody fashion, Pig Knot saw him and smiled feebly.

"I'll kill you!" Skulljigger's words came across the waves of cheering, but something restrained him, perhaps indecision or the law of the arena, yet he still flaunted his weapons as if ready to use them.

"I'll have your head," the Zhiberian shouted back. Then he dropped to one knee, wanting to stop Pig Knot's bleeding but simply not knowing where to start.

"You're cut up bad, boy." Halm forced cheer into his voice. "But you'll live. You'll be fine. Have no worries."

Pig Knot said something then, and Halm lowered his head to hear.

But the Sunjan faded into unconsciousness.

All around, the roar of the crowds peaked, frightening in its intensity.

Then a rush of arena attendants and armed Skarrs appeared and surrounded the three.

46

The Gladiatorial Chamber members gazed on, their expressions unreadable as their accountant sat at a table before their raised panel and dutifully counted the gold coins before him. A cloth sack of money deflated while dull towers rose from the table. Goll watched it all, switching at times from the accountant to the Chamber members clothed in their regal robes of gold and white and appearing more than bored with the afternoon. Goll didn't know what it took to hook the interest of one. A thousand gold coins on a table would make *him* stop and stare for a bit.

Behind him, Halm stood pensively, not wanting to be there and not the beaming picture of joviality he usually was. It had been a near thing for Pig Knot. The man had almost died from blood loss. As it was, he was still in the Pit's infirmary, delirious and cut up by Skulljigger's hand. The Zhiberian had come very close to crossing a dangerous line when he burst out onto the sands, and it took a complement of Skarrs to prevent him and Skulljigger from fighting over Pig Knot's unmoving person. It was a good thing the pair didn't have at it as arena rules forbade such unscheduled encounters. That would be a match for another day.

The first task Goll had given three of his new recruits was to watch over Pig Knot's battered and bleeding form as the healer attempted to put him back together. Borchus had disappeared, and Goll ordered Halm and two others to carry their sizeable winnings directly to the Gladiatorial Chamber. Along the way Goll revealed that he had ordered Pig Knot to lose if he wished to be a part of the house.

"He'd best be a part of it then," was all Halm said, absorbing the information in rather unsettling stoic fashion.

It had been a long walk to the Chamber and an even longer wait while the accumulated coin was being counted.

"That's a thousand gold pieces there." The accountant leaned back from the towers of coin with a sigh. "There are several hundred more left."

Goll looked at Halm, who lurched into motion with an annoyed expression and gathered up the remaining gold.

"We have plans for that," Goll said to the Chamber. "Now then… are we formally a house?"

"Can you sign your name?" spoke the oldest-looking one with the missing right ear.

"I can."

"Bring the documents then," One Ear rumbled and took a breath. Goll saw that the Chamber member habitually breathed through his mouth as though constantly fighting for breath.

The accountant produced another sack and started filling it with gold, removing the fortress he had constructed. An attendant came forth with a scroll, unravelled it, and placed it on part of the surface not covered in coin.

"This document is a legal and binding account establishing the House of, you must provide a name, on this day and year as witnessed by myself and the present

Chamber members. As a newly recognized house, you are required to observe the laws and rules of the games each season and make right with the members present if and when a disagreement or conflict occurs with one of their own or an existing house which places both or more houses at odds."

"Make right?" Goll asked.

"The language of the document," the attendant answered at once, "means you'll have the Chamber listen to any grievance you might have with another house and resolve the issue on the same day, allowing the Chamber to pass judgement. You agree to adhere to that judgement and not allow it to go beyond these walls or those of the arena."

"I see," the Kree said.

The attendant listed off more items of note in the document, some of which sounded very odd to Goll, and others he wasn't certain of at all. He asked questions at points and received clarification from the attendants, all under the weary gaze of the members present. It was going on supper after all.

At the end, Goll fumbled with his crutches and signed his name.

"You must provide the Chamber with a list of fighters," the attendant informed him.

"Ah. Active fighters?"

"All fighters, since the games are already in progress. If a man dies, the Madea will scratch that name from your house list, and you may not enter another in his place. If a man is eliminated from the tournament, he's done for the season but may fight again next year. It's your responsibility to provide us a fresh roster at the start of the every season. He may even fight in a non-tournament match if able to do so."

"I understand."

Goll provided the names as he remembered them and wrote them down with a fine feather quill.

"Careful not to use too much ink," the attendant warned him. The Kree paused and nodded, intending to try just that.

"What will your name be?" a Chamber member asked him.

Goll thought about it for a moment. He had been going to call it the House of Goll, but the Weapon Masters of Kree would not approve of such arrogance. *Greatness does not draw attention to itself*, he heard them whisper in his head. He studied the names on the scroll and considered what the name would be.

Halm leaned in, meeting his gaze and sizing up the scroll with dark interest.

"What will it be, then?" the Zhiberian asked in a low tone, wary of the brooding council. "And did you add Pig Knot's name to that document?"

"Of course I did." Goll pointed.

Halm didn't look. "Only checking."

"You think I wouldn't? He had to lose. It was the only way. The only *sure* way. Can't you see that?" Goll insisted. "I'm not arguing about what Pig Knot did for us this day or his sacrifice. Don't worry. He'll be taken care of; on that, you have my word."

Halm thought about that and nodded once, but Goll could see the Zhiberian was suspicious of him now.

"I have a name in mind," Goll said eventually, hoping to change the subject.

"What is it?"

"The House of Eight."

Halm's face darkened. "You're forgetting some."

"Muluk and Pig Knot are done for this season. Probably for the rest of their lives."

"*You're* done for this season," Halm said almost too loudly.

"Look. I've listed their names here," Goll gestured to the scroll.

"I don't care about the scroll. You should recognize them in the name of the house. This is the beginning, after all."

Goll reconsidered and, after a moment, sighed. "You're right."

But then he relented and gazed upon the scroll, the quill drooping in his hand.

"Both of them bled for this, almost *died* for this," Halm reminded him, unyielding. "They're at the mercies of healers for us. For *you*. Best to remember that. You need to show those who remain that they weren't forgotten. That *they* won't be forgotten if they fall."

Nodding slowly, Goll knew the fat man spoke the truth. And though Goll might never have believed it, Pig Knot had surprised him the most by actually following through and losing. It was a lingering question if Pig Knot would even survive the night, but Goll was grateful to the man.

He turned to the Chamber members.

"We have a name…"

"What is it?" a bored member asked.

Goll suddenly liked the name even more and caught his breath. This was a very special moment for him and for those behind him. He looked from one Chamber member to the next, holding his breath until he couldn't any longer, the excitement building in his person, making his heart pound.

"We are…" he started.

And the thought became sound.

47

As the evening drew on, shadows detached themselves from the rows of shelved tomes surrounding Grisholt like black ghosts seeking to chill the old master's bones. Long limbs, growing fat from being fed dying light, slunk towards, touched, and caressed his still face. Grisholt didn't care. He was drunk. Sweet wine, bought with his stable's recent winnings, soothed the lash of defeat. When news of the failed attempt at robbing the Free Trained had reached him two days ago, he sat and mulled and asked Ballan everything he knew. Caro was a right shifty bastard, the very reason why Grisholt employed him, and was wise enough to send his henchman with the bad news in his stead. But the real surprise was how one man had managed to execute six of his pit fighters. *Naked* even. It was beyond him. Caro had come exceedingly close to seizing the coin but had failed, and yet the failure didn't gall Grisholt. The weasel appeared at the estate the next day with a sack of coin—coin he'd won from a bet placed on the Zhiberian's head. A paltry sum compared to what was probably lost, but as Grisholt had to admit, it wasn't a complete disaster. He'd rid himself of six men who were difficult to begin with, and his involvement with the attempt had died with them. Caro was trustworthy to the last, as were the men he employed beneath him.

But the Zhiberian lived. How that thought… *galled* him.

A servant entered with a lit lamp and placed it on his desk. Another bottle of wine was thumped down beside it, and the man left without a word or a sound, retreating into the escalating gloom as though swallowed whole. The light burned brightly, the fiery curves shifting, although it barely reached the warship painting on the far wall. Grisholt stared at that fearsome beast of battle setting sail on what now appeared a moonlit ocean with nary a ripple on the water— lost at sea or waiting for a breeze. It was open to interpretation at this late hour, and Grisholt simmered where he sat and drank, smacking his lips at times.

A figure appeared in the doorway, and in Grisholt's drunken capacity, it seemed as if the shadow had magically formed.

"Master Grisholt," a voice asked. Grisholt recognized it as belonging to Brakuss. "It's late, but Ballan is here from the city."

"He's here?" Grisholt croaked, his throat slick from drink. "Step into the light then."

Ballan appeared with Brakuss's one-eyed bulk towering over him. The smaller man's eyes looked as black as the darkest corners of the study, and he had a weary look about him, as though he had travelled hard to reach his employer's home.

"What then?" Grisholt said gently, the alcohol pacifying him as effectively as a hammer to his skull. "Speak now, good Ballan. And we can all retire for the night."

"I bear news from the city," Ballan reported.

"Yes, yes, I heard that part already. Out with it before I

piss my breeches here."

"As you've asked, we've kept an eye on the Zhiberian and his companions. This afternoon, they formally registered a house with the Gladiatorial Chamber. A small house composed of ten names, ten fighters, although three of them are badly hurt. Two have already been eliminated from competition. Caro wanted you to know and sent me as soon as his contact within the Chamber informed him."

Grisholt sat and stared as though he was about to retch. "They've established themselves as a house?"

"They have, Master Grisholt."

"You hear that, Brakuss. The enemy has built a foundation for itself. We missed our opportunity and they... they didn't. Well."

"They still are unaware of our involvement with the six," Brakuss rumbled, not nearly as drunk as Grisholt wished him to be.

"That's good. Good, isn't it? We live to strike another day."

"Caro wishes to report he's seen other agents take note of the new house," Ballan said.

"Word travels fast, eh?" Grisholt grinned in the lamplight. "Sometimes, like a blood poison seeking the heart. By now, most of the others are aware of the new competition. It's an unheard-of time to introduce a house but permissible all the same. Those... *bastards*."

Grisholt didn't say anything else for several moments, but Ballan and Brakuss were accustomed to their employer's long lapses of silence.

"Go on and get some rest," Grisholt finally rumbled. "Eat something if you wish. The castle is no longer crumbling around us, and the pantry is no longer bare. In the morning, when you are rested, you'll return to the city with a few extra coins. Give these to Caro. He'll disperse them as he sees fit. Keep someone watching the Zhiberian bastard and his friends. I want to know what they are doing. Find out who the fighters are and their records. Find out everything you can about these men, for our lads will be meeting them bearing arms soon enough."

Ballan nodded and moved to depart.

"By the way." Grisholt stopped him. "What *is* the name of the house?"

"They've called themselves the House of Ten, Master Grisholt."

Grisholt, set adrift on a strong riptide of sweet wine, thought about the name before repeating it with grim feeling.

"The House of Ten." He tasted the words, attempting to grasp a greater meaning, his tongue wetting his lips like that of an old but still-dangerous serpent.

"Ten," he hissed in the dark.

131 Days: House of Pain (Book 2)
is on sale now…

Enjoy the story? Try these other titles
by Keith C Blackmore:

Horror
Mountain Man
Safari (*Mountain Man* Book 2)
Hellifax (*Mountain Man* Book 3)
Well Fed (*Mountain Man* Book 4)

The Missing Boatman
Breeds
Breeds 2
Cauldron Gristle (novella—contains *Mountain Man* short
story "The Hospital")
Private Property (novella)
Isosceles Moon (novella)

Heroic Fantasy
The Troll Hunter
White Sands, Red Steel

131 Days (Book 1)
131 Days: House of Pain (Book 2)
131 Days: Spikes and Edges (Book 3)

Science Fiction/Fantasy
The Bear That Fell from the Stars

Children's
Flight of the Cookie Dough Mansion

If you enjoyed this story and have the time and inclination, consider leaving a review. It's good advertising for me. ☺ Visit www.keithcblackmore.com for news and announcements.

Want to know when new Heroic Fantasy from Keith are released?

Visit http://eepurl.com/VK275 and sign up for fantasy news!

About the Author

Keith lives in the wild hills of Canada.

CHARACTERS

The Free Trained

Halm (Zhiberian), seasonal pit fighter
Pig Knot (Sunjan), seasonal pit fighter
Muluk (Kree), seasonal pit fighter
Goll (of Kree), seasonal pit fighter, pupil of the Weapon
Masters of Kree
Tumber (Vathian), seasonal pit fighter
Brozz "Crowhead" (Sarlandish), first-time pit fighter
Torello (Sunjan), pit fighter
Kolo (Sunjan), pit fighter
Junger (Perician), the Perician Weapon. First games.
Kolem "Sapo" (Sunjan), pit fighter
Clades (Sunjan), survivor from the Third Klaw
Skulljigger, seasonal pit fighter

The Masters, their Houses (Stables/Schools),
and their people

House of Curge

Curge, the oldest, most successful owner.
Bezange, agent
Baris, trainer
Tubrik, trainer

Bechar, trainer
Demasta, burly head of Curge's household guard

School of Gastillo

Gastillo, once gladiator, now Master of his House, wears a
golden mask
Varno, agent
Prajus, gladiator

School of Nexus

Nexus, wealthy wine merchant turned Master
Bojen, agent
Tino, spy
Bernd, trainer
Rezzo, trainer

Stable of Grisholt

Older house, which almost grasped glory within the games,
only to fall short

Borl Grisholt, owner and master of the house
Brakuss, once gladiator and head of household guard
Caro, once gladiator, now agent
Ballan, spy
Marrok, cook
Sarkus, smithy

Gunjar, pit fighter.

Turst, taskmaster.

Golki, once gladiator, now a hired thug

Kurlin, once gladiator, now a hired thug

Morg, once gladiator, now a hired thug

Sulo, once gladiator, now a hired thug

Lantus, once gladiator, now a hired thug

Plakus, once gladiator, now a hired thug

Others

Clavellus, exiled taskmaster

Machlann, trainer of Clavellus

Koba, trainer of Clavellus

Nala, Clavellus's wife

Ananda, house servant

Borchus, free agent

Bagrun, wagoner

(Karashipa, town of)

Miji, tavern owner

Thaimondus, once taskmaster

Torcul, Thaimondus's son

Neven, Thaimondus's son

Made in the USA
Middletown, DE
10 January 2021